Soiled Dove

Soiled Dove

A Novel

Michael Kennard

iUniverse, Inc.
New York Lincoln Shanghai

Soiled Dove

iUniverse books may be ordered through booksellers or by contacting:

iUniverse
2021 Pine Lake Road, Suite 100
Lincoln, NE 68512
www.iuniverse.com
1-800-Authors (1-800-288-4677)

ISBN: 978-0-595-43383-4 (pbk)
ISBN: 978-0-595-87709-6 (ebk)

Printed in the United States of America

We live in the age of the internet, I pods, games consoles and MP3 players to name but a few, but it was the written word that preceded them. Let us not lose touch with our humble beginnings, and remember the entertainment, comfort and knowledge that can still be accessed from the art of reading. Encouragement to read when young is the key. Whether it be *Treasure Island, Black Beauty, Gulliver's Travels* or the collected works of William Shakespeare that floats their boat, reading will broaden the mind.

To Evie and Harry Harding

My first grandchildren.

Acknowledgements

Firstly I'd like to thank my good friends Gil and Elaine Davies, for persistently urging me to continue writing *Soiled Dove.* My thanks also to my son Alan for his technical experience and serious knowledge of computers, Marion Emery for her proof-reading and Lyn Hopson for helping me expand my characters and for giving my story extra depth and Yolanda Smith for her superb illustration of Maddie that fronts this book, she has captured Maddie far greater than I could have imagined. A special thanks to my daughter Candice and her husband Scott for giving me two, *so far* fabulous grandchildren and of course a big thanks to my long suffering wife Elaine for all the cups of tea she brought me while I was writing *Soiled Dove.*

Chapter 1

Her name was Madeline Dubois, well that's what she told most folk. It was as good a name as any, given her chosen profession, 'Lady of the Night,' 'Calico Queen,' 'Sporting Gal,' or 'Soiled Dove.' It didn't matter how you dressed it up, to the good people of El Paso she was just another no good prostitute, another whore plying her trade in the gin palaces, saloons and parlour houses of the red-light district.

Maddie had breezed into town on the Overland stage a couple of days back. She'd have gone unnoticed if she hadn't have been one of the most attractive women the town had seen in a long time! I watched as she thanked the driver and turned towards the stage depot. She looked older than when I'd seen her last, but those eyes still carried that same hint of mischief. Older and wiser I'd bet, but still warm and affectionate. Maddie was the sweetest thing you ever did see. You could say she was the proverbial 'tart with a heart.' But don't let that fool yah, anyone back in Helena could tell you, when Madeline Dubois got mad, she was hell on wheels.

I continued to watch her as she pressed a dollar into the hand of a small boy. He doffed his cap and quickly took charge of her cases. For someone pushing forty, she was travelling light, one suitcase and what looked to be a hat box, *Maddie always liked hats.* With a few words of guidance she turned towards the red-light district and trod purposefully in that general direction. I smiled to myself, Maddie hadn't lost that devil may care attitude. With her head held high she walked the one and a half blocks to the 'Blue Eagle.'

They stood and stared. As she passed, they, the good and respectable townsfolk of El Paso, gathered together in small groups to begin their character assassination. I couldn't hear them, but I could guess what was being said. Mouths opened, tongues wagged, "Shameless, hussy, who does she think she is?" The words were mumbled, whispered and unclear. Not one of them would have guessed that she was the heroine of the Butte cholera outbreak of 84. That she'd commandeered a freight wagon, piled it high with vaccine and clean bedding and driven the hundred or so miles from Helena to Butte. Once in camp she, along with a handful of her girls who'd had the guts to join her, pitched in with nursing the sick and dying. Yes, I guess to Maddie Dubois these good people were about the same as those in all the towns that had gone before.

Brought up in the back streets of Cork, Ireland, Maddie knew suffering better than most and had felt the gut wrenching hunger pains more times than she could remember. She'd been the first born of Maggie Devlin, a young and once pretty girl from Limerick, and Michael, her drunken bully of a father. They lived in a filthy room at the top of the stairs of an old tenement building. As a young child Deirdre, *as she was known then,* liked to tell herself that her father was an honourable and decent man, but as the years passed she begrudgingly accepted the truth. He was a drunkard and a bully who kept his wife in a constant state of pregnancy. When he wasn't sating his lust, he was beating on her. It had been that way since Deirdre's birth.

From her earliest memories Deirdre had only known violence, filth and squalor. The stench that emanated from the wooden pail that served as their lavatory was overwhelming, *it was one of Deirdre's first duties of the day to empty it,* but even that didn't compare to the lingering stench of her father's body odour and whiskey-laden breath. As the years passed, she became numb to her father's loutish ways. She'd never known childhood. It had been taken from her as she watched the results of her father's drunken nights of debauchery. She'd lie awake, her face turned to the wall of that tiny room whilst he grunted and moaned as his heaving body tore into her mother.

Her mother in turn gave birth to one baby after another. Sickly and malnourished, the children soon passed into the hereafter. Deirdre, being the eldest, somehow managed to hold on, although watching her younger brothers and sisters slip away into the night was heart breaking. Her father, and she'd long ceased to think of him that way, was a drunken bully who sated his lust whenever the mood took him, but worse than that, he was a self-pitying waster. He'd no thought for his poor wife, who'd remained pregnant for twelve long years, before she finally followed the path her children had trodden before her.

With her mother gone, it wasn't long before Deirdre's father switched his attentions towards his daughter. She'd been asleep when she was woken by his laboured breath and his hands all over her. She struggled as best she could, but his weight and strength were too much. Deirdre's screams as he entered her were stifled as he forced her face into the straw filled sacking that masqueraded as a pillow. For two agonising minutes she thought she was going to die as he viciously thrust into her, but then with a grunt and moan he discharged his lust. A few brief minutes later his breathing returned to normal. He climbed off her and began to weep.

"I'm sorry Deirdre, I shouldn't have done that. It's ya ma see, I miss her so much."

If anything Deirdre found his self pitying worse than what he'd done to her. What little innocence she possessed was stripped from her on that night, the eve of her eleventh birthday. She turned her face to the wall and feigned sleep whilst he climbed back in. As his snoring ruptured the relative quiet of the night, Deirdre lay awake sobbing. She was in shock and in an almost catatonic state. There was no one in the world to turn to. 'Was this her lot, to follow in her ma's footsteps?' she thought. 'What had she done that was so terribly wrong? Why had her God forsaken her?'

It was a few days later when Michael Devlin's urges lured him once more to her bedside.

"Oh Deirdre, you're so much like your poor mother, God rest her soul." She opened her emotionless eyes, turned her face away from the disgusting smell of sweat and alcohol that permeated the air around him. She put up no resistance as he climbed on top of her. She'd lived in fear ever since that first time and had decided she'd rather die than live as her mother had before her.

Michael Devlin realised something was wrong was when he felt a stinging sensation in his leg. Befuddled by alcohol it took him a few seconds before he sat up in bed to find the sheets soaked in his blood. Surprised and shocked he rose to his feet blood spilling from the open wound.

"You bitch! You tried to kill me!" he said as he stared at the kitchen knife in Deirdre's hand. His eyes grew wide with disbelief as he stared at the severed wound in his right leg. "Oh my God!" he cried as realisation crashed through his murky drink-addled brain. Blood pumped uncontrollably from a main artery.

White faced with shock, Deirdre could only watch as the man she'd known as Da fought for life.

Michael Devlin wrapped a dirty cloth around the wound in a vain attempt to stop the bleeding and staggered outside in search of help, the blood pumping even faster as his heart raced uncontrollably. His feeble cries were heard by neighbours but as they gathered around, the pumping eased. Michael's heart grew ever fainter, until it finally stopped.

Deirdre threw the knife across the floor and sat up in bed and waited for the neighbours to find her. She felt no remorse.

For a week she couldn't speak.

"Michael Devlin was bound to die a violent death," was the universal cry. "Probably making himself a late snack," said others. "Always said drink would be the death of him."

When she finally began to recover Deidre played dumb.

"She's coming with us, we's all going to America," said her mother's friend, Breda McGillycuddy.

A few months had passed and Deirdre had been taken in by Mrs McGillycuddy. A generous act, the local priest had said. 'Unpaid scivvy,' thought Deirdre. Still everything would be different when they reached this America. 'America,' thought Deirdre, 'it must be a grand place, because everyone that Mrs McGillcuddly speaks to seems suitably impressed.'

A month later, lice ridden, gaunt and malnourished from constantly throwing up the meagre rations that were allowed her, Deirdre set foot in Castle Garden, New York.

New York must have seemed such a wondrous sight to the young Deirdre Devlin, but all too soon the realities of life quickly set in. America, that land that Mrs McGillycuddy spoke so lovingly about, was nothing more than a larger version of Cork. Poverty still ruled the day. Filth and squalor were the same in both lands.

Forced to find work or starve, Deirdre found a job in a local sweatshop. Fourteen hours a day she laboured, six days a week. On Sundays she was too tired to go to Mass, a constant source of irritation to Mrs McGillycuddy.

"She's an ungrateful little tyke! Surely it's not too much to ask, to pay her respects to our Lord. To give thanks for the chances he's bestowed upon her. To be sure, wasn't it himself that guided her to our house indeed."

By the time she was twelve Deirdre had learned there was another way of increasing her meagre wages. The foreman of the garment factory had taken a particular liking to her, and had bestowed the odd little gift for the occasional hand job. Deirdre saw no harm in it. One minute he was a rampaging beast, his hands feeling her all over, the next he was as limp as a puppy dog. She soon learned that the faster she worked him, the quicker it was over. With this method Deirdre naively reckoned to keep him at bay. The thought of him forcing his way inside her, brought back too many memories of her father.

A month went by, and then the inevitable happened. It had begun as it usually did with a quick grope, then the feverish fumbling as he undid the buttons of his fly. But this time it was different, he was forcing her to her knees. "Do what you normally do, but with your mouth," he cried, the words trembling hesitantly from his lips.

"No! No way!"

"I'll give you 50 cents! That's five times what you get for a hand job."

"How much will you pay, if I let you stick it in me?" Deirdre couldn't believe the words that flowed from her lips. The thought of her taking that thing into her mouth had caused blind panic.

"Oh Jesus, a dollar, yeah, a whole do … dollar," he stammered.

Hitching up her skirt, she quickly pulled her knickers to the side and spread her legs. "One dollar, okay." She held out her hand for payment.

Now sweating profusely the foreman peered back into the factory and ran a cursory eye over the noisy machines. Satisfied no one would disturb them for the next five minutes he plunged his hand deep into his pocket and pulled out a crumpled dollar bill.

"This better be worth it," he spat as he handed the money over.

"Don't worry it will be honey." Again Deirdre was left wondering where the words came from.

Within a few seconds he was inside her, within another few he did his dollar's worth. "Right, get back in there and make like nothing happened, yah hear."

Deirdre wiped the fast cooling sperm from the top of her legs and walked back inside the factory. The swiftness of the exchange caused her both concern and excitement. That she could be pregnant after a few fumbled minutes had her praying to the blessed Mary. That she could earn such riches so easily filled her with jubilation. Deirdre vowed that if she wasn't pregnant she'd find ways of making sure she didn't become so.

Within a week and a half her prayers were answered. That tell-tale trickle of blood between her legs caused her immense relief and with that relief a renewed confidence overtook her. She'd got away with it, and earned a dollar into the bargain. But that wasn't what Deirdre was all about. Sure, she could earn a living on her back. She could take precautions to ensure she didn't become pregnant, but did she want this? The filth, the poverty, the squalor.

She looked at herself in the old cracked nicotine stained mirror and realised that she was more than just pretty. Those deep cobalt blue eyes told her all she needed to know. There was a sexual attractiveness to her that, until that moment, she hadn't been aware of. Men, she was sure would pay a high price to bed her. More than a dollar, of that she was sure. But where would she find the right clientele?

"Get up will you! You lazy harlot! Wallowing in your pit when you should be praising God for bringing you to America!"

"I'm tired Mrs McGillycuddy! I'm so tired. I'll go to Evening Mass that I will."

"You see you do Deirdre Devlin, or the Lord will turn his back on you!"

"I will. I'm just so tired."

"Tired or not, the rents due, and I'll be having your share come Thursday."

"You will, to be sure Mrs McGillycuddy."

Moments later the door slammed behind the old matriarch and her brood. Deirdre breathed a sigh of relief. She lay there staring up at the ceiling, her mind going over the plans she'd formed. It wasn't the best idea; in fact it was foolhardy. As she continued staring at the stained and cracked ceiling she made her decision. She flung the dirty rag that masqueraded as a bed-sheet from her body and dressed quickly. Tired she might have been, but this Sunday, tired or not, she was heading down to the notorious Five Points area of New York.

In the cold light of day the Five Points didn't seem that intimidating, if you ignored the open sewers, rotting garbage and filth that littered the streets. It was past noon when Deirdre peered inside Brannigan. It was a most dangerous place for a young immigrant girl of twelve, but where else was she going to gain the knowledge that she craved? Even at that hour of the day the place was crawling with cut-throats, pickpockets, pimps and whores. It was a place of infamy, a place she should stay well clear of, yet to her young eyes there on those filthy streets lay the answer to her future.

Deirdre had thought it through very carefully. She knew about the inherent dangers of being lured into a life of vice. If she wasn't careful she could be condemning herself to living no better than an animal, selling her body for a few drams; but that wasn't in her plan. She'd already conjured up what working in a place like Brannigan's would be like. She had imagined a place filled with gaiety and laughter, of drunken bawdy men and women, enjoying themselves as they sought to bring a little excitement into their lives.

Naïve she might have been, but at twelve she'd experienced more of life than most of her friends back home in Cork. Deirdre's experience of life had made her old beyond her years. With a little luck, the right contacts and a smart business brain, she hoped that by the time she was into her late teens she'd have enough money to leave the past behind her. Start a new life, out there in the West. California maybe?

Fanny Brannigan was a hard-faced cow of a woman. A mop of unruly red hair crowned her large bulbous face. Years of hard living and drinking had taken its toll on what was once a sweet faced cherub of a girl. Fanny had always been big and the years had not been kind to her. Ill tempered and ready to gut someone at the least provocation had seen her rise through the ranks of pimps and whores to her exalted position as chief madam in one of the most notorious brothels in the Five Points. It was to her that young Deirdre came.

Fanny Brannigan was intrigued by the little tyke that sat before her. *From her own hometown no less.* She listened whilst the young Deirdre outlined her plans.

"And I'll be a rich woman by the time I'm twenty!"

"You will, will yah," spat the old madam.

"I will that," agreed Deirdre.

"It's that easy?" said a sarcastic Fanny Brannigan. "Then why ain't I dripping with diamonds and pearls?"

Deirdre looked shocked at the older woman's remarks.

"Best you forget all about it. If I was you I'd take me self off back to where's I came."

"I can't do that. I'm not going back to that stinking boarding house and Mrs McGillycuddy."

"Take a look my dear, take a look at what the future holds." Fanny Brannigan had seen it all before. One look was all it took for most of the girls that entered Fanny's.

Deirdre cast her eyes over the worn and jaded women that slouched around the rooms at the back of Brannigans. It wasn't a pretty sight to be sure, not quite what Deirdre had imagined, but her mind was set. "Yes, but I won't end up like them."

"And why's that?" said the now agitated madam.

"I shall only goes with gentlemen, those that'll take care of me."

"Is that a fact?" Fanny Brannigan was fast tiring of the waif in front of her. "Seeing as you're too good for my clientele, you'd better sling your hook. You ain't staying ere you little shit."

"But! But ..."

"There's no free lodging's ere. If you stick around you's got to earn yah keep. Gentlemen or no gentlemen." Fanny's words were harsh and final.

Deirdre's shoulders drooped and she slowly turned away from the old madam. A look of utter dejection was etched across her face. But before she'd stepped outside the door, Fanny Brannigan stopped her. She made a quick assessment of the young waif, while Deirdre stood there with her mouth open. Most girls, thought Fanny, who came into the profession were either forced or drifted into it through necessity. Not many came to it voluntarily. Fanny Brannigan made her decision.

"Old it. You sayings you ain't got no kin, least ways this side of the ocean." Fanny scratched at her head and looked the kid hard between the eyes. She weren't bad looking, that dark hair of hers piled high, a bit of rouge, and a hint of colour around those eyes. She might be worth the effort and besides in a couple of years she might fit the bill for a different type of clientele.

"That's right, I'm an orphan."

"What about this Mrs McGillycuddy, won't she be wondering where you's gone?"

"She'll rant and rave, call me for all I'm worth, then in a few days she'll forget I ever existed."

"Is that a fact?" Fanny Brannigan wasn't one to turn down a fast buck and judging by what she saw before her, young Deirdre might be worth a tidy sum. "Come to think about it, I do ave a few select clientele, well they aint what you'se call real gentlemen, but they's the best we's got round ere. I'll tell you what I'll do for you."

Deirdre turned and faced her, a moment of blind panic coursed though her. She knew that once the decision was made there would be no turning back.

"These ere gentlemen, they need special services, I'll go into that later. All I'm saying is you ain't got to be squeamish. They're paying good money but they wants their's money's worth. I'll take seventy five percent. In return you get bed and board, and the remainder."

"But that's daylight robbery!"

"Take it or leave it! I ain't no charity."

"I'll take it, but I'm only doing it for a year. Then I'm off. Understood?" She said it more to convince herself than to impress the old madam.

Fanny stifled a laugh. The girl was naïve, but that would soon be knocked out of her. That she was feisty and full of fight was to her good. In her now chosen profession she was going to need all the strength she could muster. Well, time will tell. Perhaps, thought Fanny Brannigan, she would end up a rich woman by the time she was twenty. The old madam laughed at the prospect. The girl was very naïve indeed.

Under Fanny Brannigan's tutorage Deirdre learned the mysteries of birth control. "If you'se in this game, you'se best learn 'ow to prevent those unfortunate accidents. There's the rhythm method …" The old harridan checked herself for a moment. "Ah, you ave started your periods, ain't yah?"

"I have at that," said Deirdre. "On the boat over. I thought it was the devil's work until Mrs McGillycuddy put me wise."

"Good, then you'll understand what I means by the rhythm method. Then there are antiseptic douches and rubbers. Most men don't like em, but if you don't want to get yourself knocked up on your first night, you'd best find a way to persuade them."

She listened carefully to all Fanny Brannigan had to say. Old beyond her years, Deirdre listened and took notice of everything the old madam had to offer. The future was there for the taking. If all worked to plan she'd be free of the filth and squalor within a year.

Chapter 2

Rising from the gutter as Deirdre soon realised to her cost, took more than sound planning and a place to stash her money. She learned that in an establishment like Brannigan's you trusted no one, least of all the other young whores who shared her quarters. Theft was an occupational hazard. Secondly, but more importantly, the money she earned in Fanny's establishment didn't amount to much. Twenty five per-cent of what she earned was very little indeed.

"You're lucky to see that, yah little bitch. I already told yah girl, if you wants big money you's got to earn it. You got to stop pickin an choosing who you goes with. I told yah you needs to perform those little services. It's that or you're out!"

Deirdre had been working Fanny's for three months, during which time she'd seen her plans almost evaporate. What she hadn't been told was the quota she was expected to attend to each week. Within a month Deirdre was paying almost all of her own money to Fanny Brannigan in exchange for not having to put up with as many of the lecherous drunks that pawed her constantly. Dumb as it may sound it had seemed the easiest option. It wasn't that Deirdre was opposed to sex; on the contrary, there had been times, *not many mind you,* when she'd quite enjoyed it. Something she kept from Fanny Brannigan and the rest of the girls. Admitting to enjoying sex would have been unthinkable, shameless and downright scandalous, even amongst the thieves and cut-throats that frequented Fanny's. Victorian attitudes, double standards Deirdre called them, were rife, even at the lowest levels of society.

By the time of her fourteenth birthday Deirdre still hadn't earned enough to escape the poverty of the Five Points. To her cost she'd been abused, beaten, humiliated and raped. Life was harsh and there was no crying to Fanny Brannigan. If she did, at best she'd receive a lashing from her tongue, at worst a whipping that could tear the flesh from her bones. She'd fallen into the same trap that she'd so carefully sought to avoid. Her only consolation was that despite the hardships, she'd managed to keep her looks and health, *but for how long?* Whereas most of the other girls looked far older than they were. Drink was the ruin of many, whilst others sought refuge in laudanum and harder drugs. It was a downward spiral with only one end. Deirdre tried desperately to avoid the pitfalls of others, although she did take a drink on an occasion and smoked when the mood took her. She still hoped to one day drag herself out of the poverty trap, but as each day came she found herself being sucked deeper into the quagmire that was the Five Points.

Fate was about to take a hand in the shape of a one James Fairfax the third. A gentleman in appearance, a successful businessman, a pillar of the community, the kind of man Deirdre had been looking for. But Deirdre hadn't quite learned the knack of judging character. In the Five Points area he was renowned. It was common knowledge that apart from being a waster and a braggart, he was a notorious gambler and bully. It was said he'd killed a man in an illegal duel, but that was just one of the ugly rumours that floated upon the ether of the Five Points.

He was tall and incredibly handsome, dashing in a dark mysterious sort of way. His appearance suggested a sort of danger that a young impressionable girl like Deirdre would find hard to resist. It wasn't surprising when he walked into Fanny's, that Deirdre should be fooled by his commanding presence. He greeted Fanny like a long lost Aunt, then caroused with the older more experienced girls, before sitting down to a game of cards.

An hour passed, in which time Fairfax lost heavily. His mind was on other things. Knowing he was on a losing streak, he excused himself from the game and began to survey the clientele and the chattel that was on display. The painted faces fawned and preened themselves in his presence. Anyone of them would have performed the most unspeakable acts of indecency that he desired. But tonight James Fairfax was searching for something different. His disinterest in them showed, but then his eyes latched onto Deirdre Devlin. Instead of looking away and feigning shyness, she looked him straight back and sent out a challenge. She'd learned not to appear too eager. It was a mistake she'd seen countless times during her two years at Fanny's.

"And what, I pray, is your name?" said Fairfax.

"And who would be asking?" came the curt reply.

Fairfax flinched noticeably; he was taken aback by Deirdre's defiant answer. Then quickly he forced a laugh. "You have spirit my dear. I like that in my women."

Deirdre was about to counter that she wasn't his woman, but before she could he'd turned his back and walked away. The look on her face said it all.

"What's up with you girl, ain't his money good enough? I ere tell he's worth thousands!" cried Kathleen, an old whore due for the knackers yard.

"You did right Deirdre. That's a wrong un for sure," chipped in Anne, one of the few girls who had befriended her.

Deirdre was crest-fallen. All she could do was watch helplessly as Fairfax laughingly joined a crowd drinking at the far end of the room. 'Jesus, Mary and Joseph! For the love of God what was I thinkin'? If I'd a been nice to the man I could have earned more money in one night that I'd earn in a week.' Those special services sprang to mind. She could only hope Fanny Brannigan hadn't seen her rebuffed.

Upset by her own misjudgement of the situation Deirdre took a drink. She had until then, managed to drink only in moderation, remembering how it took her Da. One drink became two, three, then before she knew it she began to feel light headed and a little sick. "To hell with Fanny Brannigan and her quota!" she said to Annie, her closest confidante. "I'm having me self an early night."

Deirdre walked outside and took a few deep breaths, then, feeling nauseous, she threw up against the wall of Brannigan's. She retched for what to her was an eternity. Then the headache kicked in before a feeling of relief wafted over her. Still unsteady on her feet she managed to walk to the side of the building and began climbing the outside stairs to the room she shared with five others.

"You never told me your name," said a soft voice from the shadows.

Startled, Deirdre spun round quickly. "Who's there?"

"I'm sorry to have startled you. That was not my intention."

"Oh it's you!" she said and stifled a giggle.

"As you're not free with your name, you leave me no choice. Allow me to introduce myself. I'm James Fairfax the third."

Deirdre, fighting the effects of the drink she'd consumed, managed as sweet a smile as she could muster. "I'm sorry. My name's Deirdre. Deirdre Devlin"

"Well Deirdre Devlin, what say we get a spot of supper?"

Deirdre smiled back dumbly. 'The accent's false,' she thought. Well, as far as she could tell in her present state of intoxication. She hadn't met many English gentlemen, but she was sure he'd put the accent on to impress her. 'Well he can impress away. If he's as generous as Kathleen said, then I might earn myself a pretty penny.'

"My carriage is just around the corner. Shall we?"

Deirdre climbed down the few stairs she'd negotiated as carefully as she could. He held out his arm to steady her and she accepted readily. Even with his gentlemanly airs she wouldn't have been in the least surprised if he pushed her up against the wall and sated his lust standing up. But true to his word his carriage was just around the corner. His driver sat ready and waiting.

'Holy mother,' she cried excitedly in her head, 'perhaps the accent ain't phoney after all,' as she marvelled at the coat of arms that was emblazoned on the door of the coach. He smiled at her and held the door open and bid her enter. Deirdre brushed aside any feelings of nervousness as she stepped inside.

The horses made a clip-clopping sound as they drove along the cobbled streets. Deirdre awe struck by her surrounding stared at the finery inside the carriage. From the red velvet padding that adorned the walls and ceiling of the carriage to the red and gold curtains that framed the windows, Deirdre had never seen the like. "It's beautiful," she exclaimed. James Faifax smiled at her outburst. Overawed by the opulent surrounding Deirdre failed to recognise that it wasn't a nice smile.

As the gentle clip clopping of the hooves gave way to a gentle padding sound, Fairfax explained, "The city makes me tired. I much prefer the country. Don't you?"

Deirdre nodded her agreement, not knowing nor caring where they were going. He pulled her towards him in the coach and fondled her breasts and then he kissed them long and lingeringly in the darkness of the coach interior. Deirdre felt a surge of passion, an unexpected and enjoyable feeling for someone steeped in the oldest profession of all. He kissed her neck and felt the wetness between her legs, but he never forced her hand or mouth down to his lower extremities. He was, thought Deirdre, an expert in the art of seduction. Then all too briefly the coach pulled onto a gravel driveway and came to a standstill next to a tall building.

"It's my country retreat. I think we'll be much more comfortable here than a filthy room out the back of Fanny's."

Deirdre's mind was working overtime. That he'd taken her back to his home suggested she'd made a big impression. Everything that had gone before, everything from her father to the ill treatment she'd received at Brannigan's, was as nothing. Special favours, she'd give him special favours and more besides. If he was good to her then she'd be good to him.

As the carriage disappeared around the side of the dark grey building, a feeling of foreboding wafted over Deirdre. Her nervousness had returned. The carriage ride had sobered her up, she sensed that something wasn't quite right, but she just couldn't put her finger on it. On the drive out James had behaved like a perfect gentleman. Well as perfect as any gentleman could be in such circumstances. But now as she approached the large ornate door to his country retreat she was beginning to believe that she'd been lulled into a false sense of security. Was it her imagination or was the moonlight playing tricks on her? She could've sworn his dark eyes had taken on a maniacal look. His voice now had an edge that bordered on the threatening. It must be the drink, mustn't it? Deirdre began to panic.

By the time she'd reached his rooms Deirdre realised things weren't as they seemed. This wasn't going to be a quickie up against a wall, nor was it going to be, as Deirdre had hoped, a gentle seduction, followed by an evening's love making. It was going to be something far more to the extreme. Confirmation came in the shape of James Fairfax's fist. She didn't see it coming. One minute she's admiring the room, the next she's out cold.

Fairfax let out a wild squeal of delight as the whore fell to the floor like a sack of potatoes. Then, with a practiced expertise, he began to secure her to the bed. As Deirdre slowly regained consciousness, her worst fears were confirmed. She was naked and bound to the four corners of the bed. Her clothes, such as they were, lay in a heap on the floor. That he was going to rape her, she had no doubt. Some men, she'd learned, needed to force themselves upon women. Even then she wasn't too alarmed. Apprehensive, disappointed maybe, but only her dreams of wealth had evaporated. He wanted to show her who was boss. It was, she thought disdainfully, sometimes the only way these men could get themselves off. Life was harsh, she knew that, but at that precise moment she didn't realise to what depths a man's depravity could sink. She could only think of what might have been. James Fairfax hadn't seemed at all like those men. He was a gentleman, so why was he doing this to her? For a dollar, ten dollars, he could have whatever he wanted.

"You look puzzled my dear," he said, as he removed his coat and shirt. Deirdre's fear grew as she looked at him, really for the first time. He was handsome and, judging by his upper torso, very muscular and sinewy. His dark neatly slicked-back hair *now ruffled and dishevelled from removing his shirt,* hung menacingly across his wide forehead. His piercing black eyes twinkled with excitement and his insane like smile spread his already thin moustache even thinner. "Answer me this bitch. Why would I take the likes of you, a common whore to supper?" He began to laugh and it was at that moment Deirdre realised that he was quite mad. "You're all the same, you filthy disgusting creatures of the night."

"Please don't hurt me," begged Deirdre now fearful for her life. "I'll do anything you ask."

"That you will my dear!"

Right at that moment Deirdre saw the knife. Its blade glinted off the flame of an oil lantern that rested at the side of the bed.

His eyes bulged and his face broke into a grin that reminded Deirdre of the devil. "I'm going to fuck you like the whore you are! I'm going to fuck you six ways to Sunday." Then his voice lowered and he added, "and then when I'm finished I'm going to cut your magnificent tits off."

Deirdre's face grew white with terror, she felt the warm wetness between her legs, and realised she'd peed herself. For the second time in her short life she asked herself the question. 'Why is this happening to me?' She stifled a sob, 'Why me?' Faced with the inevitable, Deirdre shouted at him. "You'll never get away with it. I'll be missed. Fanny Brannigan will report my disappearance to the police. They'll come looking!"

James Fairfax's only reaction was to grin as he slowly removed his trousers before climbing on top of the helpless Deirdre. She felt his weight as he roughly climbed across her naked body. In his eyes she could see the reflection of the oil lamp, flickering and crying out that there was no mercy, just carnal lust. Forcing himself inside her, with his face inches from hers, he uttered, "Fanny Brannigan and I, have a little financial arrangement. You're not the first, and you'll not be the last."

As he thrust deeper inside Deirdre, she fought back the instinct to slip into unconsciousness to escape the inevitable. Her eyes searched the room for any avenue of escape. The knife with which he intended to end her life was on the table inches from the bed. If only she could reach it, but with her wrists bound and his body between them, it was impossible. 'The lantern,' she thought. It was within her grasp, if only she could free her wrist. With a desperation only a person fighting for their life could possess, Deirdre tugged at her bonds.

"That's it! Fight, struggle, cry for help!" screamed Fairfax. Her struggles only added to his excitement. The bonds that held Deirdre's wrists chaffed and tore at her flesh, as he thrust ever deeper. In that moment when time appears to stand still, she thought about what had brought her here. In that split second before she realised her right bond had loosened she vowed that if she were lucky enough to escape, then never again would she know poverty and ignorance. Straining for all she was worth her wrist suddenly broke free just as she felt him climax. It was the distraction that Deirdre needed desperately. Her hand grasped for the lantern, and in an arching movement crashed it fully against the side of Fairfax's head. The glass splintered and the oil ignited as it splattered over him. In seconds he was jumping around the room screaming in agony, his hair and face ablaze.

Free of his body Deirdre reached across and grabbed the knife. In seconds the razor sharp blade had freed her bonds. With her heart racing frantically, she quelled the instincts to flee and forced herself to think. Fighting back blind panic she somehow managed to calm herself. Going back to Fanny Brannigan's was out of the question. Throwing herself on the mercy of the courts would only result in her swinging from a scaffold. Who would the courts believe? Whore or gentleman?

Deirdre had watched as Fairfax raced naked from the room screaming. She knew it wouldn't be too long before someone came in search of her. Dressing quickly, her eyes scanned her surroundings. She had nothing but the clothes on her back. If she was going to make good her escape she needed money. Her eyes spotted a great oak cabinet at the far end of the room. If there was anything of value it would be there. She rifled though the drawers recklessly, but in each she found nothing, that was until she reached the bottom drawer on the left side. It was locked. Using the knife, Deirdre forced the lock. She was in luck; the drawer was full of papers and a cash box. Grabbing the box, she descended the stairs quietly and slipped out the back entrance.

As she raced into the relative safety of nearby woods she could still hear Fairfax screaming. Spurred on by his screams, Deirdre raced farther and farther into the wood. When all she could hear was the pounding of her heart she slowed to a walk. Her body shook and her teeth chattered uncontrollably. Although she was in a state of shock, she fought against her fear and concentrated all her attention on the monster she'd so recently escaped from. Her life depended on it.

From what she could remember of her ordeal, it wasn't the first time he'd lured a poor unsuspecting girl to her death. She prayed it would be the last. She hoped he'd die of his wounds. At the very least, she thought, he won't be seducing them with his good looks anymore. Yet the very thought of him alive, and that old harridan Fanny Brannigan, filled her with fear and dread. Forcing her painful legs and feet to keep moving she pushed on through the undergrowth.

That she'd escaped certain death renewed her faith in God. 'Surely they won't find me. God would not be so unkind as to play that kind of trick.' She was tired and weary, but knew she had to put as much distance as she could between the house and herself. Using the stars she headed in a westerly direction. Several miles later, weary from her exertions, Deirdre finally collapsed. When she awoke the sun was reaching its zenith. As she gathered her thoughts in the unfamiliar surroundings, she went over the events of that night. That there was no going back she was certain, but where did she go from here?

Her refuge, she soon discovered, was the middle of a cornfield. That at least meant God was smiling down on her. She was shielded from view on all sides. It was then that she noticed the cash-box on the ground beside her. With the knife she prised open the metal box. Her eyes grew wide with excitement at the contents. The box was stashed full of US currency. She'd never seen that much money in her entire short life. 'There must be well over a thousand dollars,' thought Deirdre. 'Enough money,' she thought quickly, 'enough for me to make good my escape, to get away, to be safe.' To a place she'd only dreamed about, to a place called California.

CHAPTER 3

She'd heard tell of the new railroad that linked both oceans. In her day-dreams she'd often pictured herself travelling on the 'Transcontinental Railroad' as they called it. The papers, from what Deirdre had been told said you could actually cross the entire continent in a little over a week. Deirdre was full of excitement at the prospect. But because she had a head on her shoulders she realised that she had to be cautious. Turning up at the train depot dressed as she was, bare feet and all, well that alone would cause suspicion. Handing over nearly 200 dollars for a first class ticket would confirm what they already knew. Before she'd be able to do anything the sheriff would have her in irons and she'd end up in the pokey.

There were plans to consider but first she had to put as much distance between her, Fairfax's mansion and the Five Points as possible. Steal a horse? Walk? Which direction? The answer came on the wind. "Wood-smoke," cried Deirdre out loud. "I smell wood-smoke."

Sticking her head over the tips of corn Deirdre spied a farmhouse in the distance. "Where there's a house there must be a horse," she whispered under her breath. With the cover of the cornfield Deirdre was able to move closer to the farmhouse without being detected. She halted just on the edge of the field and parted the corn carefully. Her eyes grew wide with excitement. Across a dirt yard she spied the house and more importantly the stables. The stables were a safe distance from the house, so with any luck she could enter the barn without making too much noise.

The first pangs of hunger hit her as she began to wait out the daylight. Her mouth watered as she smelled fresh bacon cooking. Her stomach retched and for the briefest of moments she was transported back in time to Ireland. The temptation to walk right up to the farm-house door and beg for food almost overcame her. She was eaten up with the hunger pangs. Luckily for Deirdre her instinct for survival kicked in, just in time.

"Wait, be patient. There's plenty of time to eat," she said as if to comfort herself. Her stomach groaned in unison.

Darkness descended on the farm-house and a solitary oil lantern was lit. Nauseous with hunger Deirdre stared at the farmhouse longingly. The waiting was endless, or at least it seemed that way. Then, just as suddenly as the lantern had been lit, the flame was extinguished. Deirdre's excitement grew. Forcing herself not to rush, she waited an hour before venturing to the barn.

In the dark she fumbled her way to the stall. The horse neighed a greeting or warning, Deirdre didn't know which. Grabbing what felt like a hackamore she tried slipping it over the horse's head, but found she couldn't reach. The horse was a Clydesdale and at five feet four Deirdre wasn't tall enough to loop the hackamore over its head. She climbed the stall and balanced herself on the top. The horse let out a nervous whinny. Deirdre patted the horse reassuringly and began humming an old tune her mother sang to her ill-fated brothers and sisters. It had soothed them as they lay awake with the consumption. She hoped it would do the same with the horse. She was in luck, the animal put up no resistance as she slipped the improvised reins over its large head. She'd wanted to lead the horse quietly out of the barn, and then mount him when she was a safe distance from the house. That would have been impossible as the horse was at least eighteen hands tall. From the height of the stall she lowered herself gently onto the horse's back, all the time patting and reassuring the nervous animal. A gentle kick and the great beast moved slowly but silently from the stall. It was then that Deirdre realised she was sweating like a pig. She prayed that the farmer hadn't woken up and wasn't at that moment training his shot gun on the open barn doors.

Her luck held. The night sky was bathed in moonlight, something Deirdre hadn't realised before she entered the barn. If the farmer looked out of his window she was as good as dead. Turning the Clydesdale away from the house she gently walked it. Three hundred agonising yards she walked before giving the horse a gentle kick which moved him into a quick trot. Two minutes down the road with her confidence growing she forced him into a canter. Now the moon came into its own. Without it Deirdre guessed she wouldn't have got far.

As dawn broke Deirdre pulled the lathered horse to a standstill. Ahead of her was a small sleepy village, and from the look of its deserted streets, its inhabitants were still snug in their beds. From a ridge, hidden by scrub, Deirdre scrutinised the small hamlet. Her heart raced as she spied a line of washing outside a small cabin. Hopefully she could steal some suitable attire, anything to allay suspicion from the ragged yet gaudy red dress that she wore.

Stealthily she worked her way down to the cabin, praying she'd find clothing to suit. With her heart pounding she inspected the garments on the washing line. Again she was in luck, a man's shirt and a kid's breeches blew gently in the spring morning air. Seconds later they were gone.

Back safely on the ridge Deirdre stripped herself of her ragged garments and put on the clothes she'd so recently acquired. With the knife she hacked at the earth beneath the scrub and buried her dress. Still fearful for her life, she wasn't taking any chances of leaving a trail. James Fairfax might be dead but Deirdre reflected that she couldn't be sure. She'd seen it in his eyes. If he still breathed, and she prayed that he didn't, she'd made an enemy for life. She would never feel safe if he still walked the earth. The thought sent a shudder down her spine.

She judged her moonlit journey to have been around twenty miles. Not far enough for her to relax. She felt that she had to put more distance behind her. Leading the horse back into the trees she positioned the Clydesdale as close to a climbable tree and remounted. Checking the cash box and knife were secure she continued her journey with the sun at her back.

By nightfall, tired and hungry, Deirdre came across a good-sized town. "Big enough to hide in without causing any suspicion," she mused. She whispered a few words of comfort and gratitude into the ear of the big Clydesdale, then stroking his neck gently, she turned it in the direction of home and slapped it on the rear. As it loped off she thought about the farmer and hoped that the horse would find its way home.

At the outer edge of the town Deirdre surveyed the scene. A store in the centre was her destination. Carefully she sorted through the cash box and took out a few worn dollar bills; it didn't do to show too much money. Then with the knife she dug a small hole and buried the cash-box. Secure in the knowledge that she hadn't been spotted Deirdre strolled into the town.

In a town full of waifs and strays Deirdre went unnoticed. Looking at her reflection in a store window she soon realised her unkempt appearance made her look like a boy. In her red dress, scratched up and grubby she would have raised eyebrows. But in the over sized shirt and breeches she didn't get a second look. Even at the late night mission where she devoured corn bread and potatoes like a half starved vulture she remained just another vagrant. Years later Deirdre would often recall that she'd never enjoyed a meal so well before or since.

Still masquerading as a boy Deirdre hacked her hair off with the knife and went in search of a job. Her luck was holding as she walked by the town's livery stables. An old man poked his head out, "Hey young feller, you interested in a job?"

It was more than she could've hoped for, "Yeah," she said eagerly.

Joe Adamson looked her up and down, "Well you don't look much, but I'll give you a trial." Minutes later he'd put Deidre to work, where she cleared out the stalls, brought hay and generally looked after the town's horseflesh. She soon found out working at the livery was the place to pick up all sorts of information. Anyone new in town would automatically make for the livery stable, and invariably would bring news of what was happening in other parts of the state. It was there that Deirdre first learnt the news that James Fairfax the Third was still alive.

She was mucking out the stalls when she over heard old Joe Adamson.

"How goes it stranger?"

"Goes fine sir," replied the stranger.

"Where you from?" Joe Adamson was about the nosiest man in them parts.

"Up aways, towards the city."

"The city hah! What news from your neck of the woods?"

"Man hunt, or should I say woman hunt!"

Intrigued, Adamson pushed him for more information, "What, what's that you say?"

"Seems some local gentry up towards the city almost got himself killed a month or so back. Caught some whore red-handed, stealing him blind she was."

"Yeah," stuttered Joe, "Go on."

"Fought like a tigress, from what I hear. Damn bitch smashed an oil lamp across his head."

"Jesus! He hurt bad?"

"You could say. You hear tell it, he was a good lookin son of a bitch. He ain't that now. Half his face burnt off."

"Man would be better off dead."

"You'd think so. But from what I've heard he's for putting the noose around her himself. He even posted a reward!"

"Reward! How much?"

"$500."

"What's this no good whore look like?" said Joe greedily.

"She's about 15 years old, 5 foot 4 inches tall, pretty lookin, with medium length dark hair. There's a flyer on her too. Irish tyke."

"Hey Danny do yah hear? One of your clan," shouted Adamson.

"Not mine sir," said Deirdre as she hurried into a nearby stall. She fought down the urge to be sick and found she was shaking in her boots. Somehow or other she'd begun to believe he was dead, but now things had changed and not for the good. James Fairfax was alive and what's more he was hunting her down. Deirdre's first reactions were to run, but that would have caused suspicion to fall on her. Everyone in town thought of her as a boy, it was an advantage that was keeping her alive. That she regularly smeared horse-shit across her face also helped to perpetrate the myth that she was male. No, she had to sit tight and wait for it to blow over.

During the next few month nothing much happened in the town of Cloverville. Deirdre continued as stable lad at the local livery stable by day, but at night she worked on her plans to reach California. With the cash-box money she could purchase a ticket, but so as not to arouse suspicion she'd need to look every inch the lady. Buying store-bought dresses was something Danny the stable boy could not do without causing suspicion. The answer came almost by accident. Mr Adamson sent Deirdre to collect a package from the general store. It was then that she discovered mail order shopping.

A new invention pioneered by Montgomery Ward. Fascinated by the array of goods on sale, Deirdre cast her eyes over the ladies' fashions. It wasn't long before she put in a bogus order for the latest dress and accessories. 'Mrs Adamson,' thought the owner of the general store, 'is a mite too old for what she's ordering. But it wasn't his place to say anything.'

Six weeks went by, and there wasn't a day that Danny/Deirdre didn't enquire if Mrs Adamson's order had arrived.

It was a bitter cold day in late January 1873 and Deirdre's plans were still only half formed, when James Fairfax rode into Cloverville. She was just about to step from the shadows when he climbed down from his tall mount and handed the reins to Mr Adamson. She knew it was him the moment he opened his mouth. That fake English accent was unmistakable. But if she needed more conformation, beneath his dark wide brimmed hat, his face was half covered by a tanned leather mask. One side of him looked normal, but the other side Deirdre knew was hideous and grotesque.

"Danny, see to this man's horse," shouted Mr Adamson nervously.

For a split second Deirdre froze to the spot and then the instinct to survive kicked in. With head lowered she advanced towards Fairfax, her heart in her mouth. Taking the reins from Mr Adamson she led the horse to an empty stall. In the relative safety of the stall she felt a warm wetness in her pants. It was the second time James Fairfax the Third had made her wet herself. Her fright turned to anger as she comforted herself by vowing there wouldn't be a third.

She strained to hear their conversation.

"I'm lookin for a woman."

"Who ain't?" said Adamson doing his best to regain his composure. Fairfax's appearance had unnerved him.

"Not that kind!" snarled Fairfax.

Adamson, shaken by the quick turn round in conversation cursed himself for being a fool. "I'm sorry sir; I didn't mean to offend you."

"That's just as well," said Fairfax in a low and menacing tone.

In the cold stall Deirdre began to shake with fear. The last time she had heard him speak it was in that same tone of voice when he informed her what he was going to do.

"Do you know who I am?"

"Yes sir, that I do," squirmed Adamson. Over the last few months he'd heard many tales of this masked man and none of them were good.

"Then you know why I'm here!"

Deirdre's heart almost flew from her body.

"A dress, a bright red dress that only a filthy whore would wear, was found partly buried not fifteen miles from here."

"How do you know it's hers?

"Because I recognised it with my own eyes, from just before the slut did this!" His eyes burned into the livery stable owner. For a second, Deirdre thought he was going to strike the man down for daring to question him.

"This is a fair sized town, but not that big. I'd have known if someone like her was around," said Adamson as he tried not to let his fear show.

"That flyer," said Fairfax, pointing to the outside wall of the livery stable that doubled for the town's notice board. It's out of date. I have a likeness. Pin it up and keep your eyes open."

"1,000 dollars!" exclaimed Adamson. His attention was drawn to the reward posted. "You must want this woman pretty bad?"

"More than anything else in life." The words were slow and deliberate.

"I guess you won't rest until she's hanging from a rope."

"She ain't for hanging. I'm gonna cut her heart out, roast it over an open fire, then I'm gonna eat it!"

Adamson shuddered. The look in Fairfax's eyes told him he meant every word. The man's macabre appearance, the dark brown wide brimmed hat and matching long coat and the neatly fashioned leather mask with those savage eyes that blazed as if they mirrored hell. 'Well,' thought Adamson, 'he could be the devil himself.'

The livery stable owner watched as Fairfax strolled across the street to the hotel, glad that he'd have no more dealings with him until he left town. He was still sweating from his encounter when he glanced at the flyer he'd just nailed to the wall. He scratched his head and contemplated the picture. There was something familiar about the likeness. He couldn't put his finger on it, but given time he was sure it would come to him. A thousand dollars was an awful lot of money.

Deirdre almost screamed in terror. She'd seen the double take Adamson had made towards the flyer. It was only a matter of time before he put a face to the poster. That old man Adamson would give her up for the reward she had no doubt. She'd missed death by inches and when Adamson put a face to that picture she'd be running for her life. She watched the back of Fairfax as he walked towards the hotel. He was her worst nightmare come true. Despite her plans, despite the fact it was mid-winter, the fiend had left her with little choice, she had to cut and run.

It was a good day and a half's ride to the terminal in New York. The eastern rail network reached as far as Omaha, from there Deirdre envisaged embarking on the Transcontinental Railroad to complete her marathon journey. She could only guess, but knowing her luck it would surely leave early morning. All she knew was that once Adamson realised where he'd seen that face before there'd be no time to run. As Deirdre closed up for the evening she realised she had no choice but to run that very night. Adamson would discover a horse missing in the morning and a stable boy short. He'd kick up a noise and Fairfax was sure to get wind. With luck that would give her nearly a day's start.

In the darkness of the livery stable Deirdre packed her provisions, the cash-box and the mail order clothing. She was going to make a dash for it. With luck Fairfax wouldn't hear about her leaving until late, then when he did would he expect her to return to New York?

As she pushed open the livery stable door she walked into a blizzard. Travelling by night in such treacherous conditions was not ideal. At best she'd make slow time, at worst she'd freeze to death. It was a chance she had to take.

Chapter 4

Fairfax trudged through the snow and entered the town's largest boarding house. Through past experience he realised his appearance wouldn't have gone unnoticed. If the whore was here in town, she'd surely know of his existence and would have made herself scarce and with the weather closing in, there would be no chance for escape. This could work to his advantage, he thought. Someone would know who was missing; someone would be tempted by the reward. For a thousand dollars most of them would sell their own mother. If she was here, he was sure to smoke her out.

His crusade was on hold. Those filthy bitches could wait. He had a job to do. But first he had to find and destroy the whore who had disfigured him, cut her heart out and devour every last morsel. Then he could continue his crusade.

He washed and rested up then with the pangs of hunger he entered the dining room. He was polite and charming despite the looks of apprehension his appearance caused to those about him. The mask *it must be said* gave him a rakish appearance that seemed to draw women. A number of ladies who had bedded him since the fire found being made love to by the man in the half mask added to their sexual excitement. For his part these unions only compounded his hatred for the whore Deirdre Devlin, the name being given to him by his friend and confidant, Fanny Brannigan.

His thoughts drifted back to those months where he'd slipped between the dead and the living. Then just as quickly they jumped to the day the bandages came off. In the privacy of his rooms James Faifax the third began to unravel the bandages. As the last piece of bandage was removed he slowly turned towards the mirror.

His screams could be heard throughout the whole household. He stared in horror at the monster that he already knew he was. The vast majority of the left side of his face, from the centre of his forehead near the hairline to just above the chin, was so hideously burned that a canvas mask had to be fashioned and worn before he could look at himself in the mirror again. In addition to these injuries and disfigurements an area of pink flesh, stretching from his widow's peak to the left temple, now replaced his dark locks. He was lucky that his left eye had survived.

Alone in his room with the canvas mask strapped in place, James Fairfax began the slow road to recovery. A rage had begun to simmer beneath the mask, a rage that was about to encompass more than a few filthy whores; a rage that would engulf all hell.

Fanny Brannigan was the first to feel that rage. It was six months to the day that James Fairfax re-entered Fanny's establishment. Only this time he entered through the back door. Unobserved, he crept stealthily up to Fanny Brannigan's rooms and waited.

At three fifteen in the morning she retired for the night. The light from the lantern she'd used to find her way in the dark illuminated her room, casting grotesque shadows around the walls. Slightly drunk Fanny slammed the door shut behind her.

"Hello Fanny!"

"Jesus! Who the fuck's there!" She cried out, as she pushed the lantern in the direction of Fairfax.

"Don't be alarmed. It's me James Fairfax."

"Fucking hell James, you nigh on scared the shit out of me!"

Fairfax turned his good side towards Fanny and quietly apologised. "It's information I'm after. That firebrand nigh on killed me. I need to know just what you've got on her. I need to know for your sake as well as mine," he added quickly. "If that bitch talks, they'll find out about the others." He looked at her reaction. "I paid you good money. They'll hang you for sure. That's why you've got to tell me every thing you know about her. Her family, her habits, her dreams, anything that will help me find the bitch. We need to leave no witnesses. You understand."

"I understand," said Fanny nervously.

Within two minutes the old madam, *Fairfax guessed she was well into her forties,* plump and juicy, had spilled every thing she knew about Deirdre Devlin.

"I was sorry to hear about your misfortune." said Fanny. She'd been told how disfigured he'd been, but from what she could see in the dim lantern light he looked much the same as ever. Feeling a little randy, Fanny gave Fairfax an evil smile, "Would you like one on account?" she inquired in a low husky voice. "It's been awhile since you and I took a ride together."

Fairfax flashed a smile, and Fanny moved closer. She sank to her knees and unbuttoned his fly. But before she could take him into her mouth a leather pouch loaded with lead shot caught her on the right temple. Fanny Brannigan slumped onto her bed. When she woke up, she was bound to the old four-poster and gagged. Her clothes had been ripped from her body, exposing her white ample flesh. She stared in terror as Fairfax half hidden in shadows undressed. He turned his back and pulled off the improvised canvas mask. In the semi darkness he climbed on top of the old madam and squeezed her right tit. Then he forced himself inside her. Still keeping his left side from Fanny's view, he spoke to her softly and gently. "It's just my little bit of fun. I'm gonna fuck you six ways to Sunday. Then when I'm finished I'm gonna untie you."

Still unsure of his motives Fanny moved her body in time with his, expertly flexing her thigh muscles to give him extra sensation. She smiled to her self as she heard him moan with pleasure and anticipation.

Fairfax positioned the lantern at the side of her bed so he could read every emotion on Fanny Brannigan's face. Then slowly he turned his face towards hers.

"I want you to be the first to see the new James Fairfax the Third!"

Fanny knew what ever he looked like that she had to control her revulsion. Her life she told herself depended on it. For the briefest of seconds her eyes bulged in terror at the full horror, but with all the experience of her chosen profession she smiled though her eyes and pretended to enjoy their lovemaking. When he was finished, he climbed off her and dressed himself. Then he refitted his mask and put on his top coat. He stared down at Fanny Brannigan's more than ample body, still bound and spread-eagled across the bed. He smiled and sat on the bed beside her. Fanny's eyes bulged like two hard boiled eggs.

"Don't be frightened. I mean you no harm." Then to Fanny's shock and relief he undid the rope that held her left hand. Then he released the gag that was across her mouth.

She gasped for air, "Fuck you James. You really had me going there!"

"Yeah, well you know me. I must say for an old un you're still a good fuck." Fanny smiled at the compliment.

"Tis a pity it'll be the last fuck we ever have. I did say no witnesses, didn't I?"

Fanny tried to scream but all that came out was a gurgling sound. Dead hard boiled eyes stared up at him.

Fanny Brannigan's murder got barely a mention in the uptown papers, and even in the Five Points it caused hardly a ripple. Life in the Five Points area of New York was cheap in1873. But nonetheless

James Fairfax was unnerved. He'd taken three lives up to that point in New York, each ritualistic in their execution, but the murder of Fanny Brannigan had far more meaning than the rest. She'd seen at close quarters the hideous spectre that was James Fairfax. The look of revulsion on her face as she gazed into his eyes was too hard to disguise. That was why she had to die! Fanny wasn't like the girls, she wasn't slim and pretty, she wasn't at all like the woman who'd destroyed his life. Until she'd stared at him in that way, there was no reason why she had to die.

Things were clearer in the days and weeks that followed the murder. James Fairfax knew what he had to do. That whore, the one they called Deirdre Devlin, she'd changed his plans. Like the bitch whore before her, she'd risen far above her station. She'd fought him, she'd scarred him, much like the bitch whore, but she hadn't paid the ultimate price. "Well, she will, she will!" screamed the monster that stared back at him through the mirror.

"Money is no object, within reason," added James Fairfax. "I want you to design and sculpture a leather mask, one that will cover this half of my face!" He whipped off the canvas mask and revealed himself to the leather-smith. The leather-smith stared at James Fairfax's scarring and almost ran out the door.

"Scary isn't it. That's why I commissioned you. I understand you are the best there is."

"You're correct sir," said the leather-smith. His composure returned at almost the same time as Fairfax replaced the improvised canvas mask.

"I want several, depending on what I'm wearing. I want them snug and comfortable. I want them functional and hard wearing. And if possible I'd like them to appeal to the opposite sex. Can you accomplish that?"

"It'll take a few sittings, but I'm sure I'll be able to create just what you want. But first I need to take a mould of your head. Allowing for adjustments I should have the prototype ready within a month."

"Excellent."

Fairfax next hired a detective agency to try to locate the fugitive whore. When they hadn't shown any results after a week Fairfax sent for the detective on the case.

"I'm not asking the impossible dammit!"

"I'm sorry sir, the woman Deirdre Devlin seems to have vanished without trace."

"She's a whore, man, a goddamn fucking whore! How in the blue blazes can a whore vanish?"

"We need to put out flyers. Advertise in the papers. If the rewards great enough, I'm sure someone will have noticed her."

"Get on it."

A further week went by and then a month, before the breakthrough came.

"We ran down every misdemeanour in a twenty mile radius. We found nothing of interest until we came upon the stealing of a horse from a local farm. We didn't think much of it at first, the horse being a Clydesdale and all. She'd ave to be desperate to try to ride such a beast."

"Why the fuck are you bothering me with details?"

"Sorry sir. Without much more to go on we decided to look a little closer. The horse was found, some twenty miles from home. In a pasture, it was."

"Go on," said Fairfax, as he resigned himself to listening to the details.

"We came across a little community. They ain't seen er, but a man',s shirt and a boy's breeches went missing from a washing line about the same time the horse showed up."

"Is that it?" Fairfax could feel his face glowing red with anger.

"It would've been sir, until they told me about the dress."

"Dress, what dress?"

"It's a gaudy number. The type tarts wear, begging your pardon sir!"

"What colour?"

"Red it was sir."

A smile spread across the mean lips of James Fairfax. The bitch wasn't as clever as she thought she was; she'd left a trail for him to follow. "Get me the map. Show me where the horse was located. I want to know how far it was to where the dress was found."

A map was spread across the table. The detective pointed to where the horse was stolen and then he indicated where it was found. Between both spots was where the dress had been hidden.

"How many towns are there within ten, fifteen miles of there," said Fairfax pointing at the map.

"Twelve I think, maybe thirteen."

"Well get on it. The flyers should create an interest. I want them in all of them towns before winter sets in."

For months the detective scoured the countryside, putting up posters wherever he could. In each town he met the same response. The townsfolk speculated, accused, even lied about the waifs and strays who frequented their towns, but none fooled the detective. He'd seen the anger in James Fairfax's eyes. There was no way he was going to court his venom without having something concrete to go on.

Christmas came and went. There was still no sign. The trail had fizzled out. Then an unexpected incident forced James Fairfax to take to the trail himself. Fanny Brannigan's murder hadn't caused so much as a ripple in most quarters, but Sergeant Finbar O'Toole, of the New York police department had a vested interest. He'd known Fanny back in the old country, and from time to time had turned a blind eye to her shenanigans in the Five Points. He'd sniffed around the murder scene and against popular consensus believed someone she knew quite well had killed her. There had been no screams and it was blatantly evident she'd had sexual intercourse prior to her death. It was the third such killing Sergeant O'Toole had been called upon to investigate in recent months. All three had been found bound and at one time gagged. There had been sexual activity prior to death, and they'd had their throats cut. But this time the killer had deviated from his course of action. Whereas the first two were young and pretty, Fanny Brannigan wasn't. She'd been killed in her own bedroom, whilst the other two victims had been killed some place and dumped in another. But most puzzling to O'Toole and his fellow officers, was the fact that Fanny Brannigan's body had not been subjected to a frenzied attack.

On the face of it, it would appear that this murder wasn't related to the other two. O'Toole thought otherwise. He'd had dealings with the first prostitute a few months prior to her death. The very fact she'd been working out of Fanny's establishment gave him cause to think there was a link between them. The other woman he didn't recognise. Her body was too disfigured for identification. Neither girl had been reported missing, which wasn't unusual given their profession, but the very fact that one of them had worked for Fanny, suggested to Finbar O'Toole that Brannigan had been murdered to keep her quiet. Without much more to go on, Finbar had been forced reluctantly to put the three murders on the back burner.

Missing persons wasn't a job for the local police department. Everyone knew Finbar O'Toole's opinion on the matter. That's why he always gave the independent detective agencies his full co-operation. Without them he'd be out chasing shadows from dawn til dusk, and having to face the wrath of Mrs Finbar O'Toole when he finally got home. When Mervyn Prescott of 'Prescott Detective Agency,' stepped into his office, Finbar offered him his hand and invited him to sit.

"Do you remember me coming to you a few months back concerning the assault on my client, a Mr James Fairfax? He was that poor guy that got so terribly scarred up by a whore from the Five Points. It seems she ran off after nigh on killing him, with a thousand dollars in cash."

O'Toole scratched his bald head for a moment before answering. "Refresh my memory."

"High profile guy lives out in the country. He's now taken to wearing a leather mask to cover his disfigurement."

"Yeah. Now that you mention it, I do recall."

"Well I'll come straight to the point, the search has produced zilch. I've traced the woman to within thirty, forty miles of the city, then nothing. I'm heading for Cloverville in three days. I was wondering if you could give me a letter of introduction. Seems I recall their Captain of Detectives is an old pal of yours."

"Jimmy Flannigan. I ain't seen him in years," Finbar said reflectively. "Sure, I'll write you a note of introduction right away."

After Prescott had left, Finbar O'Toole thought about his old friend in Cloverville and remembered the good times in their early years in the department. He chuckled to himself.

During the course of the day O'Toole pondered the question of the missing whore. He thought Prescott was wasting his time, if the whore hadn't shown up by now, she was probably dead. Then in an instant his blood ran cold.

"Of course!" exclaimed Finbar, "Why didn't I see the connection?" his words were directed to the four walls. To most people what Finbar saw as a connection, was little more than clutching at straws. But the detective sergeant wasn't like most people. 'I missed it because it was down as an assault and robbery, not as a missing person. Now, if that young girl worked out of Fanny Brannigan's I'd say she was dead and my theory that there was a connection to Brannigan's was correct. Finbar's mind was working overtime.

A day later, Finbar's suspicions were founded. Deirdre Devlin had indeed worked out of Fanny's. What's more, according to the whore Annie, Deirdre Devlin had had a run in with James Fairfax on the very night of the assault. Tenuous though the meeting had been, it was enough to fuel O'Toole's suspicion.

During the course of the next few days, bribery, threats and one case of assault, *the basis of Sergeant Finbar O'Toole's own style of investigation,* brought him the answers he was looking for. James Fairfax had a long time financial association with Fanny Brannigan. He was a braggart, a lecher, a drunkard and a man seething with an inner rage, according to one of the prostitutes who frequented Fanny's. But it didn't make him a murderer, a suspect yes.

Finbar O'Toole felt the juices flowing through his veins. Whilst all he had was circumstantial it was enough to whet his appetite. He'd been a policeman for more years than he could remember, yet never in his time had he felt so sure. James Fairfax might not be a murderer, but in O'Toole's book he was mixed up in it somewhere.

Fairfax being in Cloverville rather than the private investigator Prescott was due largely to the visit of Finbar O'Toole a day later.

O'Toole's first impression of James Fairfax confirmed his suspicions. Calling on Fairfax under the pretext of following up on the assault left him in no doubt that the man was capable of almost anything. The man appeared calm and not in the least fazed by the unannounced visit. He accepted the questioning with a grace that defied the apparent disfigurement that lured beneath the mask. His calmness prompted Finbar to probe more deeply.

"Why do you think this young woman happened upon your house? Do you think she was part of a street gang? Did you see anyone else?"

"It was dark and as you can see, I wasn't in a position to notice if there was anyone with her." His demeanour remained intact, but his eyes burned with hatred. "You're right of course. The whore must have had an accomplice."

"Whore! What makes you think she was a whore?"

The question received the reaction O'Toole was after.

"She was a whore all right! A dirty filthy piece of vermin! She did this to me!"

Before the detective sergeant could say anything Fairfax undid the straps of the leather mask and stared defiantly into Finbar O'Toole's face.

"Jesus Christ!" exclaimed the detective, his face now white with shock. "Sir please forgive my outburst, it wasn't my intention to offend. If you say she was a whore, then she was a whore."

With the mask back in place Fairfax's rage calmed, but Finbar could see the hate simmering behind the man's dark piercing eyes.

"That's all right officer. You must forgive my lack of self-control. It's just that you brought back too many memories of that night."

"There's nothing to forgive sir. I'll take my leave of you if I may."

Fairfax enjoyed a perverse pleasure at seeing the policeman squirm. He couldn't get out of the place fast enough, thought Fairfax.

But the table was turned as O'Toole reached the door. He hesitated, looked back at Fairfax and threw one last disarming question at him. "Oh, just one more thing. Had you ever seen the woman before?"

"Never. But I'd recognise her. She's etched into my memory."

Finbar bit on his tongue. He'd seen the flyers that Fairfax had put out. The man had even got a name for the whore, but he'd never seen her before that night. If O'Toole had needed convincing before he didn't now.

James Fairfax seethed with rage as he watched the bald-headed police officer drive off in his carriage. That he'd given himself away, he had no doubt. "That bastard's too clever by half," he shouted in anger. "He knows I'm lying about Devlin, but he can't prove it. Whether he suspects me of the murders of Fanny Brannigan and those other bitch whores I'm not sure." His words drifted harmlessly upwards towards a dark wintry sky. Under his breath he muttered, "What I'm sure about is this, if he gets to Devlin before I do, my goose is cooked!"

The following day he paid off Mervyn Prescott, took the letter of introduction and rode out towards Cloverville.

CHAPTER 5

Deirdre's horse gave out, three quarters of a mile from the city limits. She'd ridden him hard through the blizzard, stopping only for shelter and rest when they couldn't go on any longer. The biting cold blizzard suddenly, after nearly two days of endless misery, finally stopped. She'd wanted to rest then, but the fear of the monster chasing her was too great. On they trudged until the horse stumbled and sank to its knees. Deirdre broke down and cried. They were so near. She knew certain death would claim it within an hour if it lay there. Desperately she did all she could to revive the horse, but it was no use. Fearing for her own life, tired and on the brink of exhaustion, she put one foot in front of the other and focused on the lights of the city.

She woke to the smell of horse manure and hay, and for a second, thought she'd woken up in Adamson's livery stable. But the added smell of coal from the nearby Rail Depot alerted her to where she was, and why. She was cold and hungry and she smelt like a skunk. In her present condition she looked more like the street urchin she'd portrayed for so long, than the young woman about to take up a teaching post in San Francisco. It was a cover story she'd invented over Christmas in Adamson's livery.

As Deirdre acclimatised herself to her surroundings she recalled seeing a water butt just outside the livery stable doors. Bracing herself against the cold she peered outside. It was still early and most of the inhabitants of the town would be warm and snug in their beds, at least that's what Deirde told herself. Grabbing an axe from inside the stable she raced outside and smashed through the ice that had formed over the water butt. Without a thought for her modesty she stripped down to her britches and sluiced the freezing cold water over herself. The cold water tore her breath away as it made contact. Vigorously she rubbed at her hair, her face and beneath her arms. As she gasped and thrashed about, any thoughts of discovery were whipped away. Only the single thought of keeping herself warm occupied her mind. And then the miraculous happened. As she dashed back inside the livery stable she realised she wasn't cold any longer. She was warm all over. In her excitement she danced around the livery stable, like a demented loon.

Ten minutes later Deirde emerged from the stables, dressed in the mail order dress and a shawl that she'd stolen from Mrs Adamson some days earlier. Her face was red and glowing and her hair hung lankly around the nape of her neck. For the only time in her life she feared that she'd not pass off as a woman. Many years later, as she was getting herself ready to greet her clients, she would look at herself in the mirror and chuckle. Though only fifteen, devoid of makeup Deirdre looked every inch a woman.

At the train depot she ate her first hot meal in over forty-eight hours. She tried her best to eat in a lady-like way, though the instinct to just tear at her food was almost irresistible. At a store close by she discarded her old coat and bought a travelling outfit; something that was more appropriate for the arduous journey ahead of her. Purchasing her ticket was in itself the most nerve wracking.

"San Francisco, that's a mighty long way to go for someone so young," enquired the man as he sold her the ticket. "Your ticket gets you to Omaha, there you've got to check in at the ticket counter, where they'll issue you with a ticket to Sacramento. Then pretty lady, it becomes a mite uncomfortable as you'll have to complete the rest of the journey by stagecoach."

"Yes, I know it's a long journey but my aunt has secured me a wonderful teaching position in one of San Francisco's finest schools. I'm very excited about it," Deirdre replied with all the skill her days at Fanny Brannigan's had taught her. Her confidence was growing, but so was her fear of James Fairfax. Although it was impossible, her imagination cried out that at any moment he would appear and drag her away before she could board the train.

As the train lurched into action, Deirdre's fear began to evaporate. By the time it had picked up speed, her confidence had returned. She was back to being a woman and then it dawned on her, she was on her way to another life and with the best part of a thousand dollars still intact. Her confidence grew with every mile.

By the time Deirdre reached Omaha she was feeling pretty worn out. The carriage seat she'd occupied for the past three days was cushion less, and hard to sit on and extremely uncomfortable. As the clickerty-clack of the engines wheels took her farther and farther from New York her self belief grew along with her calluses. She promised herself she'd purchase a first class ticket for the rest of the journey.

"How much?" she cried when the ticket clerk told her the price for a first class ticket.

"One hundred and eleven dollars," he'd said with an air of superiority.

Feeling foolish, she excused herself from the busy ticket office and retired to a small table in the adjacent dining room, where she furtively opened the cash-box. She'd already purchased her ticket to Omaha with a large denominational bill; the last thing she wanted was to attract attention. She was in luck, although the majority of bills were in large denominations she managed to scrape together the necessary ticket money. Deirdre satisfied that her purchase would go unnoticed, bought herself a meal. Then she counted her change along with the money she needed to buy the ticket. She had one fifty dollar bill, two twenties and two tens, plus the rest in change. Satisfied that the purchase of a first class ticket would go unnoticed, she finished her meal.

The smug look on the ticket clerk's face disappeared as Deirdre counted out the money onto the counter. "Have a pleasant journey," he just about managed to say.

"Thank you, I will," said Deirdre with a confidence she never knew existed.

As Deirdre settled into the purple velvet quilted seating she cracked a small smile. Then looking out the window at the busy Omaha station she hummed to herself until the wheels of the train gave a sudden lurch forward. Then slowly but surely the wheels of the great locomotive began to turn. It wasn't long before Omaha was just a speck in the fast disappearing distance.

At last she was free of her old life. Free to be what ever she wanted in the great city by the sea, San Francisco. But more important to her than the chance of a new and exciting life was the thought that she was free of James Fairfax the Third forever …

Chapter 6

Finbar O'Toole had been busy in James Fairfax's absence. A few discreet enquires here, a couple of favours there and slowly but surely the pieces were coming together. James Fairfax the Third was a first generation American. His accent was as false as the flamboyant title he gave himself. His name suggested he'd come at the very least from aristocracy, but that was far from the truth. His father was an English merchant called Jimmy Fairfax, who'd arrived on these shores at just the right time to make money. He was a low life from the East End of London, and his speech was a far cry from the posh accent James Fairfax had adopted. He married a cotton merchant's daughter in Boston and soon found himself working for her father. There marriage was a hot bed of lust and debauchery. It wasn't long before Jimmy brought others to the marriage bed. Martha was a willing partner and enjoyed three, sometime four in her bed at a time. You could say it was a marriage made in hell.

Jimmy's gambling and whoring soon found him in need. Not content with the generous wage her father had given him, he cajoled, bullied and eventually resorted to blackmailing his wife into asking her father to make him a junior partner. She was pregnant at the time, *fortunately during a period of abstinence from their lives of debauchery.* He'd threatened to leave her, sighting another man as her adulterous lover and the father of her child. Knowing her father's religious beliefs she knew he'd cast her aside and believe the lout that she'd married. She told herself that he wouldn't have gone ahead with his threats, but deep down she knew he meant every word.

The years came and went and eventually her father passed away, leaving the bulk of his estate to his daughter and her husband. Jimmy Fairfax spent little time at home, preferring the taverns and whorehouses around the harbour. He'd lived high on the hog for years, but now his sins had found him out. He'd siphoned off funds for years, not knowing nor caring about the consequences. His inheritance left him destitute: the business fell into receivership and the death duties of his father-in-law's house was crippling. His long-suffering wife had contracted syphilis from their philandering and was in an advanced stage of the disease. He'd long thought her mad and was on the verge of having her committed. And then it happened. The papers called it an accident, the police confirmed and the fire service concurred. A fire in the early hours had swept through the house and taken the lives of Jimmy Fairfax and his sick wife, only their twelve year-old son survived. There was talk that Jimmy Fairfax had arrived home drunk, as was his norm, that an argument had developed between him and his wife and that in the heated quarrel a lamp or other device had been overturned.

O'Toole also found out that a substantial sum of money was paid out to James Fairfax from an insurance that his prudent grandfather had taken out on his daughter. The inheritance was held in trust for him until he reached the age of twenty-one. He spent the years in between living with his mother's spinster sister in a less salubrious suburb of Boston.

It was enough to confirm what O'Toole already suspected. It now gave Fairfax the motive. Two motives in fact, thought the detective; murdering Brannigan and the two, possibly three whores, in revenge for his father's philandering was one; the other was far more sinister. Perhaps he set the fire that killed his parents. It's quite likely that he knew of his grandfather's insurance policy on his mother and it was possible that the shame of his mother's illness also contributed. After all, Finbar thought, she wasn't entirely blameless. Yet none of this would carry any weight in court. All it did was to confirm Finbar O'Toole's suspicions he knew he was dealing with a murderer.

CHAPTER 7

In the days that followed the blizzard, Fairfax asked around town for the whereabouts of Deirdre. Some sixth sense had kept telling him he was on the right track, but now he was beginning to believe his intuition was wrong. He was about to turn in for the night when he happened to overhear a snippet of conversation.

"God damn darnest thing! Made off on my best mare without a by your leave. Rode out the same night as the blizzard hit," said Adamson to another man standing next to him in the bar across the street from the livery. "Damn good worker too, it's a pity. My bet is they're both frozen to death. Only a fool would take off in that kind of weather."

"A fool or someone running from the hangman's noose," interrupted Fairfax.

Adamson and his friend turned towards Fairfax, "Nah, Danny weren't that way. He was a quiet boy," said Adamson. "I just can't figure why he'd steal my best horse."

"How'd you know he was who he claimed to be?" said Fairfax.

"Sorry stranger, but this ain't any of your goddamn business." Liquor tended to do that to Adamson. He wasn't a timid man, but he wasn't usually a foolish one either.

"I'm making it my business," said Fairfax in a tone that was both low and threatening. "How did you know he was what he claimed to be? He from around these parts, or did he drift here?"

Adamson looked at the macabre masked man and stuck to his guns, "You can't think he's who you're after. He was a boy for Christ-sake! You met him remember."

"I asked you a question, are you gonna answer it?" Fairfax's voice carried with it a hint of violence. It was just enough to sober Adamson up.

"Nope he ain't from around here. He must have drifted into town about five, six months ago."

"Where did he sleep?"

"He had a room out back."

A day later, having discovered the mail order catalogue, spoken to the woman at the general store and confirmed Mrs Adamson hadn't bought a dress, James Fairfax rode out. He now knew that Danny the livery stable boy was really the girl he was looking for. The thought that he'd brushed past the whore filled the masked man with rage. Only when he discovered a train timetable in the small room where Danny/Deirdre lodged, did his humour return. "San Francisco, the bitch is going to a whore's heaven. When I get there, it will become that whore's hell!"

Adamson had thought to ask if there was any reward, but the look on Fairfax's face when he discovered the timetable would have made the bravest man quiver. Adamson, now completely sober, wasn't that brave neither was he that foolish. The following morning Adamson watched as Fairfax rode out and prayed he'd seen the last of him.

During the journey back to New York, James Fairfax thought long and hard about his dilemma. That detective, according to Mervyn Prescott, was like a dog with a bone. He'd chew on it until there was nothing left. 'Which,' thought Fairfax, 'is exactly what I hope to leave him? I'd gut her where she stands! That the act would arouse suspicion in Finbar O'Toole, I've no doubt. The copper would do his damnedest, but wouldn't be able to prove I'd killed her or those other women. Would he?' Doubt was creeping in where there was none. 'Damn O'Toole, he'd make life a little uncomfortable, but unless he came up with proof there wasn't a thing he could do. Or was there?' Never before had Fairfax felt so threatened. His hatred for the whore consumed him as he got ever closer to the city. Then another thought crossed Fairfax's mind, his killing of whores had intensified but now that would have to be curtailed somewhat. On the other hand if the whore bitch had been successful in her plan and boarded a train to San Francisco, what was to stop her writing a letter to the authorities? That she'd gone to San Francisco he was almost certain, just as certain as he'd been that she was in Cloverville. A break from New York, even a permanent one would allow him time to shake off Finbar O'Toole and let him concentrate on finding that troublesome whore.

"Yes," said Fairfax loudly as he entered the city, "if the bitch whore's on her way to San Francisco, then I'll find her there." In his experience of whores they always ran true to form, not having enough intelligence to seek out other employment. The thought comforted him and his laughter echoed through the streets of the Five Points like the Devil's own.

CHAPTER 8

Deirdre never reached San Francisco. After many days of cramped living and sleeping conditions, coupled with the boredom of the journey, the taking on water and the stops for refreshments became the highlight of every day. Ten minutes, twenty if you were lucky, was all the time allowed to eat dinner and stretch those weary bones. The shrill sound of a whistle being blown in impatience, a cry of all aboard and it was every man for himself. At Rock Springs, Wyoming, Deirdre daydreamed over her meal, when the whistle suddenly blew. Alarmed, she looked around the dining room at the empty tables. Her fellow passengers had all gone. Panic stricken Deirdre raced out of the room and dashed back to the train, only to see a plume of black smoke hanging over the platform, and the train disappearing into the distance. At first she was overcome with panic, but then with the reassurance that another westbound train would be stopping there in three days time, her heart rate returned to normal.

She had money, she looked respectable, and from what she'd heard, folks out west were renown for their courtesy towards womenfolk. All she had to do was wait out the next seventy two hours. Lodging was simple enough. The only hotel in town was also the train depot.

Her dowdy schoolmarm attire did nothing to disguise Deidre's natural good looks and it wasn't long before a few of the male population of Rock Springs started engaging her in polite conversation. They were helpful and courteous, eager to hear news from back east. It was then that Deirdre realised the chance of passing herself off as a schoolteacher was doomed to fail. Although she'd taught herself to read and write, it was stilted and above all limited. Instead she said she had been engaged to work in service for a wealthy family and that she feared that when her train arrived in Sacramento and she wasn't on it, they'd abandon her.

Deirdre woke around five o'clock. It was still dark outside but an eerie glow had invaded her room. She'd been aroused from her sleep by the light of the moon shining through the thin curtains. Basking in the moon's glow she listened to the silence and for the first time in a long while felt at peace. Gathering an oversized top coat that she'd purchased from the dry goods store earlier that previous evening, she tiptoed across the room to the window and gazed out at the most beautiful of moons she'd seen in her entire life. She found it hard to imagine the horror that she'd left behind in the Five Points area of New York. Raising the window, Deirdre breathed in the biting coldness of a Wyoming winter but instead of it repelling, it seemed to invigorate her. It was as if those first few breaths were for her the starting of a new life.

She'd originally planned to travel all the way to the Pacific to start life anew in San Francisco, but why? It was a question that kept her gazing out of the window until first light. She was little more than a kid, no real education of any kind except that of the street. She was safe for the time being, but she knew the money would run out sooner rather than later. What would she do when that happened? Deirdre knew the answer to that one, only too well. San Francisco was teeming with bordellos and parlour houses, but here in the wilds of Wyoming, here at least she had a chance.

And the chance came in the form of Lieutenant Miles O'Bannion. He was young and dashingly handsome in a boyish sort of way. His uniform was freshly pressed and quite obviously new. He stood to attention by the side of Deirdre's table that morning at breakfast.

"I hope you don't think I'm being too forward, but would you mind if I joined you for breakfast."

Deirdre looked shocked, but was slightly amused by his stuffy politeness. She'd never been spoken to with such respect before. She stared at him for what must have seemed ages, wallowing in his discomfort, until she could stand it no longer.

"If you wish," she said, and smiled.

Her smile was so disarming that the young soldier took off his cap and sat down.

"In case you're wondering, I'm here to join up with my regiment. I'm newly commissioned and have a posting at Fort Laramie."

"You're a little off course," said Deirdre, puzzled at why he hadn't gotten off at Laramie. With nothing better to do than while away the days staring out of the window of the steam train Deirdre had noted to memory every station between New York and Rock Springs.

He looked at her sheepishly, "I overslept."

"You what," she cried, and then suddenly broke into fits of laughter.

"I know it sounds daft, but the journey was so tiring and tedious that I got myself involved in a little card playing, and …" he added sheepishly, "a little drinking. Before I knew it, I'd missed my stop."

"Then I believe we're two of a kind. You missed your stop, I missed my train."

"Be, Jesus!"

She noticed a faint Irish lilt, "Killarney?"

"No, the west coast of that fair isle Galway. And you?"

"Cork, but that was a long time ago." and the tears began to trickle down her cheeks. The Lieutenant instantly offered Deirdre his neatly folded handkerchief. "Thanks, that was silly of me."

"Ah, thinkin of home is never silly."

"I was thinking of my wee brothers and sisters, God rest their souls and me poor sweet gentle mother." It was funny how talking to another from that green land brought Deirdre's accent to the fore.

Seeing Deirdre looked about ready to borrow his handkerchief once more, he quickly extended his hand, "Lieutenant Miles O'Bannion, at your service."

"Deirdre Devlin, I'm pleased to meet you," she said and took his open hand.

During the days that followed Deirdre and Miles were inseparable. He spoke of home in New Hampshire and of his childhood in Galway and of his aspirations for the future.

Deirdre in turn told him of her miserable life with a drunken father and a mother who was forever pregnant. She told him how her father had come home one night and how he'd had an accident with a knife and bled to death. She told him of the voyage to the New World and the life of drudgery working long hours in the garment factory. The only lie she told him was about having a job in service in San Francisco. Then she told him about how she'd missed the train and how after waking up that morning she'd decided to stay in Rock Springs.

"Come with me to the fort! I'm sure you'll be able to find work there," he'd offered.

"I can't," she'd said, "It wouldn't be proper."

"Why not?"

"What would people think if you turn up for duty and you've me in tow."

"That's not a problem, marry me?"

"What?"

"Marry me. I'll make you happy. You'll have a good life. My pay's not brilliant, but with officers' quarters and the chance of promotion, I can offer you a better life than you're likely to find in Rock Springs."

"But where's love? We've only known each other for days."

"I've loved you since you first smiled at me and allowed me to sit at your table."

Deirdre was dumb struck. She'd known Miles for less than three days and here he was proposing marriage.

"Miles, you're such a sweet thing, but I don't know anything about you. More importantly, you know nothing about me."

"That's true, but it don't matter none. We've both come a long ways, and I guess we've some history, but what there is can't be bigger than a grain of sand."

It was a chance of a new way of life, a fresh start. Though she guessed being an army officer's wife at a far outpost wouldn't be all milk and honey, the thought of having a decent home and perhaps in the future raising a family, appealed to her. It was more than she'd dare dream about. That she didn't love him caused her concern, but Miles was good and kind, he treated her with respect and honour, and yes she believed that, given time, she could come to love him.

It was almost as though he could read her mind. "Given time, I known you could grow to love me. Think of the advantages that being married would give us. We'd have better living accommodation for a start."

"Oh Miles, it's so tempting, but you know nothing about me. That grain of sand might turn out to be a whole lot bigger than you think."

"You're the most beautiful woman I've ever seen. I fell in love with you almost from the moment you disembarked from the train."

Deirdre looked at him and a tear formed in the corner of her eye. Miles couldn't have known it, but he was offering her the earth. He didn't deserve such baggage.

Miles raised his voice slightly, "I don't care about the past. All I know is that I want to share my life with you. That grain of sand, well it stays here at Rock Springs. Now marry me you fool girl or I'll throw myself under that damn train when it finally arrives!"

CHAPTER 9

No one was more shocked than Finbar O'Toole when he found out that James Fairfax had sold up and left the city. He'd put his mansion on the market and had left instructions with his agent to have the proceeds of the sale forwarded to a bank in San Francisco. A smile of satisfaction spread across the detective's face, 'He's running scared.'

'Why San Francisco? Why now?' thought Finbar. It wasn't just that the so called English fop had noted his suspicions, there had to be another reason. At the train depot, the detective flashed his badge and soon learned about Fairfax's journey. He was no further forward when the penny finally dropped. 'What if the whore he was hunting wasn't dead. What if she'd escaped Fairfax's clutches and had taken the train to the west coast? It wasn't an impossible thought. Playing this hunch Finbar asked the ticket clerk if any woman of easy virtue had purchased a ticket in the days preceding the departure of Fairfax.

The young clerk flushed with embarrassment, but said he hadn't seen anyone of that description. The only women in the last few days had been an elderly lady and a young school ma'am. "I remember the school ma'am because she was kinda pretty. She was a nervous type. Said she had a post, living in too, at someplace north of San Francisco. She paid for her ticket with a big nomination bank note as I recall."

"Obliged," said Finbar a smile of self satisfaction began to spread across his face.

"Yeah, reason I remember is that fellow you was asking after, asked me the same question."

"About the school ma'am?"

"Yes sir."

In the days that followed Finbar wired the station master at Sacramento. If he could show his superiors proof that Fairfax was pursuing this woman, he might be able to persuade his superiors to let him follow up the case.

True to his word, the station master at Sacramento wired back that after going through passenger manifests on the days in question only the gentleman, a Mr Fairfax, had arrived. He remembered him because of the mask and his bad temper at being told he'd have to travel the rest of the way on the top of the coach. Most put out he was. A day later he wired Finbar again. From what he could make out, the young school ma'am had left the train at Rock Springs Wyoming.

Finbar, frustrated at not getting the proof he needed, managed to chuckle to himself. Either by accident or design the girl had given Fairfax the slip. The monster that was James Fairfax had escaped his clutches, but in turn the girl had escaped the attention of that scar-faced animal. All in all, thought Finbar, he's gone and if I'm a judge of character Fairfax will probably meet his end, robbed and beaten and his throat opened to the world by some Barbary Coast ruffian.

CHAPTER 10

Life at Fort Laramie wasn't quite what Miles had expected. On his arrival he was ordered immediately to Fort Abraham Lincoln, a new fort near Bismarck in the Dakota Territory. Originally it was named Fort McKeen but in November of 1872 it was renamed Fort Abraham Lincoln in honour of the late President. Miles was beside himself with excitement. He'd originally asked for a posting to Fort Abraham Lincoln but been assigned Fort Laramie instead. Now with an expedition out of Lincoln the post was short on junior officers. So Miles by way of default had got the posting he'd wanted.

"It's perfect, we'll have another week or so together before I have to report, it's almost like having a week's furlough."

Deirdre wasn't sure that a week of travelling across what had until recently been hostile territory constituted anything like perfect. But as the fresh young bride of an up and coming cavalry officer she conceded to his excitement. On the arduous journey by stage and then on the buckboard of an old cart they made their way to the new fort. Miles spoke enthusiastically about his chances of promotion under the new commander, a Lieutenant Colonel named Custer.

"I think that if I perform well under his command my chances of becoming a captain within two years would be quite likely." He took a quick breath and added excitedly, "Do you know that during the war he was promoted to Brevet Major General? The youngest officer ever to be awarded that rank."

Deirdre looked at her young husband and smiled. She couldn't believe how lucky she'd been to find someone as sweet and innocent as Miles O'Bannion. She knew nothing of army life but she knew a damn sight more about life in general. Though worldly beyond anything Miles could contemplate, his youthful enthusiasm was infectious and Deirdre allowed herself for the first time in her life to dream.

On their arrival at Fort Abraham Lincoln Miles explained to his commanding officer that his delay in reaching the fort was due to lousy train connections and the arrival from the old country of his childhood sweetheart.

"It's good for a man to have a wife," said Captain Forbes. "Yes, even out here in the west. A soldier's life is mostly filled with tedium and routine and the odd skirmishes if you're lucky." Miles allowed himself the briefest of smiles, before Captain Forbes continued. "It's fitting that my officers have a stable background. It helps to ground the troops, keeps them anchored," Captain Forbes realising his speech sounded pompous and dull added, "and Mrs O'Bannion is a fine looking woman."

"Thank you sir. May I be so bold as to ask after Lieutenant Colonel Custer?"

"You may indeed. He left with most of the 7th on an expedition into the Yellowstone. He's accompanying a bunch of surveyors and engineers from the Northern Pacific Railroad."

"Will they see action sir?"

"It's possible, but I believe the hostiles are few and far between. When we whipped Red Cloud, I think we knocked the stuffing out of them."

Miles stood there waiting for the Captain to elaborate.

"That'll be all Lieutenant."

"Yes Sir!" Miles clicked his heels together and saluted the Captain, then spinning on his heels, he about faced and marched swiftly outside.

In the privacy of their quarters Miles cursed his luck. Spurred on by tales of heroic exploits and courageous battles against the noble savage he'd asked especially for this kind of posting, but to have missed going on an expedition with the legendary Custer was such a frustration.

"Don't worry darling, I'm sure there will be plenty of chances for you to prove your worth," said Deirdre, doing her best to salve his disappointment.

Yet it wasn't all bad for the recently married Lieutenant, it at least allowed him time to get to know his young bride, without which those summer months would have seemed indeterminably long. Tedium and boredom, that's what the Captain had said, and he was right too, thought Miles, after yet another morning drilling the troops. Yet he was luckier than some. Most of the officers and a few of the enlisted men had wives, but none compared to the beauty of his darling Deirdre.

When the report came in from the Yellowstone that Custer and his command had experienced the odd skirmish with hostiles, Miles was ecstatic. Red Cloud might be whipped, he thought, but there were still a few young bucks out there, ready and willing to take the fight to the soldiers.

In the meantime Lieutenant Colonel Custer's wife had arrived from back East, and it wasn't long before the wives of the officers began to make a fuss over her. Shy in the ways of an army wife, Deirdre held back and allowed the older, more experienced wives to ingratiate themselves into Mrs Custer's company. She'd wanted to blend in, to become part of the furniture, but by standing back Deirdre got herself noticed and it wasn't long before Mrs Custer knocked on her door.

"It's Deirdre isn't it," said Mrs Custer. "May I come in?"

Deirdre flushed and stepped aside to allow her husband's commanding officer's wife to enter her humble quarters. "Can I get you something, tea perhaps?" she said nervously.

"Tea would be fine," said Mrs Custer with a sympathetic smile. "And the name's Elizabeth."

Deirdre flushed even deeper.

"Come, come my girl. How am I to recruit you as my friend if you keep shrinking into a corner every time I speak? You're young and pretty, just what this dreary fort needs. Do you think I want to join the knitting circle like Captain Forbes's wife Emily, and all those other officer's wives?"

Deirdre was shocked by Mrs Custer's frank and open manner and warmed to the woman immediately. "I'm sorry. You just caught me off guard. And the other women aren't so bad once you get to know them," she volunteered.

"I know they're not, my sweet child. It's just my way. I've watched you over the course of a few days, and I know, despite your reluctance to step into the limelight that there's a feisty young woman inside bursting to get out.

'If you only knew', thought Deirdre. "I guess you're right. It's just that everything is new and different. You see back home in Cork, that's in Ireland...."

"Yes I know," interrupted Mrs Custer.

"Oh I'm sorry, please forgive me Mrs Custer."

"Go on. Back in Cork, and it's Elizabeth," she smiled reassuringly.

"Well Elizabeth, you see, I came from a very poor family...."

Chapter 11

Jared McAllister examined the mechanism of the new Winchester 73. He noted that the lever action was smoother than his favoured Henry rifle, it took several rounds more, had a wooden fore stock and a loading gate in the breech, but he couldn't bring himself to purchase this new improved model of Winchester's earlier version. He had to admit that handling the Henry in a tight situation could get a mite uncomfortable when the metal fore stock overheated. But then again he never expected to need a rifle with that much fire power, besides the Henry had sentimental attachments, it had been given to him by his pa three years earlier.

"Here you go son, it'll help keep you safe if the occasion arises," said his Pa on Jared's twenty first birthday. "You take care of it, yah hear and it'll take care of you," he'd added as an afterthought. Jared took his Pa at his word and cleaned and oiled the rifle regularly.

"It sure is a handsome rifle Mr Halstead but I think I'll be keeping my old Henry for the time being, but thanks agin for letting me have a feel of it," said Jared politely as he handed it back to the local store keeper.

Jared stepped out of the relative cool of the hardware store into the hot blinding light of a late June sun. He shielded his eyes from the brightness and climbed up onto the buckboard, now heavily loaded with supplies, *enough to last them until late fall, his ma had declared.* With the sun high in the sky Jared figured it to be around noon and by that reckoned he hoped to be back at the ranch by supper time.

Supper time was Jared's favourite time of day, it was when all the chores had been done and the family could all sit around the large log hewn table and discuss the events of the day. There was his Ma, a rosy cheeked woman, strong and wilful, prepared to take whatever challenges the good Lord sent her way without complaint or reproach. Even the death of her oldest son Joshua in the dying months of the Civil War couldn't detract her from her faith. Then there was his Pa, he'd taken the death of Joshua to heart and although he carried on with life, he'd never been the same since that fateful day when they received the news. Lastly there was Sarah, his older sister and her new husband Dale, a hardworking man but with dreams of moving to California. "A man's got to have his dreams," he was often heard to say. Together the family worked the small ranch and eked out a living.

"Be grateful for what the Good Lord provides," preached Ma McAllister.

Jared had long ago realised his mother's strong will was only an act. He'd accidentally overheard her praying under a freshly planted cherry tree one night. He'd sought to remove himself from her private prayers but as he turned away he heard her call out Joshua's name. It stopped him in his tracks as he heard her sobbing. The sound made his heart ache. As he continued to eavesdrop he learned that his Ma's position as matriarch was largely down to her necessity to keep what was left of her family together. It was a lesson he kept secret, for he knew without his Ma's strength it was doubtful the family would have survived.

Over supper that night he told his Pa about the new gun. "You should see it Pa. It fires seventeen rounds if you leave one in the breach."

"Sounds like a mighty fine weapon, but don't you be rushing in to exchange that old Henry just yet. Every weapon needs to prove itself first."

It was sound advice and Jared nodded his agreement.

"Did you see Amy Halstead?" enquired his mother.

Jared coloured up, much to the delight of Sarah, who took great delight in teasing her younger brother.

"Yeah I saw her, but only for a few brief minutes."

"I hear tell she's popular with the boys in town," chipped in Dale.

Jared shot him a dirty look, "She ain't like that Dale."

"And you'd know?" replied Dale.

"Boys, boys. Settle down now," said the McAllister Matriarch.

"I've asked her to go with me to the fourth of July dance!"

"What about your work around the ranch?" said Pa McAllister.

Jared looked crestfallen.

Ma McAllister came to his rescuem, "If the boy wants to go a courting, you William Travis McAllister, will double up on your work load."

Dale sniggered.

"And you can help him too, Dale Brockett," she added.

"Thanks Ma," said a grateful yet embarrassed Jared. Amy Halstead was the most beautiful girl Jared had ever seen, which didn't amount to a tin of beans. Excepting his sister, Jared hadn't seen or been around women folk that much.

"Well I think she's nice lookin,'" said Sarah.

"Thanks sis."

After Amy, Sarah had been the catch of the county. 'Dale Brockett should count himself very lucky indeed,' thought Jared silently.

Jared McAllister lay in the damp grass, a smile of utter contentment etched across his face, and stared up at the firework display in the night sky. Amy Halstead snuggled up close to him.

The Fourth of July dance had proven most memorable. Jared and Amy had had a few glasses of punch, danced a jig or two, then Amy had pressed her body into Jared's muscled frame and looked up at him glassy eyed and suggested they go for a walk. Jared's heart pumped with anticipation. He was twenty four and about to get laid for the first time. He'd come close a time or two but never been the whole way. Something in Amy's eyes told him that was about to change. He just hoped he didn't let himself down.

As the noise of the crowd diminished Amy led him to an area of long grass where she assured him they wouldn't be disturbed.

As they lay in each others arms he clumsily fumbled with her undergarments.

"Easy cowboy, slow down, don't be so eager," whispered Amy as she expertly removed her undergarments. She grasped his hand and placed it on the cool of her inner thigh, "The rest is up to you, but be gentle. We've plenty of time."

A few clumsy moves later he was inside her, doing his best to concentrate on anything but the writhing bundle of flesh underneath him. With all his will power he managed to control himself for a full three minutes before his world finally exploded into the brightest lights he'd ever seen.

It was a month later when Amy's father called at the ranch. "That boy of yourn he best do the right thing by Amy," he blurted out before he'd got down from his lathered up horse.

"Dale, see to Mr Halstead's horse. Me an him got things to discuss." said Pa McAllister.

An hour later a shame faced Jared pledged to do the right thing by Amy.

"Well, then it's settled. I'll expect you in town within the week to formalise things."

Jared looked at his Ma for translation. "He means marry the girl."

Three days later Jared, dressed in his best Sunday going-to-church-clothes, mounted his horse and prepared to ride into town to meet his bride, "Well Ma, when next you see me, I'll be a family man."

"You will at that," replied Ma McAllister sadly.

Sarah appeared from the barn leading her bay gelding, "You want some company?" It was more a statement of intent than a question. Five minutes of goodbyes later and the two headed for town.

"Amy, I'm so sorry for what I did, but I'll make it up to you, see if I do," said Jared when he saw Amy.

"I know you will Jared, I knew you weren't the kind to shirk your responsibilities."

Behind Jared and Amy, Sarah seethed, 'It takes two, ain't you forgetting,' she thought angrily.

Mr Halstead smiled approvingly at Jared, "You was always a good boy Jared, I knew you'd do right by her. Ma, have you called for the preacher, we'll hold the wedding right here in the store."

"I surely did, he's on his way." said Mrs Halstead.

'What's all the rush?' thought Sarah as she looked across at Amy Halstead and her tell-tale bump. 'She must be three months if she's a day,' Sarah took a step back, her mind working overtime. A minute later she sprang into action.

"Jared, a word in private."

Jared looked across dumbly, excused himself from his frowning intended and followed Sarah into a small room at the back of Halstead's store.

"Jared, how many times you been with Amy?"

"I seen her on and off for the best part of a year. Why?"

"No!" cried an exasperated Sarah. "I don't mean that. What I'm trying to say is how many times did you, you know … umm do it?"

"Just the once!"

"And when was that?"

"At the Fourth of July dance," said Jared confused by all the fuss.

Sarah smiled sweetly at her brother. "Oh Jared, my sweet innocent baby brother, what am I going to do with you. The dance was a month ago. Amy's at least three months pregnant!"

"Then I ain't…."

"Got it in one, brother."

What happened then, or should I say the speculation about who sired Amy's baby, was talked about in the town of Uvalde, Texas for years to come.

Mr Halstead, when told by Sarah in no uncertain terms that Jared couldn't be the father, surprised everyone by not creating a scene. It confirmed Sarah's suspicions that Mr Halstead knew that Amy was putting it about with all and sundry and didn't have any idea who was to blame for his daughter's mistake.

Needless to say Jared's sparking of Amy or any other young women was put on hold for the foreseeable future.

CHAPTER 12

It was on a cold, white November morning in 1873 that Miles first caught sight of his legendary commanding officer. Lieutenant Colonel George Armstrong Custer rode proudly through the gates of Fort Abraham Lincoln to the welcoming sound of the Garry Owen played by the regiment's brass band.

Miles was in awe. His enthusiasm towards his commanding officer spread to the dinner table, "You should have seen him Deirdre, he rode into the fort almost like a god!"

"Well a god he ain't, Miles O'Bannion. He's flesh and blood like the rest of us, and don't you forget it!"

"I know that Dee, but it's just the greatness of the man."

"I've heard he's a hard taskmaster and a disciplinarian."

"To be sure, he's all that and more." replied Miles.

Deirdre smiled sweetly, "He's what you expected?"

"He is that."

Deirdre gave him another wry smile and began clearing the dishes. She so loved her husband's youthful innocent exuberance, and only hoped he wouldn't be let down when he met the real Lieutenant Colonel in person. Deirdre's past had left her with an understanding of men who commanded power. She'd watched from the sutler's store as the popinjay rode into the fort. His bearing and the general manner that he transported himself were all too familiar to her. He had the air of many a man she'd known, but most of all he reminded her of James Fairfax. She shuddered at the thought.

Miles met Custer a day later in the Colonel's quarters with all the other commissioned officers. He'd taken time over his appearance, making sure he'd polished everything that shone and pressed everything that needed pressing. To be virtually ignored, dismissed almost, hurt Miles more than Custer's equally ignorant manner of addressing his immediate subordinates. Custer was full of Custer, and puffed himself up at every mention of his Civil War heroics. Cigars were handed out and tales of Indian engagements were talked about. Miles's pricked up his ears as Custer related how they rode down an Indian encampment on the Washita River. He'd heard this tale before, but not the vividly detailed account that Custer and his more senior officers relayed.

That evening Miles felt more deflated than he'd a right to be. Deirdre, while sympathising with him, could see the full picture, and she told him so after dinner. Dejected and more than a little hurt, he took himself outside, 'Dee was right of course,' he reasoned. 'What did I expect, the Colonel to fall all over me? I'm a junior officer, new to the frontier and whether I like it or not I'm wet behind the ears.' Clearing his head, Miles elected to go back inside and apologise to his good wife, and he reflected that the best way to impress Custer would be on the field of battle.

Miles didn't have long to dwell on Colonel Custer's rebuff. With immediate effect all routine patrols were to be doubled. He also took to widening the field of the patrols. Miles found himself alongside the Colonel and Captain Keogh on a patrol less than a week after he'd arrived back at the fort.

"It's Lieutenant O'Bannion, I believe. My wife speaks highly of your good lady."

"That's right sir, and thank you sir." The awkwardness of his reply left Miles red faced. He'd been noticed after all. The thought swelled his heart.

It was a few months later that Miles realised to his horror that war on the red man was a one sided and dirty business. Whilst on patrol under the command of Captain Forbes they stumbled upon a small band of Cheyenne.

"Hostiles!" cried a trooper.

Captain Forbes, taken aback by the sudden appearance of some twenty Indians ordered the charge. It was only then that Miles saw to his horror that these hostiles were in fact a small band of reservation Indians on the way to the fort. Most were old men and a few squaws with papooses strapped to their backs. Miles cried out to Captain Forbes but it was too late, the bloodlust was in the Captain's eyes. Within minutes the small band of Cheyenne had been cut to pieces. Miles reined in his horse and surveyed the carnage.

To his surprise Captain Forbes rode back to him, his face beaming with pride. "Well that taught them," he exclaimed.

"They were innocent women and children!" screamed Miles.

"They were hostiles, O'Bannion. Take my word for it!" snapped Forbes.

"Yes sir!" Miles knew now wasn't the time to argue, but he intended having his say when they returned to the fort. "Shall I form a burial detail sir?"

"Leave them for the buzzards."

Miles was going to say something but elected to keep his own counsel. What shocked him more than Captain Forbes attitude was the look of glee and pleasure on some of the troop's faces.

It was a week later when Miles finally had his say. Forbes glared at him but when Custer spoke his face changed from a glare to a sickening smirk.

"What you have to realise Lieutenant O'Bannion, is that this is a savage land. Perhaps it was a mistake, we'll never know. Women folk have been known to be just as savage as their husbands. All in all I think Captain Forbes acted swiftly and decisively and possibly saved the lives of your good self and the rest of the troop. That's my final word on the matter."

Miles stood there in a state of shock. Minutes later he heard Custer and a few officers laughing.

"He's still wet behind the ears."

"Give him time he'll soon understand."

"Shooting down kids wasn't what he'd signed up for," cried one of Custer's officers in Miles's defence.

It was left to Custer himself to have the final say on the shooting down of innocent women and children. He justified it by one small sentence that seemed to carry with it an almost hysterical amount of laughter.

"Nits make lice."

He seemed to get a great kick out of his attempt at a joke. His officers concurred with hearty guffs of laughter. Miles was sickened to the pit of his stomach.

His quietness over dinner that evening caused Deirdre to ask what was wrong.

"Everything Dee, everything. I thought I was here to fight the noble savage, to tame and eventually convert, but I was wrong, Custer wants to annihilate the whole race, just for his own political gains. He doesn't even think of them as human beings. I can't serve under him, I've got to get out of this army."

"Whoa, Miles. I know you're upset, but don't do anything rash. He's liable to have you before a court martial, and then shot if you go up against him."

"Dee, I came to this country to escape tyranny, yet I find I'm now part of the machinery of a tyrant, what am I to do?"

"Miles, my darling, there's nothing you can do except go along with it. It's that or die."

Chapter 13

Deirdre's words were somehow prophetic. Within a few weeks Miles had seen the other side of the red man. Leading a routine patrol he came upon a sight that had him retching. The patrol literally walked into a scene of carnage that even a seasoned trooper would have balked at. There were seven of them, at least it appeared that way, but in truth there could have been as little as five. Miners, lured by talk of gold, had ventured into the Black Hills and paid with their lives. They'd all been stripped and scalped, some disembowelled and Miles wasn't sure but it looked as if one had been ripped in two.

"Fucking savages, that appears to be a woman over yonder," cursed Sergeant Driscoll a hard bitten veteran of several campaigns. He wiped the sweat from his weather beaten brow and pointed to a bundle of clothing scattered across a large flat rock, a woman's arm protruded from behind it.

Miles hurried towards the unfortunate woman. "Oh Jesus!" cried the young army officer. Her clothes had been stripped from her body and traces of semen, now sun baked were stuck to her inner thighs. It was obvious to all who gazed down at the poor wreck of a body that she'd been raped and beaten to death.

"Do you see Lieutenant, do you see what they did to her?" Driscoll shouted at the young Lieutenant, he was spitting with rage, as he pushed his face up close to Miles. His pale blue eyes stared at his superior officer with a look of distain as Miles turned away. "Take another look sir," he continued as he swept his curly blond hair back from his sun darkened face. The anger now subsiding, "That's why Custer and his officers act and talk the way they do. It's a violent land. They're savages sir, and since I've been out here, we've become just like them."

There was a madness in the sergeant's eyes that made Miles shudder. He was about to say something when the Crow scout who was leading the patrol rode up and said something to Sergeant Driscoll.

"What was that Sergeant?" said Miles as he began to regain his composure.

"He says they're not more than an hour in front of us, and travelling slow. We, with your permission could catch up to them."

The sardonic manner in the way he addressed his superior officer wasn't lost on the Lieutenant. Miles was mad as all get out, but what good would it do to reprimand him so far from the fort. Instead he chose to ignore the remark.

"Agreed," said Miles, "But before we do, we need to bury these poor unfortunates."

"No time sir," replied Driscoll, now addressing his senior officer with the reverence his rank deserved, "if we're to catch them before nightfall."

Miles looked upwards towards the sun's position in the sky and reluctantly gave the order to move out.

The Sergeant, buoyant about winning the argument, was also grateful that Miles hadn't questioned him further. It was a small war party, but travelling slow, which meant they were accompanied by their women folk. From past experience he suspected they were a hunting party bringing back meat from a hunt. The women would have been brought along to assist in cutting up the buffalo meat. They'd probably come across this party of miners by chance. He'd also suspected women were along because in his opinion some of the abuse to the miners had the tell-tale trade mark of Sioux women. He'd heard tell they could be as barbaric as their men folk, sometimes even worse. The miners had been stripped and every one of them had had their penis and testes cut from their bodies. There were other signs but the Sergeant didn't think it fit to dwell on it. As far as he was concerned it didn't matter: a savage was a savage, despite gender. What did interest him was the way an enemy butchered his foe. It told a lot about him. These bucks had been relaxed; they'd taken their time over their butchery, which meant that the Sioux didn't suspect a patrol was in the area. He'd thought to tell the Lieutenant that women were along, but dismissed the idea because he didn't think his young officer had the stomach for killing women, and would not have gone ahead. As far as Driscoll saw it, the women were as bad as the men, and as such, needed to be punished.

The Crow scout sighted them an hour later. They'd struck camp for the approaching night in a gully next to a small creek. From the looks of them, the Crow scout relayed to Driscoll, it appeared that they were fully relaxed, satiated by their bloody victory over the miners.

"They kill a few white folks and they think they're invincible," said Driscoll.

"How do we know this isn't a trap Sergeant?"

"The Crows are the best scouts on the plains, add the very fact the Sioux is the Crow's sworn enemy. If he says they're relaxed, you'd better believe it! I'd say this is a God given opportunity for us to administer justice."

'Justice? More like retribution,' thought Miles. The Sergeant was a veteran of a few Indian campaigns, most notably with Custer at the Washita. Miles knew what that had entailed, but he also realised that to gain the respect of his men, he would have to act decisively. He cast away any lingering thoughts of giving the Sioux a fighting chance, as the images of the horror of what he'd seen impacted on his brain.

"Sergeant, I'd suggest we send two columns; one right and one left. You take the right and I'll take the left. Sergeant O'Brien you attack from the rear. When we're in position I'll give the signal, then commence firing."

Driscoll smiled at the Lieutenant, pleased with his quick and decisive decision and quipped, "We'll make a soldier of you yet."

It was a remark which Miles chose to ignore. His views, though not generally spoken of, were known by the lower ranks.

The battle, such as it was, lasted a little over five minutes. The Sioux put up a brave fight but, with the withering fire from the army carbines, they were reduced to just a handful within minutes.

"Hold your fire! They've women-folk amongst them," cried Miles.

Driscoll seemed not to hear his commanding officer as he and his column continued to pour death into the small encampment. Miles, still shouting ran across to Driscoll who reluctantly supported his commanding officer, but by the time the firing had stopped only one woman was left standing. She stared defiantly at Miles, her hands at her sides. Miles dismounted and threw his sergeant an angry look before holstering his revolver.

"I meant you no harm," he said as he took a step towards her. Suddenly she lunged at him with a large bladed knife.

The look of pure hatred in her eyes glazed over as Sergeant Driscoll, aware of the imminent danger shot her right between the eyes. "It's a savage land, sir."

Aware that Driscoll had saved his life, all Miles could do was glare at the man. If he was going to file a report about the Sergeant's insubordination that bullet had put pay to any disciplinary action. Driscoll just grinned.

At the fort Miles filed his report. His fellow officers seemed to show him a new found respect. His flanking movement had been pure text book, straight out of West Point. He'd engaged the enemy and destroyed them with only the loss of one trooper and two slightly wounded. He also gave mention to Sergeant Driscoll's quick action that had undoubtedly saved his life. But the incident, though greeted with enthusiasm by his fellow officers, left a bad taste in his mouth.

That night he mentioned it to Deirdre.

"I'm just grateful that Sergeant Driscoll had such quick reactions."

"You should have seen the look on his face when he killed her. It was pure delight. The man actually likes killing. He knew, before I, what that squaw was about to do. It may appear that he saved my life but mark my words, the man's no better than a murderer."

"It's just this land, its so savage." said Deirdre softly.

"That's funny, that's just what Driscoll said after he'd killed that squaw."

"Well, it is! Oh Miles, I know your heart isn't in it. Perhaps you could ask for a transfer. Maybe we could go back East."

"Dee, after today, the chance of a transfer back East is out of the question. Custer treated me better today than at anytime since he arrived. Killing Indians is what he's about. He isn't going to let a newly bloodied officer of his return to the east. I've become exactly what he wanted. Like it or not, I'm bound to Custer almost as if I'd been chained to his side."

"Well at least you've Sergeant Driscoll to watch your back," she said feebly. Despite what Miles thought she was extremely grateful for the sergeant's intervention.

Miles chose to ignore her last remark. He'd seen what kind of a man Driscoll was and he didn't like him one bit. In Miles's opinion, if it had suited his sergeant's purpose, he'd have let the squaw gut him. Then as he lay dying Driscoll would have shot the squaw dead or worse.

For a time, life at Fort Abraham Lincoln settled down to a dreary pattern of routine patrols, parade ground drills and the occasional sighting of a hostile, *which almost always turned out to be a false alarm.* It was during this time that Deirdre had good reason to change her opinion about the heroic Sergeant Driscoll. She'd noticed him looking at her in a way that only a woman of Deirdre's breeding could understand. He was always polite in her company and showed her due respect but Deirdre could read the signs: the long leering looks, the oh-so-slight innuendos. It was around ten o'clock on Saturday night, *Miles was away on patrol,* when Deirdre heard a knocking on her door.

"Who's there?" she cried.

"Sergeant Driscoll ma'am."

Believing he had news of Miles, she opened the door and stared into his drunken face.

"Begging your pardon ma'am, I seen your light on and I thought as you're from the old country like me, you might like some company. Lieutenant O'Bannion being away on patrol an all."

Deirdre looked at him indignantly and said, "Sergeant Driscoll, you're drunk. I'll forget what you've just said to me, as I'm led to believe you saved my husband's life." She started to close the door but Driscoll pushed his way inside. "Get out! Get out I say."

Before she knew it he had her pinned to the cabin wall, his hot drunken breath invaded her nostrils. "That's right I saved your man's life. A little kiss ain't too much to ask for saving his fool neck."

Deirdre struggled to break free, but Driscoll's physical strength was too much for her. "Get off me you drunken fool, my husband will have you court-martialled." This caused Driscoll to loosen his grip a mite, but it was enough for Deirdre to reach her hand between Driscoll's legs and grab his balls tightly.

Driscoll's eyes grew wide with pain, but he didn't scream out for fear of being found out. Deirdre kept squeezing until she'd managed to push him towards the door. Only when his whole body was outside did she release him, then she slammed the door closed and quickly bolted it.

It was a day later when Deirdre next saw Driscoll. He looked shame-faced but not repentant. She walked up to him at the side of the parade ground and said, "In light of what you did for my husband I'm going to forget last night's little incident. I suggest you put in for a transfer as soon as possible. Good day Sergeant Driscoll."

"Cunts like you have no place in a camp like this," he said as a parting quip.

Deirdre swung around to face him, "Call me that again and I'll kill you," she said calmly.

Nonetheless Driscoll took Deirdre at her word and put in for a transfer to Captain Benteen's troop.

Month followed month and the seriousness of the Indian situation grew ever worse. The Sioux and the Cheyenne together with other tribes had for a few months been gathering at a place the Indians called Greasy Grass. Army intelligence stated that it was a vast encampment which stretched for six miles along the Little Big Horn River. Things were moving at a hectic pace and to make matters worse General Crook had suffered a set back on the Rosebud, which added to his frustration after the battle at Powder River. The Sioux were getting bolder by the day. General Terry, on orders from Sheridan, was heading towards the Tongue from the east, while Gibbon approached from the west. Crook in the meantime was rallying his men after the debacle at the Rosebud. Their orders were to engage the enemy and defeat it. Terry sent orders to Custer to scout ahead and locate the Sioux.

Early on Saturday the 24th June Deirdre kissed Miles goodbye and watched as six hundred men under the charge of Lieutenant Colonel George Armstrong Custer marched out of the gates of Fort Abraham Lincoln to the tune of the Garry Owen.

Custer was in high spirits and for good reason. Terry had given him orders to scout out the Indian encampment, but not to engage the enemy until Crook, Gibbon and Terry were in place. Custer had other ideas. There had been talk that the encampment was very large, but Custer's estimate was that there wouldn't be more than a thousand warriors at best, and with the new Springfield carbine and the Cavalry Colt the enemy were outnumbered by fire power alone.

Arriving a day earlier Custer saw his chance for greater glory. Crook's failure at the Rosebud was his catalyst; he decided to go it alone. His was to be the ultimate victory. Splitting his command, he ordered Captain Benteen to take a battalion of men to prevent any escape into the Big Horn Mountains. Major Marcus Reno was assigned two battalions and was ordered into a frontal attack. Custer took the high ground and advanced towards the main village. There was to be no escape for the warlike Sioux and Cheyenne.

On a bluff five miles from the main village, Miles pulled out his pocket watch and flipped open the brass cover. He looked longingly at the small tintype. Deirdre gazed back at him, and in that moment Lieutenant Miles O'Bannion knew he'd never look at her face again.

CHAPTER 14

Sarah never stopped ribbing Jared about his lucky escape from the promiscuous clutches of Amy Halstead until she and Dale set off for California and even then she had to have one last dig.

"Well brother, I guess the next time we meet you'll have converted to the Mormon faith and have ten wives and thirty children. Just make sure they're all yours you hear."

Jared smiled up at his sister sitting high on the seat of the Conestoga, "I'll not miss your joshing but I'll surely miss that sweet smile of yours. Take care now and don't forget to send me and Ma a letter soon as you're settled."

Jared reached out his hand to Dale, shook it firmly and said, "You take care of her."

"I'll surely do that Jared. When Sarah and I get fixed we'll send for you and Ma. You surely can't be meaning to carry on?" It was a question Jared left unanswered; he could see the look of embarrassment in Dale's eyes. Instead he just smiled his answer.

Dale took his cue, "God damn! I'm gonna miss Ma's cookin," and then came the expected "Ahhh," as Sarah playfully elbowed him in the ribs.

"And what's wrong with my cookin?"

It was left unanswered as Dale forced the horses into motion and the large Conestoga creaked into action. Jared and Ma stood watching until the wagon went past Pa's grave and then clear out of view.

"It's what they've always wanted Jared. You mustn't blame Dale. Sarah's a forceful woman. If she hadn't wanted to go she'd have stayed."

"I know Ma, I know."

"The ranch is all yours now," she said as she squeezed his hand affectionately, "although it ain't much since those darn Comanche drove off half the stock."

"They were starving Ma. Once Quanah Parker surrendered at Fort Sill those that didn't had to steal or die of starvation. We're lucky they weren't on no killin' spree."

"It's what finished your Pa," she added.

"That and you know...." Jared bit his lip.

"I know son, it's just me being melancholy about your poor father."

They both knew the truth; his father had died from a broken heart. It was a wonder he lived so long after Joshua had died, Jared thought reflectively.

"Ma with your permission I want to turn this run down ranch of ours into the one Pa always dreamed of."

"It's yours son. You don't have to ask my permission for anything."

Jared looked at his Ma lovingly, as she turned back to the house and his heart went out to her. The death of his Pa had aged her beyond words. He yearned for those days when father and son would go hunting for the night's supper. Where they'd bag a wild turkey, maybe catch a rabbit or two.

Jared had changed a lot since his run in with Amy Halstead. He'd matured immensely. His Pa had given him more say around the ranch and even listened to his talk of expanding.

"We need hard cash for that son."

"We'll get it somehow," said Jared.

He could only look on in envy as men like Charlie Goodnight and Oliver Loving blazed trails northwards. It was the time of the great cattle drives to places like Ogallala, Dodge and Miles City.

"Maybe we could throw in with some of the small ranchers and take our beeves to the trail head at Dodge," he said hopefully.

"One day," his Pa said, without much conviction.

On the monthly supply run, *which Jared had resumed after an interim period where Dale took his place,* his Pa received a telegram from an attorney at law up in Amarillo stating that Joe McAllister of said town had up and died at the age of sixty-seven leaving his entire estate to his brother John McAllister, the princely sum of three hundred and forty four dollars.

John McAllister was philosophical about his brother's passing and declared that he thought he'd died from the drink years ago, but yes the princely sum of three hundred and forty four dollars wasn't to be sniffed at.

"You brought us the news boy; I think it only proper that you should be the one to travel up to Amarillo to collect Joe's estate."

Filled with enthusiasm Jared said his goodbyes and set off for Amarillo. It was during his time away that the Comanche drove off half the McAllister herd. When he arrived home in February of 1876 he found his Pa had died and the ranch close to ruin.

Sarah noticed him a coming from a ways off. "I'd recognise that big old bay anywhere," she shouted, "but I can't make out who Jared's got riding alongside.

As they approached the ranch house Ma, Sarah and Dale stood on the porch to greet them. Jared looked past them at the empty doorway, then his Ma pointed with her eyes to the mound of fresh earth close to the cherry tree. Jared knew at once.

"Comanche?"

"No son, they run off half the herd, but they spared us. It was his heart, it just gave out."

Jared neither asked for detail nor was it offered. He just knew. "Ma, this here's Mordecai. Him and I, well we rode the river some. He'll be staying awhile."

Ma McAllister managed a half smile, "You're welcome to what vittles we got Mr Mordecai."

"Obliged," replied the stranger.

For the next few months Jared, Dale and Mordecai worked the ranch, until one day Dale told Jared, he and Sarah had talked about it and decided they'd try their luck in California.

"You and Ma, you're welcome to come along," Dale said feebly.

"If that's what you and Sarah want, well I can't stop yah," said Jared regretfully. "I wish you well," then he threw out his hand and Dale took it.

"Thanks Jared, this means a lot to Sarah and I."

Since Jared had arrived back at the ranch Dale had deferred to him, something he'd never have done before Pa McAllister died, but it wasn't just that. Jared had changed since his return. He was a different person from the boy who'd ridden off to Amarillo. Even Ma had noticed, though like Dale she kept her own counsel. It was only Sarah who continued to treat him as her kid brother.

Although Jared retained his quiet friendly nature, Dale detected a maturity beyond his years, he couldn't rightly put his finger on it, but something had happened up there on the Texas Panhandle that had changed the boy into a man. He was a man who commanded respect. He had become to all and sundry a born leader. On the surface he was still the Jared of old, but scratch that surface and you found a man ready to fight the devil and … Dale hesitated in his thoughts … maybe even God. And then there was Mordecai. He seemed to walk in Jared's shadow, 'but,' thought Dale, 'make no mistake, he is his own man.' He was a loner, sparse of words, friendly enough, but quick to anger, a man to have at your side, but a fearful enemy if you crossed him.

In truth Dale, like Mordecai, had always been his own man. He'd deferred to Sarah's Pa out of respect, but he didn't see himself second in command to her brother. Now with Jared firmly in charge and Mordecai to help out around the ranch, Dale saw his chance. California and a new life beckoned.

Ma, true to her word, left the day to day running of the ranch to Jared, but still ruled the roost at suppertime. Jared wouldn't have it any other way.

"How long do you think it'll take Sarah and Dale to get to California?" asked Ma over supper a few days after they left.

"That wagon train they're joining up with in Del Rio, leaves in about a week. I'd say they should be in California by the end of August. September at the latest," volunteered Jared.

"Do you think they'll run into Indians?" enquired Ma.

"I don't think so Ma. The Comanche are about finished in West Texas and if I'm to believe Dale, he told me the train is twenty or so wagons. They must have enough fire power to keep even them pesky Apaches away." Jared said it more to allay her fears than anything else. He knew at close hand what those Indians were capable of. A sideways glance from Mordecai and he quickly changed the subject.

Chapter 15

News of the Custer Massacre reverberated across the country. Custer's Last Stand, The Battle of the Little Big Horn, these and other notorious headlines were emblazoned across the newspapers back East. Custer's folly had turned him and the gallant Seventh into heroes overnight. In death he'd achieved the immortality he so craved. Pressure was brought to bear on the government in Washington. The wheels of history slowly turned. It was the greatest Indian victory ever, but it had marked the beginning of the end for the red man.

When news of the massacre reached Fort Abraham Lincoln, the wives and loved ones of the deceased were hysterical with grief. Mrs Custer and a small group of officers' wives, including Deirdre, rallied the women and brought them comfort and support during their hour of need.

"It's my duty as George's wife to see to these poor unfortunates, and as wives of his subordinates I expect you all to help," said Elizabeth Custer forcefully.

Deirdre looked up to her and marvelled at the noble way she went about her affairs. Stiff upper lip Deirdre had heard the English call it, but until that moment she hadn't known the meaning of the words. It was during these times that Deirdre got to know the true realities of

Miles's death. Mrs Custer was adamant that as officers' wives they should know what became of their loved ones.

One morning a week after the news of the massacre, Mrs Elizabeth Custer commanded all officers' wives to her quarters. There she relayed the tragic fate that had befallen their loved ones.

"Our Crow advisers informed my husband of the Sioux village a few miles distant. They were camped on the banks of the Little Big Horn River. Mr Custer," *as Elizabeth Custer was inclined to call him,* "decided to split the column into a three-pronged attack. Reno was rebuffed before he could reach the village, whilst my husband headed straight towards them. Mr Benteen was bringing up the rear. Our men fought bravely, but the sheer number of Sioux and Cheyenne overwhelmed them. After a few hours of fighting my husband gathered the surviving men around him and prepared for one last stand. Mrs Keogh, your husband and George's brother Tom were with him to the end. Deirdre, your Miles was there also. From the reports I've received all the men fought bravely to the last." There were tears in Mrs Custer's eyes as she finished her report.

What Mrs Custer left out was filled in a few days later as remnants of Benteen and Reno's troop rode in. All the bodies had been stripped naked and been mutilated after death, then left to rot in the summer heat. When Terry's command found them, the stench of their bodies could be smelt a mile down wind. Deirdre preferred Mrs Custer's account, though she knew the account from the ordinary soldier were probably far more accurate.

It wasn't until weeks later that Deirdre found her own personal time to grieve. But by then she had more things to worry about. She was with child; Miles's parting gift before he set off on his ill-fated campaign. Three months pregnant. That alone was enough to take in. The letter from the War Department expressing their heartfelt sympathies on one hand, and politely telling her on the other, that she was to leave Fort Abraham Lincoln before the end of the month, was another.

That's when it hit her. Custer would be remembered, folly that his campaign turned out to be. The War Office would turn him into a national hero. What bloody revenge would be taken in his name, Deirdre could only speculate. But she, like the rest of the wives save Mrs Custer and a few others, would be left to their own devices. All she would receive was a small pension, lukewarm offers of help and advice, and then she'd be forgotten. It was all too much. If nothing else Deirdre had her pride. There was no way she was going to let those bureaucrats back east give her handouts and scraps from their tables. In the loneliness of her rooms she let it all out. What should have filled her with joy and expectation was nothing more than a burden. She sat up all night considering her options. She could bring the child into this world and get a job in Bismarck, but how would she work and look after the baby? Apart from the army she had no other family, and they were no use. Deirdre thought about that first meeting with Miles and his proposal of marriage. It was the answer to her prayers. A new beginning, a new life, but it had been so cruelly taken away from her. She'd relied on others and it hadn't panned out. She was expecting a baby, a dear sweet innocent baby, but all she could think about was how much of a burden it would become. In the small hours of that night Deirdre made her decision. It would have been different if Miles had lived, but without a loving husband, the comfort of a home and the security of being an Army officer's wife, there was no way Deirdre O'Bannion could take on the responsibility of another mouth to feed. She'd known poverty; she'd lived with its deprivations and consequence's but that was in what they supposedly called civilisation. Here her problems were magnified. It was a savage land, a savage and cruel unforgiving landscape. The very words she'd uttered to Miles only weeks earlier and they had come back to haunt her. To bring a child up in those conditions was something she didn't dare contemplate.

Miles was dead. Mrs Custer had gone back East and Deirdre was now reaching full term and hitting rock bottom. She'd thought of accompanying Mrs Custer but chose not to. The West might have the Sioux, the smallpox, bad weather and loneliness, but it beat the thought of one day bumping into the monster, as she'd now begun to think of James Fairfax. For he surely would have delighted in her condition and mercy was a commodity he didn't possess. She feared for her unborn child and knew that if the child stayed with her, its future at best would be a childhood punctuated by poverty and crime, at worst.... Deirdre shuddered at the thought.

A childless couple, the local dry goods store owner in Bismarck and his wife had offered to take on the child as their own.

"All we ask Deirdre, is that we be allowed to bring up the child as we see fit and," added Mrs Langley, "to bring the child up as our own."

It was painful, far more painful than she'd imagined. Although she understood the severity and the sincerity in Mrs Langley's words, Deirdre found it hard to let go. She knew that once she gave the baby away there would be no going back, she would be giving up all claims on the child. They were a good and kind hearted couple Deirdre had known albeit slightly when she was at Fort Abraham Lincoln. In her weakened and emotional state Deirdre recognised the wisdom in what Mrs Langley was saying. The thought of giving up her child was abhorrent, but what choice did she have? At least with the Langleys, the child would have a good start in life.

Deirdre cried for days.

Chapter 16

They buried Ma next to her husband under the cherry tree that they'd planted in memory of their son Joshua. Jared thought it fitting and took comfort in the fact that his Ma and Pa were now at peace, sitting around a log-hewn table with their long lost son Joshua.

Ma had taken sick during the winter and, despite Jared's best efforts, she slipped away in January. "I expect she missed Pa. I know she missed Joshua, though she kept her grief from Pa on account he wasn't as strong as her. She always kept going, for the family I guess. She wouldn't have gone if she thought I weren't ready," he said as they lowered her into the shallow grave.

It was a month later when Jared received news that Sarah had died in childbirth. The baby was fine and Dale was bringing her up the best way he could.

"Why are we born?" enquired Jared. "We're born, we live a while, then we die. What's it all about?"

"I'm the wrong one to ask," replied Mordecai. "I expect there are some who make their mark in this life and there are the rest of us."

Jared gave his friend a look of incredulity.

"That's it!"

Jared outlined his plans to Mordecai, "We'll create a cattle empire to rival the best."

"You're crazy!"

"Crazy or not, are you with me?"

"I'm along for the ride, that's all."

"We'll be partners, straight down the middle. We'll add to our stock, we'll spend time building and then when we're ready we'll head north. Custer getting himself killed an all; well the government won't stand still."

"What are you driving at?"

"We drive a herd north, up into the Montana Territory. The army will have taken care of the Sioux and Cheyenne problem. We'll be able to make our own mark on this land. We'll leave a legacy for others to follow!"

"To do what you're talking about, you'd need at least two thousand head of cattle. You ain't got more than three hundred and fifty."

"I know that," said Jared gruffly, "but I ain't talking about doing it overnight."

"You're forgetting, we can't do all this on our lonesome," said Mordecai.

"I know that too!" The frustration in Jared's words plain to hear. "But first we got to have a plan, then we work to it."

"Al'right by me, but if you're set on it, you'll have to bend a few rules, break a couple too, I'd reckon. If that's what you want, I'll back yah."

Jared gave it some thought. He knew just what Mordecai was implying.

"This here country has thousands, possibly millions, of unbranded cattle. All we got to do is rope em and brand em."

"That's easy to say, but I ain't no cowboy," added Mordecai.

"Then we head to Uvalde and hire some."

A week later Jared and Mordecai rode into Uvalde for supplies and with the intention of hiring men.

"We need a cook above anything," said Mordecai as they tied their horses up outside Halstead's general store.

Jared nodded his agreement and reflected on the evening meals with Ma and the family, then he quickly shrugged the past from his mind as Amy Halstead walked out of the store.

"Hi Jared, I was sorry to hear about your Ma."

"Thanks Amy, it's appreciated."

"Must be lonely up at the ranch, with Sarah gone to California," she continued.

"We manage," he said abruptly then tipping his hat he excused himself. He didn't know whether Amy knew of Sarah's fate and he had no intention of telling her.

"Cook, right?" he said suddenly to Mordecai.

"In my experience Mexicans make good cooks," said Mordecai as they headed towards a nearby cantina. The food was awful.

"Good cooks hah," Jared said as they left.

Bernardo Torres was breaking a fiery mustang in the corral at the back of the cantina, just as Jared and Mordecai stepped outside. The noise from the corral attracted their attention. The wiry Mexican was unceremoniously dumped into the dirt as they rounded the corner of the cantina. Unperturbed by the horse's lack of respect Bernardo threw himself onto the dusty back of the crazed animal.

Jared looked impressed, "We need a wrangler, just as much as we need a cook."

They watched as little by little the Mexican, using a combination of strength, stamina and kind words, brought the mustang under control.

"Good job!" cried Jared.

The wrangler looked over, "Thank you senor."

"You lookin' for work?"

"I have work senor,"

"Pity. We're building a herd, taking them to Montana," said Jared optimistically.

"Ah, senor, I would be tempted, but I'm no alone. I have my Rosita to think of."

"Rosita?"

"Yes senor, my wife."

"Can she cook?"

"Cook senor? Rosita is the best cook this side of heaven."

Mordecai looked at Jared and gave a wry smile.

CHAPTER 17

In June of 1877, Deirdre O'Bannion, arrived in Helena, Montana Territory, equipped with a valise and a small suitcase containing two dresses from Paris, France. She had split what remained of the money from the old cash-box with the Langleys. The remainder totalling around three hundred dollars she'd used to purchase a 22 calibre pocket Colt, five shot, but deadly at close range. Deirdre O'Bannion had changed from that snippet of a strumpet from the Five Points area of New York. The respect of such notables as Mrs Custer and the widow of Miles Keogh had taught Deirdre one thing. The respect of your peers was paramount, whether in exalted company or dealing with the dregs of society.

She'd chosen Helena with good reason, it was growing. From a small gold strike at Last Chance Gulch it had defied other mining towns and had grown bigger. There was money to be made in Helena, big money. With her small stake, the 22 calibre Colt and her new found confidence, Deirdre O'Bannion was going into business for herself. At first she'd thought of seeking employment at Josephine "Chicago Joe" Airey's place on Wood Street, but that fateful meeting changed her mind.

"You're pretty, I'll grant you, and smart. Pretty, and yes too smart to waste your life as one of my girls." Chicago Joe was a good judge of character and in Deirdre she saw potential, that and the fact that in the hour she'd known her she'd taken a liking to the girl.

"I'm down on my luck, but I ain't begging," said Deirdre defiantly.

Chicago Joe stifled a laugh. "Feisty, ain't yah."

"I'll bid you good day," said Deirdre trying her best to hold on to what dignity she still had.

"Hold your horses a moment and listen."

The sternness in Josephine Airey's voice brought Deirdre up with a halt.

"There are two ways to go in this profession, one is up and the other, well I don't need to spell it out. Best you set up in business for yourself. There's money to me made here, that's for sure."

"I don't have much capital, how do I go about it?"

"You invest in property, soon as you can. It's the likes of me and others like me that are making it."

"But where do I start?"

"Jake Tunstall over at Clore Street, tell him I sent you. Oh and drop the accent, it reminds me too much of home."

"Oui Mademoiselle," said Deirdre, a wry smile suddenly appearing on her face.

Josephine laughed; her instincts were right on the button. This young lady could go far, with a little guidance. "Come see me sometime," cried Chicago Joe as Deirdre hurried off.

With a renewed vigour Deirdre thanked Chicago Joe and went straight to Clore Street. Tunstall's place, the Gem, wasn't much, a gin palace on it's uppers but Deirdre saw the potential. Jake Tunstall looked at her lecherously and Deirdre knew she'd be able to strike the right bargain. She negotiated the rent of four small rooms and a percentage of her earnings, whilst he kicked back fine upholstery and velvet curtains. She wanted to create a comfortable environment for her girls and their clients. Jake Tunstall wasn't opposed to the proposition; he thought that having a refined lady from France added to his reputation.

Deirdre had been working on her accent for almost a year and apart from meeting a real Frenchman or woman no one could tell the difference. Then using her charm and her accent she went about hiring a number of girls. It wasn't hard; Helena had plenty of women of that persuasion. She cast an expert eye over the women who sought her out, hardened her heart to their sad stories and soon weeded out the sickly and the old. She saw herself as a latter day Fanny Brannigan, hard but fair. She desperately hoped she'd stay much kinder and more sensitive to the plight of her girls than the madam at the Five Points.

A new life beckoned, albeit a life she'd once known, but up market like her new friend Chicago Joe. From that first meeting with the madam of Wood Street, Deirdre O'Bannion ceased to exist. She was now Madeline Dubois, Maddie for short.

If Jake Tunstall thought Maddie could be easily bullied into throwing her lot in with him, he was sorely mistaken. Within a week he'd tried to persuade one of her girls that as landlord he was entitled to a free one whenever it took his fancy. When Maddie heard what had happened she calmly walked up to him, and without warning had stuck her 22 calibre Colt underneath his chin and warning him in no uncertain terms that if he tried it again he'd be negotiating for tricks with the angels. Jake Tunstall wasn't a man to scare lightly, but the look in Maddie's eyes told him she meant every word. He was a businessman, problems with a jumped up whore just weren't worth the aggravation. Besides, he thought, within a month she'd be trying to negotiate a deal herself.

An incident a few weeks later had Jake Tunstall re-thinking his original thoughts and counting his blessings that he'd had the good sense to back off. Calling the taking of life no more than an incident seemed quite harsh, but in the realities of those days it was in fact no more than an incident.

Maddie was across the hall servicing a client, when she heard a scream from the room opposite. She ignored it at first as screams were commonplace in most houses of ill repute. When she heard it a second time she realised it wasn't a scream of false pleasure but a genuine cry of terror. Her client was in the first swells of ecstasy when, fully-clothed minus her under garments, Maddie climbed off him and reached inside her valise which she kept close to the side of the bed. Swiftly she grabbed the 22 calibre Colt and raced for the door.

"What the fucking hell's going on ...?" cried her client in bewilderment, his erect penis left flapping. Maddie ignored his outburst and cocked the small calibre weapon. His ardour cooled instantly as he watched Maddie turn the door handle and exit.

Across the hall another scream resounded from the room. Without a second thought Maddie burst through the door. It couldn't have been more than a second but the sight of the near naked blood soaked prostitute brought it all back to her. She wanted to scream, to run but the be-whiskered miner turned angrily towards the intrusion, a blood soaked knife still in his hand. Instead of running, Maddie advanced to within a foot of the man, aimed the pistol at his head and pulled the trigger. A deafening sound echoed around the room, as the man dropped like he'd been pole-axed.

Half-clad women and their clients gazed anxiously into the smoke-filled room, the smell of cordite biting at their throats. Maddie emerged, appearing shocked and devastated at killing a man in cold blood, then, without saying a word, retired to her room. Her client, now half dressed, looked at the smoking gun still in her hand and decided to make himself scarce. Maddie slammed the door hard behind him and slumped onto her bed and wept.

In the cold light of day she realised she could have stopped the man without killing him, but a red mist had clouded her judgement. Most people would have balked at pulling the trigger but she hadn't. In truth all Maddie could see was the masked face of James Fairfax. "What am I turning into?" she cried into her pillow.

A local constable was soon on the scene, so was Jake Tunstall and Chicago Joe, who shielded Maddie from his questions. He concentrated his investigations on Joanne whose condition spoke for its self.

Though shocked and frightened the young woman was able to satisfy the officer that it was a sex game that had gotten out of hand. He understood that Maddie had heard her screams and had reacted in the only way she could have. A discreet gift from Chicago Joe and the constable concluded that Maddie had acted in self defence.

"You didn't need to do that." said Maddie.

"I know I didn't, but someone has to teach yah."

The next morning Maddie questioned the girl herself. Joanne sobbed and said the man had been sweet and gentle and kind, not really the type to beat on a woman. But that after he'd finished, he seemed to change. She suspected it was feelings of remorse that had set in. He'd told her earlier that he had a young bride back East and was hoping to send for her real soon. Joanne tried comforting him, telling him that she'd never let it slip. He'd pushed her away and that's when he called her a cheap whore. Angered by his hypocrisy she'd responded in the only way she knew how. She said he had a dick no bigger than her little finger and then she waggled it to illustrate the point. He'd responded by smashing her across the face with the back of his hand. She wiped away the blood from her mouth but didn't scream out. Beatings were something of an occupational hazard. But after he'd beat on her several times he reached down and pulled a knife from his belt. It was then that she screamed. He slashed her viciously across her abdomen. Luckily for her it was a superficial cut. Before he could strike again she screamed. That was when Maddie had opened the door and ended that particular argument.

After that incident Maddie ensured that each of her girls should carry a small stiletto blade hidden in the inside of their lace up boots. It was of little insurance against the hulking brutes who frequented Maddie's rooms, but it was better than nothing. Joanne had learned a valuable lesson and so had Maddie. If she wanted to pull herself out of poverty she'd have to harden herself up, she couldn't just live on her wits and the skills she'd learnt in the Five Points bordello.

She'd now killed a man protecting one of her girls. It was a hard profession, and she'd gone into it almost blind. A string of girls needed looking after. So she made an arrangement with one of the town doctors to check her and the girls once a month. She'd seen at first hand what the ravages of disease could do to a person. The health and welfare of her girls was to be paramount if she was to succeed in her chosen profession. If she looked after them, they in turn should look after her.

Within a year Maddie was well on her way towards her own establishment. She'd toughened up, whereas before the shooting she'd been all bluff and bluster, now people listened when she laid down the law. No one fucked with Maddie Dubois, at least not unless they were prepared to pay the price. Jake Tunstall became far more accommodating. Business started to boom, so much so that she'd rented another two rooms from him.

The incident had brought her a form of notoriety which she neither liked nor wanted. But on the whole she found it was good for business. She mixed with some of the town's most influential men and, although they supported her enterprise, she had no illusions that their friendship extended past that end of town. She also counted others of a more notorious nature as potential allies.

With nine girls working for her it wasn't long before she started looking for more suitable accommodation. She didn't need to look far, just across Clore street and down a couple of blocks was Wood street and the Alhambra, a gaming house and gin palace. It had originally been built as a hotel but the owner had recently lost it in a card game to the current owner, who'd promptly turned it into the aforementioned gaming house. Maddie saw the potential of the three storied building, what it lacked she was well able to accommodate.

With her savings invested in the local bank, Maddie sought a sizeable loan. "Hell and Damnation Bill, I ain't asking for the earth. You've seen what money I'm taking each month." Maddie had a persuasive tongue and pretty soon she had her bank roll.

With her loan in place Maddie then confronted the owner Luke Plummer, another of her new found friends.

"I want to buy into the Alhambra."

"What makes you think I need a partner?" said Plummer.

"With a feminine touch this place could be a little gold-mine."

"So, I bring in my own girls and put them to work, why would I need you?"

"Two reasons," Maddie smiled, "First reason, you need an injection of cash to smarten this place up. Second reason, I'll handle the girls, they'll be my responsibility. I'll see to their welfare."

"What'll it cost me?" said Plummer, now warming to Maddie's ideas and plans.

"I want thirty percent of the Alhambra!"

"You what!" cried Luke Plummer.

"I run the place for you, I bring in the girls, and you get thirty percent of my takings. The gambling and the liquor, that's down to you. It's a win win situation."

Luke Plummer thought about Maddie's proposition for a few moments, then he stretched out his hand.

"Deal! I'll have my lawyer write up the papers," said Plummer.

"I've already taken the liberty," said Maddie triumphantly.

Plummer, it was said, had killed a man in Miles City two years earlier. Since arriving in Helena he'd acquired several businesses, some legitimate, whilst others, like the Alhambra, in shady transactions. He surrounded himself with an array of people who ensured the smooth running of all his businesses. In short, Luke Plummer had become a force to be reckoned with. His powerful friends in the more salubrious areas of Helena saw that the affairs of the Alhambra remained in house.

Maddie nurtured her new found stability and offered her favours to Plummer on an occasion, but made it quite clear it was a concession, not a right. In reality she would have preferred to go into business on her own, but her loan would only stretch so far. She knew there was money to make in Helena and the owners of gaming houses, saloons and brothels made most of it. Legitimate business also prospered, the only real losers were the men who broke their backs in the creeks, panning for gold. Some, very few, struck rich. The rest gambled, drank and whored it away.

Maddie's transformation of the Alhambra was nothing short of miraculous. Within three months its exterior and interiors were something to behold. The fine rosewood balustrade that decorated the central staircase was the most striking feature of the gaming palace. The matching rosewood bar which stretched down the entire east wall was in turn complimented by the ornate mirror at the back, which matched the rosewood doors framing the ornate glass frontage.

On the ground floor there was the usual array of gaming devices, from Faro and Blackjack to Monte and Fan-Tan, plus an array of green baize tables for the clientele to engage themselves in a friendly game of cards. In the centre of the room was an old upright piano complete with resident piano player who belted out tunes from late until the early hours. Luke Plummer's saloon girls circulated the ground floor area, entertaining, laughing and joking with the countless townsfolk, businessmen, miners, drummers, ranchers and card sharks who frequented the place, but it was up the ornate rosewood staircase to the parlour house at the top that the sexually minded clientele climbed.

Only the most respected prominent members of Helena's society, those who had the guts and the necessary wealth, walked through the impressive double doors at the top of the stairs. Once inside, Maddie would entertain them cordially with a natural friendliness that disarmed even the first timers. She would offer the gentlemen an array of girls, even suggesting which ones would be suitable for their preference. Alongside Maddie was the professor, a gentleman of musical talents who supplied the ambience of the house and played whatever tunes were popular at the moment. Two serving girls supplied the clientele with liquor and nibbles.

Maddie's choice of plush carpeting and velvet covered furnishing gave the parlour house an air of sophistication. It was a place to relax, to unwind, to escape the troubles of day to day life in Helena. A light supper was provided and only the finest of wines were served, *all at an extra cost.* Maddie had seen how Chicago Joe ran her place and did her best to make life just as comfortable for all concerned. All this was but a pre-cursor before the men discreetly climbed the rather less than ornate stairs to the top of the house, where they indulged themselves with the pleasures of the flesh. For this the gentlemen of Helena were ready to pay highly. Which was just as well as Maddie's outgoings were high, but the returns were just that bit higher. It was a far cry from the seediness of Tunstall's place and was only surpassed by the opulent establishments of Chicago Joe's.

Luke Plummer had several properties and couldn't be in all places at all times so as a condition of their partnership he'd left the running of the Alhambra to Maddie. She soon learned how to keep the books and how to weed out any crook and swindler who frequented her place. A couple of under managers backed her play.

Maddie was no longer the fresh faced officer's wife. Though still young and attractive, she'd developed a slight harshness around the eyes. To an outsider she looked every inch the stern Madam who ran the girls of the Alhambra but in private when she was alone she wept unashamedly over the child she'd been forced to give up. She'd never stopped thinking about him, but with her new found wealth she thought more and more about what could have been. She thought of Miles with fondness. She believed that given time she could have felt love for him but, alas, that was something she could only speculate upon. But it was the child that she yearned for, the child that she wouldn't see take his first steps, say mammy, or tend his wounds when he fell and grazed his knee. In the hours before dawn, Deirdre Devlin of Cork would cry herself to sleep. At noon she'd wake, put on her makeup and present herself at the top of the stairs of the Alhambra Gaming Palace as the voluptuous Madeline Dubois.

Maddie allowed herself one extra luxury; she only slept with the men who took her fancy, with the exception of Luke Plummer, a man that took his pleasures when Maddie decreed, despite being offered more for her services than she had a right to expect. She was earning well, so saw no reason to rock the proverbial Alhambra boat. She'd never been short on admirers but not one had made her heart race. She took her love where she found it, but secretly she yearned for that one true love, a knight in shining armour to whisk her away, just like in the penny dreadfuls she was struggling to read. Mrs Custer had been the instigator of that chore; she'd said that, despite their content, it would be good practice in her reading. Maddie sighed. 'Stupid girl,' she thought as she pulled on a mask of a smile and descended the stairs.

CHAPTER 18

Sedated and calmed by the opium he'd ingested, James Fairfax reflected on his failure to find the whore. He'd arrived in San Francisco six years earlier, bad-tempered and dusty, with an expectancy of finding the Irish waif and despatching the bitch to her maker as quickly as possible. Within a month he'd realised his task was harder than he'd expected. He'd established his patch on Pacific Street between Kearney and Mongomery, an area of San Francisco known as the notorious Barbary Coast. It was home to every cut-throat, whoremonger, lewd women, pickpocket, and murderer who frequented those parts. Gin palaces, whore houses, saloons and opium dens littered the rabbit warren of streets, alongside melodeons *low type variety concert saloons and halls* namely the Bella Union, the Adelphi and Albert's Melodeon, all catering for stag audiences. If the whore Devlin was in the red light district of San Francisco he would find her, but after extensive enquires he had to accept that Deirdre Devlin had vanished without trace. But, he reasoned to himself, one day she would put in an appearance and he vowed that that day would be her last. The thought continued to comfort him.

That had been six years ago and he hadn't had much to comfort him since. His curse, the dreaded half mask, had marked him out from most men. He couldn't go anywhere without bringing attention to himself. And with attention there was always someone who couldn't resist a chance remark. The first time had been in a bar in Chinatown. A sailor just off one of the frigates in the bay, fuelled by rot gut whiskey and the encouragement of his fellow sailors, became the first to find himself on the path to hell.

"Hey mistah," he shouted. Fairfax ignored him and continued to play cards. "Hey you! You macabre piece of shit!" Fairfax looked up, then dismissed the sailor and concentrated on his hand. The sailor, reinforced by the other man's reluctance to fight, decided to have some fun. "We've been talkin, I says you are an ugly son of a bitch under that mask."

Fairfax stopped playing cards and glared back at the drunken sailor. The sailor didn't detect the anger in those eyes and looked back towards his friends and laughed.

"Me mates and I are curious as to what you look like, so do us a favour and take off the fucking mask."

"You ain't gonna take that," goaded one of the card players.

"We'll back your play," said another.

The anger in Fairfax's eyes changed to one of cold hate as he stood up and calmly walked towards the sailor. "If you want to see me, I must warn you the stakes are the highest you've ever played for."

Puzzled by the calm words of the man advancing towards him, he half turned towards his friends, a stupid grin spread across his ruddy face, and then he reached out for the mask. Quick as a cat, Fairfax plunged an eight inch blade into the sailor's abdomen and then he twisted the knife upwards before withdrawing it. With his other hand he pointed a short barrelled Remington at the group of sailors.

"The man insulted me, he would have done me harm. I had no choice."

Others in the crowd took up his cry, "It was a fair fight."

"He asked for it."

"Dumb fuck sailor."

"Call the police."

Fairfax stood his ground until the police arrived. In the aftermath James Fairfax was exonerated, although he did spend a night in the local jailhouse for his trouble. The very fact that the sailor's witnesses had all embarked on another voyage the following morning, left the police without any witnesses for the prosecution. It was deemed a fair fight and Fairfax had been provoked beyond endurance.

For months James Fairfax basked in his new found notoriety. He became a celebrity overnight, a man not to be trifled with. He wined and dined in the best and worst of places. He gambled and whored at an alarming rate. Coupled with his drinking and his growing addiction to the pipe, it wasn't long before his vast wealth steadily began to evaporate. In order to stem the tide of his spending, he invested what little money he had left into a gaming house and brothel. He laughed at the irony. The whore killer had now become the whoremaster.

He killed his second man a year later, defending the honour of one of his whores. He shot him to death while the man's pants were around his ankles. This time he planted a gun in the man's hand. Again he was released without charge. His reputation as a dangerous man grew. He wallowed in his celebrity status, and vowed to kill another man before the year was out. But it was another woman who sated his lust for blood minutes before the old year died. She'd come to him for employment, a waif of a girl, skinny, with small breasts and a harelip.

"You're not what my customers want!"

She'd begged him to take her, "Please, I've nowhere else to go, don't throw me out into the street. I beg you."

Fairfax grabbed her by the hair and was about to do just that when an old familiar urge came over him. "You want work, okay maybe there is something you can do. Can you cook? Can you clean?"

"Yes, I'll do anything," she said desperately. "Anything."

Her body was found in a back alley the next morning, mutilated and drained of blood. Her throat had been cut so violently that her head was almost severed from her neck. There were rumours, there always are in such cases. The police did a routine investigation, then as in all big cities when the trail became cold the case file was closed.

Fairfax had picked up the habit of opium smoking on the east coast and found the opium dens of San Francisco very much to his liking. It was there that he met the infamous Ah Toy, a fifty year old Chinese madam. She was as unscrupulous an individual as Fairfax had ever met. He liked her and soon formed an alliance. She procured young Chinese girls for his devious favour, and he paid her handsomely.

"No sliceee, you understand," she often warned him. "No good for businesseee," although she turned a blind eye to most things for a price. A Chinese Fanny Brannigan he thought, and accordingly he accommodated her on an occasion. Whether he took her into his confidence is open to conjecture.

James Fairfax's notoriety reached an all time high in the summer of 1880. Always immaculately dressed, he'd taken to wearing a frock coat of the day over his shirt and vest. He carried a short barrelled Navy Colt 36 calibre in a leather shoulder holster concealed under the coat, plus the eight inch bladed knife which he kept in a scabbard on a belt around his hips. On his head he wore a flat rimmed black hat with a wide brim. With his matching black half mask he stood out as one of San Francisco's most flamboyant characters. The fact that he'd officially killed two men in open combat marked him as a target for others who coveted his position. Those who sought his exulted position usually stopped short before they'd committed themselves. Rufus Coe wasn't one of them.

It was in O'Neal's dining hall that Rufus Coe first called Fairfax a liar and a cheat at cards. He was holding a cocked pistol at his side at the time he spat out the challenge. The air was thick with tension. Everyone in the room expected gunplay, but James Fairfax, with his eyes blazing menacingly, wasn't a fool. He knew that any sudden move on his part and he would be a dead man. As calmly as he could muster, he spoke in his own defence.

"I'm sorry that my card playing has offended you. I have no wish to quarrel. Take the money from the table and we'll say no more about it."

Dumbfounded by Fairfax's humility, Rufus tried to goad him into a fight.

"You're a Goddamn cheat. Say it, Goddamn you. Say it!" His gun hand started to rise and Fairfax knew the man was intent on murder.

"I'm a cheat, I'm a goddamn cheat and I'm unarmed. Please don't kill me," he begged.

At that precise moment in walked the local constable. Rufus, seeing the law, lowered his gun and reached across the table and gathered up the scattered bills.

"You're a cheat; from your own mouth you've uttered it. You're washed up in this town, be gone on the morning stage or we'll have at it."

Fairfax, grateful for the intervention of the constable, scurried out and fled to the safety of his room. Sweating profusely he grabbed for the bottle of bourbon on the dresser. Angrily he pulled the cork out by his teeth, and drank from the neck of the bottle. After he'd steadied his nerves he began to seethe. He'd been given an ultimatum. 'Get out of town on the midday stage!'

Calmed by the alcoholic effects of the bourbon, Fairfax reasoned that he'd been scared into admitting being a cheat only because he was facing an almost certain death. And whilst he seethed, he realised that only the destruction of Rufus Coe could salve his damaged pride. Facing the man on equal or apparently equal terms was something he could deal with.

He awoke the following morning with a strangely clear head. He'd formulated a plan to rid himself of Rufus Coe and save face with the crowd. From his window overlooking the street he could see Coe awaiting the stage, gun hanging loosely at his side. And Fairfax noticed, by the man's swagger, that he'd already started drinking.

Carefully and methodically James Fairfax checked his pistol for loads and then he picked up a two shot derringer from the open drawer. He checked his appearance in the mirror. Satisfied that all was in place, he grabbed a half-empty valise and made for the door. At the top of the stairs he checked the ivory handle of his Colt for reassurance, then, with valise in left hand and the derringer loaded, cocked and concealed in the palm of his right hand, he walked into the daylight.

A crowd had gathered expectantly and Fairfax didn't intend to disappoint. News had travelled fast about his humiliation at the hands of Rufus Coe. Well, before the day was out they'd all be singing from a different hymn book, he thought. As he crossed the dirt street he could feel the derringer slip in his hand. Beads of sweat burst onto his brow, he knew as he grew closer that one slip and he, not Rufus Coe, would be in the hereafter.

What happened next is still disputed to this very day. All anyone could be sure of was that Rufus Coe had the first word.

"Get on that stage you yeller dog, you're lucky I didn't tar and feather yah!"

"I'll see you in hell Rufus!"

Rufus Coe's brain took a little over half a second to register, by then he realised it was too late. The twin over and under barrels of the concealed derringer were spitting flame. Rufus's own gun exploded harmlessly into the dirt road. Fairfax's first bullet hit a bystander but the second tore a hole in Coe's left side. He fell backwards as the tall half masked figure of Fairfax dropped the derringer and reached inside his frock coat and pulled out the short barrelled Colt. Rufus stared up into the face of death and could have sworn the man was laughing at him. Flames erupted from the short barrel as it pointed downward. James Fairfax emptied the gun into the chest of Rufus Coe.

"I was in fear for my life," said Fairfax at the inquest a week later. Men in my position are marked and we have to take what steps are necessary to stay alive." The jury took only two minutes to find in favour of Fairfax. In the matter of the dead bystander, the jury found 'death by misadventure' and ordered James to pay his widow two hundred dollars as compensation.

It wasn't long before James 'Half Face' Fairfax was being touted as the new Wild Bill Hickok. Fairfax, although revelling in the glory of being compared with such exulted company, didn't have any thoughts of going the same way as Wild Bill.

As winter approached James Faifax was becoming paranoid at the thought of death. He only ate in uncrowded rooms and played cards and drank moderately with his back to the wall. Even the demise of another prostitute found with her throat cut couldn't stem the tide of this sea of paranoia. He was fast becoming a recluse, preferring to spend his time dabbling with the whores who worked for him. Then four days after Christmas he went too far with one of them. He tied and gagged her, had sex with her until he climaxed then his eyes clouded over and he reached for the knife at his belt and pushed it slowly and firmly between the girl's legs. He watched her muffled scream and felt himself growing hard again. As he climaxed for a second time, he slid the knife across the girl's throat.

Lying exhausted on the bed beside the dead whore, realisation of what he'd done forced him to sit up. "Oh shit, I've really fucked up this time," he cried to himself. On his own premises, in his own bed with one of his own girls. His mind raced for an answer as he watched the girl's blood spread slowly across his linen sheets. He had to cover his tracks and fast. He reached for the kerosene lamp and poured the contents across the girl tied to the bed. He lit a match and set fire to the end of a sheet. Standing by the door he waited until the fire had taken hold before he slipped quietly out of the room. He shut the door making sure that no one saw him. Then he descended the stairs and slipped out the back door.

By the time the alarm was raised, the fire had swept along the landing trapping many of the girls and their clients. Their screams and cries, amidst the cacophony of frightened people running for their lives, were etched in every one of the volunteer fire brigades' members as they vainly fought the flames. The gaming house was soon no more than a blazing inferno. When the fire was eventually put out it had destroyed seven building adjacent to the gaming house and claimed the lives of at least twenty-two people.

James Fairfax had watched from the shadows as his business went up in smoke, but more important to him was to seek a place of safety. He sought and found refuge and an alibi in the opium dens of Chinatown. There had been an ordnance, banning such places, issued the previous year, but it was never strictly enforced. So for three days and nights he remained in an opium induced stupor, blotting out his handy work. He reasoned that the Chinks who were also as stoned as he, wouldn't be able to say how long he'd been there and besides Ah Toy would vouch for him.

Lying on his cot as the old year died and the New Year was born he reflected on the past few years. They had, he mused, been very eventful.

CHAPTER 19

As cattle empires went, it wasn't up to much, but it had the makings, thought Jared. His dream was taking longer than he'd expected. It was 1879 and his herd had swelled to just over a thousand head. The ranch now consisted of the main house, a bunkhouse where seven men ate, slept and farted their evenings away, a remuda of sixty cow ponies, thanks to the hard work of Bernardo, and a lean-to where the afore mentioned wrangler lived with his wife Rosita, the resident McAllister's ranch cook.

To pay wages, Jared supplied the town of Uvalde with meat and other produce such as eggs and chickens. With eight men and one woman on his payroll he wasn't able to put aside much more than eight hundred dollars, but more importantly the McAllister stock grew. However, what was once a steady supply of unbranded cattle was slowly drying up.

"You've got to be prepared to defend what's yours," said Mordecai on more than one occasion. It was a comment that was to be put to the test some months later.

Jared, frustrated by the slow process of gathering up maverick cattle, let out an oath, "Hell, at this rate we'll be driving them there cows up to Montana at the turn of the century!"

"We could buy cattle," said Mordecai.

"What do you mean buy?" asked Jared. It was the way in which his friend said 'buy' that caused him concern.

"I mean legitimate," replied Mordecai, having understood the concern of his friend. "Well as legitimate as any...." He left the remains of his sentence hanging, allowing Jared to digest the significance of what he was suggesting to sink in.

"Al'right, we'll do it."

A week later the two men road into Uvalde and headed for one of the many saloons. Mordecai had got word to an old acquaintance to meet them there. Jared ordered two beers and promptly found a table to sit and wait.

"Are you sure he'll turn up?" he enquired.

"He'll show."

They were nursing their second beer when a man sporting a handlebar moustache that split his face in two, entered the saloon. He was dressed in a fancy sombrero and wore an embroidered vest. To Jared he looked quite the dandy, except for the silver plated pistols that hung on either side of his waist. He was about to make a remark to Mordecai about the man's dress when the man's face broke into a wide grin and he advanced on their table. Mordecai stood up to greet him.

"It's been a long time Mordecai," said the dandy.

"Too long John," replied Mordecai, "This here's my partner Jared McAllister."

Jared nodded and shook the man's hand and offered him a chair.

"Right gentlemen, what service can I do for you?"

"We want to buy cattle!"

"How many? How much?"

Jared winced as he said, "As many as we can get for seven hundred dollars."

The man known as John spluttered in his beer, "Seven hundred!"

"It's all we've got," replied Jared, now thinking this whole trip was a waste of time.

"Make it a thousand, I'll give you two dollars a steer, take it or leave it."

"We'll take it," said Mordecai, his eyes told Jared not to interfere.

"You know my place, down in Eagle Pass. They'll be there waiting for your collection in a month's time."

"We get a full bill of sale? enquired Jared.

A look of mock hurt crossed the man's face, "And my word. These beeves ain't ever seen a Texas brand."

It wasn't until a day later that Jared learned the identity of the man he'd just done business with. Bernardo, *out of curiosity,* on hearing they were riding to Eagle Pass to bring back five hundred head from a ranch near Pendencia Creek, asked, "This man you done business with, was he, how you say, flamboyant in his style of dress?"

"You could say that," said Jared, "Why? Do you know this man?"

"Si senor, the man you speak of is John King Fisher. It is said that he is responsible for seven deaths," said Bernardo Torres, then he added, "Not counting Mexicans."

"Then I shouldn't do business with him?"

"Senor, you already have," said Bernardo.

Jared understood the veiled threat in his wrangler's words.

"I told you a long time ago that you'd have to bend a few rules, maybe even break some," said Mordecai, when Jared challenged him about the legitimacy of dealing with an infamous shooter. "If John King Fisher gave us his word, that's good enough for me."

Not another word was spoken on the matter until they rode down to Eagle Pass. On the road leading to John King Fisher's ranch they came across a sign post. It said in bold lettering "THIS IS KING FISHER'S ROAD. TAKE THE OTHER ONE.

"Legitimate!" said Jared to Mordecai in a sardonic way.

King Fisher walked out to greet them as they rode up to the ranch house, he was more flamboyantly dressed than normal. On his legs he wore a pair of chaps that had been made from the skin of a Bengal Tiger. As Mordecai had said when Jared asked about the man's dandy appearance, would you challenge the man's dress sense? Jared knew the answer.

King Fisher was a convivial host and Jared warmed to his friendly personality, although he never quite forgot Bernardo's words, about killing seven men not counting Mexicans.

Fisher, true to his word, had the five hundred head herded into a corral for Jared's inspection, although it wasn't needed. He also had a bill of sale which he handed to the tall fair haired rancher. "A pleasure doing business with you," he said as he extended his hand. Jared shook it.

They were eight miles out from King Fisher's ranch when eight Mexican vaqueros bore down on Jared, Mordecai and four cowboys from the McAllister ranch. Jared halted the herd and rode out to greet them.

"Heck, you and the boys hold the herd as best you can, I'm gonna keep Jared company," said Mordecai, as he unsheathed his Henry rifle from its scabbard. Clay Dean riding drag, saw the confrontation and instinctively pulled his Winchester from his scabbard then he kicked his horse into a trot, making a wide loop and approaching the Mexicans from the right side.

Up ahead of the herd, Jared was engaged in a one way conversation.

"Senor, zee cattle, they're from Mexico, no." said a greasy looking Mexican with bad teeth and a yellow shirt.

"They're bought and paid for," replied Jared, his eyes never leaving the three nearest vaqueros.

"No senor, they are our cattle and we're taking them," his smile now leaving his lips as his eyes grew darker.

"They've King Fisher's brand on them and I've a bill of sale," volunteered Jared.

"Gringo, I'm losing my patience," said the greasy Mexican in the bright yellow shirt which was stained with chewing tobacco.

"Better your patience, than your life," said Mordecai as he sidled up to within ten feet of the Mexican.

Unsettled by the dark gringo's threat, he began to work out his options. He hadn't expected this sort of opposition.

"These cattle ain't worth dying for," said Jared. His eyes were steely blue and his jaw was set firm. He was ready to defend what was his, no matter the cost. It wasn't the first time he'd looked death in the face, but it was the first time he'd seen fear in his opponents' eyes. He pushed the advantage, "You boys clear the path or get to fighting. I don't take prisoners!"

The fight suddenly went right out of the lead Mexican, as he backed his horse to allow Jared to pass.

"Wise move hombre," said Mordecai, "He'd have put a bullet in your heart quicker than you could whistle Dixie." And then to strike home he added, "If he hadn't those boys back yonder would've, they're ex rangers, and all crack shots with a rifle."

The yellow shirted Mexican looked to his left at Clay Dean, rifle held ready for action. He swallowed quickly, then to regain some form of dignity he said, "You win this time gringo, but if you cross the river I'll be waiting."

Mordecai's instinct was to shoot him out of the saddle, but he allowed the greaser his show of bravado.

Yellow shirt saw the look in Mordecai's eyes, then quickly he looked towards his men and uttered one word, "Vamoose!"

Later that night beside the dying embers of the camp-fire Mordecai looked thoughtfully at his friend.

"What?" cried Jared.

"I take no prisoners," he said mockingly. "What was that all about?"

"I guess it took that greaser to make me realise that to have a dream, you'd best be prepared to fight for it."

CHAPTER 20

Finbar O'Toole' sat at home and began reading the New York Times as he had done for nigh on three months since his retirement. Apart from helping his long suffering wife with the chores, this was his only form of relaxing. He was engrossed in an article about a fire in a gaming joint in San Francisco when he came across a name from the past. At first the name hadn't struck a cord, *which was strange because there wasn't a week that went past that he didn't think about the only case that slipped through his fingers,* but as he continued reading the article he read about the tragic deaths of many of the city's local dignitaries and of the nine ladies of easy virtue who'd perished with them.

James Fairfax, the name seemed to jump out of the page. 'Was it the same James Fairfax that he'd been certain had committed three gruesome murders? Fairfax and whores, it couldn't be just a coincidence, could it?' he thought as he re-read the article. The more he read it, the more his suspicions grew. From what he could glean from the paper it would appear that the owner, a one James Fairfax had been away when the fire started. The police report stated that he'd been in an opium induced stupor for days and was vouched for by a well connected Chinese woman who ran the opium den where he was found.

Finbar felt the hairs on the back of his neck rise as he continued to read on, "That's damn convenient," he mumbled to himself. From what he remembered about the Fanny Brannigan murder, she was a long time acquaintance of Fairfax. The coincidences were so uncanny. He'd been half hoping there would be a mention of whether this James Fairfax was disfigured in any way.

"Damnnit!" There was no mention of any disfigurement. "Be Jesus! If that ain't the same man, then I'm a monkey's uncle!" he exclaimed to Maggie, his wife of twenty years.

"Don't you be getting yourself hot under the collar, you're retired remember."

"Yes dear."

How could he forget? She kept reminding him daily. He nodded his acceptance of her wisdom. Women, he realised, needed to be humoured.

It had been a case that had stuck in Finbar's craw. He'd been certain that James Fairfax had been responsible for the death of Fanny Brannigan and two others, but without proof he was powerless to arrest him. Then the man had packed up his belongings, sold his house, withdrawn a large amount of money from the bank and departed for the West Coast. Finbar had tried to have him detained, but a gut feeling and the man's dubious past wasn't evidence. The case had gnawed at him for years especially since the murders had stopped.

Maggie knew that look and what it entailed. "Finbar O'Toole, you ain't a copper any more so best you forget about something you can't do anything about," she said.

"I guess you're right me dear, but it still rankles."

"That it does, I've heard nothing but that since you retired."

"Well you won't hear any more of it. This place is sold and the farm's ours."

He'd often thought about the whore who'd allegedly disfigured him, and hoped she'd gone on to better things. He didn't know her, but despite that, he had a growing admiration for her, but as the years passed he began to think more and more about his retirement. Now finally they were moving upstate, they'd bought a small farm and Finbar intended spending his days idly fishing.

Chapter 21

Ah Toy and the Chinese at the opium den had given Fairfax the alibi he needed. There were some in authority who thought his alibi too convenient, but they had little choice but to accept it. Ah Toy wasn't just any Chinese madam; *she was the Chinese madam* and had amongst her clients many high powered officials. After that, his relationship with the fifty one year old Ah Toy became far more intense. She knew what he was capable of but somehow she became infatuated with the evilness of the man. She told him as she lowered herself onto him that danger was the greatest aphrodisiac in the world. Fairfax laughed at her deviant mind but had to agree. He stayed with her for a time but soon both of them tired of the arrangement. It was an amicable parting, spliced with good humour. Ah Toy asked him how close he'd come to killing her.

"Tonight you would have found out," he said with a twisted grin across his grotesque face.

Ah Toy grinned with satisfaction, "Ah so, it best we no fuckee any-more," she said and with an exaggerated gesture of her arm she vanished back inside.

Fairfax recalled the advice the authorities had given him a few months earlier, The suggestion was that, for his health, he might be better off in another city. It was advice that Half-Face now decided to take on board.

James Fairfax, with an introduction from Ah Toy, settled well in Sacramento. His appearance and reputation opened many doors in the less reputable parts of town. Though still wary about back-shooters, he was becoming more comfortable with his own notoriety. It wasn't long before he found work as a faro dealer at the Sack o' Gold saloon. Within a week he was pimp to a small handful of celestial souls, *courtesy of Ah Toy's contacts,* who went about their business from two cribs at the back of the saloon. James Fairfax controlled his murderous urge to kill while he manipulated himself into the society of the streets. There would be time aplenty to unleash hell, but until that time he would satisfy himself with the pleasures of the flesh.

It wasn't long before he began making fresh inquiries into the whereabouts of one Deirdre Devlin. After all Sacramento had been the end of the line back then. But to no avail. Even Ah Toy's pimps hadn't heard of her. Fairfax's optimism was dashed and he raged for days but in the end he had to accept the inevitable; whatever fleshpots she'd disappeared into, it wasn't in Sacramento. 'One day, one day I'll find a clue to her whereabouts.' Comforted by these thoughts, he smoked his pipe and sank into a cloud of oblivion.

CHAPTER 22

1881, the year was still only three months old when Jared McAllister said those immortal words, "Head em up, move em out!" and two thousand five hundred beeves started on the slow drive to the grassy plains of Montana.

In the eighteen months since he first bought cattle from King Fisher, Jared had seen his herd grow to over three thousand head, but at a cost. Two men had been left crippled after a lightening stampede and another had been killed by rustlers a week earlier. It was a double set back, made more poignant as Sam, the cowboy who was killed by rustlers, was the youngest son of one of the crippled ranch hands.

A few months after the stampede, Heck the foreman and Clay Dean reported a few steers were missing. A day later Randy the youngest member of Jared's crew noticed a dozen or more had gone from the herd they kept in the south pasture. Jared would have let it go only Randy, *who knew far more about horses than people* told him that one of the rustlers was riding Sam's horse. More to the point the tracks weren't more than a day old.

Jared gathered his men around. "I'm going on a man hunt; I want three or four men that'll not balk at the job ahead. Heck, while I'm away you take charge; see to the running of things."

"Yes sir," cried Heck.

"Randy, you'll scout for sign."

In his heart he wanted to forget about the cattle, let the damn rustlers get away with it. In his eyes a few mangy cows weren't worth dying for, but he knew he had no choice. Sam's killers were only a day's ride ahead of them and to allow them to get away with what they'd done could not be tolerated. The proposed trail drive depended on the respect of the men who would ride with him. He took Mordecai, for his dependability, Clay Dean, late of the Frontier Battalion of Texas Rangers and Jake Duval a man known for his dexterity with a pistol. Much as he wanted to avoid gun play, he knew if they caught up with the rustlers it would be inevitable.

Mounted up and ready to go, Mordecai leaned across his saddle and spoke softly into Jared's ear, "If we catch em, that'll be where you fall or stand." Jared felt a cold shiver race down his spine. He knew very well what Mordecai was implying.

Randy caught sight of the rustlers late in the afternoon of the following day. They were making camp by the banks of the Rio Grande. The cattle were penned up in a makeshift corral, all twenty three of them. "There must be seven or eight Mexicans all heavily armed. It looks like they're intending to cross into Mexico in the morning," he said when he returned with his news.

"We wait until first light, then we hit them," said Mordecai.

"Shouldn't we give them a chance to surrender," said Jared.

"We'd hang them anyway," said Jake Duval.

Jared glared at the shooter come cowboy, he'd never taken much of a liking to the thin gunman. He was about to voice his opposition when Mordecai stepped in.

"They killed one of us, they ain't gonna take kindly to soft words, they'll be shooting back if we give them that chance."

Jared begrudgingly had to accept the wisdom of his friend's words, "Okay, we'll do it your way Mordecai, but if any throw up their hands do your best to show restraint."

He knew his words were falling on deaf ears, it wasn't the first time he'd gone into battle, but it was the first time he'd been in such a mismatch.

When the shooting started it was fierce and quick. Two Mexicans died in their sleep while the remaining five put up a show of crazed fire power before the guns went silent. When the smoke cleared only one Mexican was still alive. He'd been shot in his left hip and was writhing in agony. Jared recognised him as yellow shirt, although that morning he was wearing a faded blue one.

Jared knew if he was to have the respect of the men on the drive he'd have to administer swift justice to the sole survivor. To hell with justice, he thought angrily. Respect or no respect I can't just hang a man without due cause. How far the wounded Mexican would get crossing the fast flowing river he could only guess at, but a chance remark from Randy put paid to all that.

"That saddle, that's Sammy's saddle," he said pointing towards the man's bedroll. It wasn't unusual for a saddle or saddlebags to be used as a pillow.

"Senor, that is not my saddle," the Mexican pleaded in defence.

Jared reached down and undid the straps on the saddle bags. He pulled out a tobacco pouch, a few rounds of ammunition, a vicious looking knife and a bright yellow shirt thick with tobacco juice stains.

"Put him on Sammy's horse," he ordered.

"No senor, have mercy," screamed the Mexican.

Jake and Clay tied his hands roughly behind his back and then unceremoniously threw him up onto the horse which Randy now held steady. Jared nodded in the direction of a clump of trees. The youngster took his cue and led the horse and rider toward a cottonwood tree. Jake without being asked threw a rope over an overhanging bough.

"Senor, I appeal to you, don't do this terrible thing."

Jared slowly walked towards the horse and rider, "Make your peace with your God," he said sternly.

The Mexican, realising that all hope was gone raised himself up in the saddle and braced himself for his final moments on earth.

"Gringo, I hope we meet again in hell."

"Most likely," replied Jared as he slapped the horse's rump. Sam's horse lunged forward, leaving the Mexican wriggling and dancing for a full thirty seconds before his body finally went limp.

Jared felt sick to his stomach but showed no sign as he moved away from the scene of execution and mounted up. "Let's move it! We got a herd to look too."

Only Mordecai had seen the inner turmoil in his friend. To a man, the others began to see Jared in a new light. He'd always been treated with respect, along with his idea of starting a new life in Montana but until that moment when he despatched that surely Mexican, they didn't know if he had the sand to take those beeves on a two thousand mile trip to market. Now they knew.

As the herd crossed the Red River and continued up the Texas Panhandle Jared took stock of the cost so far. They'd skirted the Nueces, lost a few head in the Colorado and Brazos but been lucky with the Red, losing only a stray calf. More importantly, the men had crossed the rivers so far unscathed. With the Canadian river uppermost in Jared's thoughts, he decided to rest the men and the herd for a couple of days near Amarillo.

Jared, Bernardo and Rosita and a few hand picked men stayed behind with the herd, whilst the likes of Clay Dean, Heck, Randy and Jake Duval headed to town. Mordecai surprised almost everyone by electing to stay behind and ride night herd. Jared knew the reason behind why he sought solitude; he'd seen it coming on Mordecai's face since they'd crossed the Red, the man was hurting inside.

They were soon to be entering an area of some 35,000 square miles of open flat country known as the Llano Estacado, the Staked Plains. It was an area of semi-arid climate, bitter cold in winter and blazing hot in summer. It was good the boys were wetting their whistles. 'It would be a fair while before they'd do so again,' thought Jared.

Of the nine men who went into town only eight returned. To hear Clay Dean tell it, "The moment Jake Duval climbed down from the saddle; I knew trouble was just around the corner. He tried taking Randy under his wing, but I weren't having any of it. Lucky I did."

"What happened?" asked Jared.

"You know Jake, since he killed a man in Uvalde, he's been itching to try someone else. Killing those rustlers must have whetted his appetite. Picked the wrong man is all."

Jared hadn't taken to Jake Duval from the off, but he'd turned out to be a top cow-hand. That he could use a gun and might come in handy from marauding bands of Apaches *which was more than likely* was in itself a bonus; now he was dead. "Was it a fair shoot?" he asked.

"Depends on who tells it. Duval was out classed. He picked on a young kid around the card table, kept goading him. Feller opposite Jake, tells him to quit it. Jake, well he switches his venom in the man's direction. 'Do you know who I am?' he asks.

"I'd say you was a cowardly piece of shit, now sit back down and play cards," says the man, cool as all get out. Jake, he stands up and pulls that hog leg. The stranger didn't seem to move, just killed him with one shot, fired from under the table."

"This stranger have a name?" asked Jared.

"Yeah. The feller's name is Zachariah Trelawney. He's a ranger. Never met him before, but from what I heard when I was rangering, he's hell on wheels."

"Well we're a man down, the Staked Plains and the Canadian, not to mention Apaches in front of us. Get some shut eye." Jared never spoke of Jake Duval after that night.

The camp was awoken by the smell of coffee and the cry of, "Get your asses in the saddle, we're burning daylight!"

Two days later they crossed the Canadian.

Chapter 23

That first summer together at the farm was idyllic. Gone were the stresses of the job, in there place the long days of summer. Finbar and Maggie found farm life very much to their liking, at the close of each day they were worn out but contented with their lot. Winter was spent with the chopping of wood and the ritualistic clearing paths and carriageways of snow. Finbar, with cheeks rosy from the daily chores and winter's air, was rewarded by the smell of freshly baked bread and hot home made soup from Maggie's kitchen. He often kidded Maggie that her soups were enough to make him wish it would stay winter forever.

Spring arrived with a rush and the circle of life began to renew. The O'Tooles had never been happier. Then, just as the summer of 1881 was coming into its own, Maggie took sick and died before the leaves had time to turn brown. She'd always had a weak heart, having rheumatic fever as a child. They'd always known there was a possibility of dying before her time, but they'd put it to the back of their minds.

Finbar was devastated. The farm, the farm they had loved so much, now meant nothing to him with Maggie gone. Inevitably his loneliness caused him to turn to the bottle. Apart from Maggie, the Force had been his life. Without both of them, he started on a slow but steady downward spiral. On his long drinking sessions, his mind would drift from Maggie back to his time in the Force and the inevitable article in the New York Times.

One morning as he nursed yet another hangover he began to question whether it was worth going on. His life, such as it was, had no purpose, but then he had another thought: what if he re-opened the case that had been the only black mark in his police career? There was no reason to believe this James Fairfax was the vicious killer, but there was no reason to think he wasn't either. Realising that between his own self-pity, the bottle and dwelling on whether this James Fairfax was the murderer or not, he would drink himself into an early grave. He could do nothing about poor Maggie, but with time on his hands he could solve the one crime that had eluded him. Finbar quit drinking and began to concentrate on matters at hand.

It was late October by the time he'd made all the necessary arrangements, settled his affairs and bought himself a one way ticket to San Francisco. His brain had snapped into overdrive as he mentally prepared himself for the task. Despite his drinking, Finbar was in pretty good shape for a man pushing forty seven. He was five eleven tall, about three inches shorter than the man he sought, but muscular in frame and fist. Boxing had been in the O'Toole's blood for centuries. In his younger years he'd been the Force champion and he'd taken the honours on the firing range on three separate occasions. If he was found to be correct about the identity of the man he was seeking, the chances that his skill with a revolver would come in handy were immeasurable.

As Finbar made himself comfortable in the first class compartment, he slipped his hand under his jacket and gripped the walnut handle of the snub nosed 38 calibre Smith and Wesson that lay snugly in the custom-made shoulder holster. And strange as it seemed, he began to feel that for the first time since Maggie had taken to her sickbed that there was a purpose to his life. He'd telegraphed ahead to the Chief of Police at San Francisco stating that he was on a visit to their fair city and as an ex member of the New York police force would be interested in visiting.

As the changing scenery flashed by the carriage window Finbar began making plans for the identity and apprehension of the man called Fairfax. To tip his hand to the authorities in San Francisco before he'd arrived would have been foolish and unprofessional. He knew that doing it this way he could expect courtesy and consideration. If he asked any questions he was more likely to receive an honest answer that to be fobbed off. There was of course the matter that Fairfax might not come freely, in which case Finbar was prepared to use whatever means were possible to bring him to justice.

CHAPTER 24

When Jared first caught sight of the Deer Lodge Valley he knew he'd finally found his home. To the north was the great Grant Kohr's ranch, a land so rich and fertile it made his heart bleed. But the area south, though unclaimed as far as he could tell, was just as fertile and green. The grass lands stretched farther than the eye could see, bordered by mountain ranges to the east and the west. To Jared he'd never seen anything quite as beautiful, he only wished his Ma and Pa could have seen it. Sarah too, she'd have loved it had she lived.

It had been a long hard six months of river crossings, tornados, blizzards, unbearable heat, driving rain and the odd skirmish with hostiles, and not just the red kind. They'd fought a losing guerrilla war with the Apache on the Staked Plains. Shots had been fired but none hit their targets on either side. Their loss had been eighty head of cattle but fortunately these Indians were only interested in food for their bellies and so Jared thought it worth the loss. A man's life was far more important than a few cows.

Jared then counted the cost in lives; Jake Duval getting himself killed; moral reaching an all time low when George Tompkins got himself trampled during a stampede two days north of the Llano Estucado; and then cruelly almost within sight of their destination, losing Newt Rawlings whilst crossing the Snake River.

On the plus side, they traded cattle for Indian ponies with a bunch of Utes in Southern Colorado; ponies which Bernardo Torres said were working out as the finest cow ponies he'd ever worked on. The herd numbered around two thousand five hundred and after three days on a diet of Deer Lodge grass were putting on the pounds. The men were in high spirits, and had taken to building cabins far easier than he'd imagined.

Jared's biggest concern, apart from calling on the Grant Kohr's outfit was for his friend Mordecai's state of mind. He'd killed two men on the outskirts of Pocatello just before the Snake River crossing. It was to Mordecai's chagrin, spoken of quite freely around the camp, but after the drowning of Newt, there was no more talk.

He'd gone into Pocatello with Bernardo and Rosita to buy supplies, more for Jared's peace of mind than any trouble that might come the Mexican's way. On the way back to the herd, three mounted men blocked the road. They were all armed, but one cradled a shotgun in his hands. Mordecai guessed he was the leader.

"This is a hold up. Climb down from the wagon, greaser!" cried the man holding the shotgun. It was a mistake addressing Bernardo. Shotgun should have looked towards the lone outrider in the dark duster. In the few short years that Bernardo had known Mordecai, he'd never seen him draw a gun in anger. The suddenness of the exchange of gunfire caused Bernardo to throw himself across Rosita before he thought about pulling his pistol. By then it was too late.

Mordecai had fired even before the man with the shotgun had levelled the weapon, knocking him backwards from the saddle. The shotgun discharged harmlessly into the late afternoon sky. Mordecai's second bullet took the man to his left in the stomach and he'd turned his horse and bolted from the scene. His third shot wounded the boy to his right, catching him in the left shoulder just as he was raising his hands in surrender.

Bernardo, over the screams of his wife, shouted at the Texan, "Mordecai! Don't shoot! He's only a boy." Mordecai's Navy Colt was held at arms length and his finger was tightening on the trigger. "Damn you Mordecai! The kid's all done."

The man in the dark duster looked angrily at the Mexican then suddenly seemed to shake himself as if from a dream and eased his finger from the trigger. Then and only then did he survey the scene of death. Shotgun was lying on his back, mouth open in surprise at meeting his maker far sooner than he'd planned. In the short distance the second bandit's horse had slowed to a stop, the reins trailing in the dust. The wounded rider was slumped in the saddle and barely clinging onto the horse's mane. In Mordecai's immediate vision was a young boy of about fifteen, all sobs and bloody shirtfront, his face white with shock and pain.

Rosita climbed down and helped the boy off his horse. Then she dressed his wounds. He was lucky; the projectile had gone clean through the fleshy underside of his arm. His friend wasn't so fortunate; he slid from the horse's neck and lay on the grass. Rosita could only watch as the young outlaw looked up at the afternoon sky and coughed up dark clots of blood. Mercifully his suffering was short.

"He was just a boy!" cried Rosita as he passed.

"Wrong Rosita, he was man enough to come at us armed," said Mordecai, as he picked up the boy's Schofield pistol.

Rosita was about to challenge Mordecai, but Bernardo stepped between them. "Rosita, Mordecai is right. They were armed, they meant us no good."

The dark Texan walked away from Rosita's accusing words. 'She was right,' thought Mordecai, 'I could have spared them. I could just as easily have shot only the man with the shotgun, but I didn't. It's still there, the old instinct, and it won't ever let me be.'

The incident, though still in the minds of Rosita and Bernardo was eclipsed a few days later when Newt died. For the remainder of the drive Mordecai withdrew into himself and kept apart from the rest of the crew. It was a worrying sign for Jared, the dream of a cattle empire had been his, but if it hadn't have been for Mordecai's help, he'd never have achieved it. His friend needed help, but now wasn't the time. Jared had too many things to get done before winter set in. He reflected again on the cost of the drive: the loss of three men was bad enough, but to lose his best friend to the darkest depression of madness was possibly a little too much to take.

Chapter 25

Deirdre, that downtrodden young whore, daughter of an incestuous father, wife to a young cavalry officer, mother to a child she'd never see grow up, had indeed vanished. She was gone, dead and buried, gone forever, except in Maddie Dubois's head. No matter how much she tried blocking it from her memory, the life she'd led still haunted her dreams. But it was the nightmares of late which really disturbed her. He was coming for her, she could see his features clearly. The mask, the hideous mask, it was more unbearable than what lay beneath it. Often Maddie would wake in a cold sweat, heart pounding and stomach churning as he smiled that smile of his. As she woke and her heart rate returned to normal she reminded herself that, despite the years and miles between them, that no matter what, she always had to be on her guard.

Regardless of her profession, Maddie made friends easily. She was likeable, fun and above all generous and kind to all who knew her. Countless locals had reason to thank Maddie for her generosity, though she always denied any knowledge of the food parcels left at the doors of the poorest families in mid winter. Her donations to local charities were only matched by her friend and benefactor, Josephine Airey.

Even Maddie's own sort had first hand knowledge of her kindness. One in particular was Nellie Cushion. She was a thirty five year old prostitute dying of consumption. On her death bed she asked Maddie to take care of her seven year old daughter. Impossible as the task was, Maddie learned that Nellie had a sister back east in Chicago, married with two children of her own. She wrote to her.

When she received a letter back from Nellie's sister, Maddie realised she had no knowledge of Nellie's profession and actually thought she was an actress in San Francisco. She wrote back again and stated that Nellie's husband had died in the gold fields and she had joined a repertoire of actors touring the Northwest, *which Maddie thought wasn't stretching the truth too much.* She went on to say Nellie had intended sending her daughter to private school back east, but alas her illness had put paid to her plans. Maddie also added that there was a substantial amount of money to pay for the poor unfortunate's education. A month later the girl, suitably chaperoned, was on her way to a new life in Chicago. Maddie had her own funds transferred to a bank in Chicago which were to pay for the girl's education. All she asked was once a year the Aunt would send her a progress report from the school, at which time she would send the following year's funds.

She'd learned early that in her chosen occupation the most influential people made the best friends. A banker, the doctor who saw to her girls, a couple of very wealthy stockbrokers, the local store keeper and the town constable, these and other less respectable gentlemen, were all necessary allies in her fight for survival.

Maddie's plan originally was to make as much money as she could in the next five years, buy some property, stash enough cash in the bank and eventually re-invent herself one last time. She realised she could no longer hope to reclaim her son, but with wealth she could get almighty close to him. The thought comforted her. There was only one fly in the ointment: Luke Plummer. He was getting too big for his boots. He'd acquired another property in the Tenderloin District and had started to believe his own publicity. Sophie Thompson, the madam at that establishment, kicked back fifty percent of her girls' earnings, which didn't affect her too much as she worked her girls like dogs, and the three celestials even harder.

It wasn't long before Plummer put the pressure on Maddie.

"Doctors' bills don't pay themselves you know. Even if you don't, I care about the welfare of my girls," she shouted. She would have mentioned her other commitments, only those would have fallen on deaf ears.

"Cut costs. Sadie Thompson doesn't have a problem with it. Buy in a couple of Chinese, those damn celestials will soon make up the deficit," said Plummer.

"Sadie Thompson don't own thirty percent, and she treats her girls worse than shit, and the celestials even worse," she spat venomously.

Luke Plummer smiled, he always liked a woman with spunk, "Forty percent, my final say on the matter."

Maddie begrudgingly had to accept his new tariff, but she refused to cut back her welfare of the girls who worked for her. If anything the girls could hike up their prices and she'd become a little more active. She owned thirty percent of the Alhambra, for what it was worth. She was making a tolerable living but wished she could find a buyer. Then with the money she'd buy herself another establishment free from the encumbrance of Plummer. Unfortunately, there weren't many people prepared to go into partnership with Luke Plummer. Begrudgingly she had to admit that she was stuck with the son of a bitch, and that her long term plan of retiring in less than five years was put on hold, 'Forty percent, well okay, but from now on his fringe benefits are curtailed,' she thought.

CHAPTER 26

When he walked into the Alhambra Maddie knew he was the one. Her heart skipped a beat and she prayed nobody had noticed. She'd dreamed of him as a child, hoped and prayed that he'd sweep her off her feet and carry her away from the Five Points, and even as a dutiful army wife she'd lain awake and thought of him, 'Yes,' she mused, 'he's the one al'right.'

He'd ridden in from his cow camp forty miles south-west of Helena and the lure of a drink couldn't be ignored. Jared McAllister was a shade over six two, square-jawed with a wolfish grin that stretched from ear to ear. He was clean shaven, a fact that really caught Maddie's eye. Not many of the men who frequented the Alhambra held much store with their appearance.

Now if she'd seen him a half-hour earlier she'd probably not have given him a second look. His fair hair had been long and matted and the lower half of his face had been covered with three and a half month's growth of beard. As for the rest of him, his long greatcoat and store bought pants had all but covered up his well muscled frame and sturdy legs. He'd almost passed the barber's shop on the way to register a claim when he happened to glance at himself in the barber's window. He didn't realise that he looked such a sight. Half-heartedly he brushed at the dust and grime that clung stubbornly to his clothes. Dust and grime from spending nearly six months in the saddle herding over two thousand head of steers up from the Hill Country of Texas.

Not wanting to step on anyone's toes he'd made neighbourly enquires at the Grant-Kohrs Ranch. Impressed by Jared's consideration, Mr Kohrs, the present owner of the vast ranch, told him about a parcel of land adjacent to the immense spread. Although not as impressive as the bigger Grant-Kohrs spread it was still good grazing land.

"Young feller, if you've a hankering to settle down, work hard, then that land's your best bet," said old man Kohrs. "It takes a certain kind of man to drive a herd as big as yours all the ways from Texas."

Forthright and to the point, Jared outlined his plans to Mr Kohrs. The old man listened and took notice. He knew just how hard it was to carve an empire out of the Montana Territory. He admired the boy's sound business plan and took a liking to him almost at once.

"I reckon from what you're saying you'll make a fine rancher. You got sand, I'll give you that."

And that was it. Jared had met the most influential businessman in the area and been given his seal of approval, not that he needed it, but, as Jared had learned early on, it pays to be polite.

Having cleaned himself up and registered his claim, Jared felt a sudden urge to take himself a drink. He wasn't much on hard liquor, preferring a few cold glasses of beer. He'd drunk almost half a glass when he looked up and saw the small but statuesque figure of Maddie descending the stairs. At thirty-two Jared McAllister had known but a few women, his Ma and sister excepted, his experience around them was limited to a quick fumble behind the local school house and a disastrous relationship with a storekeeper's daughter. Because of that he'd always fought shy of the women who frequented saloons and gaming houses. Yet the sight of Maddie Dubois set his emotions racing. She was the most attractive woman he'd ever seen. Her dark hair was piled high, emphasising the delicate texture of her swan-like neck. Her blue eyes sparkled with mischief, while her lips spoke of endless pleasures. She wore a little too much rouge for his taste, but beneath the grease paint, Jared detected a vulnerable young woman. Their eyes locked and Jared could swear he saw an inkling of a smile. Embarrassed, he averted his gaze, but his body tingled with excitement. Adrenaline coursed through his veins, turning his legs to mush as he realised she was advancing towards him.

"Hello stranger," said Maddie huskily. "Welcome to the Alhambra, it ain't much, but it's the best we got around here." Self-assurance seemed to ooze from every syllable, "Allow me to introduce myself," she held out a small gloved hand, "Madeline Dubois, but you can call me Maddie." She smiled confidently, but underneath the rouge and make up, it was another story. Her heart was pounding fit to burst.

He smiled roguishly, and took her small hand in his, "I'm charmed, Miss Dubois. Name's McAllister, Jared McAllister. I just brought a herd up from Texas."

"Oh, you're here to sell?"

"My option was to sell, but on arriving in the Deer Lodge Valley, I just fell in love with the place. I'm aiming to settle in these here parts," *he left out the part that his original aim was to own a ranch and create a vast cattle empire to rival the Grant Kohr's.* He didn't want her thinking he was so full of himself.

Maddie detected that the wolfish grin was usually reserved for men's company. She knew enough about men to realise that he'd just about used up his repertoire around women so she spared his blushes.

"That's nice to know Jared. We need more gentlemen in these parts. I hope to see you in here again sometime soon."

"Yes ma'am, a pleasure ma'am. I'll do just that."

Maddie gave him the sweetest of smiles then walked off.

Jared found he was shaking. His body felt like it didn't belong. He felt disoriented, yet somehow the feelings were very pleasant. He swallowed down the rest of his beer, glanced towards the gaming tables and watched as Maddie Dubois held court. He'd seen women like her in

Uvalde, Amarillo, and San Antonio, but none who had captured his heart. He continued to stare as a few moments later she climbed the stairs with a client in tow. Crazy as it seemed, he felt a pang of jealousy and quickly averted his gaze. Seconds later he was staring at the broad-walk taking in a few deep breathes.

As he threw himself into the saddle, he told himself she was a whore, a lady of the night, a woman who could be bought for a few dollars. He tried to erase the lingering smell of her perfume, the sensuous folds of her mouth, and the smouldering passion of her dark eyes. She was all woman and then some. That he was attracted to her he had no doubt, that they could have a future together …? He cursed himself for such thoughts. It was only a brief encounter, what in God's name was he thinking?

"Damn fool" he muttered to himself and spurred his horse into a fast trot.

Maddie, in the confines of her room, stared out through the grime encrusted window and watched until Jared disappeared from view. She'd noticed the way he'd looked at her as she climbed the stairs. There was no mistaking that look of anguish. He was interested. No, more than that, he was very interested in her. She reflected that she had a job to do, but he was the one. He was the light she'd been seeking all her life. He was strong; she could see that in his build and the way that he carried himself. Yet she'd seen into those deep blue eyes. Yes, he was strong, but there was tenderness there also. She'd seen it in the way he looked at her, not lustful like all the men she'd known, but with a respect for her womanhood. She suspected that beneath the hard exterior he was a gentle man. She prayed that she hadn't frightened him off.

Winters came early in Montana. The bright days of summer were soon a memory, giving way to harsh winds and driving rain. Hailstones as big as goose eggs peppered the town, causing man and beast to race for whatever shelter was available, and then the snows came, covering the land in a blanket of white. It snowed constantly for almost a week before the skies cleared. An eerie silence had descended on the streets of Helena. The snow lay thick on the ground, muffling the sounds of horse and oxen that had been the first to venture back onto the streets.

Maddie looked down the street that she'd looked down religiously for the past two months. She'd hoped that the stranger would return, but as the days turned to weeks, then months, she began to despair. 'Perhaps the Montana winter had put him off and he'd decided to seek warmer climes,' she thought sadly to herself.

It was a week later that she learned that he was still around. She'd overheard a snippet of conversation which warmed her heart. Sam, the bartender at the Alhambra, was in deep exchange of dialogue with two of his regulars concerning three cowboys who they'd been playing cards with earlier.

"Old man Kohrs's got himself a new neighbour," said Charlie Adams.

"You don't say?" replied Sam a little absentmindedly.

"Yeah those three fellers we was a playing cards with over yonder," Charlie nodded in their direction. "They're hands for a new outfit that staked a claim to land near the Grant Kohr's ranch. Some fella named McAllister."

Maddie stopped in her tracks.

"Yep, up from Texas is what I hear. Fought off the Comanche, dust storms, a stampede, half a dozen swollen rivers and if you believe it, had a run in with Crazy Horse himself."

"Now that, I know not to be true," said Sam as he cleaned the dust from a glass. O'l Crazy Horse got himself killed way over in Nebraska, Fort Robinson I believe, back in 77'."

"Anyway," said Charlie Adams, not liking the correction from Sam. "Crazy Horse or not, that outfit is hell for leather."

Maddie glanced across at the three cowboys. They had the look of hard men, the type of men who could have driven a herd of cows nearly two thousand miles. Then uncharacteristically, *Maddie never needed to approach members of the opposite sex, she naturally drew them,* she walked across to the three men. They made to stand up as she approached. She gestured for them to remain seated.

"You're Mr McAllisters men, I hear."

"Yes Ma'am we are that, and Texans to boot."

"You find our weather different to Texas?"

"Hell! Pardon me ma'am, but we ain't seen snow like it, excepting up in the mountains," said Joe.

"Yeah and it can get mighty cold too," added Randy with a twinkle in his eye.

"Well we can fix that boys, our libations will soon warm the cockles. Why don't you let the house stand you a drink?"

"Well thank you kindly ma'am. We sure do appreciate the gesture, now if there's anything else on offer we'd surely appreciate that a whole lot more," said Randy the youngest of the crew. Drink and bravado made him stand up, "We're here for some action."

Maddie laughed at the impetuousness of his youth. "Well that's up to you, but I ain't on the menu. Go see my girls. They'd be happy to oblige" Before any of them could sound off she left them in no doubt as to where her interests lay. "When you see that Mr McAllister of yours, give him my regards and tell him I'd like to buy him a drink sometime." With that said, she gave them a flirtatious smile and sauntered off.

"Well I'll be a son of a gun! The boss is one dark horse. Him meeting her, an all," said Randy.

"Yeah I guess women-folks in these here parts are in short supply. Well, one's that look like that, that is," said Joe.

"Do yah reckon the boss will take up with her?" said Randy.

"Not if Mordecai has any say in it," said Heck his elder by ten years. "Killed those bushwhackers without turning a hair, would've killed the other en if'n Bernardo hadn't 'ave shouted out." His words dampened the spirits of his two younger friends.

"That Mordecai, he's one mean fucker," cried Randy doing his best to lighten the mood.

Joe and Heck laughed at Randy's observation. "Got brave all of a sudden," said Joe and they all laughed.

Maddie climbed the stairs, aware that the three cowboys were watching her every move. She risked a glance and then winked her eye, before sauntering down the corridor to her room. She'd thought to do some business with the local banker but on hearing Jared McAllister's name she'd quite gone off the idea.

As she climbed into bed, she thought of the handsome young rancher who she'd exchanged only a few brief words with and her heart beat a little faster. He was staying. 'He'd put down roots,' she thought excitedly to herself. She hoped the older cowboy would relay her invitation and then she smiled to herself. If he didn't, either of the two young men with him would, of that she was sure.

Chapter 27

Within days of his arrival Finbar O'Toole had discovered that James Fairfax, owner of the burnt out Monterey Palace, was a very colourful character.

"Yes, a very colourful character indeed," said the desk sergeant ten minutes after they'd been introduced.

"In what way?" asked Finbar, barely concealing his excitement.

"You've got to understand, this town's full of colourful characters, but his appearance being the most striking feature. Dressed he was, from head to toe in the latest black fashion, he presented himself as a very macabre figure indeed."

"Macabre!" exclaimed Finbar. The excitement in him was growing, "Would you please elaborate?"

The desk sergeant warming to his story continued, "It was the mask see. Well not exactly a mask as such, more a half-mask. It concealed one side of his face. Matching it was too. Black leather as I recall."

"You met him?"

"Aye I did that sir. It was after he'd killed a sailor down on the wharf."

"Did you arrest him?"

"No sir, self defence it was. The whole bar saw it. That sailor came at him mean as hell. He gutted him like a fish. It was all on account of that mask. Dumb sailor asked him to take it off."

Finbar felt an ice cold sliver of ice race up and down his spine. He'd seen the ravaged face behind the mask. It wasn't a pretty sight.

The desk sergeant, oblivious to Finbar's personal discomfort, continued enthusiastically, "It kind of leant him an air of mystique. The mask, the ladies loved him for it, and I don't just mean the ladies of the night either. I heard tell that some of the most respectable women of Nob Hill had shared his bed."

Finbar then learned that he'd killed two more men in open combat, and gained a certain notoriety. It didn't surprise Finbar in the slightest. He'd seen it in his eyes that time he'd called. The very fact that he'd killed openly meant the man was far more dangerous that he'd first believed.

"What caused the fire?"

"A lamp, seems like it started upstairs, spread the length of the landing, trapping those poor people. They didn't stand a chance."

"Call it morbid curiosity, or just a policeman's nosiness," joked Finbar, "but is there any chance I could take a look at the file on the fire?"

An hour later he was reading the gruesome report. There was nothing that suggested the fire had been started deliberately. Obviously a knocked over lamp, it wasn't unusual. Fires like this one happened more than you'd expect, although the loss of life was generally far less. Twenty or so people dead and the building raised to the ground. It didn't bear thinking about.

"Nothing to suggest arson," muttered Finbar, "But nothing to suggest it wasn't." he added as he handed back the report.

"What's that you say?"

"Oh, nothing, just seem to ramble in my old age."

The desk sergeant just shrugged and shuffled off to file the report.

'At least,' thought Finbar, 'I'm on the right track. This James Fairfax is the man I'm looking for, I have no doubt.' 'But' reflected the

New York detective, 'I'm a long way off proving he'd killed those women in New York.'

"Where can I find this man?" said Finbar on the sergeant's return.

"That's hard to say," said the desk sergeant. "He left town a few months ago, heading for Sacramento."

In his hotel room later that night Finbar reflected on what he'd been told. The desk sergeant had spoke of James Fairfax in an almost god-like manner. The killing of three men had given Fairfax a reputation as a hard man. It was a macabre phenomenon that out here in the West the killing of others was both looked up to and admired. It had brought him a currency that was better than money. As long as his luck didn't run out he could continue his murderous spree.

Despite any hard evidence Finbar O'Toole believed Fairfax had torched his own place deliberately. Why? Who knows? He had no proof just that same old gut feeling. He toyed with the idea of pursuing Fairfax to Sacramento, but what would that achieve? He poured himself a glass of bourbon and contemplated what to do. He'd already seen with his own eyes the attitudes of his peers. What was the point in going on with his quest without proof? Who would believe him? He wasn't even a policeman anymore. By the time he'd finished the bottle he'd given up the search. The best hope of getting justice was to head back to New York and alert the authorities to what he'd learned.

For the next few days Finbar idled away his time in the bars of the Barbary Coast, drinking himself into a stupor most nights. Then on the last night before he was to embark on the long train ride eastwards, he bumped into Jimmy Murphy the desk sergeant, in the bar down the road from the precinct. Seeing a familiar face, Murphy came over and joined Finbar in a drink. They talked about the job, the old country and about life in general, then Murphy made a chance remark which stopped Finbar in his tracks.

"It's funny, you asking questions about the whorehouse being burnt down. For a time there was a shortage of whores, can you believe that? The Barbary Coast with a shortage of whores"

Both men laughed, then Murphy elaborated. "Nine whores died that night, burnt beyond recognition, one stood out to me in particular."

"Why, what made her stand out?"

"I could've sworn her throat had been cut, but my thoughts were a bit muddled at the time, I'd had two whores murdered on my patch months earlier."

The hairs on the back of Finbar's neck stood up on end.

"What's so special about two whores ending up dead? It's an occupational hazard where I come from," said Finbar. Then casually, without sounding too anxious, he enquired of the desk sergeant the nature of the killings.

"Normal circumstance I'd allow you was right, we get them gun shot, knifed or overdosed, but these...."

"Go on, call it a professional interest. What made them different from the normal?" Finbar was fast sobering up.

"Right horrible it was. Butchered, they were, good and proper. Throat slit from ear to ear. Tits cut off one of them, the other, not quite so bad, but bad enough for us to link the two. Think he might have been disturbed."

"This one in the fire, did you report your suspicions?"

"No, it was probably my imagination playing tricks with me. Those two whores, well the mutilations, pure turned my stomach. I asked to come off detective duties after that. It kinda messed with my head."

The desk sergeant's description confirmed his suspicions. If Finbar hadn't been one hundred percent sure that James Fairfax was the butcher of the Five Points, he was now.

A very sober Finbar O'Toole walked up to his room in the hotel that night with things on his mind.

Finbar's journey home took him past Sacramento on the recently completed rail line, so he decided to stop off there for a few days. On the journey Finbar did some soul searching. It was no longer a matter of bringing James Fairfax to justice, the man was clever, too clever by half. He was a rabid animal and Finbar O'Toole saw it as his duty to rid the world of such a beast. As the train chugged into the station at Sacramento, he was still struggling with his conscience. He was a rough man and used to rough ways but he'd never killed a man. He'd been involved in a shooting in New York where he'd shot and wounded an armed robber and it took weeks for him to come to terms with what he'd nearly done. That was many years before and he'd hardened his heart since then. Could he, Finbar O'Toole take on the mantle of judge, jury and executioner? It was a question which he knew would have to be answered. That James Fairfax was a cunning and dangerous man he had no doubt, that he was cruel and lacked compassion was all so obvious. Finbar's only worry was in which way he would dispatch the murderer. The dilemma before him was whether to face the man and confront him, or shoot him down like the rabid dog that he surely was.

CHAPTER 28

"There's a lady up to Helena says she'd be mighty proud to buy you a drink," said Randy suddenly, just after finishing breakfast at the McAllister Ranch house. Heck frowned across at the youngster. 'Damn fool should mind his own business,' he thought.

Jared McAllister looked across, puzzled at what his ranch hand was telling him, but in the quiet depth of his brain he knew just who that lady was. His heart missed a beat, he hoped no one had noticed, as he stuttered out, "Oh yeah. Just who in the world up in Helena wants to buy me a drink?"

"Some young hellion at the Alhambra. Looks to me like you put your brand on her, Jared. She's a pretty young thing. Now if I was you…."

"You ain't me," cut in McAllister. "Ain't you and Heck got some fences to put up around the corral," he added sharply.

"Yes sir," said Randy as he grabbed for his coat and raced towards the door.

Jared muttered under his breath, "Damn fool kid, needs to get his priorities right." He was fooling no one, not the least himself.

For a week flurries of snow continued falling, blocking out the weak intermittent sun. Night blended with day until they appeared almost as one. Jared gazed out the window of the bunkhouse and surveyed his empire, not that he could see much farther than the icicle laden barn and outhouses.

"Damn winter ain't what I expected," said Jared. "We drove them cows all the ways from San Antonio, lost a few as I recall, now I don't figure on losing the damn lot because of one lousy winter!"

"Should have sold them when we had the chance," drawled Mordecai. "In my opinion this land's too hostile to ranch."

"I didn't ask your opinion," spat Jared.

"Fine by me," replied Mordecai with a dark hurt look in his eyes.

Knowing he'd spoken too sharply to the one man he could always rely on, Jared softened his tone. It was wise to tread carefully around Mordecai. "Old man Kohrs seems to be doing okay. I tell you Mordecai, this winter ain't gonna beat us. We work hard, we'll have us one of the finest spreads in all Montana."

"Your dream, not mine."

"Well it could be! It sure as hell could be, if you'd only believe it. I wouldn't have made it this far if it hadn't been for you. This ranch is as much yours as it is mine." Here was Jared's chance to turn around his friend's hurt.

"No Jared, it's what you want. I'm only here because of you, not for some godforsaken piece of land in the middle of nowhere."

Jared began to lose patience, "Don't hang that on me. You done paid me back a plenty."

"You still don't get it, do yah Jared?" What was left to be said remained unsaid. Mordecai had been down to his last bullet. He was seconds from blowing his god damn brains out when the young rancher stumbled along.

"There was eight of them murdering Comanche savages, you was shot to all hell. What was a man to do?"

Mordecai slumped back in his bunk, a dark mood descended as it always did when confronted with their fateful meeting. He knew in his heart that he would be forever in the man's debt yet there were times when he wished Jared hadn't have stumbled into his fire fight. Perhaps he would have been better off dead.

Jared, embarrassed and frustrated at his own clumsiness grunted then pushed his way out through the bunkhouse door. Snow drifts gave way under their resistance as the timber door swung open. Fighting his way across the white divide he reached the relative warmth and welcoming smells of the horse barn. He couldn't help but reflect on that first day he stumbled upon Mordecai. It couldn't have been more extreme.

The sun beat down from a merciless sky. He'd heard shooting from way back. At first he'd thought to just edge by, after all it wasn't his fight, but then a primeval urge came over him. He spurred his horse through some underbrush and surveyed the scene. From what he could make out there were a bunch of Comanche braves hell-bent on a killing. They were firing on an old broken down adobe structure. And from what Jared could tell, there was a white-man holed up inside. Without a minute's hesitation he unfurled his Henry rifle and took a bead on one of the exposed braves. As he squeezed the trigger he saw the Indian jump back under the force of his bullet. His horse bucked but somehow he managed to work the lever action of the old Henry. As he spurred his horse forward he fired wildly at the young braves, knocking another into the dust. His luck held as he jumped from his horse and sought shelter behind the walls of thick adobe.

A young buck resplendent in war-paint and crazed with bloodlust charged straight at him, a war club raised for the killing blow. Jared to this day still didn't know how his revolver appeared in his hand. He cocked and fired at point-blank range and stared into the dead eyes of the Comanche. Then the shooting stopped.

Jared scanned the horizon. The Indians had gone to ground. Killing three in such quick succession had taken the fight right out of them. Jared knew that it was pure luck; that and the element of surprise. He looked down at the injured man and thought he'd arrived a mite late;

he was shot to dolls rags. His eyes opened briefly and he begged for water. Jared grabbed for his canteen and put the water to his lips.

"Thanks…." said the injured man, before slipping into unconsciousness.

Doing his best Jared patched up the wounded man. Luckily the bullets had gone clean through without hitting any vital organ, but the blood loss was quite considerable by the appearance on his vest and britches.

For fear of being picked off Jared stayed next to the wounded man and for what was left of the day, kept watch, ever wary of a surprise attack. As the skies glowed red, signalling the advent of nightfall, the desert grew colder. He hugged the man to him to keep him warm, whilst his eyes and ears watched and listened for any sign of movement.

Morning came and to Jared's surprise the man's fever had subsided and he was breathing easily. More of a surprise, the Comanche had gathered their dead apart from the one who Jared killed at point blank range and had left.

"They killed the others, they killed them all," said the man.

"What others?" It was then that Jared learnt of the carnage that the man had stumbled across. There had been ten or twelve Comanche. Young bucks on a murder raid. Mordecai, as the man was called, had killed two or three but was unable to save a young family whose bodies were out back. Jared rushed towards the direction the injured man was pointing. He gagged at the sight before him. It was clear that the Comanche had had their sport with the woman before killing her. A man lay slumped against the wheel of a wagon. There was a burnt out fire between his legs, and a bullet hole in the centre of his forehead. The three children, two boys aged about seven and ten had been hacked to death and the youngest, a little girl, maybe three or four, had had her head dashed against a tree. Jared reeled back and stared down at the wounded man. Words were lost in that exchange of looks.

"I'll get a shovel," Jared finally managed to say.

It took him most of the morning to dig a hole deep enough, then he laid them all gently into the ground. When he was finished he returned to Mordecai.

"I said a few words over them."

"That makes a difference does it?" Mordecai's words were as cold as the grave Jared had so recently dug.

They rested up through the rest of the day and had a cold camp that night. Miraculously, the following morning Mordecai's wounds had stayed free of infection, gangrene and blood poisoning. There was little or no internal bleeding and with a plentiful supply of food and water Mordecai had regained enough strength to ride.

"Town's a day's ride. We should make it by nightfall." said Jared.

"Town ain't where I'm heading," said Mordeca coldly.

"You can't mean …"

"Them sons of bitches have to pay, every god damn one of them!"

Jared gazed though the bleakness of the Montana winter and at that moment a ray of sunshine suddenly sparkled and glinted off the snow laden prairie giving him a new hope. His thoughts turned to the town of Helena and in particular to the young wildcat that ran the Alhambra Gaming Rooms. The horror of his first meeting with Mordecai receded into the recesses of his mind.

Chapter 29

Finbar stepped off the train in Sacramento. He checked into the Sacramento Hotel, *it sounded better than it looked,* on the edge of town, washed up and went downstairs for dinner. He'd figured to spend a day or two making discreet enquiries. For what he had in mind, the least people knew about him the better. Sacramento wasn't as big as San Francisco so he had to tread carefully, especially if he didn't want to attract the attention of Fairfax. Showing his hand too early could prove fatal.

On the other side of town James Fairfax studied the early evening crowd. There were pickings to be had with the young and eager. Selecting a table with the most likely suckers, he drew up a chair and sat down.

"Mind if I join you," he said, *though why he bothered was beyond him.* His arrival in town a few months earlier caused a bit of a stir, partly because of his appearance, but mainly because his reputation as a man-killer had followed. No one spoke out against him, although there were some amongst them, *thieves, murderers and shooters* who didn't fear him and would have called him out if the situation had arisen, but all in all a mutual unspoken respect had formed amongst the crowd that frequented this side of town.

Fairfax found to his good fortune early on in his life that he was a natural born poker player. He'd learned how to read the cards and more importantly how to read faces. Cheating at cards he'd turned into an art form, although he rarely put it to practice. His skill with the paste boards allowed him that one sliver of honesty and besides, he knew his prowess with a gun could be matched and even bettered by some. His strength lay in his cunning and ruthless planning.

Half-Face, as he'd begrudgingly accepted as the name he was called behind his back, was having the time of his life. Out west he could continue his life of sexual depravity almost without being noticed, well at least by the few lawmen who ran the towns and cities close to the coast. Despite the mask, women flocked to his side. The thrill of being bedded by Half-Face drew women from all walks of life. He was charming and gallant in public, but in the bed-room he reverted to an animal, though he curbed his natural instincts to kill. He was a cause celebre, an infamous killer of men, and a fantastic lover of women. With his new found celebrity he found it harder to indulge in his fantasies.

His body cried out for blood. He needed to kill. The chance came in the form of a young farm boy, barely seventeen but eager to taste the fruits of life. He had come into town to buy supplies for his folks but the glowing red lights of the 'Sack o' Gold' drew him in. Fairfax spotted him right off. He was a big lad, strong sinewy arms and cumbersome hands, 'Fine for working a plough or baling hay but useless with a gun,' thought Fairfax as his eyes stalked his prey.

"Hey, are you dealing or not?" cried a fellow card player.

Fairfax averted his eyes and concentrated on dealing the cards onto the green baize table. He lost the next couple of hands and angrily threw his cards down in disgust. The urge to kill was uppermost in his mind. He glanced again at the farm boy and noticed he carried an old Dragoon Colt in his waistband and judging from the condition of the weapon, it looked apt to misfire. Goading him into a fight wouldn't be easy, but plied with enough whiskey, shamed in front of his lady love and called a cheat; there just might be an urge to cross the line. Half-Face watched as he took a tentative drink at the bar.

The boy looked around fearfully at the noisy Saturday night crowd. His Pa had told him to get the supplies and not linger, but on the way into town one of the wheels on his wagon came loose. By the time he'd fixed it and arrived in town the store was closed up for the night. He'd bedded his horses down in the livery stable and was about to grab some shut eye when he happened to glance across the street. What harm could come of it if he had himself one little drink?

Fairfax signalled across to one of the saloon girls, who dutifully came across to his table.

"Nancy, I'd like you to do me a favour."

"Why sure Mr Fairfax, anything."

He handed Nancy a five dollar bill, "See that boy over yonder; he looks in need of company." Nancy smiled in acknowledgement. "Tell him you think he's wonderful. Tell him you've never met anyone like him."

"Well that's for sure," said Nancy.

"Just guide him across to my table in an hour."

In that hour the kid lived a lifetime. Nancy snuggled up to him and asked if he'd buy her a drink. Unable to say no, John Denning bought her that fateful drink. Within half an hour the kid was in love. Nancy, knowing that Half-Face was going to fleece the kid of his money, decided to give the boy something to remember. An hour later he was in Hog Heaven. He'd come to town to buy supplies, met the girl of his dreams and was going home in the morning not just with the supplies but with his very own sweetheart. Then Nancy led him to Fairfax's table.

"I used to play cards back home on the farm," he said innocently.

"Okay boy, let's see what you're made of," said Half-Face smiling, as the boy sat down.

Fairfax dealt the cards expertly, so expertly that no one noticed as he dealt the boy a running flush. To his credit there was no flicker of excitement on the face of John Denning. He had four dollars to his name, besides the supply money. Without hesitation he chipped in the dollar stake, and then he raised the ante. Those around him folded. Fairfax grinned and raised. The kid looked hesitant, then raised again. It was foolhardy, the boy knew, but somehow he just knew he was going to win. Fairfax turned over a pair of Jacks. The kid whooped and hollered, then raked in the cash. This was turning into some night. Fairfax dealt the cards, again the kid struck lucky. Soon his pot increased, so much so that before long he had more than a hundred dollars.

"I think it's time to quit," he declared.

"No son you cain't quit, not yet. You've got to give us a chance to win our money back," said one of the card players.

"Yeah that's right," said another.

Half-Face just grinned.

"Okay, just one more hand, but I'm warning you, the way my luck's running, you'll be lucky to go home with the shirt on your back," said John Denning light-heartedly.

The crowd laughed, but Nancy grew nervous. The kid was nice, decent and honest, a little naïve, but way, way out of his depth. She prayed he'd lose just enough and then pull out.

Fairfax dealt the cards.

The kid's eyes lit up as the Queen of Diamonds, followed by the ten, the nine and eight, appeared in his hands. He picked up the fifth card, the Jack of Diamonds. He fought hard to conceal his excitement. Fairfax raised the bet, the player to his left rather reluctantly threw in the stake money. The next player folded. John Denning couldn't believe his luck. He'd won over a hundred dollars, been forced to play one last hand, and was now holding what he believed was the winning hand. He'd put forty dollars into the pot, he could fold and walk away with a cool sixty or he could raise. Beads of sweat formed on his brow. If he won, he'd be a rich man.

Nancy smiled at him nervously. She squeezed his shoulder. Bending closer she whispered in his ear, "Fold, Johnny, fold."

Fairfax glared up at Nancy with a look of pure hate, then his eyes shone as the boy ignored Nancy's advice and raised the stakes. The seated card players threw in their hands. Fairfax grinned menacingly, and raised the stakes higher. Johnny's look of triumph drained from his face. If he folded, he'd lose all the money he'd won, plus a little of the supply money. He looked across at the cruel leather clad face, "I'll see you. There's eighty dollars cash, and I've a horse and rig in the livery stable. It's worth more than what's in the pot."

"You're game, I'll give you that son. Plucky and game. I like you son, you've got spunk. I'll give you one last chance to fold."

He's bluffing thought Johnny. The man hasn't had a decent hand all night. He's bluffing.

"Eighty dollars, the horse and rig. I'll see you."

Pride didn't come into it. John Denning had become a man. He'd sat down with men and beaten them at their own game. He looked back over his shoulder at Nancy, a smile etched across his face. Nancy didn't see the smile, her eyes were glued to the green baize table as Fairfax gleefully spread his hand; a royal flush.

"I win," said Fairfax mockingly.

John Denning stared at the cards in disbelief. The odds of Half-Face having a Royal Flush were insurmountable, thought the young man.

"That can't be! You must have cheated!" The words spewed forth from his lips. It was at that moment John Denning knew he'd lost more than a game of cards.

"One chance kid, withdraw your accusation or have at it." The words were cold and calculated. The kid's hand brushed against the old colt, and he took his last gamble.

"Nooooooo!" screamed Nancy.

Half-Face smiled gleefully and pulled his colt from his holster and levelled it at the kid's chest. John Denning's grip on his pistol loosened but as it fell to the ground a bullet from Half-Face's gun ripped through his heart and lungs.

"He drew on me!" cried Fairfax. "I gave him a chance. It didn't have to happen this way."

'Oh yes it did,' thought Nancy. It was cold blooded premeditated murder and she'd been the Judas goat that had led the boy to his death. She looked at the kid's dead eyes then fled from the scene.

"I gave him every chance. Everyone saw what happened. If I hadn't have shot him he'd have killed me for sure."

"Yeah sheriff. It weren't Fairfax's fault. I heard him tell the boy to walk away," said one bystander.

"Dumb kid must have had a death wish," said another.

And with the telling, Half-Face's reputation grew. Even those who thought they could take him began to think twice. He'd killed four men, without so much as a murmur. Wes Hardin, the Texas killer, and the late Wild Bill Hickok were both men who killed without a second's thought. Half-Face now truly found himself in the same exalted company.

News of the shooting reverberated across town and it wasn't long before it reached the ear of Finbar O'Toole. His first reaction was to go to the sheriff and denounce James Fairfax for the murdering bastard that he was, and then have him arrested. The idea frustrated the hell out of the detective, even before it had fully formed he realised that, without proof to back up his claims, the gesture would be futile. The news filtered back, Fairfax had acted in self defence, though Finbar found that hard to believe. 'At least,' thought O'Toole, 'I've learned the whereabouts of the man I'm following.' It wasn't long after he heard the news that he realised Fairfax had an accomplice.

Nancy, tormented by her part in the boy's death took to her bed. She'd believed that Fairfax was only going to fleece the kid, up until the moment that Fairfax shot and killed him. What did she know about this man? He'd breezed into Sacramento living on a reputation that had followed him. He was a bad man, ruthless even, but weren't most of the men that frequented that part of town? She'd always believed that a man's reputation far exaggerated his capabilities, until now. She'd thought him quite mad but when she looked into his eyes she saw beyond madness: the man calmly sitting playing cards two floors down was pure evil.

Nancy was woken from a troubled sleep by a gentle tapping on her door. She rubbed the sleep from her eyes and wondered who would be calling at this hour. It was around noon, the usual time for her to think about getting up. The tapping continued. Grabbing a robe Nancy climbed from her bed and picked up a two shot pistol from beneath her pillow.

"Who's there?" she demanded.

"My name is Finbar O'Toole," came the answer from the other side of the door. "We need to talk."

"Talk about what?" said Nancy gruffly.

"The shooting last night."

Nancy let out an involuntary gasp. Who was the stranger outside her door? What did he want with her? Why was he asking about the killing?

"I've nothing to say."

Finbar played a hunch, originally he'd thought she was a willing siren, but on reflection he was beginning to think otherwise.

"I think you've plenty to say, Miss Riley. I think taking to your bed speaks volumes. And if I think that, then someone else also thinks it."

"I don't know what you're talking about," she said panicking.

Finbar decided to gamble, "I'm here to help you. Apart from me you're the only one who knows that James Fairfax killed that boy deliberately." He paused before adding, "I know Fairfax from back east. He's worse than you can possibly imagine, he's done terrible things."

"What things?"

She'd taken the bait. Now Finbar turned the screw, "Your life's in danger. Without my help you'll be dead before the week's out." He could almost feel her panic behind the door, "I used to be a policeman in New York. Fairfax was involved in the suspicious deaths of three prostitutes. And if I'm not mistaken he's killed at least two in San Francisco. That boy was just to whet his appetite. He enjoys killing! We need to talk."

"Go away, leave me alone," came the frightened cry.

"Okay I'm going, but if you need to talk, I'm over at the Sacramento Hotel, third floor, it's the second door past the staircase on the right, room 51.

Bathed in sweat Nancy listened to his footfalls as they receded down the hallway. She slumped to the floor, "He enjoys killing," the words kept echoing inside her head. She'd seen the look on Fairfax's face moments after shooting the boy to death; it was a look of pure pleasure. Her blood ran cold and her nerves turned her legs to jelly. Only a few minutes earlier she'd thought her life was in pieces, that things couldn't get any worse.

By dusk Nancy had recovered sufficiently to realise that her life was in danger and that to do nothing would only result in her own death. Her only hope was to put her faith into the hands of a man she'd never seen. She had to speak to this man O'Toole to find out what he knew.

It took Nancy an hour, by various horse drawn street cars, to reach the Sacramento Hotel. She'd worn an old shawl to ward of the chill off the evening as well as to disguise her tawdry dress. It wouldn't look well for a woman of shady character to be seen in such a respectable establishment. Passing unnoticed by the desk clerk, Nancy ascended the stairs. She noted the numerical sequence of the room numbers and ventured along the dimly lit corridor. At room 51 she paused for a few seconds to get her heartbeat under control, and then she knocked.

Finbar opened the door cautiously, a police Colt 38 in his right hand. He peered past the young woman scarcely giving her a glance. Once he was sure no one else was following, he quickly ushered the girl inside. Nancy was flushed and very nervous as she stood alone in the stranger's room, a man who only hours before, had told her that her life was at stake. For a second she stared at the gun in the stranger's hand and in a blind panic she started to scream. Finbar quickly grabbed her tightly and held his hand over her mouth.

"It's okay, I'm not going to hurt you," he said softly, "See, I'm going to holster my gun." As he slid the Colt back into his shoulder holster he slackened his hold of her mouth. Nancy, still frightened, edged towards the door, but didn't scream.

"The door's there, I'll not stop you. But I suspect you believe every word I said this afternoon, otherwise you wouldn't have come."

Nancy's tensions loosened. "He killed that poor boy in cold blood. It was murder and I was a party to it."

"What do you mean a party to it?"

"I brought that poor unsuspecting boy to the table, but I didn't know Fairfax was gonna kill him!

"You reckon he set it up just to kill the boy?"

"I do, I seen it in his eyes, just before it happened. His eyes were laughing. He murdered that boy."

"But can you prove it?" shot back Finbar. "At a guess I'd say he's got a dozen witnesses that'll testify that it was a fair fight."

Nancy nodded in agreement.

"I used to be a police officer in New York. I know the burden of proof is on us to prove that a man committed cold blooded murder, but if that's nigh on impossible then there's only one thing left to do."

"You mean ..."

"That I do," said Finbar, "but I need your help."

"What if I refuse, I've only your word he's as bad as you say he is."

"Then ask yourself, do you feel safe in his presence?" Nancy thought about it for a moment then remained closed mouthed.

"I thought so. He's got you plain scared to death."

"What do you want me to do?"

CHAPTER 30

Finbar knew that using Nancy for bait was against all he stood for, but what choice did he have? Half-Face, as Finbar now referred to James Fairfax, was an accomplished liar, a cheat and scoundrel of the highest order. In New York the law, unless he could prove otherwise, would most certainly find in Fairfax's favour and to a high degree Sacramento would also favour him, which left Finbar with only one alternative.

Nancy nervously knocked on the door to Fairfax's room. "It's open," came the terse cry from within.

"Pardon my intrusion, but I have something that might be of interest to you."

"What could you have that would be of interest to me?" his tone, already betraying his contempt. That he thought of whores and their like as nothing better than the garbage that littered the streets was obvious, but Nancy sensed an even deeper hatred.

Going back after hearing all that Finbar O'Toole had to say had taken all her courage. Her first instinct when leaving the New York detective's room was to buy a ticket out of Sacramento, but to where? As his cruel eyes stared at her, she knew that what she'd been told was true. She wanted to cut and run, to flee the room, to put distance between her and the man before her. Her lip trembled as she stuttered over her words, "The … there's a man…." She let her words trail off; afraid he wouldn't take the bait.

"What man? You fucking whore, what man?"

"The man from New York," she uttered. At least if things went wrong, she'd told him almost the truth.

Fairfax was taken aback, by the mention of his former stomping ground. Who was this man? What did he know? What did he want? Regaining his composure he asked Nancy for the man's name.

"He didn't give his name, he just said you'd pay handsomely for the information he has to offer."

Fairfax's eyes seemed to shrink into dark orbs of ebony. Could it be, could it really be the news he was waiting for? The excitement grew in his chest, "Did he say anything else?"

"Only that it's about a girl. He said you'd understand."

A malevolent smile crossed his lips, his tone became more amiable. "Where and when am I to meet him?"

"He said I'm to take you to him, tonight at 8 o'clock. He said if I'm not with you, there's no deal."

"What!"

Nancy could feel her bladder weakening. the warm sensation of urine soaking into her undergarments. She looked up at Fairfax, afraid the new knowledge she'd acquired would somehow be betrayed in her eyes. "He says he doesn't trust you! He wants me along as a witness."

Fairfax's anger turned into a malicious grin. The man's distrust of him and the fact that he knew about the whore caused him great excitement. The man did indeed need to distrust him; even more surely he needed to fear him. Once Fairfax received the information he so desperately sought then he would pay the man, but in blood. And Nancy, poor misguided Nancy! Well, after tonight he'd put an end to her miserable pathetic life.

"Very well, meet me tonight around seven. Now get away from me, clean yourself up, you stink like piss!"

Nancy led the way through a maze of back alleys while Fairfax trailed two steps behind. As he followed an aura of foreboding began to creep over the masked man. He couldn't quite put his finger on it, but he sensed something wasn't quite right. In the afternoon Nancy had seemed frightened, even more so than usual. But now, now he detected urgency in her walk, her manor and her demeanour. Strange as it seemed, he sensed he was being lured to his doom. Adrenaline coursed through his veins. He slowed his pace. Nancy looked back nervously. His sixth sense had been right after all.

"Hold up bitch!"

Nancy stared back at him and her face exposed her.

"Do you think I'm stupid, girl?"

"Nnn no!"

Half Face grabbed her by the wrists and grappled her to the ground. Nancy shrieked as a glint of moonlight exposed the knife he held to her throat. "Speak bitch, speak now or so help me I'll gut you from your cunny to your throat."

"It's the truth!" stammered Nancy "A man approached me and gave me the message to get you to come. Half Face's eyes took on a maniacal stare as he directed the knife slowly between Nancy's legs. "He's a New York detective called O'Toole! Please don't hurt me."

Half Face halted his upward thrust at the sound of O'Toole's name.

"O'Toole you say?"

"Detective Finbar O'Toole of New York," said a voice from the darkness. Half-Face spun round as the sound of a hammer being cocked exploded in his ears.

"Move another muscle without my say so and you're dead," said the detective. "Step away from the girl." Half Face did as he was bid. "Nancy get over her," said O'Toole sharply.

Half Face assessed the situation. It could have been much worst. The detective was not the type to shoot him down in cold blood. He'd said he had some knowledge of the filthy whore he'd be chasing. "What news of the whore who wronged me?"

Finbar knew Half-Face was just buying time before he made his move. Buying time himself, Finbar told Half-Face some of what he knew about the girl. "It seems she never made San Francisco. Way I heard tell it, she took up with a young army type. Got himself killed along with Custer". Sensing he'd already told Fairfax too much his finger tightened on the trigger.

At that precise moment the small Derringer slipped into Half-Face's slippery hand. As he brought the gun up level with O'Toole's chest he saw a blinding flash, then a searing pain struck him high in the chest. Half Face stared dumbly up at the night sky. This wasn't happening. It was he who did the killing, not the other way around. He continued to stare upwards as the Derringer slipped from his grasp and then he spluttered, "The son of a bitch has done for me!"

Finbar watched him fall then looked across at the petrified young woman, "Let's get out of here!" he cried to the shocked Nancy.

CHAPTER 31

It was almost nightfall when Jared arrived at the outskirts of Helena. Even in the failing light he couldn't help noticing the new buildings that stood where only a few months ago had been open prairie. 'Helena was growing and then some,' he thought quietly. Despite the snow-laden streets, the bitter cold and the icy winds, people had invested time and labour to build, and not just in wood. Stone from the mines at Butte had been transported at great cost. Magnificent buildings, some five storeys high, had been erected. Yes Helena was growing at an alarming rate. He thought about his conversation with Mordecai, if you could call it that. These buildings were his proof, it confirmed what he'd felt in his water.

Spurring his horse forward, he watched as lanterns were lit in the windows of buildings. He stared in wonder as a lamplighter went about his business of illuminating the street lights of Main. He wondered what they'd think of next. As his horse walked almost silently through the virgin snow the welcoming glow of lights from the Alhambra Gaming Rooms came into sight. A wave of excitement took his breath, before a feeling of panic and nervousness wafted over him. It had seemed so much easier back at the ranch, but here it was another story.

It was early evening and already the Alhambra was a hive of activity. Jared thought these revellers would be best served snuggled up warm in their homes rather than in a place of ill repute. It stuck in his craw, even his thoughts about this place were not to his liking. Yet why was he here? He'd always thought himself above such places, yet the sight of her had turned his world on its head. No matter how he fought it, it always came out the same. He'd met a woman, exchanged a few pleasantries and nothing more. She was a whore, oh how he hated that word, but that's what she was, a cheap whore, a woman of easy virtue, a lady of the night. She wasn't for him ...

As he walked though the door and made his way up to the bar he began again to question why he was here.

"What'll you have cowboy?" said the bartender.

"Just make that a beer." he replied.

It was already too late to ride back to the ranch. He'd freeze to death before he'd got halfway. So what were his intentions? Even if the lady put in an appearance, would she set aside her busy schedule, allow him the use of her body and her bed? No, that wasn't his style. He wanted to talk to her, grab a bite to eat, get to know her. Would he have to pay for her time? It was something he hadn't figured on until now.

"Merry Christmas," said a slightly inebriated reveller.

'Jesus H Christ,' thought Jared. 'It's Christmas Eve and I didn't give it a thought.' He took a swig of his beer and looked around. She was nowhere to be seen. I expect she's busy, the thought just jumped into his mind. It's a dumb idea, his mind screamed. Looking down at his beer glass he took a final gulp. He'd made up his mind, he'd get lodgings at O'Flynn's boarding house, and then first thing in the morning he'd high tail it back to the ranch.

He'd just placed his glass on the counter when a small delicate hand touched his, "Hello stranger, Merry Christmas."

"Miss Dubois," stuttered Jared, "Merry Christmas."

"It's Maddie to you, Mr McAllister."

"Jared," said the rancher as he slowly smiled and took off his hat.

Maddie's heart thumped so loud she was frightened he'd hear it. He was the most wonderful looking man she'd ever seen. He was everything she remembered and more besides. What's more she could detect something in his eyes that seemed *to her any ways as* to suggest he felt pretty much the same. The thought excited her to all get out.

"Buy you a drink Miss Dubois, sorry; Maddie."

"Why sure you can," said Maddie as she motioned to the bartender to bring a bottle of champagne to the table in the far corner of the barroom.

The conversation was stilted, clumsy and downright awkward. Jared felt like a damn fool. "I'm sorry Miss Dubois, I ain't that easy with talk around a lady, and especially one that's come all the ways from Paris, France."

Maddie laughed "Firstly I ain't from Paris, France and secondly I ain't a lady."

"Well I'll be a son of a gun. I could have sworn you was from France."

"It's a secret."

"Well any ways you might not be from France but you sure as hell are a lady."

"There's some in here that'll tell you different."

"Just you point them out."

"There's no need," said Maddie sweetly. It had been a long time since anyone had been prepared to defend her honour.

Jared started to his feet, "Guess I'll be getting across the road. You're probably busy tonight of all nights." The moment it had left his lips he realised he'd put his size nines in it, "I'm sorry; I didn't mean it that way."

"I know you didn't. Now sit down. I'll tell you when it's time."

Jared slowly slid back down.

"Right Jared McAllister, cards on the table. I ain't one to shilly shaddle. Tomorrow comes you'll be long gone back to that ranch of yours, and I'll be left wondering."

Jared tipped back his hat and looked into her deep blue eyes.

"I'm a whore, I sleep with men. It's what I do. It doesn't make me less of a person." Maddie paused for a moment, knowing that what she said next could shatter her dreams. "The first time I saw you I knew you were someone different. You see I've been waiting for someone like you my whole life."

Jared fumbled for the words and then they came out in an awful rush. "I just knew it, that first time I clapped eyes on you. I didn't know what it was, but I sure do now." He tipped his hat back and smiled that smile of his and Maddie knew the time of words was over.

"Its Christmas, my day off." She stood up and held out her hand to his. He took it nervously and quietly they made for the stairs.

CHAPTER 32

Despite the cold night air they were both bathed in sweat when they reached the sanctuary of Finbar's hotel room. Nancy was close to tears, "What're we gonna do? Oh God! What happens now?"

"Firstly we're gonna get our breaths back, then we're gonna calm down," said Finbar reassuringly, though in truth he was very close to panic.

"You shot him, you killed him in cold blood," stammered Nancy.

"If I hadn't have shot him, we'd both be dead by now."

The realisation that it was true hit her hard. She could still feel the knife that he held against her. It was her worst nightmare, but it was over. The Irishman had put paid to James Fairfax. She was free. More than that, she was alive. She started to weigh up the odds of her being implicated in Fairfax's death. No one had seen her leave with him, so no one would suspect her. "Okay, so we're got our breath back, what now?"

"We sleep. In the morning we take the first train out of here."

"To where?"

"Wherever it takes us."

Finbar was tired. He'd killed a man. That the man needed killing there was no doubt, but the truth was, he'd gunned a man down. Shot him down like a dog. It would take some getting used to.

At the Central Pacific Railroad Depot, Nancy said her final goodbye to Finbar. He had a notion to head back East while, to Nancy, the lure of San Francisco was irresistible. He wished her good luck with a heavy heart. He'd only known her a little over three days but during that time he'd begun to see her as a vulnerable young girl, although when it came right down to it she'd shown plenty of spunk. Not many young women, knowing that Fairfax was nothing more than a homicidal killer, would have gone back into his lair, let alone lure him to his death. He hoped the new life that awaited her would prove more fruitful than the life she'd just left, although, as he waved her off, he doubted it very much.

As he boarded his east-bound train he suddenly found himself at peace. He'd been sure, right from the start that Fairfax was no good. When he discovered, albeit without irrefutable proof, that James Fairfax was a sadistic killer he'd tried pulling out all the stops to force a conviction, but to no avail. It was the one case that had been a thorn in his side. When he retired from the force it was his only regret. But now the slate had been wiped clean. The notorious phantom of the Five Points was no more. And in the West the man known as Half-Face the infamous man killer, had met his fate in a Sacramento back alley. It was a fitting end for someone so evil. With that last pleasant thought and the clickety clack of the train, Finbar drifted off to sleep.

It was early morning when the train came to a standstill at Ogden in Northern Utah. Finbar had woken up with hunger pains, due mostly to his quick exit from Sacramento. He'd been so busy sorting out Nancy's ticket and his own that he'd not taken the trouble to eat. It was only when he'd been on the train a couple of hours that he realised.

The conductor walked through the carriages announcing that the train was taking on water and fuel and that now would be as good a time as any to grab a bite to eat. Finbar stretched his legs and went across to the train station cafeteria. The thought of a good hearty breakfast made him salivate.

It was whilst he was eating that the thought came to him. In truth he'd thought about it quite a lot during the last few hundred miles. Saying goodbye to Nancy at the train station had kinda put the notion into his head. He began by thinking about the girl who had started it all, the one who had destroyed Fairfax's good looks and had escaped death by no more than a whisker. That she'd managed to get herself out of the Five Points area, let alone the state of New York was a miracle in itself. That she'd taken a train ride across the entire country and took up with a young army officer was almost beyond belief. Finbar remembered the painstaking detective work he'd done after the abrupt departure of Fairfax not many days after the death of Fanny Brannigan. He'd checked the many stops on the journey from New York to Sacramento and beyond to San Francisco, giving them all Fairfax's description. He recalled with amusement how he wished he'd have checked with the station master at Sacramento first. It would have saved a whole lot of paperwork.

During this investigation he discovered by chance that a young woman answering a vague but not dissimilar description to the woman who had burnt Fairfax had taken the same train journey only days earlier. On further investigation he discovered that there was no ticket stub at her journey's end. Finbar had to presume Deirdre Devlin had got off somewhere along the way. He then began the long and painstaking chore of writing many letters to station masters along the route. He received a few possible sightings, but these all came to nothing. He'd almost closed the case file on Fairfax when he received a correspondence from the local station master at Rock Springs Wyoming, stating that he remembered a young woman matching Deirdre Devlin's description taking up with an army officer. 'If I recall correctly they got married here in Rock Springs.' Excited by the news, Finbar asked if the station master could get hold of the parish register and let him know the names of the young couple. A month later the station master sent his reply. 'Seems the couple you have an interest in are a Miss Devlin and a Lieutenant Miles O'Bannion.' Finbar read the letter and smiled, his hunch was right, but at least she'd managed to escape Fairfax's clutches,' he thought as he closed the unsolved murder file of the three prostitutes in the Five Points area of New York. It was with dismay a few years later that he received another letter from the station master of Rock Springs. In the letter he'd written 'It might interest you to know that it appears a Lieutenant Miles O'Bannion, the young man you seemed interested in, was killed with Custer at the now famous Battle of the Little Big Horn,.' That the young army officer should get himself killed along with Custer, well that figured. Bad luck was something that seemed to follow some folks whether and whatever they were doing. He wished it wasn't so.

Using his detective mind and the endless hours onboard the train, he'd come to a conclusion of what happened to the girl after her husband had been killed. Firstly she could have gone back East, but that was doubtful knowing that Fairfax was back there. Secondly she could have taken up with a dirt farmer or the like, but most likely she'd reverted to type, just like Nancy would do the moment she reached San Francisco. He guessed that she was probably plying her trade in some bordello in Montana Territory, or the Dakotas.

The train's whistle interrupted his thoughts as it blew a couple of bursts to announce that it was time to re-board. Finbar hurried as best he could through the newly fallen snow towards the platform. But just as he was about to board he spotted a local timetable stuck on the wall of the waiting room. The West was sure getting civilised, he thought to himself as he gazed at the Utah and Northern Pacific Railroad timetable. It announced an inaugural train journey to Butte in Montana Territory, leaving Ogden at mid-day.

Suddenly Finbar had a thought, crazy as it was, it began to take shape in his mind. What if....?

Then next thing he knew he was at the ticket office postponing his trip home, and instead he'd bought a return ticket to Butte. It was a big town and growing by the minute. He wasn't hopeful of finding the young woman: that was too much to ask. But on a whim he thought, 'What the heck.' Somehow, possibly because he'd tracked down Fairfax, he felt responsible for the girl's welfare. He'd started something when he took that train ride across the continent. It just felt unfinished. If he could trace the girl, let her know that her nightmare was well and truly over, well then maybe she'd.... He left his thoughts unfinished. It was a long-shot. The Montana Territory was where Custer fought his last battle, and Butte was as good a place as any to ask after the whereabouts of a young army officer's wife. The enormity of his task was insurmountable, but at least he'd give it a try.

As the train headed north Finbar cursed himself for being a damn fool. Making this trip in the middle of summer would have been a hair brained idea, but to attempt it during the worst winter in a decade was certifiable.

Snow drifts and several blizzards later, Finbar arrived at Butte in the Montana Territory. Lack of proper sleep and in need of a hot bath he headed to the nearest boarding house. It was only after he'd bathed that he realised he'd missed Christmas by a whisker.

Chapter 33

Jared arrived back at the ranch two days late, due he said to the inclement weather, but Randy thought he knew otherwise. One glare from Joe and he quickly realised he'd best keep his mouth shut. He'd been there when Jared hanged the Mexican, he'd seen what he was capable of but he also found him to be a hard but fair minded boss. And just about now he was beginning to get the idea that his boss was more of a private person. Randy reflected that had he been that lucky he would have broadcast the news that he was balling the best piece of ass this side of the Rio Grande.

Mordecai, like Randy, guessed his best friend had something to hide. He'd heard the talk in the bunk-house and he didn't like it one damn bit. Jared was his best friend; he deserved someone worthy, not some cheap whore from town. It wasn't his business, he had his own conflicts of conscience to sort out, now didn't seem like the time.

It was a week later when Jared said he was taking the buckboard into town to buy supplies that Mordecai declared that he had a hankering to see the town.

"Since when have you been interested in what goes on in town?" cried Jared.

"Since, you've been getting yourself all slickered up!"

"Well I guess that's really my business," answered Jared angrily.

"Not if you're making yourself a damn fool over some two-bit harlot!"

"She ain't a harlot! And I'd like you to kindly remember that."

"If she ain't a harlot, then what the hell is she?"

Jared remained silent for a moment. His face conjured up a picture and his expression softened slightly. Then with more purpose in his voice than ever before he spoke. "Mordecai, you're my friend. More than that, you're like a brother to me, so I'll tell you once and once only. She's the woman I intend making my wife, so don't let me hear you call her that again."

Jared had never raised his voice to Mordecai in all the years he'd known him, but the threat was clearly there, he hadn't given him any room to manoeuvre. It was shut up or get the hell out.

No one was more confrontational than Mordecai, so when he lowered his head and spoke it was all the more alarming. "I'm sorry you feel that way. I was just looking out for you, is all."

"I know," said Jared, regretting the harsh words he'd just spoken. Mordecai turned and his strong shoulders seemed to stoop as he walked back into the bunk-house. Jared watched his friend walk away and then with a heavy heart he hauled himself into the buckboard and drove off. On his return the following afternoon he found that Mordecai was gone.

A blizzard fell across the valley a day later and any hope of Mordecai's return disappeared. Snow drifts piled high against the out-houses and barns virtually imprisoning Jared and his outfit. It was two weeks before the men could get about their chores. Two weeks in which Jared reflected on his last night in Helena. He'd bought the supplies, loaded the buckboard and securely strapped it down. He'd rented space in Joe Kowplinski's livery and washed and brushed up at Harry's barbershop.

He'd entered the Alhambra gaming house with Mordecai's words still ringing in his ears. "She's a harlot, a cheap harlot." Hadn't he himself thought just the same after his first encounter with her. Yet those two nights over Christmas had sent any lingering doubts out of the window. He was in love with her, and more importantly Maddie was in love with him. It had come about by accident. She'd joked that on Christmas morning she hadn't bought him a present. He retorted by saying, "Dee, last night was all the present I'll ever need."

"Dee!" she exclaimed, "You called me Dee."

Jared laughed, "I could have called you Mad, but Dee's much nicer."

Maddie smiled, "Oh, I see. Only my late husband used to call me Dee."

"Oh I'm sorry, I didn't mean to upset you."

"Don't be silly you didn't. You don't get it, do you? Maddie isn't my real name, my name's Deirdre. I was born plain Deirdre Devlin."

And then Maddie had poured out her heart. From a little back street slum in Cork, Ireland, to the voyage across the ocean. From the sweatshops of New York to the brothels of the notorious Five Points. The whirlwind romance with a young junior officer, to the grieving widow after the Battle of the Little Big Horn and finally, to the madam of the Alhambra Gaming House.

Those two nights had been the best two nights in his entire life. The days and nights had been a mixture of torrid passionate lovemaking and an endless talk of life and what it had to offer them both. He'd ridden home with a promise that he'd return as soon as possible.

Filled with longing and wracked with nerves over whether Maddie still felt the same he'd been more on edge than usual when Mordecai confronted him. It made him more determined than ever to ask Maddie for her hand in marriage.

Maddie had seemed troubled, unsure, when he asked her to marry him. "You don't really know me," she'd exclaimed.

"I know all I need," he'd replied.

"There are gaps. There are things I should have told you. Things so terrible that you'd run a mile."

"I don't care. There are things I've done in my life that I'm not proud of. Bad things; very bad things." Those dark days with Mordecai descended like a dark cloud.

"I killed my own father!"

"What!"

"I killed him. He was a drunkard and he raped me!" Maddie felt her eyes watering. She remembered the stink of his bodily sweat, the ale, the sexual fluids. She wanted to let it all out, but there was more to tell. In front of her was a man, a good man as far as she knew, but what constituted a good man? Apart from Miles she'd only ever known the worst kind. But she sensed there was something good and kind and wholesome about Jared McAllister which made her continue.

"He raped you! Then you did the right thing."

"Jared, I've never met anyone like you before in my whole sordid life. I've thought about you every day every hour since I last saw you. I love you. I've known it since that first day I saw you."

"I love you too, Dee."

"That's why I have to tell you everything." Her eyes were wild with anger, with sadness, with desire, with regret and with grief. "I'm not an innocent, I never have been. I wasn't one of those who had been forced into this kind of life, I chose it. I saw it as an easy way to make money." She stared at him hard, scrutinising every flicker, every nervous twitch. She was sure he'd balk at her boldness. She searched his face for any sign of weakness, but found none. Her heart gave an involuntary skip. Most men would have cut and run. Her life wasn't pretty. There was nothing romantic about selling oneself. Jared had listened, encouraged her to go on. He knew what she was. Reinforced by his iron resolve she told him about James Fairfax, how he'd tied her down, forced himself inside her and how he'd gleefully told her he was going to kill her. She told him of her miraculous escape, how many months later she'd stood face to face with the leather-faced monster and how he'd not recognised her. She told him of her transcontinental train ride and her unexpected stop at Rock Springs. She smiled when she told him how she'd met Miles O'Bannion, how he'd fell so hopelessly in love with her and begged her to marry him.

"Did you love him?" Jared asked nervously.

The look in his eyes made Maddie feel warm inside. "No. Miles was good, kind and at times funny. But no, I never loved him. If things had turned out different to how they did, I believe I would have stayed faithful, despite my history. He was a good man, Jared." She paused for a moment, contemplating her lot, then she added uncharacteristically, "Apart from Miles and now you, my life has been one fuck up after another." Then she started to cry.

Later as they lay in each others arms she told him she was still in fear of her life. That not a day went by that she didn't look over her shoulder, searching the crowd, looking for that monster. "One day I thought I'd found him, but I was wrong and a man paid with his life." She looked at him again, only harder this time. To kill once in the eyes of God was unforgivable but to kill twice, that was something else entirely.

Jared looked her straight in the eye. "I'd heard something to that affect a while back. From what I heard he needed killing."

"Killing or not, I lost it. I saw that knife, the blood. It all came flooding back."

"After what you'd gone through, who could blame you?"

She'd told him everything and it hadn't changed a damn thing. Her heart swelled with love for this man. She felt safe with this man. Even if Fairfax ever turned up, she felt safe if he was by her side. She hugged him tightly.

Jared smiled down at her, "No harm will come to you, I promise."

"How can you be so sure?"

"He's back east," said Jared.

"No he's not," shrieked Maddie. He's out West, San Francisco to be exact."

"What!"

"Oh it's a few years ago now. Not long after I'd first begun to read. A drummer came in on the stage and left a newspaper behind in his hotel room. Because I'd made it known that I was interested in reading, the hotel porter brought it over for me to read. It was a week later that I managed to find time for it. It was front page headlines in the San Francisco Chronicle. A whorehouse and gaming establishment on the notorious Barbary Coast had burned down killing at least 20 people. The owner of said establishment was none other than James Fairfax!" At the sound of his name Maddie's blood ran cold.

"Yeah, but there's probably hundreds, thousands of James Fairfax's."

"Not ones that wear a leather face mask!"

"If he's the sort of man you say he is, then he's probably dead by now."

"I hope so." Maddie shuddered.

"Well Madeline Dubois, or should I say Deirdre O'Bannion, will you become my wife?"

"Oh Jared, nothing would give me greater pleasure, but are you sure? Are you really sure that you want me?"

Maddie knew in her heart that Jared was all she'd ever want, but she was afraid. In her profession she'd met most of the dregs of society. She'd known many a dangerous man, men that would think nothing of killing another human being. She feared for Jared's life. What would Luke Plummer do? How would he react when she told him she was leaving to get married? Would he try to stop her? Yes, under the hard exterior she was afraid. But wasn't this what she'd been planning for, wasn't this her real chance at happiness? What if Fairfax appeared and took away everything she held dear? For every reason to leave this life there was a counter reason, but the one set of reasons that worried her most of all were her mundane fears. She was afraid of being a rancher's wife. What if the life wasn't to her liking? Would she cope? Would Jared's friends accept her for who she was? Most of all she was afraid of herself....

"Can I give you my answer in the spring? It's not that I don't love you. I do. It's just that I need time to think, no that's not it. You are giving me a second chance. I'm a whore...."

"Don't say that," interrupted Jared. "I don't care what you were; it's what you are now."

And that was it, thought Maddie. Was she ready to commit to him?

Frustrated by Maddie's indecision, Mordecai's disappearance and the blizzard conditions, all Jared could do was wait out the storm and pray that spring came early.

CHAPTER 34

It was a dumb idea, probably the dumbest in his entire life, and now he was snowbound in Butte in the Montana Territories until the snows cleared and he could get himself back to Ogden so as to resume his journey home. Finbar had asked around about O'Bannion's widow but had drawn a blank. Then the snows came. Stuck in the mining town of Butte until the spring Finbar pondered his immediate future.

Copper had been discovered the previous year and Butte, even in the thick of winter, resembled many of the mining towns back East. There was money to be made, fortunes to be won or lost. The mines worked continually, and the saloons stayed open 24 hours a day. Prostitution was rife. Law and order was, for the most part, carried out by vigilantes.

Finbar, on seeing the many Irish who worked the mines and drank in those bars, saw a way of killing time, earning a crust and possibly finding out about any widow of the Seventh falling into a life of prostitution. Finbar O'Toole became a town constable, a position once held by a local man named Morgan Earp. He'd stayed around Butte until the end of 79, but on killing Billy Brooks he'd left town and headed south to Arizona. Finbar remembered reading about him in the San Francisco Chronicle, how only a few months ago he'd been involved with his brothers in a shoot out in the town of Tombstone.

Finbar wasn't interested in getting himself a reputation as a man handy with a gun, all he wanted was to while away the winter months and then when spring arrived head back East. Butte was a tough mining town, most able bodied men worked gruelling long hours in indescribable heat beneath the surface. It was understandable that when these men hit town they would play just as hard as they worked. Sometimes they stepped out of line and that's when Finbar came in. He'd found to his cost that on an occasion he'd had to crack a few heads. And as the winter months stretched on he found that his reputation as a hard man grew. He'd managed to stay well clear of any serious trouble but on the night of the 6th of March he met up with his own version of Billy Brooks.

Called to attend to a fracas at the White Elephant, it didn't take Finbar long to see he'd stepped into a hornets' nest. The Finnan brothers were virtually beating a young miner to death right in the centre of the saloon. A crazy wide eyed accomplice was covering the crowd with an Army Colt. Finbar noted the faded blue coat and rank. It was plain to see the crazy ex soldier was itching to be part of the action.

"Stomp him Rory, stomp that son of a bitch all the ways to hell!"

Finbar, knowing that the next move he made could be his last, holstered his gun and made to be no part of the action. Wide eyes covered the peace officer with the Colt.

"Best stay out of this law man, if you've a hankering to see daylight."

"It's just a job man. Forty bucks a month ain't worth dying for," replied Finbar as he edged closer to the man. "What's the son of a bitch done?" As Finbar, hands in an open and unthreatening position got close to the Army model Colt, he shouted encouragement to the two brothers. "Stomp the son of a bitch." Years of dealing with the dregs of society had taught Finbar to read men. The man covering him was probably more dangerous than the two bullies, but O'Toole could see that too much alcohol was glazing the man's vision. "Kick the shit out of him," shouted Finbar. In that second he made his move. A short punch caught Crazy square on the nose busting it wide open. With

Finbar's left he pulled his own Colt and buffaloed the man senseless. Then, quick as a cat, he fired a warning shot into the floor of the saloon. Rory Finnan looked up but his brother was too intent in applying the killer blow to notice. Finbar shot him in the side and the fight went out of him. Rory Finnan looked like he was going to join his brother in the hereafter but on seeing the open barrel of Finbar's Colt decided against it.

The young miner lingered for two days before he expired. Bram Finnan died on the spot where Finbar shot him. He was now laid out in the local undertakers awaiting burial. Rory Finnan and his crazy eyed cousin languished in the town jail cursing and threatening their jailer Finbar O'Toole.

"You killed a man. Two of you beat that poor boy to death. You're gonna hang Finnan. And you Driscoll, if I had my way you'd swing with him."

"Yeah I might at that if the army has anything to do about it," said Driscoll.

"You won't hang. The army shoots deserters," said Finbar. "I got no time for scum that shirks their duty."

"You know shit! I was a good soldier once, but I seen the light. I seen terrible things, things that don't bare thinkin about. I was with Custer see. Damn fool marched us straight into the jaws of hell."

Finbar pricked up his ears. Was this the break through he'd been searching for?

"You was with Custer?"

"Damn right I was, damned lucky too. He sent me back to Benteen's position. Bring packs, he says, bring packs. Benteen deferred to Reno who was under fire himself. He weren't that foolish. Benteen wanted to join Custer, but Reno considered his position. We dug in and fought those sons of bitches where we stood. It was pretty bad though, we were lucky we got away without losing our scalps," said Driscoll.

There was craziness in Driscoll's eyes. The terror of those dreadful hours was still with him after more than five years. It was clear to Finbar that the man wasn't right in the head. Drawing his gun he covered the two men as he unlocked the cell.

"Get in there Driscoll," demanded Finbar, as he pointed with the Colt to the vacant cell next door. Puzzled, Driscoll did as he was bid.

"Your cousin's gonna hang, that I guarantee, but you my friend might be out of this here jail cell long before the Provost Marshall gets here."

Driscoll scratched his head and immediately drew blood from the wound he'd been given by the constable the previous night. "Damn, you really know how to buffalo a man don'tca. What is it you want?"

Finbar checked himself from asking outright if he'd come across the widow O'Bannion. The Seventh wasn't the only cavalry regiment stationed at or around Fort Lincoln. Driscoll might or he might not have known Lieutenant Miles O'Bannion or his pretty wife. Telling me what I want to hear would be too damn easy, thought Finbar. "Tell me about life at the fort before the massacre."

"Not much to tell. Routine patrols, an occasional skirmish, drill, Bismarck, now there's a town."

"The officers, how well did you get on with the officers?"

"I'd say right well. Those officers needed the likes of me to clean up their mess. I was a good sergeant, until that day."

"What kind of mess?"

"You know the usual kind. Some shavetail cain't quite hack it. I clean up their mess."

"Elaborate."

"Damn shavetail Lieutenant. God I even saved his worthless hide. Was he grateful? Was he shit!" Driscoll laughed as he reminisced. "You'd have thought his wife would have been more appreciative."

"How's that?" interrupted Finbar, sensing he was on to something.

"Pretty young thing. Too good for that shavetail. Still wet behind the ears." Driscoll smiled inwardly, remembering and savouring whatever it was. "Thought she was too good for my kind. I saved her damn husband's life. The least she could have done is show me some hospitality."

"How's that?"

"I caught her alone, must have been a week before we got our orders. I was a little drunk. I grabbed a hold of her by the arms and pinned her against a building." Driscoll laughed. He was clearly enjoyed his foray into the past. "Hey missy, I says, how's about a little kiss, show your gratitude for saving your man's life. I don't know how she done it but she broke free. Slapped me good. Then she had the audacity to tell me that as I'd saved her husband's life she'd forget the incident."

"That's it?"

"Yeah, that's it, we get our orders and then the shit hits the fan." Driscoll laughed to himself. "There's a small codicil to this tale. Kinda heartening, well to me anyway. Bitch thought she was better than me, but I knew, I just knew. Up to Helena I went, must have been 77 or 78. Had me some money in my pocket. Thought I'd celebrate my good fortune. Then in she walks, cool as you like. I recognised her right off. She weren't so prim and proper now. I reached in my pants for the necessary. "Fallen on hard times," I says. "This should help," I grinned as I offered up my money. "Go to hell," she says, cool as you like. Acted like she didn't recognise me. But I knew it was her all right."

Barely able to control his excitement Finbar asked the final question. "This woman have a name?"

"Yeah." replied Driscoll, his mind alight, he added, "Why so interested?"

"I'm not, just curious is all," replied Finbar all too quickly.

"Hell! I don't care what you got going on with this woman. What's it worth for the name?"

"Your life, you son of a bitch! That Provost Marshall cain't be more than a couple of days ride."

"Let Finnan go, I'll give you her name."

"No chance. I ain't lookin over my shoulder for the rest of my life. Finnan hangs!"

"What makes you think I won't shoot you the moment your back's turned?"

"I ain't saying you ain't capable, I just reckon you're smarter than Finnan. And besides, if I let you out you're leaving town fast, because if I see you again I'll shoot you on sight. Now give me her goddamn name!"

"You'll let me go?" Driscoll said, his voice betraying a hint of incredulity.

"You have my word."

Driscoll smiled as he recalled the sexy wife of his lieutenant. "Her name was Deirdre O'Bannion," then as he remembered what she did to him he added bitterly, "but the whore now goes under the fancy title Madeline Dubois."

Butte was still in the grip of winter and posting a man out of town was a little extreme, but Finbar felt he had little choice as he watched ex sergeant William Driscoll dressed in an old army greatcoat mount his horse. The look on Driscoll's face told the lawman all he needed to know. He'd made a dangerous enemy.

CHAPTER 35

The anger inside Mordecai subsided. No man had ever spoken to him the way Jared had and gotten away with it. Yet he found himself walking away. He knew, despite the great debt he felt for his friend that if he hadn't walked away then one of them would have been sent racing towards hell. No man, not even Wes Hardin, had such a volatile temper as Mordecai. His friend Jared was tough, and he could be mean, but he lacked the instincts of a killer. Sure he'd killed, but they were people who needed killing, whereas he himself had killed for every kind of reason that existed on God's earth.

With nowhere to go, Mordecai found himself drifting towards Helena. It was approaching dusk and the chances of reaching town before nightfall were, at best, slim. Mordecai knew of an old line shack a little over half the distance from town. He'd take shelter there and continue on the following morning. There was always the chance that Jared on his way back to the ranch might stop over there too. Both men had said things that they regretted. It would be as good a place as any to patch things up. He reached the line shack but was disappointed to see the place was deserted. As night settled Mordecai unrolled his bedroll in the darkened one room shack, lit only by a shaft of moonlight, and fell to remembering how it all began.

There was a time when Mordecai had it all. A wife so pretty it made his heart bleed and two lovely kids, Tommy and Rebecca. Yes, Mordecai and Laura had it made. They lived close to the Rio Grande in West Texas. Mordecai had taken up blacksmithing as a trade and worked out of the livery stable in Del Rio. Tommy had just started school, whilst Rebecca was not much more than a toddler and kept Laura busy most of the time, although she did find enough time to become a leading member of the local Methodist church: well respected and hardworking until that fateful day in June of 1873. The day had begun like any other hot summer's day. Mordecai was busy shoeing a bay mare when all hell broke loose.

"They're robbing the bank!" shouted a terrified townsman as the first shots were fired. The street, which only minutes earlier had been busy with people going about their business erupted into blind panic. Men, women and children scattered in all directions. A woman screamed, a horse reared in panic and tore itself from the hitching rail. A young boy stood in its path. Mordecai raced from the livery stable, his Henry repeater clutched in his hand. He watched in horror as the horse trampled the boy asunder. At the same time four men emerged from the bank, guns blazing in every direction. Transfixed by the horrific scene in front of him, Mordecai worked the level of the old Henry repeater and took careful aim at one of the emerging bank robbers. The man fell backwards just as he was about to mount his horse. He somehow managed to pick himself up and stumbled into the dusty street. Mordecai worked the lever of the Henry and shot him high in the chest. Seconds later the street was alive with bullets as other townsmen joined in, but none found their target.

Mordecai jacked another round into the breech. He fired but missed the man he was aiming at. Before he could load another, the man spurred his horse forward. Mordecai dived out of the way of the lead horse losing his rifle in the process. All he could do was stare through the cloud of dust which slowly obliterated the three riders as they raced out of town.

As the dust settled Mordecai picked himself up and began to survey the damage. To his immense relief he saw the town doctor attending to the trampled boy. The kid was barely conscious but he was a sight luckier than the dying bank robber. He had suffered only a mild concussion and a broken leg.

Mordecai's heart pounded rapidly as he drew level with the dying man. There was something familiar about him. The last time he'd seen this man he'd been a boy dancing at his and Laura's wedding two years earlier. The hairs on the blacksmith's neck stood on end, as the robber gasped his last words, "Tell Laura I'm sorry…." It was a cruel twist of fate; Mordecai had killed his wife's younger brother.

The bank robbers had got away with only a few dollars and some coin, but one of their outlaw band had paid the ultimate price. However, his death was nothing compared to the anguish that Mordecai felt. He knew his brother-in-law rode with a bad crowd, but he never figured he'd try to rob the bank at Del Rio.

Mordecai was devastated, his mind was in turmoil. How could he tell Laura that he'd killed Billy? She adored the boy. That he'd gone to the bad wouldn't matter, she'd see only the senseless violent death. She would blame Mordecai, she would shut him out of her life. Why had he been so quick to act? He knew he should be the one to tell Laura, but he couldn't face her. A posse was quickly formed and Mordecai was asked to take charge. Perversely he blamed the death of his young brother-in-law on the bank robbers who had led him to this fate and thought that by bringing them to justice it would alleviate his own feelings of guilt. Events moved so quickly that before he knew it he was eating the outlaws dust.

For days the eight man posse tracked the desperados, gaining ground mile by mile. The pursuit was dogged and fresh in the memories of each posse man was the sight of the trampled boy. A bloodlust had fallen upon the posse, each one of them knowing the final outcome. None more so than Mordecai.

His thoughts kept returning to Laura. She'd doted on Billy and after their mother died she'd brought him up. She'd been everything to him and when Mordecai first came into Laura's life the kid idolised him. Mordecai became a father figure to him, which to Laura was a good thing as their father had deserted them a year before their ma died. As an immature youth Billy was becoming a little wild and was in need of direction. Laura thought that Mordecai would be able to steer him onto the right path, but when he found out that Mordecai had fought in the Sutton Taylor war he couldn't contain his excitement.

"Was you really in the Sutton Taylor war? Did you kill anyone? Was you as good as Wes Hardin? I bet you were!" 'Here,' thought Billy, was a man he could finally look up too.

Mordecai had been shocked at the kid's outburst, he thought he'd put the past behind him. He'd been wild and free and in danger of going to an early grave until Laura came along. She'd lost her husband to the Sutton Taylor Feud some years earlier and had moved away to look after her younger brother Billy and her young son Tommy. She'd returned briefly to De Witt County to pay her best friend Jane Bowen a visit when she met Mordecai. There was an instant attraction and before long they were walking out together. She was soft and warm and determined to bring her child up away from the senseless violence of De Witt County. She was, thought Mordecai, his salvation. On the day that she agreed to marry him, he renounced all violence. He even stopped wearing a handgun, carrying only a Henry rifle for hunting purposes. A few months after they moved to Del Rio, Rebecca was born. Billy idolized him.

Mordecai looked across to Laura for assurance then he turned back to the boy.

"Yes Billy I was in the Sutton Taylor war. But no, I didn't kill anyone." he lied. "Yeah, I knew Hardin, the back shooting son of a bitch. I was there Billy, but when the killin started I ran. I ran for my damn life. You ever see a man with half his head blown off? It ain't pretty."

Laura managed a secret smile of approval. After that day Billy shied away from Mordecai. He'd expected a hero not a coward, marrying his sister had been the final straw, and soon after the birth of Rebecca, young Billy drifted away and fell in with the wrong crowd.

Mordecai dwelt on the killing of Billy, he didn't know who he was shooting at, but the man was down, he hadn't needed that second shot. The killer instinct in him hadn't died after all. It had lain dormant until the bank hold up. In his heart Mordecai knew that Laura could never forgive him.

They finally caught up with the three outlaws at a shallow ford in the Rio Grande. In the ensuing fire fight all three robbers were killed, with only a few minor casualties to the posse. A week after the bank robbery Mordecai and the posse rode back into Del Rio with their prey strapped to their horses' backs.

Mordecai took no part in the celebrations that ensued when they arrived back, instead he rode home. Killing Laura's brother weighed heavily with him and he knew that he shouldn't have gone with the posse. It was a mistake, it was circumstances. However he dressed it up it came out the same. He should have put Laura's feelings first, instead of riding away from his responsibilities.

He knew, almost before he'd climbed down from his horse, when Tommy and Rebecca hadn't race out of the cabin to greet him. Laura and the kids were gone. There was no note.

Mordecai stuck it out until Christmas of that year in the mistaken belief that Laura would return to their cabin. He discovered that once she learnt the truth of the bank robbery, and his part in the dispatch of Billy, she flew into a blinding rage.

"He's a boy, he's hardly grown. Why, oh why did Mordecai have to kill him?"

On learning who the boy was some members of the community drifted away, while others showed the sympathy.

"Who'd have thought it? Our own blacksmith, cool as a cucumber he was. Stood there in the street and took careful aim, bullets flying all around him. Shot the boy outta the saddle. He was game though, he got up on to his feet, but then Mordecai shot him again."

"He what!" screamed Laura, "My brother was down and he shot him a second time?"

Sensing they'd said too much the townsfolk left her question unanswered. Laura, distraught with grief, frustration and anger quickly saw to the burial of her brother and went home and packed her belongings. She'd known the kind of man Mordecai was, yet she'd been taken in by his attempt to reform. Well it hadn't worked, she thought angrily. She'd lost one husband to the Sutton Taylor Feud and now she'd lost her only brother. She didn't want Tommy going the same way. Laura's iron will even prevented her from coming into town to say her goodbyes, she just upped and went.

Mordecai began searching for her the day after returning to town with the posse. It was a forlorn search, nearby towns threw up nothing. When that failed he swung a wider loop. With no positive sightings of his family he started thinking of the possibilities of towns like El Paso or San Antonio. Mordecai sold his business to finance his searches, but by mid winter he'd all but exhausted his funds. He had to admit that Laura and the kids had vanished without a trace. If she'd made it to El Paso or San Antonio she could have taken a stage to almost anywhere. Returning to Del Rio his frequent drunken outbursts and fits of temper did little to endure him to his friends there. Life in town held nothing for him without Laura and the kids. It was time for him to leave, and he could think of only one place where he'd be welcome, well at least by half the population. The place; Cuero, in De Witt County.

Mordecai was heading for a war zone and he couldn't care less. There were old scores to be settled, one of which had already been taken care of. Jack Helm, ex captain of the dreaded state police and an old enemy of Mordecai, had been killed the previous August by John Wesley Hardin in Cuero. The Sutton Taylor Feud was becoming the bloodiest rivalry that Texas had ever seen. Now five or six years after the start, John Wesley Hardin, the notorious man killer had thrown in with the Taylors. Somewhere along the line Mordecai heard tell he was a distant cousin. They'd met on an occasion but sought to walk in different circles. Hardin wasn't the easiest man to get along with, and since his foray up to Kansas he'd become even meaner. Mordecai decided early on that he didn't like him, but if truth be known they were very much alike. Both men had a dark side and were prone to violent action at the slightest provocation. But there the similarities ended. Hardin had thrown in with the Taylor's because of blood ties and a propensity for violence, whilst Mordecai had been there because he was with William and Henry Kelly when they were captured by Jack Helm, Bill Sutton and their posse.

It was a trivial charge and all three men went along peacefully. They'd only ridden a few miles from Henry's cabin when suddenly Helm and his men opened fire on the three cowboys, killing William and Henry before Mordecai made good his escape. Helm alleged that the Kelly's had tried to escape and been killed in self defence, but Mordecai knew otherwise. Their crime, being sons-in-law of old man Pitkin Taylor. After the murders, Mordecai swore a blood oath to avenge the killings. The Suttons had the law, such as it was, in their pocket, whilst the Taylors had mostly Southern sympathisers on their side. Getting justice meant taking the law into their own hands. Mordecai knew the identities of some of the men who had done for the Kellys and killed or took part in the assassination of some of the men responsible. The Suttons replied in kind. Taylor men were either dry-gulched or found hanging from a tree. Several bloody encounters with the Suttons later and he met Laura and everything changed after that. She'd brought him back from the brink of hell, she taught him the error of his ways, and she became his salvation.

All that changed on Del Rio's dusty main street. He should have stayed back, avoided trouble, kept his head down, but that wasn't Mordecai's way. He'd met it head on, and destroyed his marriage into the bargain. Now circumstances had changed yet again and he had returned to the carnage of the Sutton Taylor Feud with Hardin covering his back.

With the loss of Laura and the children, Mordecai thought to recapture the old devil may care attitude, but it wasn't working out as he'd planned. There was still a number of men who needed killing, bad men the world would be better off without. But Laura had taught him forgiveness. Though not a churchgoer, Mordecai had listened to the teaching of their local preacher. He'd listened to Laura, sweet gentle Laura, and he'd watched his kids grow and somehow he knew that he'd taken the right path. With Laura gone he'd reverted back to his old life. Yet it wasn't the same. Men were dying on both sides. Widows grieved, whilst the young ones cried for the fathers they lost. It was a mistake to come back, he could see it now, but Hardin wouldn't let him back out now. Ever since their last meeting Mordecai had a feeling that Hardin was itching to try him. The man liked killing, whereas Mordecai killed only when necessary. Whatever way he chose to go, it was almost certain to end in bloodshed.

It was Hardin who brought the matter to a head.

"Mordecai, you and I got some business to attend too."

"I guess we have at that," he replied.

"I heard tell you ain't got much liking for Reuben Brown."

"You heard right," said Mordecai, still wary of what Hardin had in mind.

"He with Helm and Sutton?"

"The last of em," replied Mordecai.

"What say we finish the job?" cried Hardin.

A week later Ex-Marshall Reuben Brown was shot to death in a saloon in Cuero by five unknown assailants. There were conflicting accounts of what went down but no one was ever charged with his death. An old timer many years later came up with one account. It seems a dark looking young man of Hardin's stamp walked into the saloon. Marshall Brown recognised the man as one of the Taylor bunch and tried to arrest him.

"On what charge Marshall?"

"I'll think of something."

"Like hell you will. Pull that hog leg and get at it!"

Reuben Brown was startled at the challenge and tried to pull his gun. The dark looking man grabbed at the Marshall's gun hand with his left whilst he pulled his own with his right. He fired twice at almost point blank range, hitting the Marshall high in the chest. Brown's shirt caught fire as he began to slump to the floor. At that moment four men appeared at the entrance to the saloon and fired into the already dying Marshall.

"Damn you to hell!" cried the leader of the bunch. "Why didn't you wait?"

"He was mine, he always was mine," came the cold reply.

A week after the killing Hardin came to see Mordecai. "I had a hankering to call you out, but since what happened happened, I realise you're too much like me. Bill Hickok was the same. I guess that's why he let me go that time up in Abilene."

"Story I heard, you got the drop on him."

"Believe that if you will. If I'd got the better of Hickok he'd be lying in a lonely grave. No, Bill saw himself in me. Now I'm doing the same."

Before Mordecai could say another word Hardin handed him a letter. It was addressed to Jane Bowen, Hardin's woman. Puzzled Mordecai opened the letter and read the contents. When he had finished his face was ashen.

"Sorry man, but I thought you ought to know."

Mordecai left De Witt County that morning heading toward Amarillo. Jane's letter had been from Laura. She'd been living in Amarillo for the best part of two years. During that time she'd taken up with a widower with a ten year old son. They'd met at church and judging from the affectionate way she spoke about him in the letter it looked as if they were going to set up home together. The reason she'd written to Jane was to inform her they were setting out for California.

He had to stop her; he had to explain about what happened on that dusty street in Del Rio. He'd tried to make their marriage work, oh how he'd tried! He'd even let her headstrong brother believe he was a coward. He'd done everything she'd asked, until that fateful day. Even if she couldn't forgive him she should have waited to let him explain. Now she had taken up with another man. As he pushed his horse onward his mind went through a gambit of emotions.

Montana's weather was unpredictable at best, but as winter took it in its icy grip, Mordecai slept long into the night, his mind tortured by the demons of the past. It was still dark when he awoke. The biting wind had eased but the weather was still bitterly cold. He judged it to be around five in the morning, but couldn't be sure as the ground outside the cabin was draped in a white blanket. All thoughts of Wes Hardin and the Sutton Taylor Feud were back shelved in the recesses of his mind. He didn't have a plan. He didn't know why he was drifting towards town. All he knew was his best friend didn't have much experience of the opposite sex. That he could have his head turned by some cheap town whore beggared belief. Jared wasn't dumb by any means, Mordecai couldn't figure it out. Perhaps there was more to this woman that he thought. He knew the only way to get the answer to his questions was to find out for himself. Half an hour later he had saddled up and was heading towards Helena.

Chapter 36

It was the middle of the afternoon when Mordecai, hunched low in the saddle, reached Helena. Although it was only early the bad weather had turned the afternoon sky a dirty grey. Icy winds whipped though the centre of town clearing the streets of any pedestrians who hadn't the good sense to stay indoors. Mordecai spotted the sign for Jasper's livery and kicked his mare towards the stable, where he quickly dismounted and unsaddled his horse. Within a few minutes he'd found the proprietor and was giving his horse a quick rub down and a bale of hay. Then with directions from old man Jasper, the weary horseman made for the Bon-Ton cafeteria. Inside, his appearance raised a few eyebrows but nothing more. With a hot meal inside his belly he felt almost human. Throwing payment on the table he ventured outside and braved the biting cold weather as he walked half a block to Ma Crandall's boarding house.

In his room he tried figuring out what he was going to do, if anything. He hadn't a plan. He'd walked out on his only friend over some harsh words. But it was more than that; the shooting at Pocatello had opened old wounds, it had shown that he still had the killer instinct, something he'd tried hard to contain. He was fighting his demons and losing. He desperately needed his friend's support, but it had been lacking. It wasn't Jared's fault, he could see that now. Newt's drowning on the Snake, the Deer Lodge Valley, the talks with old man Kohrs, they all took precedence over his troubled mind, but the woman, the woman had been the last straw. She was nothing but a cheap whore. His pride was hurt, nobody had ever talked that way to him and got away with it. But, he reflected, nobody ever was as good a friend as Jared.

Lying on his bed he remembered the circumstances of the first time he'd met Jared McAllister.

Sickened by the mindless slaughter in De Witt County, *of which he was no innocent,* he'd set off in pursuit of Laura and his kids. He thought about the man she'd taken up with and his mind was filled with rage and jealousy. Yet if he was to win her back he had to forego his natural instincts. He knew in his heart that she had loved him once. He prayed that when he saw her she'd remember the good times and come back to him. He so desperately wanted a second chance. He was prepared to beg if necessary. And if all else failed he was prepared to let them be, provided she promised to send him a letter from time to time.

In Amarillo he found he'd missed them by a couple of days. When he did finally catch up with them, it was too late to ask for a second chance and to beg her forgiveness.

Crossing the Llano Estucato, that vast openness of high plains in the top left hand corner of Texas and New Mexico, Mordecai heard a faint noise that was unmistakeably the sound of gunfire. Spurring his horse forward he prayed that the gunfire had been Laura's man out hunting game. On reaching a sandy ridge the Texan gazed down the other side and spied an old abandoned adobe outpost. He could see and smell the acrid smoke from a burnt-out wagon and knew his worst fears were confirmed. The blood curdling cry of a Comanche brave high on adrenaline and bloodlust filled the still air, as he danced around wearing a woman's dress. It was Laura's.

"Oh God! Please no!"

Wrapping his reins around the pommel he spurred his horse towards a group of Comanche warriors, screaming obscenities as he rode amongst them, a Navy Colt in both hands spitting death from each barrel. The charge unsettled the savages and they began to scatter. He killed one instantly and seriously wounded another. The Comanche, not knowing how many men were behind Mordecai, ran for the cover of the brush and rocky outcrops a short distance from the outpost.

Jumping from his horse, Mordecai entered the adobe compound and stared at a wreck of a man tied to the wheel of a wagon. He was screaming in agony, a small fire was still burning between his legs. His genital area was already a blackened mess.

"Kill me! For pity sake kill me!"

Mordecai ignored the man's plea and raced into the crumbling adobe structure.

"No!" he screamed, as he caught sight of Laura first, then Tommy. In that moment time stood still. In the distance he could hear the war whoops of the Comanche but he didn't care. He stared in horror at the woman who had once been his life and begged to die. Then he slowly turned his back on what was left of his wife and child and staggered outside. Tears streaked his face as he sought out the screaming man. The smell of burning flesh invaded his nostrils as he reached the tortured man. He looked up weakly and a silent thank you crossed his lips as Mordecai raised his Navy Colt and shot him between the eyes.

Where was Rebecca? Could she still be alive? These thoughts screamed through his brain as his eyes searched the compound. There was still hope. Another bloodcurdling cry pierced the air and Mordecai was forced to turn back towards the war whooping Comanche as they remounted their ponies and began to regroup. A barrage of fire tore into the adobe building as Mordecai retrieved his Henry from his saddle scabbard. Then a ricocheting bullet hit him in the side, the Henry fell from his grasp and he landed face down in the dirt. At the same time a Comanche brave spotted his fall and turned his horse towards the entrance to the compound. With the agility of an expert horseman he jumped from the charging horse and raced towards the entrance, war club held high in the air. Mordecai, seeing the danger, spun onto his back and grabbing frantically at his Henry, jacked a round into the breech and fired. The brave spun backwards, a look of bewilderment spread across his face. Mordecai rolled over several times until he managed to make cover behind the adobe wall. He fired six times with the repeater, hoping to discourage any attempt at an all out charge.

For an hour there was intermittent gunfire, but Mordecai kept close to the adobe structure, in so doing he was able to move around the small compound without being hit. He knew as the day grew longer that it would only be a matter of time, but if he could find Rebecca he could make a run for it. His mare could out run most horses in De Witt County. He reckoned against Comanche war ponies he had more than a fighting chance. He was hoping against hope that he'd still find little Rebecca alive, but then he stumbled upon a boy of ten, who he took to be the dead man's son slumped against a wall. What hope he had that Rebecca was alive were quickly dashed, his daughter lay in a still heap beneath an old cottonwood. The sight of her made him weep, there was nothing left for him to fight for; it was over. He sank to his knees and took his Navy Colt from its holster and was about to shoot himself in the eye when he heard the Comanche singing.

Madness overtook him and he lost any feeling he still had for humanity. As he eased his finger from the trigger he began in earnest to reload his revolvers. He wanted to kill, to kill every murdering son of a bitch. But his lust for blood remained unquenched; all through the day the Comanche kept peppering the walls but managed to stay out of sight of Mordecai's Navy Colts.

"The white eye is much warrior; he who kills him will be looked on by Manitou as a great warrior. Good fortune will follow him for the rest of his days," their war chief, Kills-like-the-Wolf, had spoken.

Frustrated by the lack of action, Mordecai raised himself above the adobe wall and screamed obscenities at his aggressors. He took another wound in the shoulder for his trouble, but luckily it passed right on through. He wanted it over. He was losing blood fast and knew that now the Comanche would ready themselves. He prepared himself for the inevitable rush. He re-checked his loads and cocked his Navy Colts and waited …

At that precise moment a lone horseman rode into their midst, dealing death with every shot. 'Yeah, Jared sure knew how to make an entrance,' thought Mordecai as he drifted off.

Mordecai woke to the unfamiliar surroundings of Ma Crandall's boarding house. Washed and rested, he decided to take his first look at this woman who had turned his best friend into marshmallow.

CHAPTER 37

People looked up as he entered the Alhambra, some stared and others averted their eyes. Trouble came in many packages, but none more menacing than this man. He cut an imposing figure in his full length overcoat and wide brimmed hat as he sidled up to the bar and ordered a beer. Automatically he undid his coat, exposing a claw-hammer jacket, charcoal grey in appearance, a collarless smock shirt and dark pants. But to the casual onlooker it was his waist that caused the most concern, butt forward was the unmistakeable shape of a Navy Colt. It wasn't unusual in itself, most men went armed in Helena, *it wasn't like other towns that posted ordinance notices prohibiting guns, those days were still in the future.* It was just that this man looked like he really knew how to use it.

Mordecai drank his beer down and ordered a bottle, then he found himself a table. Seating himself with his back to the wall he surveyed the scene. Through the smoke he could make out dance hall girls sparring for drinks with the clientele. He continued to observe the rough looking men, already at this hour worse for drink, and gamblers fleecing their table companions.

He drank slowly as he waited for the whore to put in an appearance. A blonde, rouged up and rowdy, approached his table. He knew at a glance that this wasn't she.

"Hey cowboy, you ready for some action."

"No ma'am. Just watching is all."

"Just watchin." mimicked the blonde.

And then he saw her. Dark hair piled upon the top of her head, a high collared white blouse with a cameo brooch attached to a velvet strap enhancing her swan like neck. Around her slim waist she wore a broad belt, whilst her free flowing black skirt with a small bustle completed the outfit. She had the deepest innocently wicked blue eyes he'd ever seen and her generous, but not overly full, lips invited kissing. Mordecai could see why this woman would appeal to Jared. She was like no other woman he'd ever known.

Regaining his composure Mordecai poured himself another drink as she brushed by his table.

"Madeline Dubois, would you sit awhile?" he said.

"I don't know you sir. Why would I sit awhile?"

"My name is Mordecai. We have a friend in common."

Startled by the stranger's forthrightness Maddie looked him up and down. He was about six one and as dark as Jared was fair. His well tanned and almost swarthy features were accentuated by the dark moustache and deep brown eyes. He was, thought Maddie, strikingly handsome in a rugged sort of way.

"Are they all like you in Texas?"

"Nope ma'am, only the good lookin ones."

He forced a smile from Maddie and soon she found herself sitting down and signalling for the bartender to bring over a glass.

"You're Jared's friend?"

"That's right ma'am," he smiled disarmingly, "and I'm here to stop this foolishness before it starts."

At first Maddie thought he was only joking, but one look at those dark brown eyes left her in no doubt. Taken aback by his forthrightness, Maddie gathered herself together.

"Did Jared send you?"

"No ma'am."

"Then I suggest you mind your own damn business!" Maddie stood up abruptly, looked Mordecai in the eye and added, "I ain't known Jared long, but long enough to know that he loves me and I him."

"Ask yourself this, could you really become a rancher's wife? What do you think it'd be like living out there in the back of beyond?"

"Goodnight Mr Mordecai whatever your goddamn name is"

Then, turning on her heels, she raced back up the stairs. Throwing herself on the bed she burst into tears. She was angry and mad as all get out. Angry because he'd disarmed her with his charm and mad because she hadn't seen it coming. But what troubled her most was that, despite the man's rudeness and forthright manner, he was only acting in Jared's best interests, misguided though it was. So why, she asked herself was she so upset? She knew the prospect of becoming Jared's wife would be thwart with prejudice. Would it work? Would Jared, when the first flush of their relationship had faded, still feel the same? There were so many questions that she didn't know the answers to.

She knew she was capable of starting a new life, she'd proved that when she married Miles. But this time it was different. She loved Jared with all her heart. Miles was a sweet and kind boy, but she'd never really loved him. And now that she'd found a man whom she could truly love, would the fact that she'd slept with hundreds of men keep him from really loving her? She wouldn't blame him. He'd known that during the winter months that separated them, that despite their oath of undying love, she might have sex with other men because of her chosen profession. Even if Jared could overcome these obstacles, what of his friends? Would they accept her so readily? Her head ached with all the unanswered questions, but one niggling thought worried her more than anything. It had been triggered by Jared's friend: would she miss this life?

Mordecai, frustrated by his clumsy and unsuccessful attempt at discouraging Maddie Dubois, thought long and hard about his next move. He'd at least found out why Jared was so besotted. She was a handsome woman indeed and he understood the attraction, he'd felt it himself. As he lay awake in the darkness of the boarding house room it came to him what he had to do.

The next night Mordecai settled himself at the same table, ordered a bottle and two glasses and prepared himself for Maddie Dubois. He waited and waited, occasionally looking at the big clock that hung on the back wall of the bar.

At nine fifteen Maddie stood at the top of the stairs and surveyed the crowd below. She spotted him almost immediately, and felt herself under his scrutiny. 'To hell with it,' she thought, 'what you see is what you get!' She held her head high and carefully descended the stairs. When she'd reached the bottom she threw him a look of distain. Then began to flirt with the regular clientele of the Alhambra, aware that his eyes were following her every movement.

Mordecai watched her for more than half an hour before he made his move.

Maddie was seated drinking with a couple of men, when he stood up and approached their table.

"Miss Dubois, we have some unfinished business," he said firmly.

One of the men looked up at Mordecai and said, "Miss Dubois ain't going anywhere."

"Mister, if you don't want grief, best you shut your mouth," said Mordecai in a mildly threatening manner.

Maddie, sensing a situation that could be avoided, cut in, "Listen boys, I don't want no trouble, best you both ease off. I reckon me and this Mr Mordecai got some things we need to discuss."

"If you're sure, Miss Maddie," said the man with a detectable sense of relief in his voice.

Mordecai gave the man a hard stare then motioned with his eyes to his empty table. Maddie's hackles rose, she felt like telling him to get lost, but instead she followed him back to his table, her face set in granite. She was angry beyond words.

"Say what you have to say," she said with venom.

"I want you for the night. I'll pay over the going rate."

Maddie's mouth dropped open. She'd been prepared to listen to him telling her she was no good, but this, this hurt worse than anything.

"You can't afford me!" she snapped back. She forced back the tears, but inside she was fighting to control her temper and to keep her dignity in tact. She didn't know much about the man in front of her, only the little that Jared had told her, and the impression was that he wasn't the type to behave in this manner.

"I can afford whatever you ask. Fifty dollars okay?" he persisted.

The disgust in her eyes said it all. The man was rude and arrogant, but above all he was supposed to be Jared's best friend. Why was he behaving in this manner?

"Alright, make it a hundred bucks. Two hundred?"

"Go to hell!" screamed Maddie as she hitched up the hem of her skirts and for the second time in two nights raced for the stairs. She didn't stop until she'd closed and locked her door behind her. Was this what it was going to be like? Would she never be allowed to forget?

Later as she gazed out of the window at the clear dark sky she tried making sense of what had happened. Jared had told her they were very close, that things had happened that had changed them. Mordecai was the only man he could fully trust, the man would die for him, for Christ-sake. Yet why did he proposition her? Maddie went over it in her head a few times before she realised the answer was in her first meeting with Mordecai. He'd warned her off, he'd told her to keep away from Jared. On their second meeting he'd tried to pay for her services. Neither action added up unless in the clumsiest of ways he was trying to drive a wedge between her and Jared. 'Yes that was it,' thought Maddie.

She'd misjudged the man. He was arrogant and rude and stupid enough to think she'd go with him and risk her happiness, but she realised above all else he was prepared to risk losing his best friend just to keep Jared apart from a woman like me.

Her last thoughts before falling asleep were as always of her child, *he'd be six now* and of the man she loved, who, unbeknown to himself, had caused her such anguish and of course his misguided friend. Misguided yes, but his intentions, she told herself, were honourable. Tomorrow, she was taking the battle to him.

Mordecai had just finished his breakfast at the boarding house when a shadow fell across his table. Looking up he was surprised to see Maddie Dubois standing over him. She was devoured of all makeup and wearing an old greatcoat, her hair hung loose and her smile disarmed him.

"Mind if I sit awhile?" said Maddie.

Mordecai slightly shocked by Maddie's presence rose to his feet and offered her a chair. Still reeling from the unexpected arrival he said, "What can I do for you?" as he reclaimed his seat.

"I thought long and hard before I came over. I think we got off on the wrong foot. Despite your clumsy attempt at discrediting me, you need to hear me out."

"I'd say you already discredited yourself," he said unkindly.

Maddie tried to ignore his deliberate slight, and then it came out in a rush. "I suppose you've lived a blameless life Mr Mordecai.," she said sharply. "I was born into poverty, do you know what its like to have cramps? Not the normal cramps, but the ones that come with hunger. The pain makes you vomit, and the more you vomit the worse the cramps get."

Ma Crandall's breakfast clientele fell silent at Maddie's outburst.

"I watched by brothers and sisters all die of hunger and dysentery. Well I wasn't prepared to lie down. I'm a whore, get over it. Jared has!"

Red faced with anger she started to get up when he laid his hand across hers.

"Sorry ma'am. I guess I asked for that."

Fighting the urge to tell him to go to hell, Maddie, red-faced with anger and embarrassment, sat back down.

Mordecai looked at her for a second or two, then he spoke, "And no, I ain't led a blameless life. I reckon I done more bad things than the good Lord could shake a stick at. It's just that me and Jared, well we done rode the river together for more than five years. I ain't had a friend like him my entire life. I just didn't want to see him destroy his life over a wh.... woman."

"Whore, you can say the word."

"I ... I meant woman, I'm sorry."

"Is it that you've been hurt by a woman? Is that it?"

"I don't want to talk about it. I came here to see for myself. I tried. Evidently it ain't worked. I done all I could. This conversation is over."

Mordecai rose from the table, "I'll say no more." He felt himself flush as he picked up his hat. "I'll bid you good day," he said awkwardly and walked out of the boarding house and into the blinding cold of a Helena winter morning.

The woman, strange as it seemed, had got to him. She was nothing like the hard faced madam that he'd conjured up in his head. In fact she'd damn nigh impressed him. She had a kind of noble dignity, though he believed she'd be a handful if trouble erupted in her establishment. Yeah the lady was a real wildcat. Fine looking woman too, without the makeup, though she didn't look to bad with it either, he thought reflectively.

Mordecai trudged through the snow laden streets, deep in thought and oblivious to the weather conditions. He'd got it wrong about the woman; she was all the things Jared had said she was. In the years he'd know Jared, his friend hadn't made one decision that he thought was wrong, until he met the woman. Mordecai questioned his own motives as to why he opposed the relationship. Was it because this time Jared hadn't sought his approval? That he'd been openly hostile to Mordecai's remarks? Or did it run much deeper? Was he jealous that this woman would replace him in Jared's affections? Was it because he no longer needed a friend to walk in his shadow? Was it because Jared was now truly his own man? As the biting cold wind threatened to turn into a blizzard, Mordecai came to a decision and stepped back inside the warmth of Ma Crandall's boarding house. He told himself that as soon as the weather broke he was heading back to the ranch. His intentions, though not as clear as he would have liked, were to make up with his friend and wish him well in his own private affairs. If things took their natural course and Jared and Maddie married, well then he'd see whether it was time to head back to Texas. But first he had one chore and one favour to ask.

It was a busy night in the Alhambra, the place was full and the gaming tables were at capacity. There was a boisterous crowd in from the Grant Kohrs spread, *which was much closer to Helena than the McAllister Ranch,* cowboys letting of steam, drinking, gambling and whoring, just like any other typical Friday night in the Alhambra. But Mordecai sensed there was an air of menace hanging over the place the moment he walked in.

He ordered a bottle and sat down in the same seat he'd occupied over the previous two nights and prepared to wait for Maddie to put in an appearance, only this time he was coming hat in hand. As he sipped his drink he cast his eye around the noisy gaming house and soon located the source of that air of menace. A group of five men, dressed in city duds but looking for all the world like the thugs they really were, sat at a table near the bar. From the shape of their clothing he could tell they were armed. Two dance hall girls were keeping them amused with their cavorting and drinking. Drunken hands pawed at the girls whilst they in turn laughed encouragingly. Mordecai observed with disapproval, how the bartender nervously ran a gauntlet of abuse on his way to keeping the five men supplied with liquor. He was obviously the butt of most of their jokes. The Texan felt his hackles rise, he'd never been able to stand bullies, but he turned away. Life had taught him when to butt in and when to keep out. Five heavily armed men, and a gaming house that might be hostile to a lone stranger was all the persuading he needed to steer clear.

When Maddie finally put in an appearance Mordecai stood up and made to walk towards her, only for her to look through him and walk towards the group at the bar. He didn't blame her one bit; after all he'd given her nothing but grief since he arrived. She obviously knew the five men at the bar as she greeted them like long lost friends.

They in turn acknowledged her with some reverence, except the guy Mordecai took to be their leader. He was, as far as Mordecai could judge, a little over six feet tall and slightly better dressed than his companions. His dark striped frock coat and pants suggested wealth, but it was his threateningly cruel eyes and his black swept back hair that set him apart from the others. Also the very fact that the others were drunk and he was not, told Mordecai a great deal. They were a noisy bunch and Maddie laughed and joked along with them.

He continued to watch as she flirted first with one, then another, before she finally settled next to the well dressed man. Not once did she look in his direction. Mordecai felt a strange emotion, one that he'd never experienced before. Then as suddenly as she'd approached them she laughingly gave the well dressed man a kiss on the cheek and sauntered to the other end of the room, joking and flirting with the clientele as she went. A feeling of relief wafted over Mordecai, 'Perhaps it's my paranoia kicking in,' he thought. After all the woman was just going about her work as hostess of the Alhambra.

Whatever it was Mordecai decided he didn't like the well dressed man or his friends. He glared across, not caring if any one of them took offence. At the same time the bartender delivered another bottle to the table. There was no chance that the men had seen him scowl, they were too busy jostling and pushing the barkeeper from one to another. Then the leader slapped the barman across the back of his head and another of the group kicked him up the butt, sending him sprawling. They laughed at the bartender's fear and discomfort. A gun was drawn and fired into the floor inches from the man's feet.

"Dance you son of a bitch, dance!"

Mordecai had had enough. Checking his revolver he began to rise, only to see Maddie race across the room and violently slap the gun out of the man's hand.

"How dare you fire a gun on my premises and treat Sam like that!" The man grinned stupidly. Maddie was as angry as she could be, "Now get the hell outta here right now. All of you." The anger in her eyes was directed mainly towards their leader.

It all happened so fast. The music in the Alhambra stopped and all eyes focused on the small group at the bar.

"Ain't you forgetting I own this joint," said the well dressed man. "Now pick up Bill's gun and hand it to him. Then you can take him upstairs and apologise real good."

Mordecai felt his hackles rise. Someone needed to teach those sons of bitches how to behave, he thought angrily. As the men laughed Mordecai rose to his feet, but before he could say or do anything Maddie spat back "Like hell I will!"

Luke Plummer breathed deeply. "Just this once I'll forget you said that. Now whore, get up them stairs and do what you're good at."

"Luke Plummer, you might own seventy percent of this place but you sure as hell don't own me." You could hear a pin drop as the Alhambra crowd held their collective breath and watched as Maddie reached down pulled a two shot derringer from her boot. In one movement she cocked and aimed it at Plummer's head, "Now get the fuck out!"

Unmoved, Plummer looked at her and smiled. "Two shots if you're lucky, then you're a dead whore."

"Pull the trigger Maddie, I'll back your play," said Mordecai coldly. "You step back," he added to the man called Bill, who was stooping down to retrieve his revolver.

"Who the fuck?"

"You don't want to know," said Mordecai threatening. Although at that precise moment he hoped they'd make a play. "As I said Maddie, pull the trigger if you've a mind."

"Luke, you and your boys get the fuck out!"

Plummer looked down the end of Maddie's derringer then looked across at the man that was siding her play, "Okay boys, let's pay Sadie a visit."

Bill tried again to pick up his gun. "It stays here," said Mordecai.

"That's a fifty dollar pistol," cried Bill.

"It ain't worth dying for," came the cold reply.

At the door Luke Plummer turned around, "I ain't finished with you yet Maddie. Best you pack your things and get out!"

"Ain't you forgetting, I own a third of this establishment. I'll go when I'm good and ready," she said more through bravado than real intent.

"And you stranger. I ain't finished with you either."

Mordecai ignored Plummer's threats and helped the bartender to his feet. It wouldn't be the first time he'd been threatened, but nonetheless he took the threat onboard. Maddie, gun still trained on Plummer, watched as he and his crowd walked across the street. Her hand carrying the derringer began to shake.

"Best I take that," said Mordecai, "before you do some damage with it." And then he saw it, the one thing that had been lacking, the woman, like most delicate objects was vulnerable. How could Jared resist her!

Maddie smiled and let him take charge of the pistol. "I reckon this just about made up my mind," stuttered Maddie nervously.

"Sorry, what was that you said?" said Mordecai.

"Oh nothing, just thinking out loud is all."

CHAPTER 38

Finbar O'Toole, constable of Butte, gunman, head cracker and jailer as he was becoming known around Butte was becoming restless. Justice was swift and brutal in the Montana Territory and Butte was no exception. After a quick trial, Rory Finnan was sentenced to hang and the constable of Butte was to guard his prisoner until the date set. On the 13th March Finbar watched as Rory Finnan dangled from a rope. He cursed and swore while Finbar looked on impassively. He'd half expected Driscoll to put in an appearance, but being the coward that he was, there was no sighting. When Rory Finnan was lowered into a pine box Finbar concluded that, as far as he was concerned, the job of town constable was over.

It had been a tough winter but the thaw came early to that part of Montana Territory. Finbar resigned from his position and loaded up his horse for the journey to Helena. His plan was to find Maddie Dubois, or whatever name she now went by and tell her that there was no one to fear, James Fairfax, alias Half Face, the scourge of the Barbary Coast and whore killer, was no more.

Finbar was surprised when he first caught sight of Helena. She was bigger than he expected and getting bigger by the day *if the new buildings being erected on the outskirts of town were anything to go by.* Big as the town of Helena had become, it didn't take the ex-New York detective long for him to find the whereabouts of Maddie Dubois.

He paused outside the Alhambra, it had been a long journey from the Five Points, but it had been worth it to put the killer of at least five prostitutes in his grave. What mayhem he would have reeked if he hadn't been checked! The gruesome deaths at the gambling den in San Francisco, which might or might not have been caused by Fairfax, gave him cause to shudder.

Finbar ordered a bottle and sat down at a table by the window. He'd handed the bartender his card and asked if Miss Dubois would see him. He knew this was risky, that she might cut and run, but somehow he judged her better than that. At the very least she'd feign no knowledge of what he was talking about.

He glanced up the stairs as a movement caught his eye. Madeline Dubois in all her glory was gliding down the staircase. A steely gaze etched upon her face.

"Mr O'Toole I presume. What is it that you want of me?"

Finbar stood up as she approached his table, an out stretched hand before him. Maddie took his hand and accepted the offered chair that Finbar held for her.

"Would you like a drink?" he said lamely.

"No, Mr O'Toole. I'm a busy woman. Kindly state your business."

"Very well," said Finbar, slightly taken aback by her demeanour. "Firstly I'm not here on official business."

"I'm glad of that," cut in Maddie. Then she smiled and Finbar began to see a thawing of the young woman in front of him.

"I believe we have an acquaintance in common. James Fairfax of New York City." His eyes darted towards her face for any change of expression. There was none. She was good, thought Finbar. A name from the past, one that had made her flee across an entire continent, and there wasn't a whisker of a flinch.

"I know no such man."

"Okay, I'll cut to the chase, if you'll allow me."

"Go on sir, as you've come so far."

"He's dead! I killed him. He won't bother you ever again."

"Dead! You killed him?"

Finbar made to stand up. "Yes dead. But as you don't know the man, I can see I'm wasting my time."

The ruse worked. Maddie softened her tone and urged Finbar to remain seated.

"Tell me, I'm curious, about this man Fairfax."

A knowing smile spread across Finbar's face as he told her about his involvement.

"He'd terrified this young woman called Nancy. He was pure evil. I shot him down like the dog he was in a dark alley in Sacramento."

"Are you sure he's dead?" The anxiety was clear in her voice.

"I put one dead centre of his chest. He's dead alright." Maddie let out a breath. Her face softened, the feelings of relief were clear to see. "I mean you no harm. All I wanted was to bring him to justice. Wipe him from the face of the earth. I just want you to live your life, Miss Devlin."

Maddie smiled, but kept her pretence in place. "Thank you Mr O'Toole. I'm sure who ever this Miss Devlin is, she's very grateful."

Giving her his best Irish smile, Finbar rose from the table, offered his hand and within a few fleeting seconds departed the Alhambra Gaming rooms.

Maddie watched as the retired New York detective stepped onto the boardwalk. She breathed a sigh of relief. She was free. The spectre that hung over her was no more. James Fairfax, sadistic killer of women, was dead.

'Free … that's a funny word,' thought Maddie. 'Free of Fairfax, yes, but not free of the dilemma I'm now faced with. Jared, dear sweet Jared, would be coming to town now that the snows have eased.'

He'd be coming to claim his bride, to sweep Maddie off her feet. She should have been excited, happy even. Why was it that she felt so fearful? She loved him with all her heart, yet things had changed since their last meeting.

Maddie had always been hot blooded, why else would she have turned to prostitution? Despite her father, and even after her near death experience at the hands of Fairfax, she was a woman that loved the company of men. She'd become, over the years, an excellent judge of a man's character. And now finally she'd met the man of her dreams. He'd stirred her heart like no man before him. He was good and kind, strong and dependable, everything a woman could ask for, but....

A lot had happened since they'd last seen each other. If only Jared had waited, if he'd asked her in the spring, things would have been so different. She was torn between her love for Jared and her growing affection for the man known as Mordecai. What kind of a woman was she? Jared was everything she'd ever dreamed of, everything and more than she could ever have hoped for. She saw in him a hope for the future, a stability she'd never known and yes, the chance to get close to her son, all that and the possibility of starting a family of her own. Whereas what kind of life would she have with Mordecai? He was like her; a tormented soul. They both walked on the dark side. But she could see the good in him. He was like Jared, a man you felt safe with, strong and dependable, but with a fault; a volatile nature that could erupt with devastating effect. Life with him would never be dull, a life that she knew; a life, strange as it seemed, where she felt comfortable. It was the life that she'd known virtually all her life.

Maddie ordered a coffee. She looked out the window and saw the New York detective walk into Ma Crandall's boarding house. "Thank you Mister Finbar O'Toole," she said ruefully, "your news hasn't made things any clearer.' She smiled sadly as she sipped on her coffee. It had only been six weeks since Mordecai stepped into her life, six short weeks she mused, as she remembered what happened after the confrontation with Luke Plummer.

It was Mordecai who spoke first after he'd taken the small derringer from her hand.

"Miss Maddie, he won't bother us for awhile. I came here tonight to apologise for my rude and clumsy behaviour and to ask you one little favour."

Maddie invited him to sit down at a nearby table and ordered a bottle. Her face broke into a sweet smile belying the facts of the last few minutes. And then she began to shake. She'd drawn a gun on Luke Plummer. Was it to show him she couldn't be treated that way or did she really intend to shoot him? It was a question she didn't want an answer to.

"Are you okay?" enquired Mordecai, "can I get you a glass of water?"

"No, I'm fine. Now what was that favour?"

"I'd ask that Jared doesn't hear of my rude and clumsy behaviour."

"It's forgotten," said Maddie as a wry smile spread across her face. 'A minute ago he was prepared to kill, now he's as gentle as a lamb, there's more to Mr Mordecai than he gives out,' thought Maddie.

"Thanks, I didn't want Jared getting the wrong idea." His relief clearly detected in his voice. "What's this Plummer to you Miss Dubois, if you don't mine me asking?"

"He owns the Alhambra, well seventy percent of it, but he takes forty percent of my takings."

"Oh I see," said Mordecai, for a moment he'd forgotten where he was.

"I'm a whore, I run the girls, it's what I do." There was mischief behind her eyes. His discomfort caused a perverse kind of amusement.

Her words made him feel awkward and dumb. Feeling he wasn't used to. Quickly he changed the subject, "What's Plummer likely to do?"

"Oh he'll raise merry hell. He won't hit me mind. He's not that dumb. Then I guess things will go back to how they were."

"If he touched you, I'd kill him," said Mordecai. His words chilled Maddie to the bone. She'd seen a fair share of brawls, been in a few too and knew quite well how they could get out of hand. Men died for the merest of insults. The Alhambra had seen its fair share of bloodshed.

"He won't hurt me," she said to reassure him.

"Nonetheless, I reckon to stay here until I'm sure you're okay."

"I don't need a chaperone, or a bodyguard for that matter." Her words were slightly indignant.

"I didn't like the man's tone so until I'm satisfied he means you no harm you're stuck with me."

It was useless to protest. Maddie put her hand on his arm to reassure him, "I'm okay, I'll be fine." She was touched. With the exception of Miles, no one had ever offered her this kind of security before, although given the same circumstances she was sure Jared would have reacted much the same. "So how do you propose to protect me when I go to my room?" she said mischievously.

Mordecai felt himself flush, then clearing his throat he said, "I guess I'll sit outside your room all night."

"Yeah, and you'll be fit to protect me without any sleep," she said sarcastically. "If you've a mind to camp outside my room, you'd be better equipped if you were the other side of the door. That way you get some shut eye yourself."

"I can't do that, what'll people think?"

Maddie revelled in his discomfort, "I don't really care what people think. Right now I've got to go to work. I'll see you later." She smiled and sauntered off in the direction of the gaming tables as if nothing had happened.

"No wonder Jared's crazy about you," he said under his breath as he watched her move through the crowded bar room, flirting and laughing like she hadn't a care in the world. An unfamiliar feeling crept over him. The thought that she'd be having a poke with one of them fat cat copper barons or some banker really stuck in his craw. She was marrying his best friend and it just didn't seem right. Yet as he watched her work the room he remembered that many of the men he had known had married prostitutes. In the west it was more than acceptable. In fact, some of the biggest cattle barons had married them and they'd made good wives. Yet it still hurt to see his best friend's girl cavorting with riff raff. That unfamiliar feeling wouldn't go away.

As she talked with a guy at the bar, Mordecai managed to catch her eye. He motioned her over to the table. "What do you want, I'm working?" She said it a little sharp and regretted it.

"Don't take this wrong. Hear me out before you go off half cocked. How much do you expect to earn tonight?"

"It's a busy night, I could expect to make a hundred dollars and upwards, if I've a mind."

"If I've a mind. What's that mean?"

"It means," and there was hostility in her voice, "I run seven girls, so I can pick and choose who I sleep with, if I've a mind," she added sarcastically. "Look Mordecai, Jared don't own me, he knows what I do."

"I bet he don't like it."

"You're probably right, but until I decide to marry him it's my business." she said, slightly irritated with the way the conversation was going.

"Okay, I get you're point. I'm slow to learn that's all. A hundred a night, I'll pay you a hundred; for your time. Nothing else."

"What!"

"Yeah, seems I like your company." He gave her a boyish smile, something she'd never seen in him the three days she'd known him.

"Spring's about six weeks away, are you sure you can afford me?" She smiled quickly in case he hadn't seen the joke.

He had, "We'll negotiate."

They were sitting drinking coffee the following afternoon when Luke Plummer walked into the Alhambra. He smiled in their direction and walked up to their table. As he did he opened his coat to show he wasn't armed.

"I'm here to clear things up," said Plummer. "Things got a little out of hand, that's all."

"Then you'll apologise to the lady," said Mordecai.

"It shouldn't have happened. There's no profit in trouble," Plummer said in way of an apology.

"I'll buy that," said Maddie, knowing that was as far as Plummer was prepared to go.

"As you're aware, this town is growing up fast. It's a law abiding place. People want to have fun, let off steam and generally have a good time."

"What's your point?" said Mordecai gruffly.

"My point is there's law and there's the law of the vigilante. You may have seen the posters all over town. What's the point in us starting a little war? We all lose. Well, what I'm trying to say is let bygones be bygones. A clean slate, start over. There's money to be made in this town."

"That's it?" stated Mordecai.

"That's it, business as usual," replied Plummer. "My men and I were a little out of order."

"Well actually Luke, I've been meaning to talk to you about business. I'm quitting as of the end of the month. You can buy me out or I'll leave it open to offers. If the girls want to work for you that's okay, but I'm out," said Maddie firmly. She'd been dreading telling him but after the night before it came easy. She also wanted Mordecai to know that that part of her life was well and truly over.

"Fine, Maddie. Whatever you say. I'll be sorry to lose you." He made small talk for a few minutes then he offered his hand to Mordecai, but his gesture was ignored. "Right I'll see you around. We'll talk some more about the business side of things after I've spoken to the bank."

"I'd appreciate that," said Maddie.

Luke Plummer tipped his hat and turned on his heels.

"That was too easy," said Mordecai after Plummer left. "A man like that is as treacherous as a rattlesnake that's been cornered."

"You're right Mordecai, but if I miss my guess I'd say it's because of the 3-7-77 posters that have been going up around town."

"The what?"

"Vigilantes; Montana's not-so-legal law enforcement. Come to think of it, Luke Plummer has the same surname as Montana's most famous badman come sheriff, Henry Plummer."

"What's this Henry Plummer got to do with Vigilantes?"

"Very little seeing as they took him out and lynched him in 1864."

"So what do these numbers mean?"

"I don't rightly know, some say it's the dimensions of a grave, others that it's some Masonic sign. All I know is, since the birth of this 3-7-77 violent crime in Helena has been low." Then Maddie added a codicil, more as a warning, "Though back shootings and stabbing that go undetected have risen of late. And I reckon Luke Plummer could well be a back shooter."

"Well Maddie, looks like I'll have to watch your back and you'll have to look after mine."

"We'll have to stay in the bright lights," added Maddie.

For a week they did just that, taking in the rounds, dining in Helena's most popular restaurants and even spending a night at the theatre, but they drew a line at going to the opera. Surprisingly Maddie found he was both charming and very eloquent. His knowledge far surpassed that of her own, revealing in her eyes an educated background, so much so that she asked him about his learning.

"It's just books. I read everything I can get my hands on. I've always had an inquisitive mind. Don't know where I get it from."

At the end of each evening he would see her to her room, observing a sense of propriety. And it didn't stop there, as Maddie found out on that first night he stayed in her room. He rigged up some kind of makeshift curtain made out of burlap sacking, which he draped across the centre of the room. It touched her that he was concerned for her privacy. 'What is it with these men from Texas that has them behaving so gentlemanly?' she thought as she retired to bed.

Maddie spoke about most things, including, though not as detailed, her flight from Fairfax, but surprisingly she'd held back on the subject of her son. Why? Was it because it might set up a barrier? Become an obstacle that Mordecai thought his friend Jared couldn't overcome? Or was there a deeper seated reason why she'd not mentioned him? Then, in the middle of their second week, after a very pleasant evening when both had retired to their side of the curtain, Maddie decided to broach the subject.

"Did Jared tell you I had a child?"

"No, he never mentioned it at all." 'And why would he?' thought Mordecai. I was too wrapped up in my own self pity.

"He lives with a nice couple over in Bismarck," she said in a tentative way. "He'll be about six now. He was my husband's child," she said by way of justification. "After my husband was killed at the Little Big Horn, I was thrown into a panic about my unborn child. How would I cope without the army's backing? I couldn't bear bringing him up in a world of poverty." She'd already told him about her upbringing but she couldn't help going over it again. "You see, I was born dirt poor and there was no way I could inflict that on my child. He's better off with the Langleys than with me. I just didn't realise how much I'd miss him." Then without warning the tears came.

"Are you crying?" he said from his side of the burlap sacking.

"I'm sorry, I'm just being foolish," she said as she tried to shrug off her emotions, but it was no use. Her body wracked with grief, as for the first time she bared her soul fully. Mordecai, uncomfortable with the situation, pushed aside the makeshift curtain and reached out for her. She let herself fall willingly into his arms where he held her tightly and waited for the sobbing to subside. When it did, it was too late.

CHAPTER 39

The weather had broken and spring was everywhere. A troubled Mordecai stared down the empty street and wondered when Jared would arrive. He kept telling himself that his intentions had always been honourable, but what kind of a man lets himself fall into such temptation? He'd known from the first time he'd set eyes on Maddie why Jared had been so attracted to her. She was the most beautiful woman he'd ever seen. And even though they'd got off on the wrong foot, Mordecai kept telling himself that he was only looking out for his friend's best interests. As he continued to stare aimlessly down the street his mind kept going over the events that would made their meeting so painful.

When he'd held her in his arms and tasted the sweetness of her tears he'd known that things had changed between them. When her crying subsided he looked into those watery eyes and saw that she felt the same. It was wrong, he knew it was so very wrong but he couldn't help himself as his lips brushed against hers. She kissed him gently in return. Then for a second they paused as if giving themselves time to back away, but it was too late. There was no guilt as he responded, kissing her with more urgency as they fell back onto the bed. He could taste the wine on her lips, wine they'd consumed earlier together as friends, but now shared as lovers. She was his for the taking, not bought like so many others, but his because she wanted him, giving of herself, as if in some primeval sacrifice. Locked in each others arms, not a word passed their lips until it was over.

The moon cast its eerie blue grey light through the window exposing his corded arm muscles wrapped around the alabaster flesh of her naked body. They lay silently transfixed in time, lost in the intimacy of each other's arms until sleep overtook them.

He awoke early with the realisation of what they'd done. Sitting up in bed he gazed down at the woman sleeping peacefully beside him and strange as it seemed, he too, felt at peace. He'd slept with his best friend's future bride but at that precise moment that didn't matter. He wanted her like he'd never wanted anyone, not even Laura. As he continued to gaze at her his heart surged and a feeling of panic caused it to beat rapidly. He prayed that when Maddie awoke she'd feel the same about him as he did about her.

Maddie's eyes flickered, then like a flower opening up to the sun they stared up at him. Mordecai searched her face, and could find no remorse, no guilt and no regret. She looked up at him with a sleepy gaze and smiled.

"Good morning. Did you sleep well?"

"Yes, I slept well. Better, than I've done in years."

It was small talk and they both knew it. They were skating around each other until Maddie broke the uneasy politeness between them.

"Last night," she said, "last night was wonderful and I don't regret a damn thing. At this moment in time I've never been happier."

Mordecai's heart skipped a beat, "I'm glad you're happy, in fact I couldn't be happier myself, bu … but what about Jared?"

Maddie face changed slightly, "I know, but don't spoil it just yet. Can't we just enjoy the moment?"

"Yes my darling. I can't think of anything I'd like more," he stuttered.

"Come back to bed," she said invitingly.

Mordecai slipped beneath the sheets.

Over dinner that night Maddie surprised him with her frankness.

"I think I love both of you. I know that's unfair, but its how I feel. Until I met Jared I hadn't ever felt that way. I've tried figuring it out, but I can't." She shook her head and stared down at her uneaten food, then she looked up into his apprehensive eyes. "I always thought I was a woman of the world, one who was able to control my emotions whatever life threw at me, but I was wrong." Her heart went out to him as she saw the look of trepidation creep across Mordecai's face. She didn't want to play games. Life was so unfair.

"You're saying last night was a mistake?"

"Yes, and no. I knew there was chemistry between us from the moment we first met. It confused the hell out of me. Like I said, I love both of you. I want both of you, but I know that's impossible. Neither of you are the type to accept those terms."

Mordecai slowly nodded in agreement. He loved this woman, yet he loved Jared like a brother. He owed him a debt. It wasn't the small matter of him saving his life; it was deeper, much deeper.

"Go on."

"You could make this easy. If you told Jared about us, he'd never look at me again, but then I wouldn't have to choose." she paused, judging his reaction. It was as she'd suspected. He looked shocked and bemused.

"I' … I couldn't do that to him," he said.

"I know you couldn't. You see, I'm weak, and I've always thought I was strong, but I'm weak where you and Jared are concerned. I hate myself for it, I've no pride left." She choked back the urge to break down. "We could go away together, but that's the coward's way out, and I know you won't do that. You love him, you love him as surely as I do and you wouldn't hurt him for the world. But you might if I chose you."

"I don't know what to say." Mordecai looked at this woman before him and knew he was in an impossible situation. "Jared's my best friend, but I can't help myself. I suppose I've known it since we first met. I didn't, couldn't believe that you'd feel the same way. I've never felt this way before. I love you."

"I love you too."

"Then lets enjoy the moment while we can," he said hopefully, although deep down he knew it would be Jared she'd choose. He knew it because there was a stability in Jared that was missing in him. He'd only known her a few days, but it was enough for him to know that only Jared could make her truly happy.

Mordecai's mind set over the next four weeks surprised even him. In Maddie he'd found a true equal. She knew the true extent of their situation but chose to put it to the back of her mind. He thought, unkindly that she was able to deal with it better because of her profession, but he was wrong. Nothing had prepared Maddie for what was happening. When he broached the subject whilst they were laying in each others arms, she began to cry.

"I'm sorry," he said, "I didn't …"

Before he could say anymore Maddie cut in, "Oh it's just me being silly. You might think me a heartless bitch, but I'm not. You see Mordecai, all my life I've had to cope with hardship. I had no childhood, all I knew was filth and squalor and heartbreak. I watched each of my brothers and sisters as they struggled into this world and I watched as they left it. I loved each and every one of them, but after a time I began to distance myself from the inevitable and enjoyed what time I had with them. That's why I'm the way I am."

Mordecai loved her then more at that moment than he'd thought possible. "Maddie, we're two of a kind. My life ain't been a bed of roses. At seventeen I enlisted in the Confederacy, fought my one and only battle at Palmito Hill where I killed my first man. I shot him from a distance with my rifle and had to watch as his life ebbed away. It turned my stomach. I wanted to take back what I'd done but it was no use. Then it was all over, the war had ended. We'd lost and then the bitterness kicked in. I drifted for a while but then I got in with the wrong crowd, killed a couple of men, and it didn't feel the same." His mind wandered for a brief moment, "They needed killing," he added quickly. "Then I met Laura and everything changed. I got married, had two kids and for a while I had it all, then luck turned against me."

Maddie put her arm around him, "I so sorry," she said softly. She hoped he would open up more but he remained silent for a minute before continuing.

"Maddie, I'm a violent man, I always have been. I managed to keep it under control for Laura and the kids. When things changed between us I became the man I'd always been. I saw lives destroyed over nothing and I didn't feel anything." The full horror of what happened after he'd found the remains of his family flashed through his mind. Quickly, for fear of losing Maddie, he banished the vision in his head. "It was Jared, he helped me change, and for that I owe him a greater debt than you'll ever know. He's a good man Maddie."

"I know," said Maddie softly. She wanted to press him further, but knew that now was not the time. She'd come to realise that Mordecai was a very private man. That he was still struggling with his demons was obvious. Something, maternal perhaps, tugged at her heart. If she chose him over Jared would she be able to fight the demons that haunted him. She was only too aware that he and Jared had some personal history. Something Jared had said led her to believe it was both sad and terrifying. But then she thought of Mordecai's last words, "He's a good man." He'd said it with love in his heart. Maddie silently cursed herself for falling into this predicament. What they had was the moment.

They enjoyed the moment for a little over three weeks, and then the thaw set in. Neither one of them mentioned it but both knew that Jared would soon be coming to claim his bride. Up until then Maddie had put off making a decision about her future. She had to admit the past few weeks had been wonderful, and deep down she didn't want it to end. She knew that with Mordecai the devil was not far from the surface, but she knew she had unlocked a softer gentler side to his nature.

When Finbar O'Toole had walked into the Alhambra and spoke about killing Fairfax she'd felt a great weight lift from her shoulders. Yet the lightness she felt caused her even greater concern. With Fairfax gone, nothing or no one could stand in her way of settling down, the scales *and she hated to think of it that way* had tipped in Jared's favour.

Maddie was quiet over dinner and Mordecai knew that the subject of his best friend couldn't be avoided any longer.

"I had a visitor this morning, a New York detective called Finbar O'Toole."

"What did he want?"

"He told me Fairfax was dead, that he'd killed him in an alley in Sacramento."

"Why'd he tell you that? How'd he know you'd be interested?" The tone in his voice showed concern.

"I dunno. From what I can gather he'd been tracking Fairfax for years. Said he knew all about what happened with me, that now I could breathe easier at night. I reckon he wanted to give me peace of mind."

"Nonetheless I reckon I'll pay this Finbar O'Toole a visit."

Maddie looked worried but did little to persuade Mordecai to cease his endeavours on her behalf. The man might be who he said he was but then again he might not.

Finbar was getting ready to pack when Mordecai knocked on his door. "Who is it?" said O'Toole as he concealed his revolver under a jacket that lay across the bed.

"Name's Mordecai, I'm a friend of Maddie Dubois. I'd like a few moments of your time."

Finbar reached under his jacket and felt the familiar feel of the walnut butt, a feeling that gave him some degree of confidence.

"You'd better come in, I was kind of expecting Miss Dubois herself."

Mordecai entered the room cautiously and noted the hand of the man seated by the bed. "Easy Mister, I mean you no harm."

Finbar removed his hand from beneath his jacket and pointed the snub nosed Colt at the stranger, "I mean you no harm either, state your business."

"It pays to be cautious," said Mordecai amiably. "Your message this morning caused Miss Dubois some distress. She'd like to know your part in this affair."

Finbar lowered the revolver, "I'm sorry, you can't be to careful. Has Miss Dubois told you anything of our conversation?"

"You mean her real name's Deirdre Devlin and she worked out of a whorehouse in New York. Well, yeah I'd say she told me about that conversation."

Finbar relaxed and pushed the gun back under the jacket. "What is it you want to know?"

"Well to begin with, where do you figure in this?"

Finbar produced a half full bottle of bourbon and offered Mordecai a swig, then he told him everything he knew about Fairfax, Maddie's miraculous escape, the fire and the killings and finally how he'd corned Half-Face in a back alley in Sacramento. "He was a monster, he deserved killing and that poor girl needed to know that. I can only imagine what torment she's been through over the past few years."

Mordecai could see the killing of Fairfax weighed heavily on his conscience.

"He the first man you killed?"

"First man in cold blood, yeah. I killed a man up in Butte a few weeks later. It's funny how much easier it was the second time."

Mordecai nodded his agreement.

"Ain't that the truth." Then he thanked him for his honesty and bid him farewell. As he crossed the street to the Alhambra he made a decision. The bald detective had crossed a continent to rid Maddie of the vermin who had stalked her. He'd gone against his God and taken a life in cold blood. His sacrifice had cleared the way for Maddie and although it hurt like hell, Mordecai knew he'd have to make a similar sacrifice. He loved the girl so much that he could see no other option.

Chapter 40

Maddie could sense the tenseness in Mordecai over dinner at Waldo's restaurant. She knew he was troubled over the impending return of Jared and he'd been unusually quiet after his meeting with Mr O'Toole.

"What is it my love? What's troubling you?"

Mordecai shifted awkwardly in his seat, his eyes cast down.

"I think it's about time I told you what happened between me and Jared. I want you to know just what kind of a man I really am."

"I know what kind of a man you are. You're good and kind, gentle but firm. I know you killed in anger, but there's no one man or woman for that matter here in Helena who hasn't done something dreadful in their past."

Mordecai looked up at Maddie's sweet, but sensuous face, stared into those dark almond shaped eyes and knew he could never love anyone as much as he loved her. His smile was tinged with sadness. He so wanted this woman, but he knew that, after he'd told her of the horrors that still haunted him, she would never look at him in the same way again.

He began by telling her about catching up with Laura and his kids to find he'd arrived too late to help them. How he'd decided to take as many of the red devils with him before he died. Then came the timely intervention of this stranger called Jared McAllister.

As he began his narration it all flooded back.

"You're in no fit state to take off after the Comanche."

"They killed my family! I've no other choice. Did you see what they did to them? They need killing, every last one of them sons of bitches."

"They were your family, oh Jesus I'm so sorry!"

In the space of twenty four hours Jared had killed at least three men. Before that he'd never fired a shot in anger, now he was left with the choice of more killing or of leaving the man to fight them alone. Judging by the signs, there were eight Comanche braves, more than enough to overwhelm the two white men in open country. It was sheer madness but Jared felt he had little choice but to accompany the man called Mordecai.

That first night they made cold camp Mordecai sensed the Comanche were close by. They slept in shifts; Jared taking the first watch, while Mordecai lay in his bedroll with a revolver in hand. Later as he willed himself to sleep, Jared prayed that Mordecai would cease his pursuit of the Comanche.

He awoke before dawn, cold and hungry. Mordecai handed him a slice of jerky, it was the only rations they had between them. Jared had stashed it into his saddlebags before the nightmare. He ventured once more to try changing Mordecai's mind.

"We've followed them savages for nigh on a couple of days, what say we call it a day?"

"Would you if it had been your family? You call it a day. You done enough for me. I can't. I'll ride on alone. I ain't quitting until they are all dead or I'll die trying." He checked the loads in his pistol as if to make a point, "It ain't really your fight."

"I didn't say I was quitting, all I said was we'd given it our best shot."

"Well our best shot just ain't good enough. I know we're close, I can almost smell them."

Mordecai forced the pace and by mid afternoon they caught their first sight of the Comanche. They were like dots on the horizon at least half a day's ride away. To follow was impossible. Across the staked plains they'd be spotted easily.

"We have to wait until nightfall," said Mordecai. "Best we rest up until then."

As night came they made their way with only the North Star to guide them. When they were close Jared suggested tying rags to the horses' hooves to muffle the sound. It was almost dawn when they crested a small bluff. As they reined their horses to a halt they spied the band of Comanche taking their sustenance at a small watering hole. Both men quickly brought their horses back below the crest and prayed the Comanche hadn't seen them. Tying their horses to some brush they inched forward on their bellies towards the crest. They were in luck; the Comanche were too busy drinking from the hole that they'd failed to post guard. They'd taken a beating at the adobe outpost but had left the occupants of it in no fit state to follow, *or so they thought.* There were eight braves and fourteen horses, five carrying their dead. From the bluff Jared and Mordecai had a clear view of the wasteland. There wouldn't be a better opportunity.

"How are you with that Henry?" whispered Mordecai.

"Pretty good at shooting turkeys, but injuns....?"

"We got us a chance to reduce the odds. We ain't gonna get a better chance."

Jared looked at his companion and realised that within a short while they could both be dead. It was a prospect he didn't take kindly to. He levelled his rifle and took careful aim.

"Let's do it!"

Mordecai jacked a round into the breech of his Henry, "Why not!"

'Crack, crack, crack.' Two Comanche fell like they'd been pole axed. Another spun around and grabbed at his shoulder. The remaining five raced to their horses.

"Shoot the horses! Shoot the fucking horses!" screamed Mordecai.

Jared quickly took aim and fired off four rounds killing two outright and wounding one other. The heat from the forestock of the Henry burnt into his hand *reminding him of the new Winchester he'd examined at Halstead's hardware store in Uvalde.* At the same time Mordecai worked the lever of his Henry and brought down five more. The remaining Comanche kicked their horses away from the range of the Henry repeaters. They circled and let out bloodcurdling war cries but they didn't come within range.

"Jesus H Christ!" exclaimed Jared, "I think I know who that one is," he added breathlessly, as he pointed to a tall brave wearing a wolf's head with the skin and fur draping over his broad shoulders, "That's 'Kills like the Wolf,' if I miss my guess."

Kills like the Wolf reared his horse and held his rifle out in defiance as he shouted profanities at his unknown assailants. His men circled and war whooped but came no further than Kills like the Wolf. These Comanche had learned of the white man's prowess with the long gun. Undoubtedly some, if not all, had fought at Adobe Walls, where twenty eight buffalo hunters had held over five hundred braves at bay with their Sharps buffalo guns.

Frustrated by the inactivity and taunts of the Comanche, Mordecai raged. Jared cautioned about him doing anything rash.

"Them fucking Comanche, they'll wait until dark then they'll either collect their dead and wounded or they'll come for our scalps. I ain't waiting for neither."

"What you planning on doing? I ain't in this for the fun of it!" spat Jared.

"I know you ain't," said Mordecai. "I just mean to stir them sons of bitches up some."

Before Jared could do anything Mordecai had mounted his horse and rode back down their side of the bluff. Jared waited. Sweat trickled into his eyes, stinging them in the process. He retrained his rifle on the mounted Comanche, who, to relieve their boredom, were showing off their horsemanship to each other by racing their horses across the staked plains in zig-zag patterns. His growing curiosity as to what Mordecai was up too, mounted. He wiped away sweat from his brow and hands and waited.

As two of the Comanche raced towards each other in a display of horsemanship, the like of which he'd never seen before, a lone rider raced towards the watering hole. Kills like the Wolf saw him first and levelled his rifle across his strong forearm and took careful aim. Mordecai raced forward, reins in his teeth, guns blazing. Then, with bullets flying past him, he reined in his horse near the dead Indians. His eyes scanned and searched the area until he found what he was looking for. Kills like the Wolf fired repeatedly but missed his target. With a bow or a war club he had no equal, but he hadn't yet mastered the white man's weapon, but he was not foolish enough to come into the range of Jared's Henry rifle.

"What the fuck's he doing?" mumbled Jared. Then it became obvious as Mordecai remounted his steed and began the race back to relative safety. A body seemed to move, to follow the rider. It was then that Jared realised what Mordecai was up to, he was dragging the wounded Comanche by a rope he'd attached to the pommel of his saddle.

"Jesus H Christ!" swore Jared.

Kills like the Wolf and his band made to follow but Jared's Henry *now with a rag wrapped around the forestock* kept them at bay. Minutes later Mordecai arrived back on the ridge with his captive. Suffering from loss of blood, battered from being dragged for half a mile, he looked more dead than alive.

"What the fuck's going on?"

"You'll see, watch and learn."

Close to the top of the bluff was an old gnarled tree. Mordecai dragged the half dead Indian to the tree and hauled him up with the rope around his neck until he was standing on tip-toes.

"Shoot him, Mordecai. Put the son of a bitch out of his misery."

"No Jared, you don't get it. Do we fear those red devils, you bet your sweet ass we do, but do they fear us? No! But they sure as hell will after I've finished with this bastard."

There was craziness in his eyes which left Jared rooted to the spot. He was sure that at that precise moment if he made the wrong move he'd have been as dead as the Indians lying at the watering hole.

Mordecai splashed some water over the man's head to revive him. Then he hurriedly gathered sticks and brush which he placed around the petrified Comanche's feet.

"Oh Jesus No!" cried Jared.

Mordecai ignored the plea, and reaching into his pocket, he found the makings and lit up an old stogie. Then he bent down and nurtured a small fire from the brush and dried sticks. Within seconds the brush crackled and spat. The Indian's screams pierced the air as the flames licked at his feet.

Kills like the Wolf stared in horror, as the flames began to engulf the warrior. His powers were diminishing; he could only watch as the brave began writhing in agony, his screams pierced the morning sky.

For Spotted Horse, it was too much. He couldn't watch as his younger brother was being burned alive. He spurred his horse forward. Two other braves followed.

"Stop!" cried Kills like the Wolf.

But it was too late; the screams from the bluff muffled his command.

"Now you see," said Mordecai as he trained his rifle on one of the fast approaching braves. Jared, still shocked by what he'd just witnessed stood for a second before he too took up a stance and raised his rifle.

'Crack, crack, crack.' One brave flew backwards from his horse, another ducked behind his mare and continued his suicidal charge.

Spotted Horse his face contorted by rage, spurred his horse first to the left, then the right. He fired at the two men and would have hit Jared if he hadn't over balanced at that very moment.

Mordecai laughed as the two braves descended on him. He dropped his rifle and pulled his Navy Colt from its holster. He held the gun at arms length and squeezed the trigger. He fired twice more before he saw the rage slip from Spotted Horse's face. The Comanche slipped harmlessly to the ground in front of him.

Jared, using his rifle as a club, downed the remaining Comanche. He was up almost immediately, knife in hand. Jared swung the rifle again and the Indian dropped to the ground. He swung it twice more breaking the stock before the man died.

The screams from the burning man ceased at almost the same moment as the fight ended. Mordecai stood on the crest of the bluff and let out a blood curdling cry as he raised his hands, still clasping his pistol high into the air.

"Now they fear us!" he screamed.

The smell of burning flesh choked the morning air. Jared gagged as he stared at the back of Mordecai and beyond to the two figures on horseback on the desert floor.

Kills like the Wolf glared back. Rage and anger gave way to a very strange feeling. It was an emotion he'd never experienced before; it was the smell of fear. This white man, this crazy white man had ridden after them and killed six of his men and one in a way that matched the cruelty of his own methods. Something told him the man was not finished yet, that before the next moon one, or both of them, would be dead. He gave the man on the bluff one last look before turning his horse. As he rode away from the carnage he began to chant his death song. Plenty Coups looked at his leader and he too began to sing.

Jared looked back as the buzzards started circling, while Mordecai looked straight ahead. It was only a few hours since the fight but it seemed like a lifetime had sped past. Jared felt old, older than he'd thought possible. The man in front was obsessed and only the complete destruction of Kills like the Wolf and his companion would satisfy Mordecai's bloodlust. Jared had tried persuading him that his mission had been accomplished.

"He's a walking dead man. He led a war party of fifteen men and he lost them all save one. I know these people, to lose face is everything. He was a great war chief, now he's nothing. Give it up Mordecai."

"I can't, it's not in my nature," he said coldly, then added almost as an after thought, "It's who I am." Mordecai managed a weak smile and turned towards Jared, his hand extended. "You've been a good friend. You've done more than was asked of you. From now on I'll go it alone."

"The hell you will! I never said I was quitting, I just thought that today would have been the end of it for you."

"It's over when I say it's over." Mordecai turned and mounted his horse. He looked towards the distant horizon then kicked the animal to a walk and headed east. Jared stared after him, and then he mounted his bay gelding and fell in silently behind.

With provisions salvaged from the dead Comanches they continued the pursuit, but they'd kept at a deliberate slow pace. Loss of face or not, the man known as Kills like the Wolf was still a dangerous animal, now probably more so. For two days they followed sign, ever wary that Kills like the Wolf could double back and kill them in their sleep.

On the third day Jared looked at the terrain and surrounding countryside.

"Jesus H Christ. I think I know were Kills like the Wolf is heading!"

"What do you mean?"

"He's heading for the Clear Fork of the Brazos. It used to be a Comanche reservation until they moved them to Oklahoma. I heard tell a few Comanche have been seen loitering in them parts. That was a while back, but I reckon it's worth lookin into."

Mordecai pondered Jared's hunch, "If we travelled by night do you figure we could get there before Kills like the Wolf."

"It's possible."

"Then let's get to it."

To avoid bumping into Kills like the Wolf in the dark Jared had suggested they ride in a wide loop to reach the Brazos River. The sounds of the fast flowing waters of the river alerted them that they'd almost reached their destination. In silence both men dismounted and walked their horses along the bank of the Brazos. Not a word was spoken as they inched their way forward. Within minutes the acrid smell of smoke twitched at Jared's nostrils.

"We're close," he whispered.

Leaving the horses tied to an old Cottonwood they stopped and inspected their weapons. Mordecai turned the cylinders of his two Navy Colts to check that the powder was dry before moving forward. Jared did likewise.

The smoke had told them they were not alone, but was it Kills like the Wolf? The answer came as dawn broke across the silent desert. The source of the smoke was coming from a lone tepee.

A woman emerged suddenly from the tepee causing both men to flatten themselves into the sand. They watched as she approached the Brazos with a clay pot in her hands. As she bent down to catch the water from the swift flowing river her eye caught a sudden movement to her right. She glanced up and looked straight at the two men. She screamed, dropped the pot and raced for the tepee.

"Oh shit," cried Jared as he and Mordecai scrambled to their feet.

From the tepee raced two small children. The woman quickly grabbed them and gathered them behind her. Her eyes were wide with terror, she was shaking and she shouted something in Comanche. Jared guessed she was just terrified at seeing two white men. Mordecai and Jared stood in the open, guns held firmly in their hands.

"We mean you no harm," cried Jared in broken Comanche. The fear in the woman's eyes told them they'd beaten Kills like the Wolf to his destination.

"Easy," said Jared in a subdued tone, as he crept slowly towards the Comanche squaw and her offspring as they backed into the tepee.

Kills like the Wolf heard his woman's cry. He motioned for Plenty Coups to circle behind the camp. It did not surprise him much. The crazy one carried much bad medicine. It must have brought him from the sky.

Plenty Coups trod silently to within forty feet of the unsuspecting white men. Hidden behind some Cottonwoods and brush he watched as Kills like the Wolf crept ever closer to the tall dark crazy man. Then he switched his attentions to the fair headed man as he moved toward the woman. Plenty Coups drew back his bow and measured the distance his arrow would take to reach its target. He would count coup before he killed the white eye. At this distance he couldn't miss, but where would the honour be in killing from hiding?

Plenty Coups unleashed the arrow. 'Swoosh.' The arrow hit its mark and spun Jared around. He'd been hit so hard in the leg that the impact knocked him off balance. Shocked and full of pain Jared retched into the sand just as Plenty Coups let out a bloodcurdling cry and hurled himself forward, war club in one hand a coup stick in the other. Jared's eyes grew wide with terror at the fearsome sight of the advancing Comanche. He fired wildly, missing the Indian as he advanced. It all happened in a split second, but somehow Jared pulled himself together. He knew he faced certain death and an eerie calm came over him. He cocked the hammer, aimed and fired in quick succession crack, crack, crack, crack, click. His gun was empty yet the Indian kept on coming. Plenty Coups hurled himself at the wounded man, who flailed at the Comanche with his unloaded Navy Colt. They grappled for what seemed like an eternity, but in fact was little over a few seconds. Plenty Coups's grip on his war club loosened, his eyes glazed over and he died. Jared kept hitting him with his pistol until suddenly and violently it was kicked from his hand. Startled he looked up into the barrel of an old Dragoon Colt held menacingly in the hand of Kills like the Wolf.

"Crazy man, listen to me!" roared Kills like the Wolf, his face menacingly turned towards Mordecai. The swiftness of the attack had surprised even the Texan, who'd also fired into the body of Plenty Coups. He trained his gun on Kills like the Wolf, but did not fire. "My fight is with you Crazy man. The Gods have spoken."

At that moment his woman and his children appeared at the entrance to the tepee. In the guttural tongue of the Comanche he ordered her back inside.

"I shoot him, you shoot me. We fight you and me, one great warrior against another. You win he lives. I win he dies quickly."

"You speak good English," said Mordecai without emotion. The Comanche stared defiantly at Mordecai but the Dragoon Colt was still pointed only inches from Jared's head. Mordecai's finger tightened on the trigger. He knew that if he fired the Comanche chief's last reaction would be to blow Jared's brains all over the desert floor.

Suddenly Kills like the Wolf lashed at Jared with his moccasin bound feet, sending the white man sprawling in the dirt. His Dragoon Colt was now trained on Mordecai. It was a Mexican standoff.

"Why? Why did you track us so hard? The woman, she was nothing to you"

"She was my wife! The children were my children!"

"Ah, I understand," said Kills like the Wolf, "and you want to kill me, slowly I think."

"Any way it comes."

Kills like the Wolf puffed himself up to his full height, which was about six four and grinned, showing off a set of perfectly white teeth. "She fought, your woman, she fought me hard, but she liked it when I was inside her." His words were supposed to anger Mordecai into a mistake, but he didn't flinch. "The brat, the youngest, I dashed her brains out against a tree," he laughed but his eyes were searching for a reaction.

"Which is what I aim to do to those kids in the tepee after I've killed you," replied Mordecai coldly.

Kills like the Wolf's eyes glared with anger. "We fight, me and you," he grinned defiantly at Mordecai. That the white eye would accept his challenge he had no doubt. Mordecai nodded.

Kills like the Wolf lowered the Dragoon Colt slightly and with his other hand produced his war club. Mordecai in turn pulled a knife from his belt. As one, both men dropped their guns in the dirt. Jared had regained consciousness and had pulled himself up with his arms and watched in horror as both men prepared for battle.

Kills like the Wolf's grin faded from his lips as Mordecai reached behind his back with his right hand and pulled another Navy Colt from his belt. He aimed it at Kills like the Wolf's mid section and cocked and fired twice. The look on Kills like the Wolf's face contorted even more when Mordecai stepped aside and fired once more into the Comanche's right temple. The big Indian dropped like a stone.

The pain in Jared's side began to hurt. It was over, they'd survived against the odds, but then he saw that Mordecai's wrath was not nearly over. He'd grabbed the woman by the hair and had thrown her onto the ground with her man.

"I made your man a promise, I intend keeping it!" he screamed at her.

Jared shouted, "No! Mordecai it's over let them go!"

The dark haired Texan was crazy with vengeance, there was no way Jared could reason with him. His eyes blazed pure hatred. He watched helplessly as Mordecai cocked and aimed his Colt at the scared woman.

Without a thought for his wounds Jared grabbed up the old Colt. "Don't do it! So help me God, I'll drop you where you stand!" he cried, now half standing but pointing the cocked Dragoon Colt at his friend. "I'll blow you fucking brains from here to hell if you even twitch."

"He killed my family...."

"I know he did," said Jared sympathetically. "I know he did. But killing them won't bring your family back. You'll be as bad and evil as that son of a bitch lying at your feet. It's over Mordecai, it's over...."

Mordecai weary from reliving the horror of that time turned to Maddie, "We stayed like that for almost an hour, before he collapsed. By then the woman and her kids were gone. Jared had shouted something to her in Comanche, she ups and runs with the kids. She caught Kills like the Wolf's horse and that of the other brave and high tailed it outta there."

"We all do things we're not proud of," said Maddie as her gentle hands brushed the side of his head.

"But don't you see, if Jared hadn't have stopped me, I'd have killed his woman and kids and kept my promise to Kills like the Wolf."

"But you didn't. You're not like the Comanche."

"That's just the point if Jared hadn't intervened when he did, I'd have killed them all. I owe him far more than I can pay."

CHAPTER 41

Maddie hardly slept a wink that night. She'd listened intently to Mordecai's story and understood why he felt such a debt to Jared. Their story was horrible in the extreme but it only confirmed to her what her heart had been saying for weeks. Mordecai was like her; damaged goods. He'd been carrying this guilt around with him for nearly six years and even though Jared had saved him from himself it had brought little comfort. He now saw a way to repay his best friend. It wouldn't heal the wound but in Mordecai's mind it would go a long way towards repaying the debt. He'd sought to sacrifice his own happiness, misguidedly believing she'd be better off with Jared. That he loved her, she had no doubt. But, did he believe her when she said she reciprocated that love? His clumsy attempt to kill off any feelings she had for him hadn't worked. He'd only succeeded in strengthening them.

As she struggled with sleep her thoughts returned again to Jared. She'd thought about nothing else since Mordecai told her about the great debt he owed his best friend. That she loved both of them there was no doubt. Between them they'd left her with an impossible choice. On the one hand with Jared she had stability and a chance to get closer to her son, but on the other, Mordecai needed her and she so desperately wanted to be needed.

On the surface Mordecai had seemed the stronger, but now she'd seen beneath the surface. He was a dangerously damaged man, prone to excessive bouts of violence, whereas Jared had an inner strength and stability. Perversely Maddie believed his strength of character made him far more able to cope with her decision.

When she awoke her mind was made up. She was not surprised to see that Mordecai was already up. He was an early riser. Maddie washed her face and dressed quickly. Hurrying down the stairs she looked towards the table where Mordecai always sat and ate breakfast. It was empty.

"He ate breakfast early then I saw him heading out of town, about two hours ago," said Sophie the Alhambra's resident cleaner.

"Oh," was all Maddie could manage. She walked outside into the fresh spring air and looked down the street. It wasn't unusual for Mordecai to saddle up and take an early morning ride now that winter was gone, but this morning troubled Maddie.

She slowly turned and walked back inside. Sitting herself at Mordecai's favourite table she asked Sophie to get her a cup of coffee. It was cold by the time she decided to drink it. Then just as she was about to order another, Mordecai walked through the doors of the Alhambra.

"Oh, I was worried about you," she said weakly.

"No need. I told you all about me last night. I'll survive, I always have. I guess Jared should be arriving pretty soon."

"I don't care about Jared, it's you I want. What you told me last night ain't changed a damn thing. I love you Mordecai Jones!"

"But, but, bu.... You cain't. After what I done, after what I would have done."

"I love you. I've loved you since I first met you." It was said. Finally they could get on with their lives, thought Maddie.

"Jared's a strong man. He'll understand. Given time, he'll understand." Her last words were more wishful than truthful. "I'm selling up my stake in the Alhambra. Jake Tunstall might not like Plummer, but he's always had a hankering to buy out my share of the business."

"What about Luke? He ain't gonna like it one bit."

"Jake helped me set up when I first arrived, I owe him that much. He'll make me a reasonable offer. Plummer would only offer me a fraction."

Mordecai looked thoughtful. He knew that he and Maddie couldn't stay around Helena after they'd told Jared. They'd head south, maybe to Cheyenne. Buy a stake in a saloon or gaming house. He was a dab hand at Faro and Maddie could run a few girls, if that's what she wanted. Maddie deserved better and he knew it. She'd chosen him against the odds and he knew enough about her to know she wasn't going to change her mind.

With her mind firmly made up, Maddie started to fret about Jared's non-appearance. She'd felt sure he would have arrived by Saturday at the latest. The mystery was solved on Tuesday afternoon. Two riders, one on horseback, the other riding a two horse rig, pulled up at the Alhambra's door early in the afternoon. Maddie had watched them from an upstairs window and recognised the young one riding the horse. It was Randy, the young cowhand who had flirted with her last year. She hurried down the stairs and watched as Randy and the other cowboy brushed the dust from their clothes.

"Hello Ma'am," said Randy politely as he took his hat off. "Mr McAllister is indisposed; he broke a leg two weeks ago." Randy's companion quickly added, "Its okay, the Doc took a look at it, just a fracture is all. He strapped it up real good."

"Is Jared okay?"

"Oh sure Ma'am," cut in Randy, "Just belly aching. He reckons he'll be out of bed, and riding before the weekend." Randy screwed his hat up. "Begging your pardon Ma'am but the sooner you gets to him the better it'll be for us. He ain't stopped hollerin an yellin since the Doc strapped him up."

"Yep, he's a mean son of a gun," said the other cowhand.

"But he's okay, I mean really okay."

"He sure is. That's why we're here to take you to him." said Randy.

"You've got to see him. If you're sure about your decision, then you have to speak with him," said Mordecai after she'd told him about Jared's broken leg.

"I know I must, but it's so damn hard." She had missed it. Later when it was all over, she realised than even if she'd spotted the missing 'we' it wouldn't have made the slightest difference.

Mordecai had thought long and hard about Luke Plummer. Both men acknowledged each other cordially when they chanced to meet on the street, but other than that they kept apart. It wouldn't be long before Plummer heard that Maddie was selling out to Jake Tunstall. Plummer wouldn't do anything while Mordecai was around, but if he wasn't, Maddie's life wouldn't be worth a plugged nickel. There was no way that he would accept Tunstall as a partner and equally there was no way he would offer Maddie the asking price. Which meant, as far as Mordecai could tell, the co-owner of the Alhambra would meet with some kind of accident. With no known next of kin, the Alhambra, minus a few taxes, would revert to Plummer.

Darkness arrived early as a few rain clouds clogged the evening sky. Mordecai fastened his black Fish Brand slicker and stepped out onto the rain splattered street. To an onlooker he looked like an ordinary man taking in the evening air but Mordecai had murder on his mind. Leaving Maddie was the hardest thing he'd ever done. He could so easily have told her to pack, but he knew she deserved better. Jared would give her the love and stability that she so desperately needed, whereas he could only give her an uncertain future. He owed it to the both of them. With those thoughts in mind he entered the Red Dog.

'Gas lamps, I'm impressed,' thought Mordecai as he familiarised himself with the lay out of Luke Plummer's latest acquisition. Seating himself at a table close to the doors he ordered a bottle. Undoing his slicker he brushed a few droplets of rain from his sleeves, then he spread his long legs, poured himself a drink and waited. It wasn't long before one of Plummer's cohorts caught sight of him.

"You owe me for a pistol," challenged Bill.

"I ain't here for a fight. You want your pistol, its over at the Alhambra. Ask the bartender politely and he'll hand it back to you."

"I ain't afraid of you. Luke tells me you're some shooter from down South."

"Luke's right." said the Texan. Bill's gun hand brushed the walnut butt of his Colt. "You reach for that hog leg, I'll cut you down."

The fight went out of Bill's eyes as he stared death in the face. "I don't want any trouble," he said as his hands spread out to the sides in submission.

"Tell Plummer I want to talk to him."

Ten minutes later Mordecai looked up at the beaming face of Luke Plummer. "Mind if I sit?"

"Be my guest. Drink?" said Mordecai cordially.

"Not that rot gut." Luke Plummer gestured to the bartender to bring over a bottle of the finest Louisiana bourbon, "You'll like this a whole lot better." He poured two generous glasses and handed one to Mordecai across the table. "What can I do for you?"

"You can buy Maddie out at the right price, or let Tunstall buy in."

"I could, but why should I?"

"Because I'm asking you politely." Mordecai stare intently into Plummer's eyes, gauging the reaction.

"If I refuse?" A sickly smile spread across Luke's face.

"Then I guess we got some business of our own," replied Mordecai coldly. He noticed an almost undetectable flinch in the big man opposite.

"We can dicker, can't we?"

"We can if you've a mind."

"I could use a man like you in my organisation. I've very powerful friends. They could be yours too. Come work for me."

"And Maddie! What of her?"

"She's a whore. If she's got herself a notion to move on, that's her business, but I ain't giving her a red cent. You sir, are a different proposition altogether. There's money to be made. Within a year you could be a very rich man. Are you going to let a cheap whore come between you and a fortune?"

Mordecai felt his hackles rise, but more importantly he knew Luke Plummer was gauging his reaction. "And why would you be offering a man you don't know a fortune?"

The question threw Plummer for a split second before he replied, "Why indeed? I heard tell you were a man quick to anger. I want you on my side."

"I'll ask you one last time. Buy Maddie out at the right price," said Mordecai, his voice deadly calm.

Plummer let his right arm drop casually to his side. "Go to hell!" screamed Plummer as he jumped to his feet, sending his chair flying. His hand gripped the ivory butt of his Remington and he drew and aimed at Mordecai's seated figure. A smile crossed his lips as he began to pull back the hammer. The world exploded in his face. Fragments of wood and glass tore at his cheek, his neck and his forehead and ripped his immaculate clothing to shreds, but Luke Plummer didn't seem to care as two loads of buckshot blew him halfway across the barroom floor.

Mordecai rose to his feet, the sawn off Greener dropping to the ground. He covered the shocked Red Dog crowd with his Navy Colt, "He pulled on me first!"

The crowd made angry noises. Bill, of the confiscated pistol, glared hatred but neither he nor anyone else had the stomach for a fight. Plummer's dead body laid testament to that. Mordecai backed out of the saloon and walked swiftly to the nearby livery stable.

As he saddled up and kicked his horse into a swift trot he thought about what he'd left behind. The way was now clear for Maddie. Luke Plummer was dead. Fairfax was dead, killed by the detective from New

York and he, Mordecai was a fugitive from Montana's Vigilantes; a man no longer in a position to marry the woman he loved. Yes, thought Mordecai, now Maddie could have all the happiness she deserved. Soon she would discover the note he'd left her. She'd see in time that it was for the best.

Shocked by the news of the killing of Luke Plummer, Maddie took herself to her room. She was beside herself with worry. She feared for Mordecai's life. Those posters weren't a warning, they were notices of intent. She'd been told that after Mordecai killed Plummer he calmly walked out of the saloon and made his way to the livery stable. She guessed he was heading back to the McAllister spread. Then she saw the note lying on her pillow.

My darling Maddie,

By the time you read this you'll know what I've done. I told you I wasn't good enough for you. I told you I was a killer. I guess I'll never change. One day I'll meet someone who'll put paid to all the misery I've caused. So you see darling why I couldn't take you with me. I'm going to say my farewell to Jared, I'm going to beg his forgiveness for ever doubting him, then I'm going to tell him that he's a very lucky man and that he couldn't have found a finer woman.

I've never met anyone like you. You're the most wonderful person I've ever met. I love you, and I guess I'll continue to love you for the rest of my days. Take heart my love. I'm leaving you in good hands. You said it yourself how you loved Jared, how I could make it easy for you to choose. Well now I have.

Don't mourn my passing from your life, embrace your life with Jared. If you don't then this gesture of my undying love will have been in vain. Tomorrow go to him, declare your love, sell your share of the Alhambra, become Mrs McAllister.

Mordecai.

I beg you don't ever tell him about us. I couldn't bear for him to know.

Don't look for me. I'll be long gone by the time you arrive.

M.

Maddie wept.

CHAPTER 42

It was late afternoon when Randy arrived back at the ranch. He'd pushed the horses at an alarming rate on the insistence of Maddie, who was sitting at his side on the buckboard. Jared was standing, propped up by two crutches on the porch. His face told Maddie that Mordecai had already broken the news.

"Hey boss! Mordecai gunned a man down in the Red Dog," cried Randy as he reined the well lathered horses to a halt.

"Yeah I heard. Now help Miss Dubois from the buckboard, then get them horses rubbed down and fed." He smiled weakly at Maddie. 'God, dusty as all get out, but still as pretty as ever, even after a neck breaking ride from town,' he thought as he gazed down at her. "Maddie darling, I'm sorry I cain't come down and greet you like I want. As you can see, I'm a little bit crocked. Come in I've some fresh lemonade waiting."

'It wasn't the most romantic of meetings but given the circumstances it would have to do,' thought Maddie as she climbed down from the buckboard with Randy's assistance. Her mind was racing, she wondered just how much Mordecai had told him. On the porch Jared stepped aside and held the door open and bid her enter. Nervously she stepped past him and walked into the main room.

"Joe, has every man been issued with a rifle?" said Jared.

"They sure have boss, and they're in position."

"Good," said Jared as he closed the door.

"Maddie, my darling, I cain't tell you how much I've missed you, come here."

She froze for a second, then years of acting kicked in. "I'm sorry my love, it's just with all the excitement, it's thrown me."

"Yeah Mordecai told me you'd be a little distant. Which is understandable, given what's happened in the last twenty four hours."

Maddie sat down on a leather couch, "My, this is comfy," she said politely.

"Yeah, I had it shipped in from back East. That and a few other home comforts." He seemed uncomfortable and a little unsure of what to say next, then it came out in a flood, "Maddie say you haven't changed your mind about what we discussed. I've been going out of my mind since this happened," he motioned towards his leg.

She looked into his eyes and all she could think about were the words Mordecai had written. *Tomorrow go to him, declare your love, sell your share of the Alhambra, become Mrs McAllister.* On paper it looked so easy, but in reality Maddie was finding it unbearable. It was true, she loved him, but to begin their life together with as big a secret as she possessed would not be easy. She'd chosen Mordecai over Jared, but he'd turned the tables on her. Killing Plummer had indeed burned their bridges. "Jared I love you, nothings changed. It's just terrible what happened."

"Mordecai said the man needed killing. If he hadn't have killed him then I would have. What did he mean by that?"

Remembering the words Mordecai had written she began to tell Jared how Mordecai had come to warn her off.

"That's so typical of him. Pig-headed ain't the word."

By the time Maddie finished telling him her version of what happened she almost believed it herself.

"And he insisted on a piece of burlap sacking to guard your privacy. Well don't that beat all!"

Maddie smiled at Jared's innocence, and began to believe that Mordecai was right after all.

"Sorry to bother you boss, but riders are heading this way," said Joe as he burst in on them.

"I'll be right out. Maddie get yourself in that room, there's liable to be some shooting if I cain't convince them that Mordecai's gone. From what I've heard these vigilantes don't take prisoners."

"If you're going out there, then so am I!"

"No Maddie, leave this to me," he said forcefully.

Maddie retreated into the back room.

As the riders converged on the ranch house Jared, watching from a window, counted them. There were at least thirty in the bunch, all wearing burlap sacking masks. He worked the lever on his Henry rifle and opened the door. "What can I do for you gentlemen?" he said in way of greeting.

"We're looking for the man called Mordecai. We heard he works here. Killed a man back in Helena. We aim to see him brought to justice."

"He ain't here. He no longer works for me."

"Mind if we take a look?" said the leader.

"As it happens I do mind. You arrive at my ranch uninvited wearing hoods and shouting orders. I told you he ain't here. He's long gone."

"You sir are missing the point. We ain't asking, we're doing!" His tone had turned ugly.

"You die first," said Jared as he levelled the Henry rifle at the man's belly.

"You can't kill us all," said another of the lead group.

"We can give it a good try," shouted Randy from the barn. His rifle aimed at the group of horsemen.

"We're appointed by the citizens of Helena," protested their leader.

"My name is Jared McAllister. My word has always meant something. If I say the man you are looking for is gone then that should be an end to it."

The leader, unnerved by the shout from Randy scouted the out houses and barns. There were at least twenty rifles pointed at them. "If you say he's gone, I'd be obliged if you'd point me in the direction he was headed and how many hours head start he's got."

"Now that's more like it," said Jared as he slowly lowered his rifle. "He arrived at first light, picked up his grip and some wages that was owed and lit out about six hours ago. Said he'd got into a shooting scrap and had to kill a man. Said, it was self defence."

"Self defence my eye! He gunned Luke Plummer down with a twelve gauge."

"I don't know the whys and the wherefors and frankly I don't care. I've a ranch to run and I'm a man down. He was a good hand."

The leader looked around at his men as if to seek approval to move on, then Jared spoke again, "Can we rustle you boys up some grub before you get on your way?"

"Obliged," said the vigilante.

"Randy, tell Rosita to fix these gents up with some vittles."

Randy raced across from the barn and entered the house.

"I don't know who you gentlemen are but I'd suggest that the next time you visit you do so without the Halloween masks. I don't turn any man away from my door." Then Jared paused for a few seconds before adding, "I heard tell that son of a gun had some folks lived over in the Dakotas. Deadwood I think."

Half an hour later the group of hooded horsemen left and headed east towards the Dakotas. Jared watched them go with a wry grin on his face. Maddie joined him at the door and reached her arm around him, "It ain't every day you save a life. I reckon I've saved nigh on a dozen. Mordecai would have seen their dust and found himself a spot and picked them off one by one."

Beneath the burlap hood it didn't take their leader Jake Tunstall long to suspect they'd been sent in the wrong direction. The man called Mordecai might have mentioned he had relatives in Deadwood but that didn't mean he was heading that way. Tunstall thought to split his men and send half in the direction of the Dakotas while he led the remainder south. But he had other plans, he had no interest in Mordecai. In fact the man had done him a big favour. Now after two or three days scouting the plains he could return to Helena having done his civic duty and begin working on his new empire. Maddie, when she returns to Helena, would sell out to him and the shareholders who sponsored Luke Plummer would be only to willing to deal with him.

"Jared, what of Mordecai? Do you know where he's headed?"

"Mordecai's a law unto himself. From what he told me I'd say he was heading towards Cheyenne. He'd done his time at ranching, I guess the lure of town life was still in his blood."

"Did he say if he was ever coming back?"

"It's funny you asked that, we had a falling out before he met you. I guess you know all about that."

Maddie felt her face flush slightly but in the oil lantern light Jared never seemed to notice, "Yeah, he did tell me something of the sort."

"I guess coming to see you for himself were his way of making sure he'd leave me in safe hands." He gave her an affectionate smile, "You see I think it was his time to move on. He didn't take much to ranching. Preferred town life and what it entailed."

"So you're saying he's gone for good."

"It looks that way. You could say shooting Luke Plummer was like burning his bridges."

Maddie smiled weakly, she'd thought the same after reading the note. "He didn't have to do that, you know."

"In his mind he did. He told me that if he hadn't, then your life could have been forfeited."

"He didn't know that for sure. He couldn't have, could he?"

"Trust me, if Mordecai said your life was in danger, best you believe it. The man has an instinct for these things. Like Plummer, he's a man killer."

"I know," said Maddie recalling the narration of how he hunted down Kills like the Wolf, "but he was a very nice man. Well to me anyway."

Jared pulled her into his arms and kissed her tenderly. It was a kiss so warm and comforting that Maddie melted into his arms. He was everything she'd ever wanted; strong, dependable, tender and loving. Mordecai was right. She'd fallen in love with Jared from that first moment when she descended the stairs of the Alhambra. How could she have been so blind? How could she have been as stupid as to think she could have a life with anyone else? The man she'd fallen in love with during the winter was long gone. It was as if he'd never been. Maddie tried pushing all thoughts of Mordecai from her mind, but deep down knew that there would always be a small place in her heart that belonged to the dark and troubled man from Texas.

During those early days Maddie and Jared spoke about many things but the subject of Mordecai was never mentioned again. Jared wanted her to stay over, but Maddie insisted on getting back to Helena to sort out her business interests.

"I've been here for three days, I need to get back. My share of the business needs taking care of. I have a responsibility to my girls."

"You don't have to. You can leave it all behind. I'll take care of you from now on."

"I know you will my darling, but this I have to do for myself."

"How long will you be gone? I hope to be up and about within another week."

"You better be! We've some catching up to do." The mischievousness in her voice promised so much. As they walked out onto the porch Randy was readying the buckboard for the ride back to town. Maddie turned her face up to Jared's, a look of concern etched across it. "I love you, but if you're having second thoughts tell me now." Her fears for the future had returned.

Jared swept his hat from his head and a lock of hair fell across his forehead, "Maddie," he said seriously, "I told you once that what's gone on before ain't gonna change a damn thing. I love you darling and when you get back you can start planning the wedding."

Maddie kissed him passionately and at that moment would've changed her mind about going to town if Randy hadn't pulled up with the buckboard and let out a rebel yell just as they were saying their goodbyes.

Jake Tunstall's offer for Maddie's share of the Alhambra was not as generous as she'd thought. It was a fair offer considering the circumstances, but that's all it was, a fair offer. As Jake put it. "I'm doing you a favour with a fast sale. Buying Plummer's share done almost turned me into a poor man." Maddie gave him a look of disapproval, but he came back at her with, "You can still stay as partner until a better offer comes along. It's your choice."

"Jake, all I want to do is sell up and put this place and business behind me. I'm getting married."

With the deal done Maddie crossed the road to the bank and deposited the cheque. Then she re-crossed the road, looked at the Alhambra sign, smiled, then she walked through the doors and went upstairs to her room to pack.

It was in the quiet of her room that she thought about her actions. She'd sold up. She was packed and Randy was picking her up first thing the next morning. She was heading for a new life. Then it hit her. She loved Jared, of that she was sure, but could she marry him and live with the secret of her love affair with Mordecai? She guessed she knew the answer.

CHAPTER 43

Finbar wasn't a westerner by birth but he could see the attraction. Away from the polluted air of Butte he found Helena more to his liking. Now that the weather had truly broken and spring was all around, he'd taken to riding out a ways to sample the fresh morning air and to take in the scenery. Tempted by the vastness of this wonderful land, he knew that if he didn't move on soon he'd stay in the Montana Territory. Perhaps head north to the great glaciers or even further. But his wanderlust was matched by his desire to return home, to his farm in upstate New York and to Maggie. He could see that being close to her final resting place would give him comfort in his declining years.

As he looked out over a majestic valley his thoughts took in all he'd achieved since boarding the train for San Francisco. He'd seen the Pacific Ocean; cleared up the unsolved murders of prostitutes in the Five Points area of New York; been town constable in Butte and most important of all met the woman now known as Madeline Dubois and had liked what he saw. He was glad he'd been able to reassure her about Fairfax. Yes, thought Finbar, all in all he could be proud of his achievements.

It had surprised him how he could speak so candidly to a complete stranger, but that's what he did when the man called Mordecai had visited his room. He'd seemed to care a great deal for Miss Devlin, *or whatever she called herself*, so why did he throw it all away and kill a man in a bar fight only days after their meeting? It was a question he knew would remain unanswered. He was heading home.

It was late in the evening when he arrived at Butte. He checked at the railroad depot for the first available train to Ogden, then on finding the answer, he fixed himself up lodgings for the night and then made his way to The Bucket of Blood. It was a wild and raucous place just a few blocks from the White Elephant, but far enough away to go unnoticed and undisturbed as he had himself a few glasses of cold beer. Sometimes the more crowded a place the less people see. He'd been a face around town, but that was during the winter months. Now, clean shaven and sporting a Prince Albert suit he guessed he was safe from any back slappers or kids hell bent on a killing. He'd hated shooting Bram Finnan, but the bully of a man had left him no choice. Notoriety in any form was something he could well do without.

Finbar was lucky. The Bucket of Blood was heaving with drinkers, whores and card players and every one of them intent on extracting whatever pleasures took their fancy. As he drank he reflected on his decision to go home. He'd grown accustomed to the Westerners wild and woolly ways, but it was on a night like this that he missed home. He longed for the peacefulness of his farm in upstate New York. It would take some fixing up before winter came. That was good because he'd keep himself busy. He began thinking about those lazy spring mornings when he'd get up with the birds and take himself down to the river's edge. Trout cooked on an open fire was something to die for. His heart swelled at the thought of it. Only the loneliness of being without Maggie marred the thought.

Boarding the train to Ogden gave Finbar a lump in his throat. It wasn't the polluted air of Butte of that he was sure. He smiled to himself as he realised the reason. The man called Mordecai had shown genuine concern for the woman now known as Maddie, yet he'd thrown it all away. It didn't make sense, nor, he thought, did his dwelling on the subject, and then it hit him. He'd looked into the woman eyes, and at first he'd seen the look of concern but then as he told his story, they changed and all he could see was warmth. It surprised him some, that he should feel this way with Maggie not even a year in the ground. He couldn't help chuckling to himself. She was a fine figure of a woman and Finbar guessed if he'd been fifteen or twenty years younger he'd have given that young man a run for his money.

"You're an old fool Finbar O'Toole," he said out loud as the wheels of the train slowly chugged their way out of the station.

When he reached Ogden he found the place buzzing with heavily armed townsmen. As he stepped down from the train he asked a porter what was happening.

"There's a killer on the loose and the vigilantes are heading this way. The town council don't take kindly to vigilante law so they're getting a reception committee together," said the porter, "Yessiree, Ogden don't hold with unlawful killin."

"Tell me, this killer, where's he coming from?"

"Heard tell he's fleeing from the Montana Territory."

It was a big country and it could be anybody, thought Finbar, yet something told him it was the man called Mordecai.

"Yes, but where in the Territory?"

"Don't rightly know but somewhere up to Butte or Helena. The stories run thick and fast here in Ogden."

Finbar enquired at the depot when the next train heading east would arrive. He was hoping the train wouldn't be arriving for several days as he had a hankering to hang around Ogden and see what panned out. If it was Mordecai and he handed himself in to the law in Ogden he'd be safe from the vigilantes. Finbar guessed if that was the case then the young man could do with a friend.

"You are one lucky son of a gun, the train's due in less than an hour. If you'd arrived a little later then you'd have been stuck in Ogden for over a week."

Finbar looked disappointed but paid his fare and took the ticket, 'Some things in life are not to be,' he thought wearily. There was no point in postponing his trip home on the speculation that if it was Mordecai he might be heading his way.

The New York detective ate a light meal at the depot and watched as the eastbound train steamed into the station. He thought once again of Maddie and realised his motive for wanting to hang around Ogden wasn't so much curiosity, more a reluctance to leave behind the memory of that woman, 'She was a handsome lookin woman,' he told himself. Again he cursed himself for being a damn fool. An hour later he boarded.

Finbar awoke with a jolt as the train came to a screeching halt. Awoken from his slumber he quickly gathered his thoughts as he looked at the puzzlement on the faces of his fellow passengers. He realised the train wasn't derailed but had halted on its own steam. He looked out of the window towards the trains tender. A barricade of rocks had been laid across the tracks. Beyond the barricade Finbar spotted a large group of riders. All were heavily armed and wearing burlap sacks on their heads.

"Them's vigilantes I seen them before," cried a fellow passenger.

"What're they stopping the damn train for?" cried another.

"Say, you don't think it's a hold up!"

"These men must be the ones the towns folk of Ogden were so riled up about," cried yet another.

Minutes later it all became clear as the train porter moved through the carriages informing the passengers that there was no cause for alarm, that the men outside were looking for a known killer and once they'd searched the train the rocks would be removed and the train could be on its way.

Finbar didn't take kindly to vigilantes, but being out numbered and out gunned he prayed they'd move quickly through the carriages and that they wouldn't find the fugitive on the train.

As the hooded men moved through Finbar's carriage he watched as his fellow passengers fretted and cowered at the sight of the burlap masks. He smiled to himself. He guessed that most of the frightened passengers wouldn't have looked so scared if the masks were off. In his experience most vigilantes looked like regular go-to-church-on-Sunday kind of people.

When they reached Finbar several hooded men stopped as if to scrutinise him, then to his surprise a burlap sack nodded to another and then several guns were cocked and pointed in his direction.

"Get up you murdering son of a bitch!" snarled one of the hooded men.

"What's going on? I'm not the man you're looking for," bewilderment was etched across Finbar's face. A pair of strong arms grabbed at the lapels of his Prince Albert coat and lifted him out of his seat. Finbar, aware of what was happening, smashed his head into the man's hooded face, and then he tried pulling his colt. With the swiftness of a man who knew what a trapped animal was liable to do, a Dragoon Colt's barrel caught Finbar behind the ears. All he felt was a blinding pain and suddenly the world went dark.

He awoke to see the wheels of the train lurch into sudden movement. With an instinct to survive, Finbar searched the dusty trackside frantically with his eyes for his missing gun; it was nowhere to be seen. All around him were hooded men milling about and all he could do was watch helplessly as the train built up speed. He wiped at the blood as it trickle from his ear. Shaking his head to clear his addled brain he stared up at his abductors.

"You're making some kind of mistake; I ain't the man you're looking for!"

"Oh but you are!"

Finbar stared at the man who'd singled him out, his voice was strangely familiar.

"Driscoll!"

"The one and the same," said the man as he took off the burlap sacking.

Finbar stared at the row of burlap hooded riders.

"Yes, I killed a man in Butte, but it was in the line of duty. I was the town constable. Bram Finnan was beating a man to death. Driscoll there," he pointed, "was helping."

"Relax," said Driscoll, obviously enjoying Finbar's distress, "We ain't here to hang you for killing Finnan."

"You ain't?" Finbar's face showed relief and surprise.

"Nah, we're hanging you for killing someone else."

"Who?" cried Finbar as panic returned to his voice.

"Me!"

The detective looked up at the mounted horseman who had spoken. He stared back menacingly. Finbar felt his blood turn to ice as the hooded horseman pulled off the burlap sacking.

"Oh my God!" cried Finbar.

"No, I think I'm closer to the Devil than your God," replied Fairfax.

Finbar stared at the shining tan leather mask and beyond to the two cruel eyes staring back at him. In that moment realisation hit him deep in the gut; this was no ordinary group of vigilantes, not with him leading them. He was without hope. Fairfax would show no clemency.

He was lifted violently from the ground and a noose put around his neck, then he was hoisted onto a horse and led towards an old gnarled oak. The trailing end of the rope was thrown over an outstretched bough.

Still in shock at seeing the ghost of Half-Face all Finbar could say was, "This can't be happening! You're dead, I killed you myself."

The mounted horseman roared manically. Startled by his rider's outcry, the horse reared and kicked. Fairfax fought to bring the horse back under control. After several circles the horse settled down. He was taking great delight in reliving that night in the alley in Sacramento.

"When you intend murdering someone make sure they're dead. Your bullet destroyed my timepiece, a family heirloom, and then alas it tore into my left shoulder. The pain was excruciating, but I managed to stop myself from crying out. I thought that double crossing Nancy was sure to put a bullet in my head, but you hurried her out of there, for that I thank you," he added mockingly.

Finbar was desperate to buy time; every second had become a precious commodity.

"How did you find me?"

"The same way as I found Nancy," he sniggered, "You remember Nancy don't you? She wasn't best pleased to see me." There was a glint in his eye as he recalled their last meeting. "She'd gone back to whoring, a fatal mistake."

"You killed her, you bastard!"

"Let's just say I put her on the right path." He laughed at his little joke. Then suddenly he turned serious, "I only wanted to find that harlot from the Five Points, but you, it seems, beat me to it, according to my good friend Driscoll." He looked away and motioned for one of his men to secure the rope to the tree, "You should have gone back East, I wouldn't have bore you a grudge. But Driscoll spotted you in Butte."

"Yeah, I wanted to drop you as you walked out, but Mr Fairfax had other plans," said Driscoll, clearly revelling in O'Toole's discomfort, "I must say his way is far more enjoyable."

"But how'd you know each other?"

The detective in Finbar wanted to know the connection and time was fast running out.

"After you ran me outta town I drifted south. Had me a card game in Pocatello, where I met Mr Fairfax. We got to talking and guess what, we had someone in common. You!"

Half-Face took up the story, "I sent Driscoll back up to Butte to watch out for you, while I busied myself with a little recruiting," indicating the hooded horsemen.

"Yeah, you saved me a ride to Helena. All I had to do was find out where you were heading, then I sent a telegraph to Mr Fairfax in Pocatello. The rest, as they say, is history."

"The whore, I trust she is both alive and healthy?" said Fairfax.
"Go to Hell!" shouted Finbar.
"You first!" replied Fairfax as he lashed the horse savagely.

CHAPTER 44

Maddie thought long and hard about her decision. Despite everything she stood to lose she knew she couldn't embark on a life with Jared without being truly honest. All her life she'd been trustworthy. It was the code she'd lived by, but now Mordecai was asking, no, he wasn't asking, he was telling. In spite of everything that had happened between them he had no right to dictate her life. Whatever the outcome, it would be of her making. Maddie was going to tell Jared about her relationship with Mordecai.

As Randy steered the horses towards the big house Maddie's heart pounded uncontrollably. Her bravery about her decision decreased as the horses brought her nearer to her destiny. It was all wrong she told herself. Instead of the anticipated excitement a new life would bring she was fearful of how Jared would react when she told him. Her heart skipped a beat as she saw the big oak doors of the ranch-house open.

Jared's face beamed with excitement as Randy brought the buckboard right up to the steps of the ranch-house. Maddie smiled back nervously and then, steeling herself for what she had to do, she took a deep breath and thanked Randy as he helped her down.

Within seconds she was in Jared's strong arms. True to his word he was free of crutches. "They're gone," she said automatically, and then she melted into his arms. Warmth seemed to come over her as she felt the security of his hold. He kissed her softly, then he looked into those dark almond shaped eyes and an involuntary breath escaped his lips.

"Maddie, you've never looked so beautiful."

She could hardly look at him as she stuttered, "I'll look a whole lot better if you'll allow me to freshen up. That trail is mighty dusty."

"I'm sorry, just seeing you has made be forget all considerations."

"It's not your fault," cried Maddie guiltily.

Sensing her discomfort he pointed to a small door just off to the left of the room she'd just entered.

"You can wash up in there," he said awkwardly. "You must be hungry. I'll have dinner prepared."

Maddie excused herself and ducked quickly into the room. It was small but roomy. An oil lamp hung from the centre rafter illuminating a small table and chair. On the table Maddie found a bowl and a jug of hot clean water. Placed carefully beside them was a bar of scented soap, a bottle of perfume and a vase containing a few sprigs of sage. Across the chair were draped two smallish towels. Maddie was taken aback at the trouble Jared had gone to. He'd undoubtedly noticed the cleanliness and the feminine touch to her rooms at the Alhambra and had done his best to make her feel at home. She smelt the strong fragrance of the soap and smiled. Her heart skipped a beat. He was the most thoughtful man she'd ever known. Telling him would be the hardest thing she'd ever done. He was a good man, Jared McAllister. A strong independent man, a man who deserved better, but over all a man who deserved the truth, she thought regretfully. If only she hadn't fallen in love with Mordecai.

Washed and refreshed, her make up delicately applied she looked in the small mirror Jared had thoughtfully placed at the back of the small table. Satisfied with her appearance, Maddie took in a deep breath and ventured into the room she'd occupied with Jared some forty minutes earlier.

"Oh!" she cried involuntarily. The sun had gone down and the room was lit with candles. Maddie stared at the room in amazement.

In the time it had taken her to freshen up Jared had transformed the room. In the centre stood a large oak table draped in an Irish linen tablecloth. Place sittings for two, strategically placed opposite each other at the shortest point. Expensive wine glasses, like in some fancy restaurant, completed the picture. The scene was set undoubtedly for a romantic dinner for two. Maddie sighed, she knew that Jared was a special kind of man, but until that moment she didn't know how special.

Jared appeared instantly, "Well," he said nervously, "Does it meet with your approval? I sent back East for all the finery."

"You set this out by yourself?"

"I did," he replied proudly.

"It's, it's wonderful."

Jared escorted her to the table and held out the seat for her, "I take full credit for the place settings, but the dinner—that's Rosita's speciality."

"Rosita?" said Maddie enquiringly. She'd heard him mention her name before, but didn't know what she was to him.

"Yeah, she's my chief wrangler's wife. She acted as our cook on the drive."

Maddie, still thinking of when to break it to Jared, smiled, "It smells so good."

"It is."

The candles had burned low. The plates were empty and the conversation and wine had blended together perfectly. Gone was the awkwardness of their meeting. It was, thought Maddie, the most romantic of nights. The moon was high in the heavens and cast a ghostly light across the room. For a time she allowed herself to forget, but as the evening grew longer she began to realise that what she said in the next few minutes could change everything.

"Did you enjoy many evenings like this with Mordecai?" It came right out of the blue. Maddie blushed uncontrollably. "You know he's a strange one, late dinners then back to your room. Burlap sacking, that's so typical of him," he laughed.

There was no putting it off, if she didn't tell him now she never would.

"Jared, I've something to tell you. I tried to spare you, but it's not right, I can't keep it from you any longer!" It was coming out wrong. She could feel the tears forming, knowing that the next few words could destroy her world.

"Whoa, Maddie, you're frightening me. What's wrong?"

Maddie took another deep breath. She loved this man so much. It would be so easy to forget what had happened.

"Jared, you know what I am."

"Yeah. You're the most beautiful girl in the world."

"No! Be serious. I'm a whore. I've slept with men for money. Doesn't that bother you?"

"Maddie, this is a wild frontier. People do what they do to survive. I'm okay with it all."

"So you were okay with me working this winter?" It was a cruel weapon to use, but Maddie was fighting for her life.

It was Jared's turn to blush as he took onboard what she had just said.

"Maddie, I love you for you, for the woman that you were, to the woman that you are. Nothing can change that."

"I slept with Mordecai."

Jared's face looked ashen in the candlelight.

"I slept with him because I wanted too," then quickly she added, "But I never stopped loving you."

Jared sat back in his chair like he'd been hit hard in the gut.

"I couldn't start a life with you not knowing what I'd done." She felt the tears as they trickled from her eyes. She dabbed at her cheeks with a handkerchief as she rose from the table, "I'll pack my things and go in the morning."

"Maddie, sit down," said Jared softly. She looked down at him with tears stinging her eyes and slowly did as he bid. Jared remained silent for what to Maddie seemed an eternity. When he spoke, his words sounded almost like velvet. "Maddie, I know. I've known since Mordecai came back."

"He told you?"

"No. That's not his style. It was the way he spoke. I could tell he'd fallen in love with you. And why wouldn't he? I did. I'm not that worldly around womenfolk, but I'm not that naïve to think that nothing happened between the two of you."

"Oh Jared, I'm so sorry."

"No, you've nothing to be sorry about. It's me that's sorry. I should have been more forceful. I should have insisted that you quit what you were doing and married you back then, but I didn't. I put the ranch first, and for that I'm truly sorry."

"But, we betrayed you."

"I know, but it doesn't matter, I love you." Maddie looked across at Jared and saw tears in his eyes. He sighed and then he spoke again, "I love both of you and nothing's gonna change that, ever." He paused for a moment and grinned wolfishly. "It's funny, but bizarre as this sounds, you've unwittingly helped repay a debt."

"How? I don't understand."

"Mordecai thought he owed me. It was stupid really, but it was something he carried with him. On the day when he said goodbye, I knew that in his eyes that debt was now paid in full."

"I know all about that debt, Mordecai told me everything."

"You know! Then Mordecai really loved you." For a moment Jared was taken aback. It was foolish to think that only he could love her so. "Now I understand why he's gone, but I regret that I'll never see him again." Then he smiled and Maddie knew she was lost forever, "But he's left me in your care. And Maddie Dubois, like it or not, you're stuck with me."

"Oh Jared!"
Maddie flung herself into his arms.

Chapter 45

As Fairfax stared back at the hanging body of Finbar O'Toole, *now bullet riddled from the target practice his men had thought necessary,* he found a grim satisfaction on how things were turning out. His shoulder still gave him pain, but nonetheless it was a reminder of how lucky he'd been. He hadn't expected the New York detective to shoot. When the bullet struck his father's pocket watch and smashed into his right shoulder he wanted to scream in agony, but self preservation caused him to play dead, there in the dirt and grime of that Sacramento back alley. He cursed himself as a fool, being led like a lamb to the slaughter, and by a whore. He could have laughed at the irony of his situation if his life hadn't been at stake.

He lay in the filth and stench of that alley for fifteen minutes, where he drifted in and out of consciousness. In that time his life flashed before him. They were scum. They were angels of death and depravity. All his life he'd been plagued by them and now one of them had almost succeeded in leading him to his death. Like the others who had gone before, he knew that if he lived Nancy would pay.

Not one of them could be trusted, not even his mother. She'd been the catalyst. She was a whore, she was Queen of whores. When his drunken father had refused her advances, she'd forced him into her bed. He'd been eleven at the time and didn't know what was happening, except afterwards he remembered immense pleasure. She'd come to his bed many times after that but around his twelfth birthday his father had come home early.

Outraged by what he saw, he beat his son badly then set about his mother. Young Fairfax crawled into an alcove and whimpered. Then he heard the words that changed his life forever.

"You fucking whore! You're infected with the pox, and now you've given it to the lad!"

He rained blow after blow upon the woman while the boy could only look on helplessly. Then he tired and fell asleep beside his badly beaten wife. James Fairfax ceased to whimper and a terrible rage came over him. He was cursed. He was unclean! He was diseased! Minutes later the house was a blazing inferno.

For years he lived with the terrible secret that he was cursed, seeking sex wherever he could, not caring who he was infecting. But then at eighteen he fell in love. Not wanting to give her his curse he sought help from a local doctor. On examination he was found to be clear of any infection and that he was a normal healthy young man. The syphilis which had taken his parents had mercifully not transferred to him. For years he'd been living with a terrible secret, a secret that had warped his mind, but now he was free. Free to marry the girl of his dreams. When he asked her to marry him she was taken aback by his proposal. She was sixteen and the thought of marriage was the furthest thing from her mind. She said it was sweet of him to think of her in that way, but she was too young. Her parents thought it laughable and told him to come back when he was fully grown. Enraged by her refusal and her parents obvious amusement, Fairfax stormed off. The girl refused to see him after that.

For months the hurt festered until it became a murderous rage. It was a rage that he found strangely easy to suppress. Seeking solace with the whores of Boston, he formulated a murderous plan. At nineteen he lured a young prostitute called Daisy into the darkness. Up against a dirty wall of a dark alley he forced himself inside her.

"Take it easy deary. It doesn't have to be rushed," exclaimed Daisy. To her relief she could see in his eyes that he was about to climax. But she was surprised that when he did she felt a searing hot pain low in her abdomen. Realisation hit her instantly, but it was too late. The blade plunged frantically again and again, and Fairfax climaxed like he'd never climaxed before, except strangely during that first time with his mother.

It was supposed to have been a dry run before he extracted his revenge on Emma, but he'd found more pleasure in the act than he'd anticipated so that he knew he'd do it again and again. A month later Emma was found at the back of her father's large house on the Kingsford estate, raped and brutally murdered. A few weeks later Fairfax moved to New York.

The stench of rotting vegetables and human faeces forced him to gag. Awoken into the hellhole of that alley, Fairfax somehow managed to stagger to his feet. To stay there was to die there. Weak through lost of blood, his hideous mask and smart clothes now covered with blood and human faeces, he emerged into the lamp-lit street. Some people fled at the sight of him, but fortunately the streets of Sacramento still carried men of decency. When he woke up he found himself lying on a cot in the back room of a saloon. He learned that he'd been lucky, far luckier than he had a right to be. He'd staggered through an area where, even in his terrible state, he could have been knocked to the ground and robbed. As it was, he was found by a citizen who helped carry him into the saloon. There he was patched up, but the proprietor didn't hold out much hope and the last rites were read over him. He'd lain asleep for two days. Weak from the loss of blood he took what nourishment was on hand. The more he realised how close to death he'd come, the more anger churned inside him. He'd gone past the point of no return. His hatred had plumbed new depths. He no longer wanted to kill from the shadows, he wanted to kill openly—to kill and maim, to rape and pillage. There were bands of men in the West who did just that. Apache renegades, Comancheros, outlaw gangs and vigilantes. As he began his recovery he started making plans.

The Barbary Coast was just as he'd left it. Old acquaintances were rekindled, drinks downed and his lust sated. A discreet enquiry here, a not so discreet enquiry there and it wasn't long before Half-Face had the whereabouts of Nancy.

Down on her luck, she was scraping a living in a crib out the back of O'Shaunessy's. In Sacramento she was a saloon girl, ready to do favours, but at a price. Now, she'd do anything just for a fix. He watched from the shadows as she took a client back to her crib. Impatiently he waited for the man to finish, even toying with the idea of killing them both, but as he thought about it, he realised it would be too easy. Nancy had to know she was about to die.

Stealthily, keeping in the shadows cast from the full moon over the ocean, he walked in.

"Be with you in a minute," she snarled. The intruder would have to wait as she ingested a quarter of the contents of a small bottle of laudanum. Fairfax lurched in the shadows, his breath coming thick and fast, "Okay deary, don't get yourself worked up. I'll soon ave yer as right as rain."

"You will at that," said Fairfax pleasantly as he advanced on her. She put up no resistance as he forced her onto the filthy mattress, his hand across her mouth. Her eyes cleared from the mist of the laudanum, then grew wide with terror. Half-Face smiled maniacally then released his grip on her mouth. Open-mouthed she stared up at him, a silent scream on her lips. It was the nightmare she'd always feared.

"Cat got your tongue?"

Then in a flurry of movement he reached inside her mouth and with a razor sharp knife he sliced off her tongue. "Sorry," he said insanely, "I've got your tongue." Then he began to laugh.

Nancy sat up suddenly, her face ashen with shock. Blood spurted from her mouth as she tried to scream. Half-Face pushed her down on the bed. He was still laughing when she drowned in her own blood.

An hour later, Fairfax lay on a cot in the Chinese quarter of town and let the opium vapours waft over him. In his stupor he recalled the words O'Toole had said to him in that alley in Sacramento. The bitch whore, she'd taken up with a soldier in Custer's regiment. He smiled to himself as he felt the opium working its magic.

Pocatello was like any other cowtown of the day. Smoke laden saloons, painted women, liquor and cards. It was the same as all the towns that had gone before. His month long search had produced nothing, but across the card table from him was a man dressed in a faded blue uniform. He was unkempt and suffering from too much drink, but the man interested Fairfax. He'd noticed the faint gold braided stripes but what excited him the most was the emblem of the 7th Cavalry.

"You ride with Custer," remarked Fairfax as he stared intensely at the emblem.

"Maybe. What's it to you?"

"Nothing! Everything! I'm lookin for a whore"

"Ain't everybody," replied Driscoll.

"Her husband rode with Custer."

"You don't say," said the ex-soldier. There couldn't be many, if any whores whose husbands had rode to their deaths with Custer—except for a certain widow woman. He sensed that the freak seated opposite him had business with an old acquaintance of his. What was it with O'Bannion's widow that two men should seek her out? He looked Half-Face in the eye, "Supposing I knew the woman you was looking for, how much would that be worth to a gentleman like you?"

"Nothin if it ain't the woman that I seek."

"Oh, I think this woman would interest you. You're not the only one who's lookin for her."

Fairfax felt the hairs on the back of his neck stand on end.

"Who's lookin?"

"An Irishman from New York," Driscoll read the look in Fairfax's eyes. "How much are you prepared to pay for such information?" The answer chilled Driscoll to the bone.

"You didn't die with Custer, you don't want to die on the floor of this place, but you will if you don't tell me her whereabouts."

Driscoll was no coward, but the man opposite him looked crazy enough to carry out his threat. "Easy mister, I'll tell you what you want to know."

Within an hour Driscoll had told Fairfax all he knew about Finbar O'Toole, town constable of Butte and the whore now known as Madeline Dubois.

'At last,' thought Fairfax, 'I know where the bitch whore is and what a bonus! The New York detective is also within my grasp!'

An alliance of evil was formed that night, as both men realised that they had many things in common, "I want that fucker O'Toole dead. I want him badly, but more than that, I've unfinished business with O'Bannion's widow myself," spat Driscoll.

"The bitch whore is yours to do with as you like. But remember, I do the cutting," declared Half-Face menacingly.

Driscoll, chilled to the bone by Half-Face's last remark, knew not to argue.

"What you've got to remember is that Helena is, to some extent, a law abiding town. It's growing fast. I hear tell it's in line to be the capital of Montana Territory and they're looking towards statehood."

"So!" cried Half-Face rather irritated by Driscoll moving off the subject of the bitch whore.

"You're missing the point," persisted Driscoll. "You can't just go up to O'Bannion's widow and snatch her off the street. They got law."

"Law! Since when have I been frightened by the law?"

"It ain't just ordinary law, its Vigilante law." Driscoll could see the anger in Half-Face's eyes and sought to appease him. The man frightened him, but he feared the Vigilantes far more, "Begging your pardon, Mr Fairfax, but you'd not go unnoticed in or around Helena. O'Bannion's widow, if I remember correctly, had some important friends and if she fears you and we ride in, by sunset we could be swinging from a rope."

Fairfax stifled his anger. Driscoll wasn't afraid to push his point and he liked that in the man. He wasn't a fool either. What he'd said was quite logical. Of course it wasn't inconceivable for him to sneak into town under the shadow of darkness, find a way into her rooms and wait, but that way could be too risky. She might scream, she'd definitely fight and if he did succeed it would be too quick. He wanted her to know it was coming. He wanted her to suffer, and besides, Driscoll wanted a piece of her. No, there had to be a way of having it all.

"Vigilantes!" cried Fairfax.

"What!" exclaimed Driscoll.

Fairfax outlined his plans.

A month later having formulated their plans, Driscoll returned to Butte. When he found out that O'Toole had resigned his position of town constable he broke into a cold sweat. He'd promised Fairfax so much and here he was in Butte with nothing to show. He needed to get his head straight, he needed a drink. He avoided the White Elephant, too many ugly memories and so he decided to have a few drinks in The Bucket of Blood. It was there he got lucky.

Fairfax's daydream was interrupted by Driscoll.

"Ain't that a pretty sight?" he said motioning towards the remains of O'Toole.

"It makes my heart burst with pride to see justice done," replied Fairfax. The killing of Butte's ex-town constable had been more satisfying than he'd thought possible. His plan had worked like a dream.

Driscoll, having only just returned from Butte, was troubled. As a leader of men he wasn't too sure about the calibre of men whom Fairfax had recruited in his absence. He voiced his observations whilst Half-Face was in such good humour.

"Too many in my opinion. We need a small nucleus of men. We can always pick up extra men when needed."

Driscoll, assuming his place as second-in-command behind Fairfax, didn't trust his life to the judgement of just one man, even if he risked the wrath of Half-Face.

Fairfax laughed, "I like that about you Driscoll, when it comes to your own welfare you're not afraid to voice your opinion. I respect that."

Encouraged by Fairfax's comment, Driscoll continued, "We need no more than ten men. Ten, that'll take orders, no matter what. With your permission I'll hand pick them?"

"Go ahead. But in two days we ride for Helena."

CHAPTER 46

Maddie had never been happier. Jared was the most considerate of lovers. Though he hadn't been around many women, his natural instinct to please excited her. He was passionate, yet gentle. Considerate, but strong. He was as much a man as she thought she'd ever need. Yet as she lay by his side with the moon slowly passing behind dark clouds, she thought guiltily about Mordecai. She loved Jared with all her heart but one tiny corner of it was reserved for the man she could never have. As she looked at Jared's sleeping form, she considered herself the luckiest woman alive.

They awoke to the gentle warming rays of the early morning sun. He kissed her tenderly on the lips, "Take all the time in the world, I've horses to attend. Rosita's gonna prepare breakfast, I'll see you in an hour."

"Do you have to go?" she said pouting.

"The ranch doesn't run itself," he said mischievously. "I'll see you at breakfast."

All through breakfast Maddie had a feeling that Jared was holding something back.

"Okay, I can't stand it any longer. What are you up to?"

Jared laughed, "Am I that obvious?"

"I'd say."

At that moment Randy came through the front door. Jared waved him silent.

"As a rancher's wife you'll need to survey the ranch, and" he paused as he led Maddie towards the open door, "you'll need a horse. Her name's Fawn. She's yours."

Maddie's eyes grew ever wider as she looked at the most marvellous bay mare she'd ever seen. "Oh Jared, she's beautiful."

Jared's face took on a worried look, "You can ride?"

Maddie smiled, her hands clasped against her hips, "You forget. I was married to a soldier and as it happens I can ride pretty damn good."

"Yeah, I knew that," said Jared with a wry grin.

"You didn't," joshed Maddie.

Maddie climbed into the saddle like she'd been born to it. Jared stared with admiration as she gently walked the horse around the yard, talking, patting and generally getting to know the animal. Ten minutes later she rode up to him and said, "Well are you going to show me this ranch or aren't you?"

"I guess I am at that," replied Jared, as he climbed into the saddle. He smoothly brought the horse alongside and smiled at this woman whom he loved so much. Then Jared swung his horse around and pointed it in a northerly direction and loped off at a gentle pace. Maddie followed and soon they were riding together across a carpet of sagebrush buttercups and pink bitterroot flowers. He led her up through the foothills weaving between rocks and boulders, Douglas fir and lodge pole pine, through dense forests, cool mountain streams and across open meadows until they reached the summit of their journey.

As they gazed down upon the valley from the relative cool of the timberline Maddie exclaimed, "It's, it's beautiful."

"Only matched by your beauty," replied Jared.

"Oh Jared McAllister, I love you."

There was warmth in Maddie's voice which dispelled any lingering doubts. Jared knew what she was, what she'd been, what she'd done and he didn't care worth a damn. He loved this woman to death.

"I love you Maddie. What say we get hitched this Saturday? I can't wait any longer for you to become my wife."

"Oh yes Jared. Yes, yes, yes!"

Justice of the Peace Tom Lusk looked around at the flamboyant surroundings of the Red Light Saloon and thought how different it looked in the daylight. He was more accustomed to seeing it through the bottom of a glass, with a pretty whore across his knee. The Red Light Saloon was the brainchild of Josephine "Chicago Joe" Airey and her new husband James T "Black Hawk" Hensley. When Maddie had knocked her door down and told her she was getting married Chicago Joe was ecstatic and gave her The Red Light Saloon as the venue for her pending nuptials.

"Girl, I said you was smart. Finding a fella of wealth, that's something, but you've bagged yourself a real live one."

Maddie blushed at Chicago Joe's outburst and looked imploringly at Jared, "It ain't like that, honest."

Jared laughed, "I know that you silly girl. I ain't been around much but I ain't dumb."

Maddie smiled the sweetest of smiles and mouthed, "I love you."

As Jared looked at the woman on his arm he forgot about Maddie's choice of venue. She wasn't wearing white. No, she was wearing a high collared navy blue laced dress, and it was, as Jared learned later, her best Sunday going-to-church outfit. She was doing her best with what clothes she had. She needn't have bothered, thought Jared. She'd look good in anything. As it was, she looked stunning. His eyes cast down to her feet. He hadn't realised until then just how small they were. Her feet and legs were adorned in a pair of the finest black lace up boots he'd ever seen, he could only guess at the stockings she was wearing. His thoughts involuntarily switched towards the bedroom. "Yes siree," he thought. "The Red Light Saloon was the right venue and then some."

Heck acted as best man, while Randy motioned people to their seats. His eyes were all over. He felt in his pockets to make sure he had enough, if and when the chance came for him to get some action. Bernardo and Rosita were the only other guests on Jared's side on account of the work at the ranch.

On Maddie's side there was a vast amount of people. Some came out of pure curiosity, while others like Josephine and Mr Hensley came because they loved Maddie. Duke Hamilton and Lillie arrived late with Annette in tow. Joanne was Maddie's matron of honour, though she seemed the worse for wear from the night before.

Alex Lavenberg, one of Chicago Joe and Maddie's chief lenders looked on in bewilderment. He'd financed many of the Tenderloins businesses over the years but the likes of Maddie and Chicago Joe had proven far shrewder than most of the madams who frequented Wood Street and surrounding areas. Maddie took a leaf out of Josephine's book and made sure she paid off her loans before the note was due.

Jake Tunstall nodded across to Jared, no doubt remembering the wild goose chase the rancher had sent him on, thought Jared wistfully.

"Do you … "Tom Lusk began. He looked quizzically at Maddie. She urged him to go on. "Do you Madeline Dubois, nee Deirdre O'Bannion, take this man Jared Thadeus McAllister to be your husband?"

"I do," said Maddie.

Minutes later the crowd in the Red Light Saloon drank a toast to the bride and groom, then they vacated to the fire proof stone dance hall next door for the celebrations to continue. It was another of Chicago Joe's shrewd investments.

Unobserved by the wedding party, an uninvited guest watched the proceedings from the shadows.

Chapter 47

Fairfax had to admit Driscoll was good at his job. Being a sergeant in the 7th had honed Driscoll's ability to read men. Of the thirty or so who had rode with them when they stopped the train he'd noticed only a small handful had pumped bullets into the dead body of O'Toole. It was something Fairfax hadn't spotted, a fact that he stored away for future reference. Paying off the remainder of the bunch had left Half-Face in dire need of funds. His powers of planning and cunning were about to be put to the test.

Through a network of spies, Fairfax learned that a payroll shipment of cash was being delivered to the copper mines at Butte. It was being guarded by a hand picked bunch of hardened, but honest, men.

"And there be their weakness. We block off the road in full view dressed as vigilantes."

"What if they don't buy it," said Driscoll.

"It worked with O'Toole, why wouldn't it work with the payroll shipment? By now everyone in the territory will know about the exploits of the Vigilantes. We block off the road, they have to stop. We show ourselves. I tell them there's a possible fugitive amongst them and that we only want to check. Close up they won't have a chance, then we slit their throats. Easy."

"What if they don't let us near the buckboard? What if they fire at us?" said Lucas Graham, a noted shooter from Virginia City, Nevada.

"It'll be me nearest them," said Half-Face as he shot a murderous glance at Graham.

As Half-Face went over his plan to steal the payroll he realised that he had to make an example, show the men who was boss. Driscoll had done a good job selecting the men. They were all mean and dangerous. Lucas Graham had spoken up when he should have listened. He wasn't the most dangerous among them, but his reputation had preceded him. He'd got into a bar fight in Virginia City, wounding a man. When the sheriff came to disarm him he'd handed over his weapons meekly. With the sheriff's hands full he pulled a hide away pistol from beneath his jacket. He gut shot the sheriff in the middle of the no 5 saloon. Then he pushed the sheriff's body to the ground and walked out as calm as you like. Since then he'd been on the dodge, taking what work he could get and stealing horses. As far as Half-Face could tell that was his only fatal shooting.

They camped out in a clearing that first night on the way to Butte. The men were sitting around eating and chatting amongst themselves. Three were playing cards and cussing each other. All in all the camp was very relaxed, 'too relaxed,' thought Half-Face. Now was the time to show them who was the leader. Casually he called Lucas Graham over.

"Hey Lucas, come here."

Graham looked up quizzically from his plate of stew, "What's up boss?"

Fairfax laughed, "I like that. We ain't earned any money yet and Lucas here calls me boss."

Driscoll looked up, uneasy at Fairfax's happy demeanour. Lucas put his plate down, wiped the grease from his fingers down his pants and walked over to Half-Face.

Fairfax smiled and put his arm around Lucas Graham's shoulder, "You asked how we'd get close to them, well this is how!" With lightening fast speed Fairfax ran his razor sharp knife across Graham's throat.

"Jesus!" cried Micah Levy "What in the hell did you do that for?"

Levy, a dark and swarthy hook-nosed thin excuse for a man, realised he too had spoken out of turn. But unlike Lucas Graham, he never underestimated friend or foe. He'd killed swiftly with a knife on five occasions and knew better than to get to close to any man. His victims had found that out to their cost. He remembered the sodbuster and his young wife. They'd invited him to stay for dinner, his demeanour was non-threatening and both felt at ease. She'd begged for her life on all fours beside her dead husband as he sodomised her. She went without a whimper as he ejaculated. Sly and devious, he realised that Fairfax was more than his equal.

"He doubted my word. We ain't going on a Sunday school outing. There's big money to be had, but with that comes risk. Lucas Graham weren't up to it."

Half-Face had only just finished speaking when the gurgling sound coming from Graham's neck ceased. He turned away and without looking back, helped himself to a plate of stew.

The two Logan brothers turned back to their plates and continued eating. John Larch just grunted.

"That's fine by me," said Micah Levy doing his best to keep the fear from his voice. "Lucas Graham talked a good fight, but I'm like you Mr Fairfax I reckoned he didn't have enough sand for what you got in mind."

Half-Face grinned; his little exhibition had brought his men together. Now they feared him.

"We hit the payroll then you boys can take your pleasures in Helena. You'll see working with me has its own reward."

News of the massacre of the payroll guards reverberated across the territory. Only the stripped and mutilated remains of the guards and their burnt out wagon were found. A scout from the army confirmed that the mutilations were consistent with previous massacres attributed to the Sioux. The only concern he had was that the vast majority of Sioux and Cheyenne had very recently retreated over the border into Canada. He could only assume that a small renegade bunch had come across them by chance. He cautioned everyone in the Territory to stay vigilant.

Fairfax laughed when he heard the news. Driscoll and his knowledge of Indians had proved invaluable. His military background and his willingness to take whatever orders Fairfax threw at him were truly admirable. He was an asset and deserved to be rewarded.

"Rest up men, for tomorrow we head for Helena." He looked directly at Driscoll and could almost see him drool at the thought of the O'Bannion widow. Then in a quieter voice he added a note of caution, "The woman is yours to do with as you see fit, but remember I am the last person she'll see before I send the bitch whore to her maker."

Driscoll took Fairfax's words for what they were, an offering and a threat of certain death if he went too far. An understanding was already forming between them.

Two days later they drifted into Helena, the Logan brothers arrived first and headed for the nearest saloon. Then came John Larch and Micah Levy. Both men were lean and hungry looking, but the uppermost thought in their minds was for the women of the town. They headed for the Tenderloin district. Kid Briscoe and Tom Bender arrived late, taking a roundabout trip to approach from the other end of town. Kid Briscoe had been impatient to reach town and wanted to voice his opinion, but Tom Bender advised against it, "I ain't frightened by him, fucking freak show."

"Well you should be boy. You might have killed a couple of niggers down south, fair or otherwise, but you ain't a match for Half-Face. I seen him in San Francisco one time, killed Rufus Coe clean as you like, dispatched him almost as quickly as he did Lucas Graham."

"I'll bear that in mind," said Kid.

"See you do." Tom Bender, like John Larch, was a man killer with a reputation to boot. Both men killed without question. Death walked in their wake, but Fairfax left Bender cold.

Fairfax and the two Mexicans, Gregorio and Rufio the half breed, camped out at the edge of town in a thicket. Fairfax knew his appearance about town would cause a stir and that was something he didn't want. Besides, he was happy around the campfire with the two Mexicans. Gregorio and Rufio had ridden together with the Comancero's until the Texas Rangers chased them out of the South West. They'd done their share of killing and more, but Fairfax had a new found respect. He'd seen how both men had quickly dispatched a number of the payroll guards with an expertise he could only admire. They were useful men to have at your side in the months ahead.

Sergeant William Driscoll and Finn Harpe were there not for pleasure but to scout out the whereabouts of Maddie. Harpe had no liking for the drink, but loved the card table. He was a card sharp of dubious talent. He'd killed two men who'd accused him of cheating and murdered the friendly jailer whilst waiting trial.

Harpe was to be Driscoll's front man while he stayed in the shadows waiting to eyeball O'Bannion's widow. They made their way to the Alhambra and soon found out that she had sold up. Panic stole over Driscoll as he visualised what Fairfax would do if she wasn't found.

"So Maddie sold up, where'd she say she was heading?" He said it as casually as he could, hoping against hope that the bartender knew.

"Oh she ain't headin far, caught herself a young rancher, out towards Deer Lodge."

"How far is Deer Lodge?"

"Oh you ain't to be worrin about that, she's here in Helena. Getting hitched she is. This afternoon, or so I heard tell. Over to the Red Light Saloon on Wood Street."

"Obliged," said Driscoll, the worried frown disappearing almost as quickly as it came.

From the shadows ex sergeant William Driscoll watched as the O'Bannion widow recited her vows. She's a fine lookin woman, he thought. She was, he mused too young and too pretty to die. 'If only she'd succumbed to me at the army post, all this could've been avoided.' Then he remembered the rebuff, the air of superiority she gave out when she told him to leave her alone or she'd inform Mrs Custer of his intentions. 'And all the time,' he thought angrily, 'she was nothing but a low down whore. Well soon she's gonna find out what she's been missing,' he mused as he felt the hardness come upon him.

CHAPTER 48

The wedding party was up early the next morning. Their plans were to reach the ranch by nightfall, stopping off to rest the horses at the old line shack and take on more water and then push on into the afternoon. If their progress was slowed in any way, they had the advantage of a full moon.

Randy, *worse for wear from too much alcohol and carousing with one of Maddie's girl's,* rode point with Heck, who was teasing the life out of the youngster. Bernardo with Rosita at his side followed closely behind in the first buckboard, while Jared drove the trailing buckboard at a deliberate slow gait. It was his honeymoon and whatever privacy he could get, was earned only by keeping a discreet distance between him and the rest of the group. Maddie clung to his arm, *still not quite believing she was now Mrs Maddie McAllister,* with the birds singing to a chorus of creaking wheels. It was the most perfect of late spring mornings.

The buckboards made good time and arrived at the line shack by a little after noon. Jared, Heck, Randy and Bernardo saw to the horses while Rosita and Maddie prepared a cold lunch.

Maddie found she was enjoying herself far more than she'd thought possible. Rosita was so naturally bubbly, she'd already put the new Mrs McAllister at her ease. Maddie thought she was going to become a true friend. She could already tell that Bernardo was devoted to her. Heck was stiffly polite but Maddie could see that given time he'd relax. Randy, well he couldn't do enough for her. He was like a little puppy dog in his behaviour. Gone were the reservations she'd had during the winter. Ranch life wasn't going to be easy, but then again nothing had come easy to Maddie McAllister. "Maddie McAllister," she mouthed the words in wonderment. The name itself suggests a frontier woman, a woman to stand at her husband's side against all odds, to love him in sickness and in health and perhaps to bear his children. She had visions of bringing them up good and strong. To watch them together as they took their first steps. Her thoughts were like an endless daydream. Maddie thought she'd burst with happiness.

Maddie's daydream was interrupted by Jared.

"This idleness ain't gonna get us home before dark if we don't mount up soon."

Heck nodded in agreement and stuffing what was left of his sandwich in his mouth, he gave Randy a playful kick. The young cowboy swiped at his foreman with his hat then he slowly dragged himself up from the dusty ground, brushed himself off and began to attend to his horse. The others followed and within five minutes the wedding party was all mounted and ready to continue their journey. Heck kicked his horse into a slow walk and remarked to Randy what a beautiful afternoon it was going to be.

"Look at that sky, boy. It don't get better than that."

Randy looked into the distance at the blue sky dotted with puffy white clouds high above the distant purple hue of the mountain range.

"Yeah Heck, mighty pretty." He was still recovering from his hangover, but his thoughts of Lillie and last night seemed to ease it somewhat.

They'd travelled about five hundred yards from the old line shack when Heck saw, in the distance, a group of riders heading towards them.

"Looks like we got visitors Jared."

"Can you make em out?" replied Jared. He checked his Henry repeater and laid it down on the front foot rest. "Just in case," he said to Maddie reassuringly. He looked forward and saw that Bernardo had done the same.

Randy, without waiting to be told, spurred his horse forward to get a better look. Within a minute he was back smiling. "It ain't hostiles, from the way they're riding I'd say they was white men."

Maddie looked relieved. She'd seen at close hand what the Redman had done to soldiers at the fort.

"They're probably heading back towards Helena. It doesn't do to travel in small groups when there are hostiles about." said Jared as he smiled back at his young bride reassuringly.

As the riders drew closer Heck called back to Jared, "Mr McAllister, it's those damn vigilantes again."

Jared reined the buckboard to a halt and stood up to get a sight of the approaching riders. There were eleven of them, all hooded and heavily armed. They were in open country, why were they hooded? It didn't make sense, thought Jared. Calmly he reached down and picked up his rifle.

"They're just the bunch who came to the ranch," he said to Maddie. Though in his heart he knew they weren't the same group.

Then as the hooded horsemen drew closer they brought their horses to a walk and began to fan out.

"Jesus Christ, what are they at?" Jared mumbled under his breath. With every step they moved closer, his uneasiness grew and he sensed it was felt by the rest of the group. "Bernardo, follow my lead," barked Jared.

The wrangler nodded and tapped his Winchester.

The vigilantes closed to within thirty yards, their intentions as yet still unknown, but Jared could feel it in his water. The threat was growing minute by minute. Standing up in the buckboard he adjusted his stance and levelled his Henry. Bernardo did the same.

"That's far enough," shouted Jared. "State your business!"

Randy slipped off the rawhide thong from the trigger of his new Colt. Heck positioned himself between the group of horsemen and the buckboard, his gun hanging loosely in his hand. These men had driven cattle all the way up from Texas, they were seasoned trial herders and trouble was something they were used to.

"We're lookin for an escaped prisoner from Deer Lodge," said a rider in a faded greatcoat, army issue.

"All we want is to take a look at you all. If you ain't who we're after you can go on about your business," shouted Driscoll. He hadn't wanted to speak but the small group in front of him had out manoeuvred his bunch. He hoped against hope that O'Bannion's widow hadn't recognised his voice.

"Jared!" cried Maddie, "Something's wrong, something's really wrong."

"I know, I know," he said trying to calm his young bride. The urgency in her voice prompted the Texan into action, "He ain't amongst us. I'm Jared McAllister from the Circle M. I can vouch for everyone here." To emphasize he meant business Jared jacked a bullet into the breech of his Henry, "Ride wide of us friend, or have at it."

He'd hoped his aggression would take the fight out of the hooded riders, but it was greeted by a wild scream which tore into the still air. All eyes turned in the direction of the scream to see Kid Briscoe tearing the hood from his head and pulling his revolver from its holster. His horse reared as he spurred it straight at Jared, his gun raising. Jared swung the Henry in Briscoe's direction and waited until he was almost on him, then he fired. Briscoe was blown from the saddle and the gates of hell let loose. Bullets flew in every direction. Bernardo fired off three quick shots at the hooded horseman then seizing the reins of the buckboard he whipped the team into a broad curve and headed back towards the old line shack. Jared followed his lead. Caught in the open it would only be a matter of time before they were cut down. Heck, holding his horse as still as he could, took careful aim and fired his pistol at the largest rider, catching him square in the chest. Bull Logan dropped like a stone. Randy, with his horse turning back and forth, gave covering fire as the two buckboards began to pick up speed. Amidst the gun smoke and swirling dust Heck whirled his horse around and shouted for Randy to beat a retreat to the line shack, but before he could put spur to his horse he was cut down by a withering barrage of fire. Jared threw the reins to Maddie and shouted, "Drive like the wind!"

Maddie grasped the reins and whipped the horses into a neck breaking gallop across the uneven ground. As the buckboard shook and bucked under the insane speed of the horses, the relative safety of the line shack grew ever closer. Jared whirled round in the seat and fired repeatedly with the Henry, downing a horse and unseating its rider. His satisfaction was short lived as he saw Bernardo whipping his two horse team in a frenzy of panic. He was fighting hard to bring them under control.

Jared grabbed the reins from Maddie and swung the buckboard in front of the line shack. A cloud of dust flew up as he brought the team to a halt. Through the dust he judged the distance to the door to be about twenty five yards, "When I say run for it, run!" Maddie nodded. Jared swung his Henry in the direction of the chasing horsemen and fired. "Get inside now!" he screamed. With bullets flying past her ears Maddie crashed through the line shack door.

Maddie stared out the window and watched helplessly as Bernardo's buckboard slew uncontrollably from side to side. Rosita, white with fright, gripped the handrail as hard as she could. The buckboard righted itself, but then the right hand wheel hit a rock and Rosita lost her grip on the hand rail and flew out of the buckboard. A bloodcurdling scream alerted Bernardo, "Rosita!" he cried fighting hard to bring the horses under control. Bringing them to a screeching halt he jumped from the buckboard and raced back to the crumpled figure of Rosita. Hooded riders thundered towards him their guns blazing. Bernardo pulled his pistol from its belt and returned fire. "Bernardo!" screamed Rosita as he bravely stood over her. He fired his pistol until it was empty. Thumbing fresh shells into the cylinder of his Frontier Colt he looked down at her and mouthed, "I love you, my little Rosita," then a bullet smashed into the side of his head killing him outright. Rosita screamed in horror as she saw the side of her husband's head explode.

Randy reined his horse in beside Jared. As the Henry spat flame Jared screamed an order at Randy, "Stay mounted. Ride to the ranch get help!"

"No I'm staying here with you and Miss Maddie."

"Don't be a damn fool. You're our only chance, now get outta here."

Randy's horse reared at the abrupt change of direction, his eyes wide open in fear and panic. Through tear-filled eyes he looked down at his friend then kicked his horse forward. The sound of firing deafened his final words.

"I won't let you down."

Instinctively knowing what Randy had said, Jared cried, "I know you won't." His heart was in his mouth as he watched the young rider gallop away. At the same time he jacked another round into the breech and fired. He heard a satisfying scream of pain as a rifle spun uncontrollably into the air. But other rifles cracked away at the lone rider. Jared fired quickly in their direction and watched in quiet anticipation as Randy, an expert horseman, proved his worth. He dodged and weaved through the high sage, bullets flying in every direction. Jared felt a sense of relief when none of the bullets hit their target.

A fresh horror eclipsed Rosita as three hooded horsemen brought their horses to a screeching halt and jumped down, each eager to be the first. Micah Levy panting with anticipation grabbed her around the waist as she kicked and screamed. He slugged her roughly with the barrel of the gun he brandished in his right hand. Rosita went limp and lifeless and then Levy swung the gun around and pointed it at Tom Bender and Ruffio.

"I'm first! You can have her after me!" The crazy look in his eyes told Bender and Ruffio not to argue. Instead they watched in lustful anticipation as Levy quickly undid his trousers. Then from behind them came the rapid firing of a handgun. They turned as one to see Caleb Logan emptying his gun into the dead body of Heck.

Jared fired his Henry at anything that moved, then an agonising scream tore into the afternoon sky as both team horses were shot to death in front of him. He took his cue and ran the twenty five yards to the open doorway. Maggie had already begun pulling the big oak table towards the door.

"Good girl, now take this," he handed her the rifle. Just point and shoot, but only if you see someone. We ain't got much ammunition." Jared upended the table and jammed it in place against the door. "That should stop them for a time."

"Oh Jared, what's happening to us?"

"We're going to survive, that's what."

"Who are they? What do they want? They ain't any kind of vigilante that I ever saw," said Maddie.

Her question was answered seconds later as they heard Rosita scream.

"Oh Jesus, they're raping her!" The words came out before he knew it. "I'm sorry. I didn't mean...." even as he began to speak he realised the redundancy in his words.

"Jared, don't spare my feelings. I've been around too long. That man who spoke, I think I know him. I recognise his voice. He used to be a sergeant in Miles's regiment. It's me he wants! If I go out there, they might let you alone."

"Do you really believe that?" replied Jared, "He ain't getting any of us without paying a price. Check my pistol belt. How many bullets we got left?"

Maddie did a quick count, "Eleven."

"I've two left in my pistol and eight in the Henry."

"I've five in this," said Maddie, producing the 22 calibre Colt.

"Then we've got more than a fighting chance," said Jared with a conviction he neither felt nor believed.

In the lull between firing Maddie and Jared were tormented by Rosita's screams, "Oh Rosita!" cried Maddie.

Then a hail of bullets peppered the cabin. Jared pushed Maddie to the ground and looked through the crack in the door. He could just about see five or six men taking up positions behind rocks in the brush and two behind the buckboard.

"They want me to return fire. That might work in our favour," he muttered to himself.

"What'd you say?"

Jared grabbed the pistol belt and fed two bullets into the chamber leaving the next two empty. Another hail of bullets cut off his answer. "A little trick Mordecai taught me."

Away from the line shack, Tom Bender stared down angrily at Micah Levy.

"Hurry up you Jew bastard, you're taking too long. I want my turn." The Jew looked up, his eyes glazing over, as he finished with a final thrust. "She's all yours," he said as he staggered off the spread-eagled Rosita.

Tom Bender unbuckled his belt and let his pants slip to the floor. Then he slipped to his knees and pushed her legs farther apart.

"Now she's gonna feel a real man," Rosita opened her eyes and screamed as his heavy body fell upon her.

Ruffio, the half breed stared down as Bender thrust into her. He undid his pants.

"I'll stop the bitch screaming." His eyes betrayed only lust and cruelty as he advanced on the screaming Mexican woman. Bender looked up and laughed.

Caleb Logan looked down at the writhing mass of bodies.

"They killed my brother," he said almost in a trance as he walked towards the line shack. He reloaded his gun as he approached. Micah

Levy joined him laughing like a cat that's got the cream. "What are you laughing at? They killed my brother."

Micah's face changed and he snapped.

"That ain't my fault, take it out with them in the shack." He broke into a grin as Caleb Logan, without any thought of safety, advanced on the cabin.

"Get down you stupid bastard!" screamed Driscoll.

Driscoll's words fell on deaf ears as the six feet five giant advanced on the cabin cocking and firing his gun as he moved closer.

Jared, alert to the new danger gauged the time between cocking and firing, then he made his move. He opened the door slightly just as the last bullet splintered the door. Jared fired, 'Crack, crack, crack.' The big man kept advancing but the Henry stopped him as Jared switched from the chest and shot him in the forehead.

"Shit, I didn't want to use up ammunition," he said more to himself than to Maddie. At the same time he stared at the dead man, then at half a belt of 45 calibre cartridges around the big man's waist. Jared thanked God that he'd traded the old Navy Colt for the Peacemaker. He quickly told Maddie his plan, "If we can hold out until nightfall I might be able to get that cartridge belt."

"Do you think we'll get out of this alive?"

"We've got this far, if we hold out Randy should be able to get back in time with the boys. But whatever happens there's something you need to know." Maddie looked at him and tears rolled down her cheeks as he said, "I love you Maddie McAllister." He smiled at her briefly and Maddie thought that despite their situation she was with the man she loved and in her eyes that's all that counted.

"I love you too."

Then as quickly Jared changed the mood. "If I can get my hands on that cartridge belt we've as good a chance as any to get out of this alive," he said, though in his head he knew that unless help arrived soon, they were done for.

They kept a vigilant watch. Occasionally a shot was fired into the cabin but little else happened. Then Driscoll's voice broke the silence.

"Hey, you inside the cabin. We only want the woman. Send her out, we'll let you live."

"Go to hell!" cried Jared.

"I said it was him, if I do as he says he might let you go."

"I ain't letting you go anywhere. You know what happened to Rosita."

The memory of Rosita's screams reverberated in Maddie's brain. She knew men, she knew just what they were capable of, she'd been raped, she'd been abused but she'd never been subjected to the horrors Rosita had to endure. Maddie made up her mind that she'd rather die than subject herself to gang rape. She smiled at Jared and said in a darkly humorous way, "Some honeymoon this is!" Jared grinned at her and knew that despite everything he'd made the right choice.

It was dusk and the sky was turning flame gold as the sun began to sink beneath the horizon, masking the nightmarish horror that was unfolding beneath it. Only the strong smell of cordite as it dispersed into the air, and the occasional flurry of gunfire betrayed the tranquility of the scene.

Jared and Maddie heard a scurry of movement and knew the time would soon be upon them.

"They're gonna rush us as soon as it's dark. We've made it difficult for them. They know they haven't much time before Randy arrives with help."

"Oh Jared, do you really think so?"

He didn't answer her question.

"When they rush the cabin I'm going out to meet them. I want you to use that pistol of yours to keep them at bay. If I can get that pistol belt I reckon we'll be able to hold out until help arrives."

As the sun vanished and the sky turned a midnight blue, the moon took up its rightful position and illuminated the sky. Jared, thankful for the blue grey light looked up and saw clouds drifting across the moon. He knew that with the next cloud that obliterated the moon's glow, the fight would be on. He waited until he saw the first wisp of cloud touch the moon, then he looked at the nervous Maddie.

"Are you ready?"

She nodded. Her mouth had dried up, but she still managed a smile.

"I'll always love you," he said and Maddie detected a tear in his eye, then he was gone. She fired wildly, emptying her gun into the darkness. With his Henry in one hand and a razor sharp knife in another he managed to get to the body of Caleb Logan. He sliced through the cartridge belt and pulled it from the body. He turned and raced for the door. He'd almost made it, when, from his left side, an ugly Mexican quick as a cat, plunged a knife into his side. He caught the Mexican a glancing blow with the butt of his Henry. The Mexican stumbled and Jared turned the rifle around and fired from the hip: crack, crack, crack. Then turning, stumbling, blood seeping from the wound in his side, he staggered towards the door. At least five bullets tore into his body.

Maddie screamed, "Jared!" Then holding his Peacemaker in both hands, she fired at the approaching horde and backed further into the room. Driscoll was the first inside, his eyes afire with lust. Screaming in terror Maddie fired, she missed him by inches. She fired again and still they came. She felt the wall at her back and knew it was all over. With terror in her eyes she turned the gun upwards, cocked the hammer and closed her mouth over the barrel.

"No!" screamed Driscoll as Maddie's finger pressed hard on the trigger.

"Click," she cocked the hammer again, "Click."

Maddie's nightmare was just beginning ...

Driscoll slapped the empty gun from Maddie's hands and caught her with a blow under the chin. Then, screaming in triumph, he dragged her out of the cabin into a clearing. The moon shone down creating an eerie blue glow over the grinning men who stared hungrily at Maddie's semi conscious body.

Driscoll, gun in hand, looked defiantly at the still hooded figure of Fairfax.

"You said I go first!"

"And you shall," replied Fairfax, "You above all have earned your reward, but first I want her to know."

Driscoll relaxed, his lust for the woman beneath him was at breaking point.

Maddie, head bowed in defeat mouthed, "Why, why....?"

Driscoll grabbed her by the hair and made her look up at the hooded man.

"Why? You ask me why!" His anger was in danger of overtaking his lust. The bloodletting had taken its toll as he fought to regain his composure. With her still facing the hooded horseman, Driscoll brought himself under control, "You could have shown me some respect, but no. I was beneath you, O'Bannion's widow. But you're nothing, just another cheap whore. I saved that poor fuck's life and you wouldn't give me the time of day. Well now it's judgement day and you are about to reap the whirlwind."

"Enough!" bellowed Half-Face, tired of his histrionics.

Driscoll went silent and Maddie looked up at the hooded man who commanded such respect. She stared transfixed as he took off the burlap hood, his mouth breaking into a maniacal grin, the same grin that she'd seen just before she smashed the lantern across his face.

"It's been a long time," Half-Face said slowly, "we have so much to catch up on," then he laughed.

Maddie stared up at the masked face of Fairfax, but instead of surprise, a look of resignation was etched upon her face. She'd questioned God on many occasions, but this time she saw no point. She knew. She knew that it was God's punishment for taking her father's life.

She didn't hear as Fairfax continued his oration, "But before that you can entertain my men as only a bitch whore like you can." He gestured towards Driscoll, "She's all yours, but don't be greedy, the men all want their share."

Driscoll slapped Maddie viciously across the face several times and then he ripped her dress from off her back. The others looked on, all shouting encouragement. He threw her to the ground and quickly undid his belt and let his pants fall around his ankles. Driscoll looked down at her, the woman he'd lusted after for so many years, and felt nothing, nothing except an urge to inflict pain and humiliation. As he sank to his knees he looked longingly at O'Bannion's widow hoping for a reaction, but none came. He forced himself inside her and the pain of his penetration snapped her out of her catatonic state and she began to scream and struggle. In those brief seconds when he'd thrown her to the ground Maddie renounced God. He'd forsaken her but she wasn't giving up without a fight. Rough hands and arms pinned her to the ground. She struggled until all the strength went out of her and all hope was lost. Driscoll thrust into her for five long minutes then he turned her over, to an immense roar of approval. A look of perverse pride spread across his face. He was sweating profusely as he began to sodomise her.

"See what you've been missing all these years." The ordeal went on for several more minutes as he ripped into her. When he climaxed, there was a great roar of excitement. Eager hands tore him from her body and threw him to one side. Then in ones and twos the men took their turn. Only John Larch didn't partake.

"You don't want the whore?" asked Fairfax.

"I ain't no animal. I've killed many times, but I take my pleasure where it's mutual."

John Larch looked at Fairfax disdainfully and walked into the darkness. Half-Face watched him walk away. Of all the men under his command John Larch was the most dangerous. His thoughts were interrupted.

"Ain't you had your fill Micah," cried Bender.

"I didn't see you refusing seconds," laughed Levy. "I aim to fuck her every which way."

Fairfax stood over Micah, "Fuck her anyway you wish, but hurry the fuck up, I want my fun with her before them cowboys get here."

The men were like rabid dogs ready to turn at the slightest provocation. One on one he thought he was a match for all of them with the exception maybe of John Larch, but as a pack he knew he could be ripped apart. He so wanted to cut, to hurt, to see her scream out in terror but as the moon crept higher in the sky he knew he would have little time. With the men's lust sated apart, from the Jew, he decided to make a stand.

"Saddle up, we're out of here in ten minutes!"

The men turned away from the spectacle, tired and spent from their exhaustions and slowly began to mount up.

Micah Levy was still humping away at the unconscious body of Maddie when Fairfax dragged him off. Micah turned with a murderous rage and stared straight at the eight inch Bowie in Half-Face's hand. His ardour cooled some what.

"Go mount up, we're movin out," snapped Fairfax.

Alone at last, thought Fairfax. He stared down at the bloodied unrecognisable face and then he knelt down and shook Maddie's limp body. Panic set in as he felt the sticky mess between her legs. His hands were covered in blood. 'That stupid fuck has done for her,' his mind screamed. He shook her again. He fumbled for a pulse. He put his ear to her mouth. There was nothing. 'The Jew fuck has killed her!' His brain screamed out for vengeance.

He glanced towards the Jew who was already mounted just as John Larch rode over to him.

"There's a group of riders heading in our direction. I'd say there's about twenty of them." He held out the reins of Fairfax's horse. Fairfax looked down at the battered translucent body of Maddie and was in two minds to mount up or follow his urge to slash her throat. "It's now or never. I ain't hanging around," Larch said as he dropped the offered reins.

Fairfax nodded. He could see the wisdom in Larch's words and in one swift movement climbed into the saddle. As he turned his horse he looked down at Maddie's broken body for the last time, then spurred his horse into the night.

CHAPTER 49

The moon's blue grey light, spread across the prairie floor illuminating the silent cabin. Ghostly shadows danced across its walls as the men from the McAllister ranch brought their horses to a grateful walk. An eerie silence descended upon the men as they surveyed the scene of recent carnage.

"Oh Jesus, we're too late!" cried Randy, breaking the silence. "Spread out, search the whole area."

In stunned silence the men obeyed his orders to fan out from the line shack. Randy and Joe Buckley climbed down from their horses. Their nostrils were greeted by the stench of death emanating from the bodies of the two harnessed mares, still, even in death, attached to the bullet ridden buckboard. Buckley gagged and pulled his bandana up over his nose. Randy, over-awed with grief, ignored the smell and began the search for his friend. He'd made a promise, one that he'd tried so hard to keep, but alas he felt he'd arrived too late.

They stepped over the bullet ridden body of Caleb Logan, "Looks like Jared messed him up good," said Joe, doing his best to alleviate Randy's feelings of guilt. His words fell on deaf ears as Randy's fears were becoming fact; he'd spotted Jared lying in the doorway close to the body of a Mexican. *Later Randy was to learn the Mexican was Gregorio.*

"Oh fucking Jesus!" cried Randy as tears began to form in his eyes.

"He's still alive!" cried Buckley in astonishment. "But only just," he added, as he noticed the many wounds on Jared's body.

Randy brushed aside his tears and rushed to his boss's side, "Get a blanket quick!" he shouted. Then he too looked at his friend's blood soaked body, "Ah fuck, it don't look good." His words were lost on Joe Buckley as the man rushed back to his horse for his bed roll. The biting cold night air of the prairie caused Randy *now back in leader mode* to begin to think on his feet.

Seconds later Joe returned with the blanket.

"Help me get him inside," barked Randy. Then more softly he added, "As gently as we can." Joe, without questioning, knelt down and took a hold of Jared's legs. "Best we keep him warm," sobbed the grief stricken Randy, as they gently carried Jared's body inside the shack.

Then something in the darkness of the doorway caused Buckley to jump. He pulled his Colt from his holster and cocked the hammer.

"What is it?" cried Randy.

"It's the damn Mex, he's still breathing. I'll soon fix that," said Buckley as he pointed his revolver at the wounded man's head.

"What the fuck! Don't kill him we need him alive!" shouted Randy.

Joe Buckley looked perplexed but un-cocked his Colt and brought it down hard upon the side of the Mexican's head. "That'll keep him quiet some," he replied, pleased that he'd inflicted just a little pain on the murdering scum who had waylaid the boss of the Circle M.

With no doctoring between them, all Randy and Joe could do was to keep Jared warm and as comfortable as was possible. Just as they'd seen to that chore, three of the boys from the Circle M walked their horses in. The look on their faces said it all.

"They're all dead, Bernardo and Heck been shot to pieces," said a shocked Jake Timmons.

"Maddie and Rosita?" questioned Randy.

Timmons looked at his two companions for support. They replied by bowing their heads.

"They.... they raped Rosita. God damn it Randy, they raped her and then they killed her."

"Oh God!" cried Joe Buckley. His words summed up the collective shock and grief of the men in the shack.

"What about Maddie?" cried Randy. His words remained unanswered as a shot pierced the night sky. "Stay here," ordered Randy. "Keep Jared warm and for fucks sake keep an eye on that greaser." He mounted up and kicked his horse in the direction of the shot, several torches guided him and within less than a minute he arrived in a clearing.

"We found Maddie!" cried Clay Dean sternly. Clay, ex Ranger that he was looked shocked at what he'd found. He'd fought hard against the Comanche, cleared up after they'd raped and pillaged, he was a man who had seen it all, but the look on his face said everything, "I thought she was dead, but then I noticed there was a faint breathing. Clay had thrown a blanket over her to cover her dignity and to keep her warm. Randy lifted it up, "I wouldn't, it ain't pretty. Those sons of bitches done messed her up good and proper."

Randy picked her up as gently as he could and carried her back to the line shack.

"Light a fire, we got to keep them warm. At first light we're heading for Helena. It might kill em, but without a doc we ain't got any choice."

Maddie's scream woke Randy from a fitful sleep. He knelt down beside her and did his best to calm her. "It's me, Randy, you're with the boys from the Circle M, you're safe now, no one's gonna hurt you anymore." The tortured look of unbridled fear tugged at Randy's heart, all he could do was talk gently, try to allay her fears. He thought of the first time he'd seen her, how pretty she'd looked, then he looked down at the quivering swollen wreck of a face and swore vengeance against those who had done such a crime, then thankfully Maddie slipped back into unconscious.

"At least she's showing signs of life," said Dean, "which is more than can be said for the boss."

"He ain't dead yet, so don't you be writing him off," cried Randy.

"No need to get riled at me," said Clay Dean. Dean was a hard man and wasn't used to a whippersnapper sounding off at him, but given the circumstances he let it slide.

"Sorry," cried Randy as he stood up. "I should have stayed with the boss. We might have had a better chance."

"Randy, don't blame yourself. From what you've told us, Bernardo, Heck and Rosita were beyond your help when you left. At least the boss and Maddie have a chance, thanks to you," said Buckley.

"That might be, but I wish I could've done more." He was the youngest of the bunch and until today no one had taken much notice of him. But his ride back to the ranch and his leadership since, had turned the boy into a man. 'Yeah,' thought Randy, 'there is something I can do.' He'd stopped Joe Buckley from putting that filthy Mex out of his misery, but until now Randy hadn't reasoned why. Now he knew. "I'm taking a walk, clear my head," he said apologetically.

Randy found the Mexican bound hand and foot and covered with a horse blanket. The young cowboy kicked him roughly awake.

"I want names and I want them now."

By morning Randy had that list of names; James Fairfax, Ex army sergeant; William Driscoll, the man killer; John Larch; Finn Harpe; Tom Bender, a Mexican half breed called Ruffio and a Jew called Micah Levy.

"The four dead are Kid Briscoe, Bull Logan, Caleb Logan and the Mexican ..." he told the hands of the Circle M.

Everyone of the boys had heard the gunshot just before dawn, but nobody spoke of it.

"Expired in the night," said Joe.

"Yeah, kinda peaceful like," said Clay Dean.

Randy felt a strange sense of pride, killing a man in cold blood wasn't something he'd ever dreamed could happen to him. But having Clay Dean, famous Indian fighter and ranger giving him the seal of approval, kinda made it right. But it was the feeling of impotency over the killers who had escaped that caused him the most concern.

When the buckboard finally reached Helena, Doc McClaren was there to greet it. Clay and Joe had rode on ahead and told the authorities about the killings and rapes. Chicago Joe waited anxiously by the Doc's side as the Texas cowmen rode in with Randy, driving the buckboard at a slow gait.

"They're in a bad way Doc, but Mr McAllister he's strong, he'll pull through, won't he?" Concern was written all over Randy's face. "Miss Maddie, she's been beaten badly; those son's of bitches really done for her, begging your pardon ma'am."

Chicago Joe replied, "You cuss all you want too." Hardened to the life, she was unprepared for the state of Maddie's injuries. Both eyes were swollen shut, ugly blue and yellow bruising and dark dried blood covered the entire lower half of her face. She was unrecognisable to Josephine Hensley. To put it mildly the poor woman had been beaten to within an inch of her life. Probing inside Maddie's battered and bloody mouth she found miraculously that all her teeth were still intact. She sobbed at the sight of her friend, "Those bastards will pay for this."

While Jared was housed in the backroom of Doc McClaren's, Maddie was moved to a bedroom in the Red Light Saloon. Chicago Joe and her girls cleaned Maddie up and saw to her wounds. The doctor came and administered painkillers and potions to help her sleep. She'd been damaged internally; her private parts were black and blue with ugly red and yellow bruising down both sides of her inner thighs. The blood loss from her vagina alone led the doctor to believe that, in his opinion, if she survived she wouldn't be able to bare children. "Not," he added, "that she'd have the need, in her profession." Chicago Joe shot him a murderous glance, but bit her tongue. Doc McClaren also discovered Maddie had sustained a broken wrist, three fractured ribs and as many cuts and bruises as the doctor had seen in a long time. Oblivious to his insensitive remarks, the doctor began to berate the perpetrators of the crime. "The bastards treated her worse than a wild animal. No human should inflict such wounds on another. But she's luckier than she has a right to be given the circumstances. She has a chance, provided she doesn't have any major setbacks with her internal organs."

Chicago Joe thanked the doctor and said they'd call on him if necessary. Concerned as she was with Maddie's physical condition, it was her mental state that worried her most. She'd seen girls over the years who had been abused and raped; their suffering probably less than Maddie's, who had taken to the drink and dope. One, in particular, that sprung to mind committed suicide. The emotional and violent trauma could affect Maddie in many ways. She could die or at worst she could end up in an asylum.

Over the course of days Maddie slipped in and out of consciousness. Twice Josephine called for the doctor and the priest, but each time Maddie seemed to bring herself back from the brink and then around the fourth day she began to show signs of improvement. In her lucid state she seemed to be aware of what had happened to her, asking constantly after Jared and the others, but then she'd slip back to talking about her childhood and eventually, exhausted by everything, she'd fall into a deep but troubled sleep. That she was showing signs of recovery was welcoming, but the prospect of having to tell her that Jared was barely holding on worried Chicago Joe.

Jared died without gaining consciousness six days after they brought him in. "Oh dear Lord. She's gonna take it badly I fear."

"I'll get over there right away," said Doc McClaren.

"No, I'll do it. Best she hears it from me."

Chicago Joe climbed the stairs to Maddie's room with a heavy heart. Closing the door behind her she sat down at Maddie's bedside and broke the news.

"No! He can't be dead, he can't be." For an indeterminable time she refused to listen to Josephine's news, but then as she looked imploringly to the others in the room, the truth seemed to knock what stuffing she had left, out of her.

"I'm sorry Maddie, he's gone. He died peacefully an hour ago."

Maddie slowly resigned herself to the awful truth, "Why? Why him? He was good and kind, he wouldn't hurt a fly," and then suddenly she went silent.

Now that Jared had gone Maddie had nothing to cling on to. Chicago Joe despaired for her condition and sought Doc McClaren's advice.

"Keep her busy. Keep her mind busy. Tell her she's a ranch to run, tell her she needs to look to the future. Tell her it's what Jared would have wanted. Just tell her anything."

"I'll tell her Doc, but I don't think it'll do no good."

"She's able to walk, well almost. She can stand at least. Just keep her mind occupied." Doc McClaren was struggling to find the words, "Time's what she needs, you've got to buy time. Mr McAllister, he'll have to be buried. I know it's harsh but tell her she's a funeral to take care of."

"What! I can't tell her that!"

"Believe me, the woman needs to feel her worth. She needs to feel wanted. Arranging the funeral could bring her out of herself."

"Yeah, or push her over the edge."

"What choice have you got?"

"None," said Josephine 'Chicago Joe' Hensley.

It was a tall order, but somehow Chicago Joe managed to get Maddie to break her silence. She told her in no uncertain terms that she had to pull herself together as she had Jared's burial to arrange. This seemed to bring Maddie out of her trance like state. Then Chicago Joe told her that, as sole owner of the Circle M, she had the livelihood of around twenty men and three women in her responsibility.

"I don't want the ranch! It's not mine. Jared must have some family down south." It was as if she wanted to wash away any thoughts of what might have been.

"He had a sister but I think she died back in 77, other than that he had no one," said Randy. "Begging your pardon ma'am but I know how fond Jared was of you. I reckon he'd a wanted you to keep it."

Randy's innocent words seemed to hit home, "I don't know the first thing about ranching, would you and the others run it for me temporarily?"

"Let me talk with Clay Dean, Joe Buckley and the others. I'll get back to you."

Maddie, dressed sombrely in a black full length dress, walked slowly behind the black plumed horses as they carried Jared's coffin to the cemetery at Helena. She held her head high as she walked through Helena's streets. 'At the very least,' she thought, 'Jared needed a dignified burial.' From the corners of her eyes she could see people lining the sidewalk, heads bowed in respect. She felt like crying, but knew in her heart that she was all cried out. The manner of Jared's death, the tragic end for Rosita and Bernardo and poor Heck forever stiff lipped and formal, had left their mark on her. No, crying was not an option.

As the funeral party reached the gates of the cemetery it had grown in size. To an observer it looked like a who's who of local dignitaries. At the graveside Alex Lavenburg, Jim Hensley, Duke Hamilton and Jake Tunstall stood alongside the rough Texas cowboys of the Circle M and sung from the same hymn book. Josephine and the girls from the Red Light Saloon supported Maddie who seemed a little fatigued by the slow walk to the cemetery.

As Jared's coffin was lowered into the ground, Maddie stood there tearless. Her mind was a whirlwind of torment and hate, fighting against the general good of others. The last few days had been a revelation to her. The kindness shown by her peers and the sympathy shown by her betters had somehow stiffened her resolve. She had three ways to go. She could take on the ranch, become a successful female ranch owner, or she could sell up to the highest bidder and disappear from the state forever. Both of these options were sound, even sensible, but what if Half-Face, the monster of her nightmares, came back? What if he learned of her new found success? She knew that despite the dangers he would return. Even if she disappeared she'd live with the dread that one day he'd find her. She wanted justice, she wanted protection, but there was no recognised law in the Territory, at least none that would effectively track these men down. She wanted to see James Fairfax and the others dangling from a rope, but above all Maddie sought retribution.

The last remnants of Rock of Ages floated into the night sky as dusk crept over the small cemetery. Maddie knelt down and threw a small bouquet of wild flowers on to Jared's coffin.

"Goodbye my love."

Then with a lace handkerchief she wiped at a solitary tear and stood up. She looked at the bowed and sombre faces of the mourners as they filed past the open grave, each one of them lost in their own private thoughts, and then over the shoulders of the mourners she saw a lone horseman approaching the cemetery gates. Transfixed she continued to watch as he stepped down from his horse. Her heart skipped a beat and for that she felt guilty. The man was some distance away and the fading light was poor but Maddie knew. Her eyes couldn't make him out in the twilight but her heart knew. As he walked up the small hill towards her, she let out a gasp. Then without thinking she forced her tired legs to race towards him.

"Mordecai, Mordecai.... I just knew you'd come. If you'd news of what happened, then I knew you'd come."

He held her in his arms and she cried, and she cried and it all came flooding out. The dark Texan held her tightly, afraid to let go, afraid of what she might think when he gazed upon her poor damaged face. His eyes would betray him; they were the windows to his soul. She'd see the pity, the hurt, the pain, but most of all she'd see the anger that raged inside.

"Maddie, my dear Maddie. I'm here for you. I'm here for you ..."

CHAPTER 50

Jake Tunstall was the first to recognise Mordecai. He looked towards his fellow townsmen, but Clay Dean calmly stepped in front of him.

"If you're thinking what I think you're thinking don't, unless you intend staying up here permanently."

"It can wait," said Tunstall with a conviction he didn't feel.

"Damn right it can wait. Be warned if we see any men in hoods we'll shoot them down on sight."

"I understand, but he's got twenty-four hours. After that the town Marshall will come a lookin," replied Jake Tunstall.

"Twenty-four hours."

"You got my word. Believe what you will, but Miss Maddie's been more than a friend to this town. We owe her that."

In a private room of the Red Light Saloon Maddie and Mordecai sparred around each other. Their initial meeting was filled with emotions that they both shared, but in the privacy of the room they appeared awkward. Mordecai looked longingly at Maddie and said in as soft a tone as he could muster, "Maddie you look done in, best you rest now. We've important things to discuss and now ain't the time."

"I am tired and I'll take my leave of you, but yes there are things we need to discuss. Today we buried my husband and bad thoughts should be left for another day."

While Maddie slept, Mordecai quizzed Randy about the ambush.

"They rode up to us, hooded to all get out, but almost friendly like. We had a visit from the vigilantes when they were looking for you at the ranch."

"Except," broke in Clay Dean, "these weren't vigilantes. I've spoke with Jake Tunstall and he reckons he ain't ever seen the men that Jared and the boys killed."

"So who were they?"

"I got their names from that dying Mex," said Randy.

Mordecai listened as Randy went through the names. He froze as Randy mentioned Fairfax.

"Fairfax! What did he look like?"

Randy was startled by his response, "I don't know Mordecai, honest I don't. They was all hooded when I last seen em." He looked hesitantly at Mordecai.

"The boy done good Mordecai," interrupted Clay. "He rode through the afternoon and into the night to get us."

"That Mexican, he … he said something. Yeah, that's it, he called that Fairfax guy Half-Face, or something like that."

"Jesus H Christ!" exclaimed Mordecai.

"You know him?" cried Clay Dean.

"Nah, I ain't had that pleasure, but I will."

Randy felt his blood run cold. Whoever this Half-Face was, the young cowboy wouldn't have wanted to be in his shoes. Mordecai's eyes burned pure hate.

The Circle M cowboys posted guard around the Red Light Saloon, not that they expected trouble, but if the vigilantes wanted Mordecai then they'd have to fight for him. To avert bloodshed Clay Dean paid a visit to Jake Tunstall at the Alhambra.

"We don't want any trouble, what we do want is time. Miss Maddie's still in a bad way and needs to recover. We also need to know that our mutual friend will be left alone during that time."

"Look Clay, I think we got off on the wrong foot. Maddie and I have been friends since she first got here. All I want is what's right for her. If our mutual friend stays out of trouble we won't be paying him a visit."

"That's all I'm asking," said Clay.

Jake Tunstall held out his hand, "What happened to Maddie and her husband ain't right, but this town is growing up. So it needs to be seen to be doing the right thing, you understand?"

"Yeah I understand," replied Clay Dean, ignoring Tunstall's open hand.

Next Clay sent a telegram to Texas Rangers headquarters in Austin. He had friends there who could possibly give him a lead on the band of killers.

Mordecai knew what he had to do, but first he had to clear the air with Maddie. There were so many things left unsaid, so much guilt. He felt he had to unburden himself. He checked with Chicago Joe on Maddie's condition the very next morning.

"She's still pretty weak, but physically she's on the mend, it's her state of mind that bothers me," said Josephine.

"I won't tire her out," replied Mordecai, "it's just there are things we have to discuss."

"I understand," replied Josephine knowingly.

Maddie, on hearing the door creak opened her eyes and looked at Mordecai and smiled.

"I … I thought for a while that I'd dreamed you'd come."

"I'm here right enough, but I'm feeling that it's a mistake. Perhaps I shouldn't have come."

"How can you say that?"

"Jesus Christ Maddie, I done a terrible thing. You was engaged to Jared, what possessed me."

"We both done wrong, but it can't be fixed. We have to live with it."

"How can you be so calm about it?"

"I'm not calm. I felt as guilty as you. I couldn't go ahead and marry Jared with a lie hanging over us, so I told him before we were married."

"You what! I told you not to say a word."

"Mordecai, I couldn't live with myself if I hadn't told him. But he knew! He knew already."

"How?"

"You told him; I don't mean in the normal way. It was when you said goodbye. It was your awkwardness around him." Maddie could see the hurt look in Mordecai's eyes. "But it didn't matter. It didn't matter to him," she said hurriedly. "He was strong, stronger than either of us. He knew why you were leaving and he knew you were never coming back. He loved you, just as…." Maddie stifled a sob, "just as he loved me."

Mordecai reached out for her and she responded. For ten minutes they held each other in a comforting embrace while Maddie sobbed her heart out. Mordecai remained silent, still not sure of why he came.

It was a day later when Clay Dean received the telegram he'd been waiting for. It read…. *John Larch, shooter stop considered very dangerous stop known to frequent Cheyenne stop. Others unknown stop.*

Clay Dean gave Mordecai the telegram, "It ain't much to go on, but in my opinion if I was them I'd get the hell outta Montana Territory. Cheyenne is a wide open town and it's far enough away to feel safe."

"It's where I'd go," said Mordecai. "Maddie needs looking after, so I'd suggest as soon as she's ready to travel you take her back to the ranch."

"And you, what are you going to do?" It was a question that didn't need answering; Clay Dean already knew the answer.

"I'm heading for Cheyenne."

"You're not going alone," said Dean. "We're coming with you."

"And if this Half-Face gets wind that Maddie ain't dead who's gonna look after her?"

Clay thought about it for a moment, "You're right, she's better off at the ranch with the boys for protection, but I'm coming with you."

"If Clay's going, then I'm going too," said Randy.

"Jesus H Christ!" exclaimed Mordecai. He knew too well that to argue would have been futile. Clay Dean was a good gun and the youngster had shown his worth against the murdering scum, "If you come with me, don't stand in my way."

"I ain't going back to the ranch. I'm staying here with Josephine," she told Clay Dean when he outlined their plans to her. "I just ask that you be careful, all of you."

She'd only spoken a few words to Mordecai since their reunion, and those were fraught with an awkwardness that she found unnatural. It was as if their shared guilt was turning them into strangers. Now that Mordecai was going, Maddie felt a strong urge to talk. She sat up in her bed and asked Chicago Joe to send for Mordecai.

He was just saddling his horse at the livery stable when he received Maddie's message. Turning to Clay Dean and Randy he said, "I'll meet you outside the Red Light in fifteen minutes."

He was surprised to find her dressed and sitting upright in a large ornate chair. Her dark hair was piled high, the bruises and swelling around her eyes had all but gone, she wore a little makeup around her eyes. Mordecai could see she'd gone to a great effort, but she was still deathly pale, a mere shadow of her former self.

"You're looking well," he lied.

"You never could lie," she said, and gave him a weak smile. "I asked to see you because I know where you're going and I know that if you survive things will have changed between us. It would be hypocritical of me to ask you to stay, to take care of me, to take me in your arms and love and protect me, to be as we so easily could have been, but I can't. I've changed Mordecai." Her eyes remained cold and unmoving as she continued, "What those bastards did can't be undone. I still hear Rosita's screams, they haunt my every waking hour. The guilt I feel is overwhelming. If I hadn't fallen in love with Jared, he'd still be alive, him, Rosita, poor sweet Bernardo and Heck, they're all dead because of me."

"Maddie, don't. It wasn't your fault. No one asked Jared to fall in love with you," he protested.

"Nevertheless, I feel a great debt towards them. That scum killed without mercy and they have to be punished. I only wish I was strong enough to go with you. I'm alive but I'm dead inside." She looked at him with a sad longing and Mordecai knew that whatever it took he'd hunt those killers to the ends of the earth. "They killed me as certain as they killed Jared. Find them Mordecai, find them and kill them all."

Mordecai looked into Maddie's deep cobalt blue eyes, that once held such sparkle, such sassiness, such life, but all that remained was a dark emptiness.

"Whatever it takes," he mouthed. Then, without another word spoken between them, he turned his back and walked out of the room.

Jake Tunstall stood on the sidewalk outside the Alhambra and watched with relief as the three men rode out. Behind them trailed two packhorses loaded with provisions and an array of weapons that Mordecai had bought at the general store the day before.

Three days saw them reach Butte where they boarded a Utah and Northern Railroad train to Ogden in Utah. Whilst in Ogden, Clay Dean heard about an incident on the Union Pacific six weeks earlier. The train had been forced to stop by a large group of hooded vigilantes. Mordecai's ears pricked up.

"Yeah it seems they claimed they were looking for a fugitive from up in the Montana Territory. Finding their man they forced him off the train and then strung him up to a nearby oak tree. Not content with taking the man's life they then used his body for target practice. He was shot to dolls' rags," according to the ticket attendant.

Half an hour later, Mordecai asked the ticket clerk more about the incident.

"Buried in Ogden cemetery he was, got a proper marker an all. Seems he had luggage which is how the authorities were able to identify him."

"What was his name?" enquired Mordecai.

"Don't rightly know, but you've got until tomorrow morning to go pay him a visit," added the attendant.

"I might at that," said Mordecai as he walked away from the train depot.

They boarded the Union Pacific eastbound train to Cheyenne the following morning. Mordecai was in a morose mood when he sat down. He made it quite clear that he was in no mood to talk. As the train gathered speed he mused on the name on the marker of the newly dug grave. It had confirmed his suspicions. The marker read Finbar O'Toole, nothing more, nothing less. It didn't seem much like a fitting epitaph. He'd only met the man on that one occasion and he'd seemed the most capable of men. He'd enjoyed their talk together and had felt comfortable in the man's company. That he'd been caught off guard and dragged from the train by an ugly hooded mob told Mordecai these men were cunning as well as ruthless. No doubt he'd been beaten to within an inch of his life before being killed.

Mordecai had known violence probably more than most men. He'd seen it in the war, he'd been part of it during the Sutton Taylor Feud, seen the mutilated bodies of his family by the Comanche and finally become as bad as the rest of them, but he'd never enjoyed killing. This bunch was the worst kind and Mordecai vowed to himself that they had to be wiped from the face of the earth.

He glanced across at his companions and judged the task in front of him. Clay Dean was strong and dependable, ready to kill if the time came, but young Randy, he'd killed in anger, yes he'd killed in cold blood, but would he be up to facing this bunch? Mordecai didn't know the answer. He was a good kid, always joking and acting the fool, but now all that was about to change.

As the train pulled into the depot at Cheyenne, Randy remarked that he couldn't believe the time they'd saved. It had taken less than a week to transport the three men and their horses to the wide open town of Cheyenne. 'Yeah,' thought Mordecai, 'he's a good kid but still wet behind the ears.'

At the railroad depot they remounted their horses and trotted into the heart of town, where they booked into Dyer's hotel on Eddy Street, across the way from the Bon Ton and Harris Billiards parlour.

It was a Saturday night and the Bon Ton was heaving with revellers. Clay Dean and Randy pushed open the double doors and walked into the dimly lit saloon. A few minutes later Mordecai followed. He ordered a drink then sat with his back to the wall at the opposite end of the room. Randy ordered drinks and asked the bartender if John Larch had been in.

The barman shook his head, "Don't seem to recall anyone of that name, nope never heard of him."

"You can do better than that," said Randy persistently. He placed a five dollar bill on the counter.

"I could if I didn't value my life." The bill was ignored, but the question was answered.

Clay stepped up to the bar, smiled and placed his Colt on the bar counter. The bartender began to look worried.

"He ain't been in for awhile. Does most of his drinking at the Occidental on Taylor street, but I ain't seen him in a coon's age." His greedy paws reached out and expertly made the five dollar bill disappear.

"Obliged," said Randy.

Mordecai pulled his Peacemaker from its holster and spun the chamber, then he checked the loads in the sawn off shotgun which he had concealed under his coat.

"Randy, if you find any of them stand clear, because this is the only warning you'll get."

Randy gulped involuntarily, "I understand."

Clay Dean felt the walnut butt of his revolver for reassurance, before he pushed open the doors of the Occidental Gaming house. As expected the place was crowded, so this time all three men walked in unnoticed and took up different positions in the room. Clay stepped up to the bar and ordered a whisky. Mordecai scanned the room for the man known as Half-Face. Apart from him there was no one who would stand out. Their only tool was to ask around, but this carried an inherent risk. Asking if anyone knew John Larch in a crowded saloon was risky at best, but if they asked the wrong person then all hell could be let loose.

Mordecai walked up to Clay Dean and explained his fears. The ex ranger concurred.

"Best we concentrate on lookin' for Fairfax. If he's in Cheyenne he should be easy to spot. Get Randy, we'll try the next saloon on our list."

"Will do," replied Clay.

It was nearly midnight when the trio decided to call it a night. All agreed reluctantly that to get a result on their first night in town was a little too much to ask. Then as they neared Dyer's Hotel, Randy stared across the road at the hitching post outside Harris Billiards Parlour.

"Damned if I ain't seen that horse before!'" he exclaimed.

"What's that?" cried Mordecai.

"That horse, the one with the three white socks, I've seen it before!' Me and Heck were the closest when they rode up to us and I remembered looking down at the unusual markings on that bay."

Mordecai relaxed, "Three socks ain't that unusual."

"It's the same horse," insisted Randy.

Clay Dean pulled his revolver, "Anyone else, I'd agree with you Mordecai, but the kid really knows his horses."

Mordecai thought about it, the ranger was right; Randy did have an uncanny eye when it came to horseflesh. "Take a look through the window," he cried.

Randy raced to the corner window and peered through the grimy window pane. In the dimly lit room he could just make out two men with billiard cues in their hands crouching over the green baize table. To the left of them was a long bar, with one bartender and two customers drinking. Over to the right of the table there was a card game in progress; five men sat around the table. "I count ten men."

"I'll take the card table, Clay you cover the bar and you, watch the billiard players."

The bartender looked up as the three men entered, "Three whiskies," said Clay as he strolled up to the bar. Randy followed close behind and peeled off to the left and appeared to be watching the billiard game with interest. No one paid them any attention.

Mordecai walked purposely over towards the card table.

"Which of you owns that bay outside with three socks?"

"Who wants to know?" came the reply from a dark bearded man sitting farthest from Mordecai.

"You was asked a question mister," said an impetuous Randy.

Ignoring Randy the bearded man addressed himself to Mordecai, who gave a weak half smile. "You don't look like law dogs, who are you?"

"We're, well I am, a friend of John Larch and I heard he rides with a man that rides a bay like the one out front. I heard tell he was in town." Mordecai hoped John Larch wasn't in the room.

"Larch ain't here," said a sandy haired card player. Now state your business or get out while you still can."

"John Larch and me rode together back in Texas a while back. I heard from someone back in Pocatello that he hired on with a mean crew, figured we'd join up with the son of a bitch." Then Mordecai recalled that Finbar O'Toole had been taken from the train by a posse of vigilantes maybe thirty strong, but only about a dozen had attacked

Jared and Maddie. "Heard he'd gone into the lynching business," Mordecai feigned a laugh.

The bearded man was about to say something, but the sandy haired one silenced him with a look. "Lynching, how'd yah mean?"

"Man I spoke to reckons they took this law dog from a train clean as you like. Spoke a few words over him then hauled him up to the nearest tree. That's John alright."

Sandy began to relax, "He's gone. He took off a couple of days ago. Said he had business back in Texas. I reckoned he didn't have the stomach for it."

"Stomach for what?" roared Randy.

Tension once more filled the room. The card players all looked handy and the two men at the bar seemed ready to join in.

"If he ain't here let's go," said Clay. All eyes looked towards the bar. "The kid's young, he didn't mean anything."

"Didn't mean anything maybe, but I'm sure I've seen that kid someplace before."

"Damn right you've seen me, only you was wearing burlap sacking over your goddamn head."

Realisation came to Sandy in an instant. He cocked and fired his pistol from underneath the table just as Randy raised his own gun. The sound echoed around the room as the bullet struck the young cowboy in the fleshy part of the thigh.

'Boom, boom.' Mordecai's Greener blew Sandy from his chair and into oblivion. All around the room guns were cocked and pointed, some at point blank range, but miraculously no one fired.

Clay Dean screamed into the melee, "Don't fire, no one else has to die!" Mordecai had dropped the Greener and now covered the table with his Peacemaker and his Navy Colt. Four guns were pointed at him while the two men at the bar had half turned towards Clay with their hands full of fire power. Clay pointed his revolver straight at the nearest man's head, "We'll just take our friend and back out of here."

"Easy on those pistols boys, the man's got a point. I ain't dying for a two bit card sharp," said the man standing closest to Clay's pointed revolver.

"Me neither," said another.

"You know who you just killed?" said the bearded man, all the fire now having gone out of him. "That's Finn Harpe, heard tell he killed a couple of men in Nevada."

"You a friend of his?" spat Mordecai.

"Didn't know him long enough to call him friend. He rode into town a week ago with a mean lookin bunch."

"Barkeep, can you vouch for every man in the room?" asked Clay Dean.

"I can at that," said the bartender.

"If we find out you're lying we'll be back," added Mordecai.

"Everyone save him," said the bartender pointing towards the bearded man. "He, I've only known a little over three months, oh and the drummer playing billiards, he comes in about once or twice a year."

"One of you men go fetch a doctor for the boy?" demanded Clay. To his relief Randy had managed to prop himself up against the bar counter, the lower half of his body soaked with blood. "Move!" shouted Clay as he looked down at Randy.

"Sure," said one of the billiard players, glad to be out of there.

"The sheriff will want to see you." said the bartender, after all guns were lowered.

"He can as soon as the Doc fixes our friend." said Mordecai.

"We've got no problem with you men, all we wanted was Harpe," added Clay Dean.

The men all made to file out of the Billiards Parlour but Mordecai motioned for the bearded man to sit down. "I ain't with him honest," he squirmed.

"If I thought that you'd be long dead by now."

"Oh Jesus!"

"What we want is descriptions of the men that rode in with Harpe, that and any other information that might be of use to us."

"The leader, I can give you a full description."

"Yeah, other than him."

"There's the man in the army greatcoat. He's about six two in his stocking feet, dark complexion with dirty blond hair. That's all I can say."

"The others?" spat Mordecai, with anger in his voice and murder in his heart.

"The ... there's the Jew," stammered the bearded man.

"Yeah go on."

"He's about five ten, thin sallow faced, pockmarked with a thin moustache."

"What about the breed?"

"Just a breed, can't tell them apart. Oh, carries a silver handled knife with a carving of a snake's head on the grip."

"Larch and Bender?"

"John Larch, he scared me."

"Yeah sure," said Mordecai his impatience showing.

"I'd say he was about six feet, thin, oh and he's a lunger. Bender's easy. See the sheriff tomorrow he's got a flyer on Bender."

"Obliged," said Mordecai.

It was three days before Randy was able to sit up in bed. He'd been luckier than any man had a right to be. He'd lost a lot of blood, but fortunately the bullet had gone clean through. He'd slept the best part of a couple of days before he awoke fully, and then he wished he hadn't. The chewing out he got from Mordecai made him wish he could sink back into that blissful peaceful sleep.

"Damn fool kid! You could have got us all killed. You provoked a reaction we could have avoided."

"I'm sorry, I just lost it." Randy replied weakly.

Mordecai wasn't finished, "I needed that son of a bitch alive."

"I just didn't think."

"We're lucky that some idiot wanted to emulate them. If that bearded fool hadn't been in awe of those sons of bitches we'd have been no farther forward than befor' we started."

"You found out where they're heading?" asked Randy.

Mordecai looked angrily at the kid. His temper frayed to a frazzle. He'd finished talking.

"Not exactly, but we ain't likely to catch them this side of Christmas," said Clay Dean.

"How's that?" said Randy, oblivious to the murderous rage still seething inside of Mordecai.

"On account Mordecai and I are on bond to appear before the circuit judge this time next week."

"What!"

"We killed Finn Harpe lawfully, but this here country is getting itself civilised," spat Mordecai.

"We have to wait around until we get a hearing next week," added Clay Dean. "We could have taken off, but we ain't got any idea which ways to go and besides, if we left town the Sheriff said he'd have to light out after us and I don't relish being hanged for killing no lawman," said Clay as Mordecai stormed out the room. "We done run into a dead end."

Three weeks later they arrived back in Helena.

CHAPTER 51

Finn Harpe had been right about John Larch. He was bad tempered in a fight, ready to kill at the blink of an eye, but he had no stomach for the senseless killing and rapes that Fairfax seemed to thrive upon. John Larch thought long and hard about his ventures with Fairfax. They'd acted like a rabid wolf pack, well John Larch was nobody's wolf. He'd ridden along for the promised cash. He'd been ready to kill for it, but Fairfax was a different kind of animal, he killed for the fun of it. He was heading straight to hell and Larch wanted no part in it. He had his own hell and that was more than enough.

When he'd told Fairfax that he was up and quitting he'd expected some resistance, *even craved it,* but had received none. Then, Finn Harpe, taking his cue from the Texas gunman up and say's he'd like to spend a few extra days in Cheyenne. That masked fiend surprised the whole camp by accepting with good grace. John Larch could only figure that Half-Face was just that, half a man. His aggression might frighten some but it sure as hell didn't cut the mustard with him.

It was a month later, down in Amarillo, that he first heard the news of Finn Harpe's demise. A drummer off the stage was full of it. He'd been shooting billiards in a saloon in Cheyenne when three men walked in.

"Within a few minutes of them entering all hell broke loose," said the brush salesman. "This young un' he gets real mad at the card sharp, goes for his gun only for Harpe to shoot him in the thigh. Then cool as you like this other man lets go with both barrels of a shotgun. Finn Harpe was dead before he could see how much damage he'd done."

"Did they say what it was over?" Larch enquired.

"Nah, but I heard tell the mornin' after that Harpe and some others done killed a bunch o' people up in the Montana Territory."

John Larch left it there. He'd known that something like that was bound to happen sooner rather than later. You can't just go around killing without pissing someone off real bad. He hoped that leaving when he did he'd be spared any wrath that was brought down, though he thought reflectively he'd be ready when the time came.

Fairfax was glad to be rid of Larch and Harpe. He'd figured Harpe was nothing more than a card sharp that had gotten lucky, while Larch was another thing entirely. He was cold and ruthless, a man who would kill for the slightest provocation and for that Fairfax thought he was better off without him. Like everything else in Fairfax's life, he'd weighed the odds of a confrontation with Larch and decided that it was in his own interests to let the Texas gunman go.

Leaving Cheyenne they headed in a westerly direction. With Driscoll as his second in command and the ex Commanchero Ruffio on side, he didn't expect any trouble from the Jew or Tom Bender as long as he kept their lives profitable and pleasurable. Several stagecoach hold-ups outside of Laramie sated their bloodlust and lined their pockets. The last stagecoach to be robbed was so terrified of the gang that the guard climbed on top of the stagecoach and with a sharp bladed knife cut the straps holding the cashbox. His actions and that of the driver probably saved their lives and the lives of the passengers. Two previous robberies had left three passengers dead, one woman brutally raped, and four company men dead at the roadside. When the cashbox cascaded towards the outlaws they lost interest, *much to Half-Face's annoyance,* and reined in their horses. The cashbox burst open as it hit rocky ground and the contents flew into the air.

"We should have gone after the stage. We shouldn't have left anyone alive!" screamed Fairfax. No doubt remembering how he'd sliced the neck of that woman after Levy had finished with her. "Now we're gonna have to move out of the Territory." No one questioned his decision.

For the next few days the gang headed west to Brown's Hole, a notorious hideout of thieves and killers. A town, Powder Springs, *well not more than a few shacks* had been built and the inhabitants even had their own drinking hole called the Rock saloon.

When Half-Face and his gang rode in they were exhausted, dirty and trail weary. They'd been pursued for days by a posse of army cadets and townsfolk from Laramie. There had been sporadic firing but none of the gang were injured. Brown's Hole was an oasis, but an expensive one. The area was impenetrable and most posses would balk at entering the high rimmed canyons. Those who did were usually picked off by rifle fire.

The camp, though inhabited by law breakers was run on much the same lines as an ordinary town, though the prices of food and liquor were higher. No one complained because justice came swift and final.

Fairfax knew that he was a marked man in Wyoming and he guessed in the Montana Territory, but he didn't care. The country was big and vast. There were plenty of places further south that he could plunder. He began to revel in his infamy. Now he was a face, a name. Half-Face, it struck fear in men's hearts. Not quite a legend, but certainly a phantom of the plains.

Winter came early to Brown's Hole.

CHAPTER 52

In the months since Jared's death Maddie withdrew into herself. Her scars healed and thankfully she hadn't any complications down below. Josephine tried talking to her and eventually persuaded her to try walking to the town stores, but the sympathetic looks she received soon drove her back to her room.

"I know you mean well, but leave me be!" she shouted.

Josephine thought that with the return of Mordecai things would change. But she was wrong. Maddie screamed when he told her they hadn't found Half-Face. Josephine thought it was a scream of terror, but Mordecai saw it for what it was, a scream of anger and rage. He tried telling her about Harpe but to Maddie he was faceless. He was just another man who had forced himself inside her. It wasn't enough to quell the demons.

Mordecai tried in vain to talk, to tell her he'd get the bastard. But his words fell on deaf ears. She was as cold as the day he'd left to extract vengeance. Didn't she know about the rage that was building up inside of him? Didn't she know how badly he wanted to destroy the mad man who had caused her such grief? She couldn't see it. She couldn't see the love he had for her which he yearned to pour out. He could see it now. The Maddie he knew and loved had died alongside his friend. It was in her eyes. Those eyes that once held such warmth now burned with an unquenchable anger. He could see it was eating her up, destroying her from within. He so desperately wanted to save her, to stop her from becoming just like him, but words and actions failed him. He left her alone then and in the quiet of his room he wept.

By late fall she was unapproachable; her body had healed, but her soul was now with the Devil. She was consumed with a bitter hatred, a rage against all men. The woman who had loved so freely now could feel only loathing. Mordecai rarely visited, but when he did she looked at him with expectation. When she saw he had no news she turned her back. It was destroying Mordecai. He had hung around Helena *much to Jake Tunstall's chagrin*, for one reason; to protect her if that creature ever came near, and to one day maybe make her whole again, but even he was beginning to think of it as a lost cause.

Then just as the New Year dawned Mordecai received a telegram from Texas, it was from Clay Dean. Clay had found he missed the old days and had returned to his homeland and signed on with the rangers again. He'd told Mordecai, "Ranch life ain't for me, I'm heading back home. I miss the old life." Mordecai understood only too well. In another life he'd probably have joined him, but there was Maddie. There was always Maddie.

Received word through Pinkertons stop Stage hold-ups near Laramie late summer stop Masked man suspected stop Ferocious attack stop Woman raped stop Throat cut stop Gang last seen heading Brown's Hole. Stop Good luck stop Clay.

Brown's Hole was an outlaw stronghold. It could figure in Fairfax's plans, thought Mordecai. Already his mind was going over how he was going to get there. But first he had to show Maddie the telegram.

"I'm going with you!"

"You're what!"

"You heard. I want this over. I want that son of a bitch dead at my feet," she cried.

"You can't go with me," Mordecai was thinking about Randy's rashness. It had almost got them all killed, "I'm going alone."

There was fire in Maddie's eyes as she whirled on him, "You can't stop me. I'll do what I damn well please, with you or without you!"

Mordecai saw in those eyes a flicker, it was enough to melt his heart and then it was gone, "Shit Maddie, you could get yourself killed!"

"And this, what do you think this is—living!" She was on fire. She was stirring into life, but there was a grey ugliness to it.

"If you go with me, you do exactly as I say. Do you hear?"

"I want him dead Mordecai, I want them all dead. I want an end to this nightmare, this living hell!" Then she broke down and cried.

It was blowing up a blizzard when Maddie and Mordecai stepped off the train in Laramie. It was mid February of 1883 and Wyoming was seeing its worst winter for a decade. Wrapped up in a dark great-coat, buckskin pants, boots and blankets no one would have given Maddie a passing look. Devoid of makeup, her hair severely tied at the back, a black bearskin hat pulled low over her ears and leading a horse from the box car, cussing as the animal balked at the inclement weather, she was a far cry from the elegantly dressed attractive madam of the Alhambra.

Mordecai emerged from the box car similarly attired. His broad brimmed southern hat now replaced with *for want of better words* a dark semi-derby type. With a firm strong hand he led his mare into the elements, then handing his reins to the still struggling Maddie, re-entered the box car and led out a third horse, this one loaded with supplies and provisions.

Half an hour later they checked into a hotel. The relative warmth of the hotel was inviting. The harsh realities of travelling in winter were now becoming abundantly clear. When Mordecai read out Clay's telegram to Maddie she'd wanted to set off at once, but as Helena was snowbound they had to wait for a break in the weather. Even then Mordecai had advised against it.

"Are you a hunter sir?" said the desk clerk, referring to the small arsenal of weaponry they had brought along. Mordecai looked harshly at him and the clerk thought better of asking anything further.

In their room, Maddie looked again at the weapons Mordecai had brought. Along with the Peacemaker, which he carried butt forward on his belt, he also had his 36 calibre Navy Colt and another long barrelled Colt Peacemaker. She still owned her 22 calibre Colt and also a 38 calibre Lightening Colt double action. His arsenal was completed by his faithful Henry repeater and a new Winchester model 73, and a single shot Sharps 'Big Fifty' 50/90. "Just in case we catch them sons of bitches in the open," he'd remarked when he purchased it from a store in Ogden. Maddie had not questioned his ethics or the manner in which he was prepared to dispatch the killers. Conversation between them was both stilted and awkward. Neither spoke of their brief affair, preferring to speak only when spoken to and then always about the mission in hand.

"Maddie, no one moves in this sort of weather. Best we rest up until the weather breaks."

By now Maddie could see the foolishness of her impatience and bowed to Mordecai's request. She knew if she'd said go on he'd have obliged without question, but she'd waited this long, another month wasn't going to make much difference.

Their sleeping arrangements were much like they'd been on the train and at the hotel in Ogden. Maddie slept on the bed whilst Mordecai slept on the wooden floor. She'd wanted to offer him the warmth of her bed but felt it inappropriate. Maddie had gone through a transformation since her ordeal, though to be fair neither felt easy with their intimate knowledge of each other. Comfort was a luxury that neither of them felt able to give the other. They were together for a killing and nothing more.

They endured a month of enforced confinement before the weather broke. During that time Mordecai spoke with the eyewitness from the attempted hold up and was satisfied that the men who had been chased towards Brown's Hole were the men they were hunting.

"They're a mean bunch at the Hole," volunteered a mule skinner in the North Star. "Best you and the boy make a wide loop around, if I was you."

"I ain't you."

Back in the room Mordecai turned to Maddie, "Way I see it, I've got to go it alone. The Hole ain't no place for a lady."

Maddie reeled on him, "Ain't you forgettin' I ain't no fuckin lady. Where you go, I go."

That came as no surprise to Mordecai, the woman was mean enough to take on all of Brown's Hole, "I guessed you'd say that. So here's what I figure we do when we gets to the Hole."

They rode out the following morning. There was still a chill in the air, but Mordecai didn't notice. He knew that the next few days camping out in the open would be a test for Maddie. The days were warming up, but at night it became bitterly cold. A lesser person would have balked at the conditions, but not Maddie Dubois. She camped as close to the campfire as possible, but during those four days of travel she didn't complain once.

On their last night Mordecai went over what they'd planned. Maddie was, to all intents and purposes the younger brother of Mordecai. She almost smiled*; it wasn't the first time she'd masqueraded as a boy.* Mute as well as daft, she wasn't to look anyone in the eye and she always had to stay close. She still wore the black greatcoat but now wore an old battered derby which concealed her raven hair. The dirt she'd collected along the trail disguised the fact that she didn't shave.

"All I ask is you watch my back. If they're in the camp, we back away. An outburst like Randy's will get us both killed." He looked Maddie squarely between the eyes, "This is my backyard. I call all the shots. I don't want no killin' at the Hole. Do you understand?"

Maddie had never seen Mordecai so keyed up before. It took her a little off guard, but then she wasn't going to any church picnic.

"Mordecai, you can trust me. I've waited this long I can wait just a little longer." She sounded sincere, but Mordecai wasn't convinced.

The next day they rode into Brown's Hole.

CHAPTER 53

The primitive and endless days at Brown's Hole had a profound effect on Fairfax, that and his brush with the law. It was as if this break in his wanton bloodlust had given him time to reassess his actions. Up until then, no one knew him as a law breaker, but if he continued in his actions he'd soon be a known outlaw. Then there would be no going back to the lifestyle he'd enjoyed in New York or on the West Coast. With this in mind he decided that the gang needed to pull one last job to set him up for a return to San Francisco. He'd heard from a source at Brown's Hole that the bank at Leadville received a large cache of bank notes on the last Tuesday of each month. There was reputed to be upwards of 60,000 dollars deposited for distribution to the various businesses that had shot up in Leadville's short history.

Fairfax spent the long winter months carefully planning the robbery. They were five in number but he'd recruited four extra men. He'd chosen three for their youth and their horsemanship. The other was Jack Curshaw, the man with the plan. He'd been part of a gang which had originally planned the robbery but before they could rob the bank at Leadville, three of the gang members had been shot down attempting to rob the Overland stage line between Cheyenne and Deadwood. They lucked out. The coach was laden with six Pinkerton men heading towards Deadwood. Curshaw was the only man to get away. He'd made it to the Hole in the Wall, then headed south to Brown's Hole where he thought he'd be safe. Confiding in Fairfax was his biggest mistake; his luck was soon to run out.

The more Fairfax thought about the plan the more he liked it. Four men would have been hard pushed to carry it off, but nine, that made it like taking candy from a baby. There was only one problem; in Fairfax's book nine into $60,000 didn't go. Nor, as he thought about it, did two.

All nine would ride into town from three directions and arrive at the First National Bank just as it was opening. The three new recruits would attend to their comrades' horses whilst the six would enter the bank. As each man entered they would don a burlap hood, so as to strike terror into the hearts and minds of the bank clerks. They would kill the first person they saw, thus striking fear into the workforce. According to Curshaw there was no time-lock on the safe and even if there was, it would have to be open for business at 9 o'clock. With a detailed plan of the inside of the bank, Fairfax couldn't see his plan failing. Stage one was all set. Stage two involved Driscoll. Stage three would follow immediately after.

As the weather broke at Brown's Hole, Fairfax, Driscoll and the others climbed up on their horses and rode out. Their departure was watched with a degree of relief and a relaxing of tensions. Almost from the day the Half-Face gang arrived, *as the inhabitants of the Hole now called them,* the air was thick with an uneasy feel. Fairfax's appearance and his maniacal laugh as they climbed down from their horses had set the tone. That they were killers was plain to see, that they possessed not a single ounce of decency became evident during their first week.

Micah Levy took a shine to one of the Mexican whores. The only problem with this was that she was spoken for. An argument broke out and Levy cut his rival's throat before making the Mexican whore his. An angry mob wanted to lynch Levy but Driscoll and Bender stood between them and Levy. Fairfax and Ruffio flanked the mob.

"Gentlemen, this doesn't need to escalate," *in truth if the mob hadn't agreed to Fairfax's terms he'd have let them lynch Levy.* "A fine would seem more appropriate, don't you think?"

The mob fell for Fairfax's bluff and Levy begrudgingly paid out $500.00 of his own money. "This fucking whore had better be worth it!" he snarled.

Fairfax was lucky during his stay in Brown's Hole. Sometimes the Hole had upwards of two hundred desperados living in the vicinity, but most of these were either at Hole in the Wall or Robber's Roost. If there'd been some who had a stomach for a fight, life in the Hole would have been a whole lot less comfortable.

As it was, the inhabitants of Brown's Hole viewed their going as a relief. The fact that Jack Curshaw had ridden off with them came as a surprise. It didn't surprise anyone however that the three young rustlers had thrown in with them. They'd been in awe of the bunch from the moment that Fairfax rode in.

A day later Mordecai and Maddie rode cautiously in to Brown's Hole and stepped down from their tired and weary horses.

CHAPTER 54

Mordecai and Maddie took up positions and sighted their rifles in what the Texan called the kill zone. It was three minutes to nine and Leadville was just awakening. They watched as first Driscoll then Bender and a third unidentified rider approached from the west side of town, then with almost uncanny timing, a thin swarthy bearded man who they identified as Levy, along with two others, rode slowly towards the double doors of the First National. From the cover of her horse in the narrow alley across the street from the bank Maddie began to sweat. She knew what she had to do. She'd had five days of gruelling riding to understand.

On arriving at Brown's Hole a reception committee began to form. Mordecai walked his horse slowly towards them but viewed the crowd with apprehension. One wrong move now could prove to be their last. They'd ridden through the deep narrow canyons knowing that rifles were trained on their every move. Getting in was easy, getting out could prove a whole lot harder.

"Hold it, that's far enough." A dozen rifles were trained on them.

"Me and my brother, we're on the dodge from the Pinkertons," said Mordecai to the crowd.

"You look like a hunting party to me," said a voice from the crowd. "Do you always travel light?" The sarcasm wasn't lost on Mordecai. The man was looking straight at the pack animal and its load. The Big Fifty and the Winchester barrels were poking out of the canvas sacking.

Mordecai felt the hackles rise. They'd strayed into a hornets nest. His hand inched inside his coat for the Colt Peacemaker. He knew they were dead in the water.

"Hold your horses, this man might be packing, but I know he ain't dumb. Howdy Mordecai." It was Old Man Pitkin Taylor's nephew, Isaiah, "Hell I ain't see you in a coon's age."

With that the rifles were slowly lowered and the crowd began to disperse.

"Isaiah! My ain't you a sight for sore eyes? That was quite a fix we was in."

"Yeah, well we've had us some mighty bad peoples visit us lately."

"Oh yeah. What kind of bad people?"

"The kind you can't wait to see the back of is all."

"Isaiah, what kind of bad people?" said Mordecai barely concealing his impatience. It triggered a quick response.

"An outfit, a bad outfit came in just as winter took a hold. Mean sons of bitches. Guy leading em' wears a leather mask across this part of his face," said Isaiah, motioning with his hand downwards across the left side of his face. Mordecai's face said it all, "You're a hunting. I seen it in your eyes. Those men need a killin'"

A day later, with warm food in their bellies, they rode out of Brown's Hole with the knowledge that Fairfax was hitting the bank at Leadville at nine o'clock on Tuesday the seventh of April, "We got us five days of hard riding if we're to get there before em'."

They'd arrived late on Monday afternoon, enough time to check out the bank and seek vantage positions. The First National was situated in the centre of town, with two narrow side roads opposite and another main road on the left corner leading south through a wooded area. Mordecai judged that the gang would take the south road when they made their escape. The best possible vantage point was in the building adjacent to the bank, but to avoid tipping the sheriff about the expected bank robbery, Mordecai had to settle for the alley opposite. Maddie had said they should inform the Sheriff, but Mordecai had said any sudden changes might tip Fairfax as to what was afoot.

"What about the four others?" said Maddie, concern etched across her face.

"What about them?" replied Mordecai. "They threw in with Fairfax. When we start shooting, you can bet they'll be shooting back."

Sweat dripped into her eyes as she glanced back at the bank. Then she saw him. He turned the corner just as the bank doors were being opened. As he pulled alongside the others and dismounted she saw them all don burlap hoods. It made her shudder with fear. Not since the ambush had she allowed herself to think about it. Her hands began to shake.

"Oh God!"

She turned her back and everything came flooding back. Tears stung her eyes. She'd waited for this moment and now she didn't know whether she had the courage to go through with it. Fighting the first signs of panic, Maddie forced herself to turn around and watched as they enter the bank. Three of the men who she didn't recognise, stood waiting, holding the reins of three horses apiece. They were so young, she thought in a blind panic. Their boyish looks so evident. She forced herself to focus on their young faces. Again she thought about not going through with it.

Mordecai checked the loads in his Henry and watched eyes level with the saddle of his horse. He wiped the sweat from his hand on the sleeve of his coat. In less than five minutes he was going to open the ball.

Inside the bank Fairfax and his men fanned out. Levy grabbed a junior clerk and with one hand jerked the man back by his hair, whilst with the other he sliced his throat. A young bank clerk quickly stifled a scream as Fairfax snapped his orders.

"Scream and you'll all suffer the same fate. Now open the fucking safe!"

Within five minutes their saddlebags were full and the vault was empty. The four terrified bank workers were then marched into a back room.

"If you make a sound, you're all dead," spat Driscoll.

Fairfax let out a chilling laugh as they walked towards the doorway. Jack Curshaw and Bender were the first to emerge.

Maddie, transfixed by the youthfulness of the boys outside, was about to call the whole thing off, then she saw the hooded figures framed in the bank's doorway. She brought the butt of the Winchester up to her shoulder and took aim.

"Come on, come on," cried Mordecai. He prayed Maddie would hold her fire until they were all out. Two men rushed from the bank, and then another. The shit truly hit the pan, as Maddie's Winchester began to spit death.

"Fuck!" cried Mordecai, as he too rained death upon the bank entrance. "Crack, crack, crack, crack." Maddie's first had gone wild, but the second found its target hitting Bender in the knee.

"They're robbing the bank," cried Mordecai as loud as he could. Horses bucked and reared up in terror. The young men holding them went white with fright as the rifle fire was joined by the return fire from Half-Face's gang.

"Oh God!" cried Maddie as she saw one of her shots cause a shoulder wound to one of the youths holding the horses. Townsfolk, alerted by the shooting and Mordecai's cry had taken up positions in building across the way and had commenced firing. Three hooded riders made it on to their horses.

'Crack, crack, crack,' went the Henry in Mordecai's hands. His first shot caught one of the hooded riders high in the thigh, but he managed to hold on. The other two missed their target. As the outlaws began to return fire, a townsman who'd ventured out into the street went down like he'd been pole-axed. Another took a wound in the groin. A hooded man grabbed a hold of the reins of a bucking horse and threw himself into the saddle only to have three slugs from Mordecai's Henry smash into his chest. In seconds Mordecai saw him crash to the ground, dead before he felt his bones crunch on the hard dusty road.

Maddie raised her Winchester to her shoulder and stepped from the relative safety of her horse and the alley. Another hooded man made the saddle and he spurred his horse towards her. She coolly aimed and fired, oblivious to the bullets zinging about her. His hooded mask turned a dark crimson as two bullets found their mark and he somersaulted from the horse.

The whirling of dust made it difficult to see, but Mordecai could just about make out two hooded riders turning their frightened horses around. He watched helplessly as they galloped southwards, snapping two quick shots after them. The hooded man with the thigh wound kicked his horse into a gallop and followed his comrades, keeping low in the saddle as the bullets flew all around him.

One of the youths managed to swing himself into the saddle but a townsman blew him out of it. Another of the youths, using his horse as a shield, managed to get out of the kill zone. Then as quickly as it started it was over. Nine men had rode in, four rode out, and at least one of them had taken wounds. As the townsfolk surveyed the scene Maddie was drawn to the man she'd killed.

"Please God let it be him," she kept saying as she drew level with the dead man. A townsman tore off the mask. Maddie let out an involuntary cry, it wasn't Fairfax. From what she could make out, it was the half breed Ruffio. The sight of his face half shot away made her want to vomit, but somehow she managed to keep it down. Turning she walked up to the second dead man and tore the hood from his head. She didn't recognise him, but from what Isaiah Taylor had described, this man was possibly Jack Curshaw. Maddie ignored the youth she'd shot in the shoulder and advanced towards the last hooded man. He'd been the first to be hit. His knee was shattered. She recognised him at once as the man known as Tom Bender.

Mordecai kicked his shattered knee and he screamed in pain.

"You son of a bitch, sit up and take what you've got coming!" Bender looked up, surprised at the venom coming from the stranger who had inflicted such pain. He looked up into the morning sun and shielded his eyes. "Do you remember me?" said Maddie softly as she took off her hat and let her dark curls cascade down.

Bender squinted into the sun and somehow managed to focus on the woman's face in front of him. Slowly it began to dawn on him who he was looking at. His eyes grew wide with terror as Mordecai pulled his iron from his holster and cocked the hammer of his Peacemaker.

"No! No!" cried Bender as Mordecai shot him three times in the face. Maddie turned her head in horror. She knew her quest wasn't going to be pretty, but this, this....

Chapter 55

Mordecai waited until the tears subsided, then he went to her. He held her in his arms and told her everything was okay. She looked up at him, at the man that only an hour since had killed a man in cold blood. Executed in front of her, for her, because of her. She never knew until that moment how she'd feel, but now she knew. She wanted it to be all over, she wanted it to be just a nightmare but she knew that this was one she'd never wake up from until it was over.

"If you want, we can stop now," he said gently. "Someone out there'll take care of him. It doesn't have to be us."

"Mordecai, today I stood in that street and took part in gunning men down. It wasn't something I'd ever thought I'd do in my wildest dreams." She stifled a sob. "We can stop now, you say. Well, as much as I want to stop, I can't. I can't until he's dead. Until I see it with my own eyes, it will never be over."

"You think today was ugly. If we go on, it'll get much worse. I owe Jared, and until I get all those responsible I won't quit. Let me go on alone."

Maddie swung round on him, steeling herself for what was to come. "No! We're going after them together. Whatever it takes, I promise I won't fail you."

The posse arrived back in Leadville in the late afternoon. One man was nursing a shoulder wound, and another was lying belly down across his horse. They'd tracked the four outlaws to the edge of the forest but then they ran into a fusillade of gunfire. It would have been sheer suicide to venture into the trees.

"It's as I figured," said Mordecai. "Fairfax planned his escape route well. He knew that if they reached the trees, they'd be home and dry." Mordecai lifted the greaseproof tarp and unrolled it across the bed. He lifted the Big Fifty Sharps and checked that everything was in working order. Maddie watched him as he cleaned and oiled the weapon. He looked up at her and smiled, but it wasn't a nice smile.

"What Half-Face didn't figure on was us tracking him the day after. That forest goes on for miles, but then it becomes wide open country."

Maddie didn't sleep well that night. The events of the day kept flashing before her. Not just the shoot out at the bank but the callous way Mordecai had despatched Bender. He'd told her what he was capable of, yet somehow she didn't believe him. Now she did. What worried her more was the fact that she too had killed in cold blood. She'd killed her father, by accident, in self defence. She'd killed the miner in fright and anger, but the killing of Ruffio had been premeditated. She knew before the shooting started that there would be no prisoners. When Mordecai fired into Bender it just underlined the fact. She'd killed and she was prepared to go on killing. In her eyes she was now as bad as Mordecai.

It was early the following morning when they set out. They walked their horses slowly past the bank that less than twenty four hours ago had been the scene of such carnage. Splash marks of dried blood still adorned the walls of the bank and sidewalk. Fresh wood shavings put down to blot up the blood swirled around the dusty street as their horses rode by. Maddie shuddered. An early riser doffed his hat in respect as the two, with Mordecai leading, passed by. He noted the determined look on the Texan's face but his eyes were riveted to the sight of the arsenal of weapons which now adorned his horse and his personage. Both the Henry and the Sharps lay in a makeshift scabbard on the left flank, while he carried his Navy Colt and the Peacemaker in holsters around his waist. His dress was sombre, from his dark hat to the black Prince Albert frock coat and matching pants and finally to the collarless grey linen shirt. The bystander felt the hairs on the back of his neck rise.

In contrast the woman, the woman who, only yesterday, had fought as savagely as her companion, brought up the rear. As the weak morning sunlight cast its rays across her alabaster skin he was surprised to see such beauty. She rode passed him without so much as a downward glance. Sitting upright in the saddle, her hair now hastily pinned back beneath the battered derby. Tell-tale ringlets carelessly hanging down, gave testimony to her femininity. She wore a short buckskin jacket which matched her pants. Around her waist, a dark leather ammunition belt with a Colt Lightening hanging, butt forward, in its scabbard. The Winchester that she'd used to such deadly effect was located in a leather sheath below her saddle. In her saddle bag she carried her old Colt 22.

Late in the afternoon they picked up Fairfax's trail. They followed until it grew dark, then at Mordecai's insistence they made a cold camp and ate jerky.

He shook her awake as the stars faded from the sky.

"If we start out now we should make time on them varmints," he said in way of explanation. The trail was arduous and at times tortuous as they wound their way though the thick mountainous forest, stopping only for Mordecai to climb down and examine the scats from their quarry. "We're gaining on them," were the only words he spoke in way of encouragement. By day three the forest had begun to open up. Here and there the trees gave way to grassland. They were making good time. Then Mordecai reined his horse in and instructed Maddie to do the same. They were at the timberline. Ahead, as far as the eye could see lay miles of open country. Mordecai scanned the vast expanse until he found what he was looking for, "Got em'" he cried. Then he reached into his saddlebags and brought out a pair of field glasses. Raising them to his eyes he focused in on the four horsemen. “It’s them!” he exclaimed.

Mordecai climbed down from his horse and bid Maddie do the same. Maddie blindly did as she was told. He pulled the Sharps ‘Big Fifty’ from its scabbard and fished in his pockets for the 50/90 calibre cartridges. He then instructed Maddie to secure the horses. She did this silently, and then walked back to where Mordecai was positioned. “We’re in luck, they’re in range of the Sharps, but far enough that they won’t be able to shoot back.”

Maddie watched as Mordecai lined up six bullets on a boulder and settled himself behind it. The Sharps ‘Big Fifty’ he rested across the rock. His unhurried manner caused Maddie some concern, but he seemed to know what he was doing. Mordecai gauged the distance, then he checked the wind. It would be a difficult shot but he suspected he’d have a pretty good chance of hitting something before they out-distanced the Sharps.

Mordecai lined up the big gun on the four riders.

CHAPTER 56

The shoot out in Leadville had shaken Fairfax to the core. The subsequent fight against the posse had caused him concern, but the hard days and nights of flight were where it was taking its toll. The only saving grace being that Driscoll had been the only one of them to hold onto the bank's money. Counted out on their first night it had totalled eleven thousand one hundred dollars. Nowhere near the amount needed to start life afresh in Frisco, thought Half-Face, but just enough to get me out of this God forsaken country.

Fairfax was deep in thought as he felt something whoosh past his ear, then less than a split second later he heard the faint pow.

"What the fuck!" cried Driscoll.

Seconds later they heard a dull thud, and Micah Levy's horse fell from under him. He was pitched head first onto the grassy ground.

"Jesus Christ!" he screamed as he struggled to his feet. All four men looked into the distant timberline. With an instinct to survive Micah Levy shouted to the kid.

"Hey Jimmy!"

The youth turned his horse towards Levy and stared down the barrel of the Jew's 44 Remington. His face froze in terror as the Remington spurted flame and two projectiles smashed into the boy's chest.

Maddie watched the scene unfold though the field glasses, "Oh my God, He's just killed the boy," she gasped. Mordecai, unfazed by Maddie's outcry, sighted on the rider as he started to race after his two companions.

Micah Levy pulled the slumped Jimmy from the saddle and swung himself onto the boy's horse and in one swift motion kicked the gelding into a gallop. He laughed nervously, and then with relief as his horse put distance between him and the deadly fire from the timberline. A sickening thud wiped the smile from his face as a 50/90 calibre bullet severed his spine. His body went limp and like a rag doll he slipped effortlessly to the ground.

"Got the son of a bitch," cried Mordecai.

Maddie looked at him with dismay. He'd killed a human being at distance and regarded it as little more than shooting a deer. She stifled her disgust, as she realised why she was there. He'd told her, he'd warned her of what he was capable of; he had known what she could only speculate. That she had loved him seemed hard to believe, what feelings she had for this man were slowly evaporating. She prayed that when it was over she'd feel something more than she did at that moment.

The boy was dead, but the horse was still breathing. Mordecai climbed down and calmly pulled his Peacemaker from his holster, then speaking softly to the dying horse he stroked its mane and fired. When he arose Maddie detected a tear in his eye and she remembered his gentle side. It was something else for her to ponder on.

Fifty yards further they found the body of Micah Levy. He was lying on his back; a faint audible gurgling could be detected. Maddie thought Mordecai would climb down and put him out of his misery, but instead he just rode by. Again Maddie questioned the Texan's sensitivities.

"Hold up," she cried, as she reined her horse in and dismounted. It would have been so easy to ignore the piece of filth as he lay dying in agony, *she remembered only to well her last conscious moments before she passed out were of his pock-marked face as he violently tore into her body.* Mordecai halted his horse and waited, his expression never wavered.

"Well you son of a bitch, you finally got your desserts," said Maddie as she approached Levy's prone body. "I should leave you to die slowly." She pointed the 41 calibre Colt Lightening at Micah Levy's head, looked away then pulled the trigger.

Mordecai sat his horse and waited for Maddie to catch up. Standing up in the saddle he brought the field glasses to his eyes and stared after the two distant horsemen.

"From now on it becomes a little trickier," he said as she pulled up alongside him.

"Did you take a look at those two back yonder?" said Maddie, "apart from the wounds you caused, neither man had been hit in Leadville."

"I noticed," said Mordecai, his demeanour unaltered.

"Which means either Fairfax or Driscoll is in need of medical attention."

"Let's hope whoever it is dies from the gangrene," added Mordecai.

Mordecai slowed their pace deliberately, they were in open country and he had no intention of giving Half-Face and Driscoll the chance to double back and ambush them. It was getting towards dark when Mordecai noticed a light in the distance.

"There's a few buildings up ahead, I'd suggest we wait until dark before going in," said Mordecai.

Maddie nodded in agreement.

An hour later the single light had become four then seven and the heavens opened and it began to rain. The settlement was a collection of rundown shacks, but the inhabitants had seen fit to post a sign welcoming visitors. Burnt into an old plank was the legend, Wagon Wheel Gap. The town was a sight bigger than the two hunters had first thought. Keeping close to the shadows, they pulled up at the livery stable.

"Hello the livery," called Mordecai. The double doors remained closed. The Texan climbed down from his horse and rattled the doors roughly. The rain had become heavier. A full minute later they both saw a lantern being lit through the crack in the doors.

"Hold your damn horses, I ain't accustomed to being woken up in the middle of the night." The livery door opened and a be-whiskered old head poked out. He pushed the lantern towards Mordecai's face and gazed into it, and then he did the same with Maddie. "Well if I'm a seeing things, I could have sworn you'se was a woman!"

"I am, and we need a place to store our horses and maybe a place to lay our weary heads. We're willing to pay for some warm straw and hot vittles, if you've got the makings."

"Ten dollars!"

"Ten dolla...." began Mordecai.

"We'll take it," said Maddie.

With some hot stew in their bellies Mordecai inspected the horses in the livery. Not finding the horses he was looking for he asked the livery man if he'd seen any strangers.

"Damn place is crawling with em'," he exclaimed. "Since they found a trace of ore peoples been drifting in and out for the past year."

"Recent, old timer," cried Mordecai impatiently, "like in the last couple of days?"

"No need to take that tone with me boy!"

"Sorry, I'm forgetting my manners. We ain't slept well the past few days."

"Apology accepted," said the liveryman, "Can't say as I've noticed any strangers, but you might try O'Hara's saloon down the track a ways."

"Obliged," said Maddie.

They trudged through the rain soaked streets until they came to O'Hara's. Maddie looked across the top of the batwing doors into the noisy smoke filled room, but couldn't make out anyone.

"Shit!" she cried.

"You wait here, I'll go take a look. If Fairfax is there he shouldn't be hard to spot."

"Be careful," the words escaped Maddie's lips before she could stop herself. It surprised her that despite everything she felt something more than companionship towards him, but what, she wasn't prepared to admit.

Mordecai walked into the dingy darkly lit saloon, and scoured the room thoroughly, searching for that one particular face from hell, but despite the rough mixture of faces, none matched or even came close. It might be Fairfax who took the bullet in the thigh, he thought. This left Driscoll.

All around him he noticed that the men were heavily armed. Miners mixed with drummers, lumbermen consorted with gamblers and freshly painted whores mixed with everyone. It could be a tricky situation if either man was here. It would be best to face them on the open street rather than a crowded saloon.

Satisfied that Half-Face wasn't on the premises he familiarised himself with the lay out of the saloon, before switching his attention for the search for Driscoll. O'Hara's was a single storey building with a double frontage and a single door to the rear. There was a Faro game going on at the left side of the room and a poker game in the far corner. Here and there a few tables and chairs, but nothing else. Then he noticed two men who might or might not be Driscoll. He edged closer to the card table to get a better view.

A roar of satisfaction greeted his arrival as one of the men reached across the table to rake in his winnings. Mordecai noticed the worn faded blue jacket with the tell-tale darker blue outline of chevrons. From Maddie's description he could be Driscoll, but without her say so it was hard to decide. A shiver ran down his spine. He wanted to take the fight to the man, but what if he was wrong? If this was Driscoll then he had a fight coming, but a fight on Mordecai's terms.

Before he walked out front to tell Maddie, he checked out the back. There were four very small shacks and a couple of tents, from each he could hear a cacophony of sexual pleasure. He looked in on all, just in case. His interruptions were greeted with profanity and further slights about his parenthood. Secure in the knowledge that Fairfax wasn't on the premises he walked back through O'Hara's and found Maddie.

Reprised of the situation, Maddie insisted on confronting Driscoll.

"Fuck no!" cried Mordecai.

"He doesn't know I'm still alive. That gives me the edge. I'll walk up to the table with my pistol in hand. Just trust me on this Mordecai, it's what I've got to do."

Knowing that now wasn't the time to talk sense into Maddie, he conceded to her will.

"But if he so much as twitches I'll send him into the hereafter."

Maddie pulled her 22 calibre Colt, checked the loads, then with her arm at her side she walked into the saloon.

Mordecai whispered in her ear, "If it's him, leave it be, we'll take him when he comes out."

Maddie nodded her agreement as Mordecai indicated to her the right direction. Through the dimly lit smoke-laden room Maddie pushed and eased her way confidently towards the poker table in the far corner. She felt a slight shudder of nervousness as she drew level with the green baize table. It was him.

Driscoll didn't look up until he heard the noticeable click as Maddie cocked the hammer, "Stand up you son of a bitch!" bellowed Maddie.

Mordecai, concealed by the crowd, silently drew his Peacemaker and pulled back the hammer.

The look of surprise soon disappeared from Driscoll's face and was replaced with a look of concern and then he smirked.

Maddie squeezed the trigger. The pistol bucked slightly as the 22 calibre bullet smashed Driscoll's right wrist. "Now I've got your attention, where's that ugly cocksucker?"

"Who the fuck are you lady? Calamity fucking Jane!" cried a bystander.

"Who wants to know?" said Mordecai slowly as the man felt the barrel of the Peacemaker in his side. His voice sunk into silence.

Clutching his shattered wrist, Driscoll stared up at his assailant. Any colour he had left drained from his face as recognition registered.

"I thought you were dead!" His brain went into overdrive, "It was you! It was you who ambushed me!"

Maddie ignored his small talk, "I'll ask you one last time Bill! Where's Fairfax?"

The contemptuous way she used his name caused Driscoll to shout angrily, "Go to hell!"

The pistol bucked in Maddie's hand for the second time. Splinters of wood and green baize covered the table. Driscoll clutched at his destroyed manhood.

"Jesus fucking Christ, she's shot me in the balls!"

The crowd having moved back, cowed by Mordecai's two pistols looked on, some out of curiosity, while others with anger at the woman's violent intrusion.

Maddie, aware of the situation she'd gotten them both in, sought to get the crowd on side.

"This man is a coward and a rapist!"

"He told us he rode with Custer!" shouted one of the angry bystanders.

"My husband died with Custer," cried Maddie, "this piece of shit ran out on him and he raped me!"

There was an audible sigh. The crowd were subdued by Maddie's remarks.

"I'm waiting," said Maddie coldly. Her finger began closing on the trigger.

Writhing in pain, Driscoll saw the look in her eye, and knew he was seconds from death. "Don't kill me!" he begged, "The fiend that you're after took a bullet in the thigh. He's over at the doc's on Front Street."

"Thank you," said Maddie as she lowered her pistol. It was done, she'd humiliated Driscoll in public, destroyed his manhood. She didn't need his life. She was better than that.

It was instinctive, foolish, but an attempt to restore some kind of dignity.

"You always were a stuck up cunt!" cried Driscoll.

Without a word, without a noticeable flicker in her near perfect features, Maddie brought the pistol up and shot Driscoll between the eyes, then without waiting to see him fall she turned her back and walked out. Mordecai backed out behind her, both guns pointing menacingly at the shocked crowd.

Maddie was physically shaking when Mordecai joined her in the darkness of the street. He held her in his arms and waited for the shaking to cease, "I killed him in cold blood! I watched you kill Bender, and the others and I judged you for it. I'm no better than you!"

"Maddie, you're a good woman, you've been wronged. You did what you had to do." It wasn't much in way of comfort but it was all he could muster, "Leave Fairfax to me."

"No!" screamed Maddie. His name still struck fear into her heart. Shrugging off her self pity, she punched out the used cartridge cases and thumbed in three more. "Let's go!"

As they approached the doctor's shack they heard, through the driving rain, the faint sound of receding hooves on the soft earth. They'd missed Half-Face by a whisker.

Chapter 57

Maddie cursed and cussed like the she-cat she could so easily have been. She so desperately wanted to pursue Fairfax into the darkness.

"We've got to go after him," she shouted in frustration.

"It's too dangerous; he could pick us off before we even catch sight of him. Best we wait for first light, then we'll pick up his trail. We've come this far, a little more patience will see it through," he said hopefully.

"I want it over, I'm so tired, I can't take much more of this," she said weakly as she succumbed to his advice.

Maddie awoke to find Mordecai gone. Frantically she pulled her boots on and ran across the livery floor to find horse and rider missing. Instinctively she reached for her saddle blanket and threw it across her horse. Just as she was about to throw her saddle up she noticed a note which had floated to the floor from between her saddle blanket. She read it frantically.

My Dearest Maddie,

Please forgive me for running out on you. I believe that what I'm doing is right. You've been through so much pain and suffering I couldn't bear for you to go through any more. You have the right to seek ven-

geance on this monster, but I believe that in so doing you'd only destroy yourself. This is something I couldn't allow. Fear not, I shall track him down and administer justice, this I promise with all my heart.

Yours as always

Mordecai.

I don't believe it!" exclaimed Maddie as she crumpled up the note and began to saddle up. A shaft of sun light illuminated both horse and rider.

"Mornin missy."

Maddie swung round to see the livery man opening up the big wooden doors.

"What time did he ride out?" she said sharply.

"I can't rightly say, but he's been gone at least two hours, unless I miss my guess."

Maddie turned back to her horse and begun buckling up the cinch. All the time she was mumbling obscenities. At the doctor's shack Maddie picked up the trail. Mordecai's tracks were hard to follow but Fairfax's trail was easy to pick out. The early morning sun had baked his horse's footprints into the earth.

"How could he do this to me?" she screamed in frustration.

Mordecai had seen the looks. He knew the last few weeks had been a revelation to Maddie. He could see that his callousness when he dealt with her attackers caused her much pain. He knew that whatever love she'd felt for him was fast trickling away and he knew that when he found Fairfax those remnants of that love would just evaporate. It was better she didn't see.

As Mordecai caught sight of the San Juan mountain range he forced his thoughts to focus on his foe. Out there, somewhere in the mountainous and rocky terrain ahead of him, was the monster known as Half-Face. Since Jared's death, Mordecai had made it his business to find out everything he could about the man. He was surprised to learn that he'd killed at least three men in apparently fair fights and that he'd killed Rufus Coe, a known gunman. This proved in Mordecai's eyes that the man could not be underestimated.

Though the trail led through rocky outcrops and vast forests of pine, Mordecai neither feared nor suspected an ambush. He had enough country boy still flowing through his veins to be able to understand the silences of the forest. His judgement of Fairfax was that the man would like distance between him and his hunters. It was the vast open grassy plains that Mordecai feared, stopping often to take out his field glasses to survey the vistas. Even then he'd hold back for an hour checking intermittently with the glasses, before cautiously beginning to cross this ocean of swaying grassland.

Beads of sweat stung at Fairfax's eyes as he patiently looked back across the open country he'd travelled through that morning. He'd wanted to make it to Purgatory before nightfall. He didn't know who was following him at such a relentless pace, but he sure as hell wasn't giving his trackers another chance to kill him. He could only speculate on Driscoll's fate, but that first sound of gunfire he heard while lying in his cot at the Doctor's office was enough for him to know instinctively that it was his pursuers.

He was in far better shape than he had a right to be, having persuaded Driscoll to part with half the money from the bank hold up. It wasn't enough, but it was travelling money. Enough to book passage to San Francisco and beyond, but first there was the little matter of his trackers to take care of. From his vantage point high up in the foothills he watched endlessly. As the sun beat down he looked towards the 'Window'. It was his short cut through the San Juan's to the town of Purgatory and beyond to Durango and a welcoming bed for the night. As the sun beat mercilessly down he began to question why he should wait much longer. 'Even at this late hour, I could still reach town before nightfall.' But as he was a naturally cautious man he forced himself to continue playing the waiting game.

At the other side of the vast clearing, Mordecai ran the glasses over the surrounding country. In the background he saw what he took to be the landmarks of the Rio Grande pyramid, towering above the rest of the San Juan's and to the right 'Spanish Window' an almost precision-cut gap in the mountain range. Beyond the 'Window', a few miles south west, lay the town of Purgatory. When Maddie had been cussing in frustration at not following Fairfax into the darkness, he'd sought advice upon the trail he was taking. He figured that, given no hold-ups, he'd camp the night at 'Spanish Window,' so called because Coronado and his conquistadors in their search for gold camped there. Legend has it that Coronado himself carved his initials into the rock of the 'Window.'

The lure of a bed for the night was getting to Fairfax. He'd camped out and scanned the horizon for hours without success. Now with the sun creeping ever westward his thoughts were now contemplating camping at the 'Window.' Then, just as he'd made up his mind, he spotted a rider venturing onto the grassland. He was surprised there was only one of them. A good surprise he thought, but a surprise nonetheless. Fairfax levelled his Winchester and waited. He wanted to wait until he could be sure of a decent shot, but close enough to hit him with a second or third if necessary.

Mordecai looked up towards the pyramid and the 'Window'. Sunlight bathed them both in a golden glow. In that moment his thoughts turned to the woman he loved, then all too late he caught a glint of sunlight hitting against a metal object.

'Crack.'

Fairfax screamed in delight as he saw the man fall from his horse.

"I got you, you son of a bitch, whoever you are!" he shouted excitedly. Then he shot the horse for good measure. He stayed there for a good hour gloating over his grisly handy work. Then a hare ran into the open and, surprised by the sight of man, froze. Fairfax couldn't believe his luck as he sighted on the poor animal. He laughed hysterically. He was alive and he was free. Tonight he would camp in the shelter of the 'Window' with warm food in his belly. Tomorrow would be as good a time as any to pay a visit to Purgatory. Yes, tomorrow he promised himself, he would sleep in a warm bed, then the short ride to Durango where he could sate his desire for bloodshed with the flesh of a young whore. From there he could ride the train back to civilisation, where he would be free to wreak havoc on the whores of San Francisco.

CHAPTER 58

The inviting smell of spit-roast hare permeated both sides of the 'Window.' Eerie shadows cast demonic pictures across the enormous high walls. None more so than the hulking form of Fairfax as he ravenously attacked the cooked hare. His face and mask were shiny with grease from the partly digested animal. He burped loudly with satisfaction. Looking up at the dark starlit sky he thought how good it was to be alive, to continue the devil's work. Now with his belly full, his mind full of evil thoughts, he looked towards his bedroll. He yawned once, then the urge to sleep became too great. He threw another log on the fire then climbed into his bedroll. Within seconds he was asleep.

The dream woke him from his slumber with a jolt. He sat up abruptly and cast his eyes around the canyon walls. Satisfied that nothing more than his dreams had disturbed his sleep he lowered his head and waited for his heart rate to slow. He was getting paranoid in his old age, he thought, as sleep once again began to overtake him. How long he'd slept he could only guess, but at least an hour, he thought as his eyelids became heavy. Then a sickening wave of terror welled up inside him as a sudden thought occurred to him, 'If I slept for an hour, why was the fire burning so brightly?' Fear gripped him as he forced open his eyes, and stared at a strange shadow against the wall of the 'Window'. At first his mind couldn't take in the flickering shadow, but then realisation came to him in an instant as his eyes grew wider with fear. Then he heard the sound of footsteps, undisguised, deliberate and closing in.

Fairfax threw himself from the bedroll and attempted to get to his feet. A deafening sound tore through the night air and Half-Face screamed in pain as his right leg collapsed from under him. The sound of gunfire ricocheted around the walls of the 'Window'. Sick with shock Half-Face stared up at the dark clad figure. He'd seen him many times and in many towns. He was the undertaker of his nightmares. Forcing down the pain, the instinct for survival kicked in and his hand edged towards the underneath of his bedroll. Another deafening sound tore through the night sky as the 45 calibre lead projectile smashed into his right hand, turning it into a bloody pulp.

Screaming with terror and fighting the pain, Fairfax swore and blasphemed.

"Oh Jesus! What the fuck do you want? I've money. Is that it?"

He was clutching at straws and he knew it. He'd seen at close hand, many times, the intention in the man's dark eyes. He felt the warm sensation as he pissed his pants, but he ignored the humiliation and the pain as he begged for mercy. He grovelled, he pleaded, he screamed in terror and his bloody stump of a hand pumped blood. The stranger grabbed him by the throat and pulled him from his bedroll towards the fire. Then he grabbed Fairfax's destroyed hand and plunged it into the glowing embers. Half-Face screamed in pain and then mercifully fell into a state of unconsciousness.

When he came to he stared at his charred stump and looked up at his assailant.

"It needed cauterising, can't have you bleeding to death can I?"

Fairfax looked in horror at the dark dried blood at the side of his attacker's head. He was the lone rider, the one he'd waited all day for; he cursed himself for not making sure. His mind raced back to that time in the alley in Sacramento, to O'Toole's fatal mistake. The advice, the advice he'd given the New York detective at the side of the railroad track, oh how he'd tormented him about his tardiness, before he killed him.

There was a wild uncaring look in Mordecai's eyes. There was no anger, just nothingness.

"What do you want? Who are you?"

Mordecai pulled his razor sharp knife from its sheath. The wounded man flinched in horror. Then carelessly he sliced through the leather throngs that tied Fairfax's mask in place, taking an ear into the bargain.

Fairfax shrieked with pain.

"My!" laughed Mordecai, "you are one hell of an ugly cocksucker."

"Who are you?" screamed Fairfax angrily.

"It doesn't matter who I am. You just need to know, the lady says hi."

Puzzlement formed on Fairfax's fevered brow.

"Who?" It was a question he all but knew, but he had to hear him say her name.

"You knew her as a naïve young waif called Deirdre Devlin."

"She's alive?"

"And kickin'. Ask your pal Driscoll when you see him!"

The screams continued into the night.

Mordecai fastened the strap of his saddlebag and mounted Fairfax's horse. Tired and weary he pointed the horse back the way he'd come. It was a long ride home and his head ached and he could feel the chills of a fever. The night's bloodletting had seen him reach the brink of madness and go beyond it. He'd killed before, but never like this. Kills like the Wolf would have been proud. He had become as one with the devil and no matter how much he tried washing Fairfax's dried blood off his hands in a nearby creek, he could never wash away the great sin he'd performed, nor the memory. He had avenged his best friend's death and destroyed Maddie's nightmares, but at what cost? She was lost to him forever, but in truth he knew she was lost to him before he started on the trail of vengeance.

It was late in the afternoon when Maddie saw a lone rider heading in her direction. She halted her horse and commanded it to stand. Then as the lone rider, who appeared to be slumped in the saddle grew nearer she slowly pulled her Winchester from its scabbard. The horse looked like the one rode by Fairfax at Leadville. Covering the man she waited until he was within ear shot. "You there! State yo.... Oh Jesus! Mordecai....!"

Mordecai slipped from the saddle and fell slowly to the ground. Maddie jumped from her horse and raced towards him. She saw the dried blood from his head wound and felt his sweat soaked body. Panic tried to overtake her, but she cast it aside as she explored his torso for tell-tale wounds and on finding none, she breathed a sigh of relief. Maddie knew enough to know that he wasn't out of the woods. He was burning up and would die just as surely as if he'd been hit in a vital organ if she didn't manage to get his fever down. She had to get him out of his clothes and into the warm.

Maddie made camp where they stood and after getting him under blankets she gathered wood and lit a fire. Then despite the possible danger of Fairfax, she soothed his fevered brow. Around midnight with his temperature at boiling point she thought he'd go into shock, but his fever suddenly broke. Maddie stared up to the heavens and mouthed a silent 'Thank you'. Exhausted by her exertions, she wrapped her arms around him and slept.

Mordecai awoke the following morning to the smell of coffee brewing over the fire. He smiled weakly at her and she wanted to cry. Last night she thought she'd lost him, she thought he would pass during the night, but he'd survived. Yet she could see in his eyes that he was lost to her. They'd been through so much together, but those shared experiences were what would forever keep them apart.

She asked the inevitable question.

"Fairfax?"

He'd replied simply, "He's gone."

She thought she'd need more closure, more proof, but it was the look in his eyes and the way he'd said, "He's gone," that told her everything.

Two days later they arrived in Durango. They'd camped the first night in the foothills below Spanish Window skirting the far right wall of the Window at first light. Mordecai neither looked right nor left as they rode through the gap. They rode in silence for most of that day and made camp about five miles out from town.

Exhausted by the day's riding, Maddie turned in early, while Mordecai put logs on the fire and stared aimlessly into the flames. She watched him for a while, knowing he was fighting his demons and that sadly he alone was the only one to be able to defeat them.

As Mordecai stared into the fire, that night beneath the towering walls of Spanish Window revisited him. Defenceless, the man had at first begged for his life, then as the torture became too hard to bare he'd cursed and uttered vows of damnation. When everything he said went unheeded he'd pleaded, begged and grovelled for Mordecai to end his life. He was a screaming bloody mess when Mordecai dragged him like a large bough of a tree and threw him on the fire and burned him alive. It brought back memories of the dying Comanche he'd burned in his search for Kills like the Wolf. He had become as one with the Comanche and as cruel as Half-Face.

Tempted as he was to return with Maddie, who he could see was slowly beginning to heal, he knew that if he did go back to Helena his scars would become her scars. It was the last noble thing he could do for her. Then he reached across to his bedroll and saddlebags. He slowly began to unwrap the soft tan leather mask, the only reminder left of Half-Face. He stared at the bloodstained leather for a few seconds, before throwing it onto the fire. Then he wept silently as the flames devoured the last physical presence of the man known as Half-Face.

Chapter 59

Maddie boarded the Denver & Rio Grande Railroad car bound eventually for Helena a week after they rode into town. Since the coming of the railroad and the construction of the line to Silverton, Durango was building itself a reputation.

Maddie and Mordecai checked out the train timetable and then booked two rooms in a nearby hotel while they waited for the train to take Maddie northwards. With almost a week until Maddie's train they spent the days purchasing new clothes in the town's stores with the money Mordecai had taken from Fairfax. In the evenings they dined in the hotel's restaurant, retiring to their respective bedrooms early. It was a week of mixed emotions, complicated by Maddie's upfront suggestion that as it was their last night, they should spend it together.

"Mordecai, I'm ready," she said over their dessert that last night.

"Sorry," said Mordecai, his heart racing.

"I said I'm ready. I want you to take me to bed."

Mordecai flushed with embarrassment, and felt at the stiff collar around his neck. He looked at this woman, this woman who he'd fallen in love with from the moment he'd first clapped eyes on her. The evening had been chock full of emotions, being their last night and all, but this was more, much more than he'd bargained for. He stared into those cobalt blue eyes and he saw that familiar flame flickering into life.

He knew then that Maddie would survive, both physically and mentally, from their ordeal and his heart wept with joy.

Ten minutes later they were in Maddie's room. In the darkness he held her gently and then she turned her head upwards seeking his lips. He kissed her softly and was transported back to that night when she'd torn down the burlap sacking.

"I love you Mordecai, I've never stopped loving you."

"Nor I you," he responded.

Their kissing became more intense, but Mordecai held back. When they lay in each others arms Maddie tried guiding him inside her, but in seconds she realised he couldn't do it. She caressed him, she coaxed him and then he wept. He'd wanted to so very much, but the pain, the guilt, the anger wouldn't cease. He thought for that fleeting moment in the hotel restaurant that everything would be all right. But deep inside he knew. Maddie kissed away his salty tears and held him gently in her arms until they both fell asleep.

At the train depot, Maddie cried as the train chugged into life. She knew she'd never find another man to match him. She'd known only two other men who had been as kind. Both were dead, but his departing seemed even more final.

"That my friend was the last time I saw her until the other day."

Governor Charles Culberson sat back in his leather backed chair and thoughtfully pondered on Mordecai's story.

"So what happened to her after she arrived back in Helena?"

"As I said earlier, she helped run a parlour house with Josephine 'Chicago Joe' Hensley, then she took Butte by the scruff of its neck during that cholera epidemic, she bought property from the sale of the ranch, invested it wisely and became a very rich woman. But she never left the life she was born to. I guess with her wealth she felt able to look after the many waifs and strays who crossed her path and hopefully steer many of them away from poverty, disease and suicide."

"Yet with all her wealth she never really achieved the happiness that she deserved. And you think I can help?"

"Yes I do sir, yes I truly do." replied Mordecai as he slumped back in his fine leather chair and took a sip of cognac and puffed away at the best Cuban cigar he'd tasted in a long while. As Chief of El Paso's police department the odd luxury was something he enjoyed.

Since Maddie had arrived in El Paso he'd been keeping a discreet eye on her movements. His first reaction after seeing her disembark from the Overland stage was to rush over to greet her, but he'd pulled back from fear that the sight of him might bring back too many painful memories. Instead he'd assigned a man to monitor her whereabouts.

She'd visited the Madam of the 'Blue Eagle', stayed a few hours, then took a carriage to the Freemont Hotel on Paseo de Rio, where she checked into a suite. At least, thought Mordecai with a wry smile, the lady has style. What she wanted with the Madam of the Blue Eagle wasn't important, how long she was staying was all that mattered. With an assurance of help from the Governor, Mordecai made his way to the Freemont Hotel.

Nervously he checked his appearance in the large ornate mirror in the Freemont's lobby. Satisfied, he ran his hand through his greying locks and took the stairs to the second floor. He checked himself once again as he reached her suite, then he ran his tongue around the inside of his mouth in an attempt to lubricate his tonsils. Pushing forty nine, Mordecai had butterflies running around his stomach. He gulped, cleared his throat, gathered his nerves and knocked on the door.

"Who is it?"

"The Chief of Police," he said gruffly.

Maddie sucked in her breath and counted to ten. Since the early nineties big cities like Helena had taken on an air of sophistication and working girls were treated as social pariahs, she guessed El Paso was no different. She flung open the door, prepared to do battle.

"What do you want?"

"I'd like to take you to dinner," said Mordecai with a smile. He looked into those deep blue eyes, *which thankfully still held that same sparkle,* as they blinked with incredulity.

She gave a startled gasp and then her breath caught in her throat. She felt foolish, surprised and a little overcome.

"Mordecai! Is that really you?" She looked deeply into his eyes, past the pain, the hurt, the suffering, and found them smiling back at her, "Tell me I'm not dreaming."

"You ain't dreaming."

She stared at him without saying another word, for what to Mordecai seemed like hours, but was in truth just enough time for Maddie to take in the tall distinguished gentleman who stood framed in her doorway.

"Will you do me the honour of dining with one such as I?" he repeated. Nervousness was still getting the better of him.

"Chief of Police. My, that's a turnaround," she said with that same old sassy attitude that he'd fallen in love with all those years ago.

In a flash it had all come flooding back. She had wept for days on the train journey back to Helena. She'd questioned herself many times as to why she hadn't tried harder with him. Yet deep down, she knew she couldn't persuade him. Too much had happened between them for life to go back to normal. He'd thought he'd spared her the final confrontation, but his feverish ramblings on the night she'd found him had left her in no doubt as to the fate of Fairfax. His outbursts had been so nightmarishly graphic; she could only feel compassion for his tormented soul. But there he was large as life, standing framed in her doorway, the man she'd thought of every night since.

"Chief of Police, and at your service, as ever."

He'd checked that she had already made a reservation in the dining room so knew that if he timed it right she'd be dressed for dinner. His timing was impeccable. As expected she was dressed to kill in the latest fashions that France had to offer. Victorian in style but with more than a hint of the scandalous Parisian to satisfy any hot blooded American male.

"And if I may be so bold, you look stunning!" he added as an after thought.

His words brought her back to the present.

"Well thank you kind sir," she said in a falsely mocking tone. Then from under lowered eyelids she added, "I'd love to dine with you."

"Maddie, I can't tell you how many times I've dreamed of this."

Maddie smiled, her very own thought now put into words.

"Questions! I've so many questions, I fear it will be a long dinner," she said as she extended her arm for him to take.

The maitre d' led them to a suitably secluded table, reserved for only the most important of their clientele. Once seated, Mordecai nodded to the maitre d' and ordered a bottle of 'Krug'.

Mordecai stared at her across the table, his eyes feasting on the beautiful specimen of womanhood before him.

"Maddie, you're more beautiful than that last time I saw you. A feat until this moment I thought impossible."

Maddie smiled and felt the warmth creep up over her neck and rush to her cheeks.

"I don't think any man has ever been able to make me blush before," she added saucily.

It was as Maddie had predicted, a long dinner.

"What are you doing in El Paso?"

"How long have you been a policeman?"

"Where are you going after El Paso?"

"Did you marry?"

"Did you?"

Questions, questions, questions and more questions. It was a night where they talked about life, of the changing world around them, of old friends, *Clay Dean and Randy in particular.* They skirted around the obvious and talked light-heartedly of many things from the past and from the future, but neither had spoken of love.

An exaggerated cough from the maitre d' broke the spell as they realised that all those around them had departed for their beds and that the entire catering staff were eagerly anticipating theirs.

Mordecai escorted Maddie to her door, a feeling of desperation wafted over him. He wanted the night to go on forever, but he feared that in his eagerness he'd ruin what had been until then, a perfect night.

"Maddie I've never stopped loving you." It was said, the words he feared would destroy all his hopes.

In her old devil may care attitude Maddie smiled that seductive smile and said, "I haven't slept with anyone since our last night in Durango," she searched his face for a reaction, "but tonight I'd like to change all that." She got one.

Mordecai looked at her and couldn't believe his ears.

"You what?"

"You heard," she said as she turned the key in the lock.

Maddie's saucy manner was matched by her inner feelings. She wanted this man more than life itself. As the door closed Mordecai reached an arm around Maddie's waist and pulled her to him.

"Maddie, those words I just spoke, I want you to know I mean every word. There hasn't been a day gone by that I didn't think of you."

Maddie brought her face up close to his and tantalisingly brushed her soft lips against him. His lips responded to hers, dancing and flirting, pressing softly, then retreating only to brush against the tenderness of her neck, then return to her eager lips, playing with them until finally they locked together as one. In an instant he was transported back to her room at the Alhambra, to the burlap curtain that, until that night, had preserved her honour, and then he knew, he knew so clearly how much he loved this woman. He didn't want to let go, to break the spell, he wanted it to go on forever.

There was no frantic ripping off of clothes, just a gentle understanding that each garment discarded brought them slowly and deliciously to their own paradise. As he gently laid her upon the bed, he kissed her naked breasts and caressed between her legs. She let out a gentle moan as he climbed on top of her. He returned her cry with one of his own as he slowly entered her. They were lost in each others arms, oblivious to the outside world. They wanted the night to last for an eternity.

After their lovemaking was over and their passions spent, they lay with their naked bodies locked together as one and talked intimately of their feelings for each other. Freed from the bonds of uncertainty, free to express their own personal fears and free to express their hopes and their dreams for the future. It was a little before dawn when they both succumbed to sleep.

Mordecai's duties kept him busy during the day, but as night fell he hurried to the Freemont hotel and Maddie. Their night of lovemaking and plain speaking had freed the demons they both shared.

Maddie told him about her return to Helena and how she got involved in the cholera epidemic in Butte a little less than a year after her return.

"It was the turning point in my life. I had the money and resources and I couldn't stand by and do nothing. It was there that I realised I could do some good. On my return I put the ranch up for sale and made a tidy profit. I bought property on Wood Street and rented it out to several businesses. I even invested in Chicago Joe's Red Light Saloon."

"Did you ever get to see your boy over in Bismarck?"

Maddie looked sad, "You know Mordecai, that, along with letting you go were my biggest regrets in life. About a year after I returned from Butte I finally plucked up the courage to pay the Langleys a visit. When I arrived I found they'd sold up the general store and headed West. California I think. I never heard after that. I guess he had his life, he didn't need no interference from me."

"I'm truly sorry," said Mordecai, at a loss for something more adequate to say.

"It's okay. It was for the best." Maddie smiled and dragged herself out of the melancholy mood. "Back in Helena, things were becoming more sophisticated and the city fathers barred prostitution and declared all hurdy-gurdy houses immoral. Chicago Joe she was hopping mad, she told me she wasn't going to take that lying down." Mordecai was relieved to see the sparkle back in her eyes. Maddie laughed as she recalled the events that followed, "Josephine, well she hires an attorney and takes the matter to court. She won too."

Mordecai stifled a laugh, Chicago Joe was one feisty lady.

"Not content with winning in court, Joe realised she needed a more stylish business. So she set about building a large, elaborate establishment which she called the 'Coliseum'. It was a combined theatre and variety house. She packed the place with well groomed ladies from back East and entertainers of all ilks. Josephine really had an eye for business, prostitution and bawdy entertainment. What a combination!"

"And you invested in the 'Coliseum'?"

"I invested a little," she said modestly. "But as you know only too well, nothing lasts forever. I sold all my interests in the Red Light and the Coliseum along with my properties before the depression of 1893. Chicago Joe wasn't as fortunate. She lost everything except the Red Light Saloon. Last I heard she was living a quiet life with her husband in an apartment above the Red Light."

"So where did you go after leaving Helena?" Mordecai had during those years exchanged letters with Randy who left the cattle business and bought into a half interest in a bar in the tenderloin. He'd kept Mordecai appraised until 92.

"I had a hankering for San Francisco, where I bought a share in a bawdy house. This Madam had twenty Chinese girls working there. Their conditions were appalling, they were treated like dogs. My profession's hard, but I hadn't bargained for the extreme cruelty. I did my best for the poor unfortunates, even used my own money to buy a couple of the younger girls' freedom. I'm happy to say I helped a number to quit the profession altogether. One even married a wealthy business man and became respectable. It was an uphill struggle and to be honest

I was losing it. San Francisco wasn't to my liking, it cared nothing for these poor souls, so after that year I headed south and I've been heading south ever since."

"You always was a sucker for the under dog."

"Enough of me. What brought you to this high office?"

It was Maddie's sense of fun that charmed him the most. She'd faced adversity and it had dealt her many cruel blows in her lifetime, but no matter what, she'd come through. Mordecai couldn't help but laugh at her dig about his role as Chief of the El Paso police department.

"Within an hour of your train leaving Durango I saddled up and drifted south. My mind was in torment, I hated myself far more than I'd thought possible. I was a days ride out of Durango, when I made camp that second night. I'd bought a bottle and began drinking it by the fire. Within an hour it was empty and I felt I was drunk enough for what I had to do. I took that old reliable Navy Colt from its holster and bit down on the barrel. I cocked the hammer, looked up at the stars and pulled the trigger. The percussion cap failed to ignite, damp I guess and the pistol misfired. I woke the next morning with a thundering headache, my mouth was dry, I had sick down the front of my shirt and wet pants."

"Oh Mordecai," cried Maddie.

Mordecai smiled at her. "I can tell you Maddie, I was fucked up big time. I'd reached rock. That gun misfiring got me to thinking. I took it as a sign. I knew that God wasn't ready for me. He'd barred the gates and until I'd atoned for my wickedness there would be no real forgiveness. So I went down to this little creek washed myself down and thought about what I was going to do with the rest of my life. Fighting my corner was the only thing I was good at, so I decided to channel my talents to law enforcement. On reaching Amarillo I contacted Clay Dean. Within a month I became a Texas Ranger. It was a thankless job, but someone had to do it. For seven and a half years I rode with the best; James Gillete; Ethan Book; John Armstrong; Zachary

Trelawney and Clay Dean. Incidentally Clay caught up with and despatched John Larch in Brownsville. Larch died game. It was sometime around 1890 that I retired from the Rangers and moved to El Paso where I took on the role of town constable. My reputation had preceded me, but I managed to get the job done without much bloodshed. I got re-elected and soon received promotion. I'd made a few strong and powerful friends who needed El Paso to change before we ran into the 20th Century."

"Tamed at last," said Maddie provocatively.

Mordecai laughed, "Not quite, I ran into an old adversary, John Wesley Hardin. Seems he studied law whilst up in Huntsville. We had a few drinks together, remembered old friends but that was about the size of it. I told him to keep his nose clean. I guess he didn't heed my advice, as a town constable John Selman put a bullet in his brain. I can't say I missed the son of a bitch. But he got me to thinking. El Paso was a wild and lawless town. It needed people like me, but I could see the changes coming, so I took a degree in law. Figured with my connections to try my hand at politics or become an attorney or the like."

Maddie smiled, she could see that what Mordecai was saying had merit, but above all she could see the enthusiasm he had for his subject.

"I think you should," she said seriously.

"Maddie, I've got to go away for a few days, meet some important people up in Washington, attend a reception or too, pretty boring stuff really, but I wondered whether you'd like to come along?" Mordecai's heart was in his mouth. His whole future was tied up with meeting these people, but if Maddie said no, he didn't know whether he could leave her.

"You don't want me around, I'd just cramp your style," she said sweetly.

"On the contrary Maddie you would be an asset, and besides if you say no, then I ain't going." He'd produced his ace card; he hoped it would be enough.

"You really want me to go that bad?"

"You'd better believe it."

Washington D.C. wasn't like any city Maddie had ever seen. From the moment they stepped off the train at Union Station she was in awe of her surrounding. From the grandeur of the Capitol Building to the row houses of Capitol Hill with their electricity, running water and inside plumbing, to the quiet elegance of the White House, she openly declared her admiration.

"It's, it's so beautiful!"

Of course Maddie had seen changes and modernisation in cities like Helena, San Francisco and El Paso with their so called air of sophistication, but none compared to the advances in the capital.

"And the people," she added enthusiastically, "Their clothes, they're so elegantly dressed."

"But none come close to matching your style my darling," countered Mordecai with a roguish smile.

"Oh Mordecai, do you think so?" Concern crept slowly across Maddie's face as for the first time in her life she began to have doubts about who she was, "Will these important friends accept me?"

"If they don't, they'll have me to answer to!"

"But I might say the wrong thing; perhaps you'd be better off going without me."

"Nonsense Maddie, if anything you'll be an asset. The women will be in awe of you, and the men ... The men will envy me to high heaven."

"But, bu...."

"No buts," he replied forcefully.

Maddie need not have feared. At the various functions they attended during those few day she was treated with the utmost kindness and warmth from both men and women alike. In truth some, if not all, of the gatherers had had shady pasts.

"An empire such as ours wasn't won by milksops, but by hardened rough men and the women who backed them. Women who weren't afraid to tackle whatever life threw their way."

"Oh Mordecai, I'm having such a wonderful time."

"You wait until the presentation at the White House," Mordecai threw in casually.

"The White House! You mean the President…." she couldn't finish the sentence. She was so overwhelmed with it all.

"Yeah, on our last day we're attending a ceremony on the White House lawns. The President, William McKinley himself, is presenting the Congressional Medal of Honour to our servicemen who fought so bravely in the Spanish American War. That war was a turning point in our future. From now on in, we'll be treated as a World power."

"It that good?" remarked Maddie with all the cynicism she could muster.

"I don't know Maddie, I truly hope so. It's just that with the 20th Century just around the corner it's as if America has come of age."

Maddie clung lovingly to Mordecai's arm and looked up into his dark eyes filled with enthusiasm and loved him for it. She squeezed him tightly and realised that she'd never been happier in her entire life than at that moment.

Epilogue

It was during the Medal of Honour Ceremony that Mordecai asked Maddie to be his wife. They'd arrived amidst a crowd of local dignitaries and senators where a lot of hand clasping and back slapping seemed the order of the day. Then they were offered champagne and canapés before being shown to their seats on the White House lawn. They sat next to each other in the spring sunshine and looked up at the ribbon bedecked platform with anticipation.

A few minutes later the President's aide mounted the podium, "Ladies and Gentlemen, I give you the President of the United States."

As one the assorted crowd of dignitaries rose from their seats as President McKinley stepped up to the podium. He smiled awkwardly and motioned everyone to their seats. Then after a short pause he began his speech. The essence of it was much as Mordecai had outlined to Maddie the day before.

Then the medal ceremony began. Maddie and Mordecai clapped enthusiastically as each serviceman stepped up to receive his medal from the President. Maddie couldn't help but remark under her breath.

"They're so young to have faced the enemy amidst such carnage. Their parents must be very proud."

"Yes," replied Mordecai, "That boy's mother in particular." He said as he pointed to a young soldier just ascending the platform.

Maddie looked puzzled for a moment before staring deeply into the face of the young man, his boyish features sending her back in time to the railroad station at Rock Springs and to another young equally boyish looking soldier.

"Oh my!" she exclaimed as the tears began to trickle down her cheek. The boy was the spit of his father. He could so easily have been Miles. Recovering her composure she dabbed at her eyes with a handkerchief and turned towards Mordecai with a look of incredulity on her face. He just smiled. It was then that Maddie knew why she loved this man Mordecai Jones so much.

On the White House lawn after the ceremony was over he asked her the question.

She said 'Yes.'

The End

27th September 2006.
Revised 2nd January 2007.

Throughout this work of fiction I have interspersed it with historical figures, whilst this was just my imagination; these people did lead colourful lives in real life.

Elizabeth Bacon Custer, wife of Lieutenant Colonel George Armstrong Custer. After Custer's death at the Little Big Horn, she became an outspoken advocate and ensured his gallant heroic image would live on for more than a century before historians took a more accurate look at his actions up to the famous battle. Elizabeth remained devoted to her dead husband and never remarried. She died in New York City on the 6th April 1933 two days short of her 92nd birthday.

John Wesley Hardin, was probably the most dangerous gunman that existed during those violent times after the Civil War. He was a vicious killer that would kill for the slightest of reasons and legend has it that he killed a man just because of his snoring. His hay days of killings were during the Sutton Taylor Feud. Killing of Sheriff Charles Webb in May of 1874 led to Hardin leaving the state. He was captured by Texas Ranger John Armstrong on a train outside Pensacola Florida, allegedly he tried pulling a gun but it got caught in his suspenders. Armstrong promptly knocked Hardin out. After nearly seventeen years in Huntsville penitentiary, Hardin left prison and set himself up as an attorney at law in El Paso. On the 19th August 1895 whilst throwing dice in the Acme Saloon with the bartender, Old John Selman stepped up behind him and shot him in the back of the head. He was 42 years of age.

John King Fisher was indeed a flamboyant dresser, but also a deadly gunman. His exploits were talked about more by others than himself and he never admitted to more than seven killings. His death in an ambush at the Vaudeville Variety Theatre in San Antonio Texas, was not intentional, it was more to do with the company he kept. Ben

Thompson, notorious shooter, originally from Yorkshire England was the real target, both men perished in the ensuing gunfire.

Josephine 'Chicago Joe' Hensley Of Irish descent, real name Mary Welch, she arrived at New York at the age of 14, where she took on menial work before moving to Chicago. By then she'd changed her name to Josephine Airey and had become a member of the demimonde. A few years later in 1867 with the nickname Chicago Joe she invested in a ticket to Helena, Montana Territory. Her savings, experience and Irish charm soon brought her what she'd craved. With the success of her first venture Chicago Joe reinvested in property. Helena began to become more sophisticated, so Josephine built a large theatre come variety house which she named the Coliseum. For many years Chicago Joe prospered but eventually the Coliseum lost its novelty value and in 1993 the financial panic and depression caused her to lose everything except the Red Light Saloon. Joe and her husband James T Hensley moved into rooms above the saloon and lived out a quiet life. Sadly on October 25th 1899 Chicago Joe died of pneumonia, she was 55years of age.

Ah Toy arrived in California in 1849. Her husband had died on board ship and Ah Toy took up with the ship's captain. When she set foot in San Francisco her pockets were filled with gold. Opening a peep show soon after she arrived proved a great success. A natural progression followed and she became mistress to many men of wealth and power. She became a prosperous dealer in Chinese prostitution, opening several brothels throughout California. Ah Toy was an unscrupulous woman who bought young girls cheaply from China, some as young as 11, and trained them in the art of prostitution. She was known as the first Oriental madam. Sometime, during these halcyon days she disappeared, some said she went back to China. Her notoriety was so great that many ladies of the night called themselves after her.

Governor Culberson served as governor of Texas between 1895 and 1899 and then became a United States senator from 1899 to 1923. During his career he'd served on the committee investigating war crimes in the Philippine—American War. He retired from public duties through ill health and died of pneumonia in 1925.

President William McKinley served as president of the United States between 1897 and 1901. Foreign policy dictated his administration. Public indignation at the plight of Cuba caused him to deliver his message of neutral intervention and thus the result, the Spanish American War. America emerged from it as a major power. During the early months of his second term of office he was assassinated by a deranged anarchist.

Notes

My spelling throughout this text has been in *English-English* rather than *English-American*. My apologies if this has distracted you in any way.

Michael Kennard

978-0-595-43383-4
0-595-43383-9

Printed in the United Kingdom
by Lightning Source UK Ltd.
119360UK00001B/184-261